NIGHTWATCH

Robin Wayne Bailey

Cover Art
FRED FIELDS

NIGHT WATCH

©Copyright 1990 TSR, Inc.
All Rights Reserved.

All characters and names in this book are fictitious. Any resemblance to actual persons, living or dead, is purely coincidental.

This book is protected under the copyright laws of the United States of America. Any reproduction or other unauthorized use of the material or artwork contained herein is prohibited without the express written permission of TSR, Inc.

Distributed to the book trade in the United States by Random House, Inc. and in Canada by Random House of Canada, Ltd.

Distributed in the United Kingdom by TSR Ltd.

Distributed to the toy and hobby trade by regional distributors.

ADVANCED DUNGEONS AND DRAGONS, AD&D, and DRAGONLANCE are registered trademarks owned by TSR, Inc.
FORGOTTEN REALMS, PRODUCTS OF YOUR IMAGINATION, and the TSR logo are trademarks owned by TSR, Inc. ™ designates other trademarks owned by TSR, Inc.

First Printing: May 1990
Printed in the United States of America.
Library of Congress Catalog Card Number: 89-52093

9 8 7 6 5 4 3 2 1

ISBN: 0-88038-914-1

TSR, Inc.	TSR Ltd.
P.O. Box 756	120 Church End, Cherry Hinton
Lake Geneva, WI 53147	Cambridge CB1 3LB
U.S.A.	United Kingdom

Faster and faster Duncan's hands flew, casting the dice and sweeping them up. The lamplight danced on the amethysts. They sparkled with flashes of purple and violet fire, and Duncan's eyes glistened with a black brightness.

Suddenly she cried out. Her hand froze, on the verge of sweeping the stones up once more, and trembled above them instead. Slowly she withdrew it and bent closer. "I see!" she gasped. "I see!"

Above the dice, a nebulous violet light formed and swirled, and the crystals rose slowly into the heart of the smoky radiance. Like tiny stars, they spun and whirled, throwing flashes about the room. Garett felt a pressure on his ears, behind his eyes. A great invisible hand seemed to press on his chest. The crystals spun faster and faster until they could no longer be seen individually but formed a single orbit around some unseen center. The violet light burned hotter.

Then something smashed Garett to the floor. A scream rang in his ears. A light exploded in his head and burst into thousands of colors.

Other TSR™ Books

STARSONG
Dan Parkinson

ST. JOHN THE PURSUER: VAMPIRE IN MOSCOW
Richard Henrick

BIMBOS OF THE DEATH SUN
Sharyn McCrumb

ILLEGAL ALIENS
Nick Pollotta and Phil Foglio

THE JEWELS of ELVISH
Nancy Varian Berberick

RED SANDS
Paul Thompson and Tonya Carter

THE EYES HAVE IT
Rose Estes

MONKEY STATION
Ardath Mayhar and Ron Fortier

TOO, TOO SOLID FLESH
Nick O'Donohoe

THE EARTH REMEMBERS
Susan Torian Olan

DARK HORSE
Mary H. Herbert

WARSPRITE
Jefferson P. Swycaffer

For Lucille and Ralph Piper, Denise and Greg Chesney, Don and Vanessa Piper, and of course, Diana.

For Jim Washek and Mark Wise.

For Steve, Wayne, Willie, Jerry, and Don, with thanks for the music and the good times.

Free City of Greyhawk

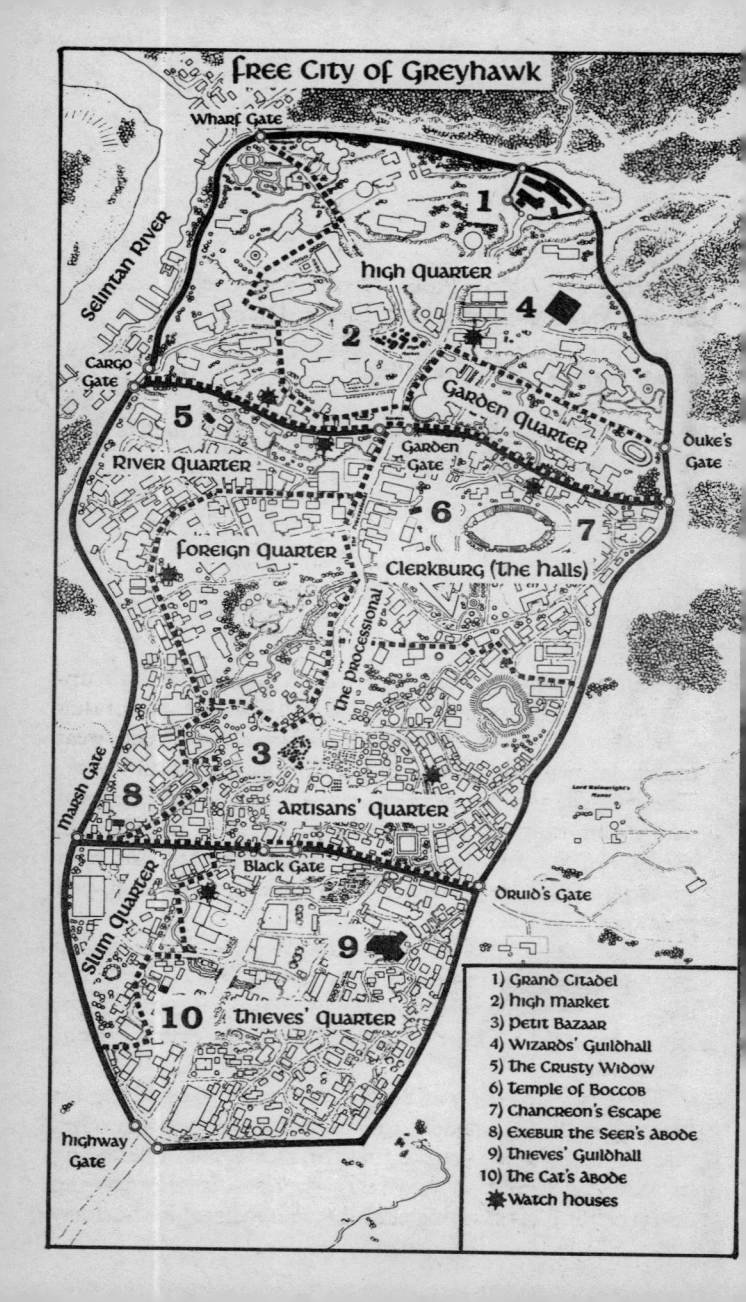

- Wharf Gate
- Selintan River
- Cargo Gate
- Duke's Gate
- Garden Gate
- Garden Quarter
- High Quarter
- River Quarter
- Foreign Quarter
- Clerkburg (the halls)
- the processional
- Marsh Gate
- Artisans' Quarter
- Lord Wainwright's Manor
- Black Gate
- Druid's Gate
- Slum Quarter
- Thieves' Quarter
- Highway Gate

1) Grand Citadel
2) High Market
3) Petit Bazaar
4) Wizards' Guildhall
5) The Crusty Widow
6) Temple of Boccob
7) Chancreon's Escape
8) Exebur the Seer's Abode
9) Thieves' Guildhall
10) The Cat's Abode
✶ Watch Houses

ONE

With a choked cry, Acton Kathenor sat bolt upright in his bed and stared into the gloom that filled his sleeping chamber. A cold fear-sweat trickled down his face and chest, down his arms and back. The sheets beneath him were soaked. The thin blanket that had covered him was a tangled knot between his old legs. He sucked in a desperate breath, held it too long, and let it go explosively. He squeezed his eyes shut, then snapped them open again.

The dream. He'd had a dream. Already it was fading from his conscious mind. He tried to grasp it, tried to call it back, for he knew somehow that it was important, but it slipped away like a mist, or a shadow, leaving only a reasonless unease.

The old man threw aside the blanket and, grabbing his bedpost to steady himself, rose to his feet. He drew another breath and stood there, waiting for the trembling to leave his limbs. A dim lamp flickered in the drawing room beyond his sleeping chamber. He lurched to the doorway and leaned against the jamb. Dim though the light was, it was grateful relief from the darkness of his bedroom. He drank in the light as if it were water, as if it could quench his fear.

Leaning over the small table where the lamp sat, he stared at the flame, feeling the heat play upon his face. Of a sudden, something moved there, something black and shadowy. A fragment of his dream flashed through his mind again. He snatched at it, but it was already gone.

He backed away from the lamp, one aged hand clutched over his heart. The flame offered no solace now. It seemed dirty somehow, as foul as the darkness of his bedroom. Snatching a thin night robe, Kathenor left his quarters. He eased open the door to the outer hallway, then padded down the empty corridors as quietly as his bare feet could carry him.

An unnatural silence filled the Temple of Boccob. What time of night was it? Acton Kathenor wondered. Surely there should be an acolyte or two awake, even if it was a very late hour, indeed. He encountered no one else, though, as he hurried through the temple's labyrinthine passages.

Acton Kathenor forced himself to be calm. Why should a dream so upset him, especially a dream he could not remember? Because that, in itself, was an oddity, his inner voice answered. He always remembered his dreams. They were a source of great creative power for him. The smallest details he always remembered. He had trained himself to remember.

A wind blew through a temple crenellation suddenly and wrapped itself about Kathenor. It fluttered his sleeves and crept up under his robe. It followed him through a passage and up a narrow, winding stairway, which was unlit by cresset or torch. It teased the nape of his neck and rumpled the few hairs he had left on his head.

The stairs led to the rooftop of the temple's highest tower. Thrusting open the door with both hands, Acton Kathenor emerged into the night. The checkered marble tiles were cool and smooth against his feet, though the air was summer warm. He went straight to the low wall that ringed the rooftop, and gazed outward.

The stars burned like diamonds against the rich velvet of the heavens. A slender waxing moon limned the dark silhouettes of Greyhawk's highest buildings with silver fire. The roofs of the university, imposing in their nobility; the more distant Citadel, way up in the High Quarter, rising like a stern parent over the rest of Greyhawk; the watchtower atop Duke's Gate; these sparkled under the generous moon.

The rest of the city, though, belonged to the shadows. It spilled below him in all directions like a black vomit. Not even the wind could mask its stench. Little of the moon's light penetrated the twisting streets and alleys, and few windows in any dwelling, as far as Kathenor could see, betrayed the fire of any lamp or candle.

Without meaning to, Boccob's priest shivered again. "Necropolis," someone had nicknamed this city, and certainly tonight, Acton Kathenor understood why. Something rode the air, some force. He knew it as surely as he knew his name. He had sensed the thing in his dream state, though it eluded his conscious mind.

Some shadow eclipsed the moon, causing him once more to look up. Not a shadow, he discovered to his surprise, but a flock of birds, huge black birds. Their eerie calls reached him faintly, the only sound he heard in the night.

Then, something else snatched his attention away from the birds. From the corner of his left eye he barely caught a streak of light incising its way earthward. For the briefest instant, it flared with a wondrous radiance, but that glory faded and winked completely out before the bolt quite touched the border between heaven and earth.

"A shooting star!" Acton Kathenor whispered, clutching the edge of the wall, though there was no one to overhear. He slammed a bony fist weakly down on the stone, gathered his robe about himself, and left the rooftop. I might have been the only one in all of Greyhawk to see it, he told himself. Surely it was a sign from divine Boccob to his high priest!

He descended the stairs as quickly as he dared in the dark, running one hand along the wall to steady himself while he gathered the folds of his robe in his other hand to keep from tripping on them. The wind brushed against him again as he reached the bottom stair and passed the open window.

The flames in the lamps and cressets flickered strangely. The corridors swirled and twisted, suddenly unfamiliar. Acton Kathenor groped and stumbled his way along, panic swelling in his breast. He reached the massive doors of the temple's great hall, where assemblies were held and instruction was given to novitiates. Against tradition, the doors stood half open when they should have been closed tight. On either side of the doors, torches burned in sconces on the walls. Kathenor seized one and pushed the doors wider.

The hall was dark, and he lifted the torch higher, casting a circle of amber light. He moved at its center, hurrying toward the huge roanwood chair on its small dais at the far end of the hall. From there, he delivered his teachings and lectures each morning when the hall was full. He gave the chair only a cursory glance as he passed behind it and parted the colorful arras that hung upon the rearmost wall. A small corridor there led to yet another chamber. He opened its door and stepped inside.

Only he, Acton Kathenor, was ever allowed to come to this room alone. It was his sanctum, his private place of meditation. There was no solace waiting for him here, though, not tonight. Hands trembling, he set his torch in a sconce near the door and moved to the center of the room.

A great brass cauldron stood on an iron tripod base at the chamber's center. Bands of runes were raised in relief around the cauldron's belly. They danced in the sputtering torchlight, seeming to move in an unnatural ring-around-the-rosy. Kathenor caught his breath and covered his mouth with one hand as he watched the arcane choreography. Still, he summoned his courage and bent over the cauldron. There was no seeing down into the huge kettle, however. Its top was covered with a grand, perfectly fitted mirror of rare, polished glass.

Kathenor stared at his own frightened face. Then, another fragment of his dream flashed through his mind as, for an instant, the image darkened and clouded over and something else swirled there. He whirled with a tiny cry, thinking something had followed him here, even to his sanctum, and that it had crept up on him from behind, revealing itself in the Eye of Boccob. But nothing was there.

He could wait no longer. He had to know what was happening, what force had disturbed his sleep with such a troubling dream. The Eye of Boccob would show him. Boccob was an indifferent god, taking little interest in the affairs of men. Yet, to his high priest he had given this mighty scrying glass. With it, nothing could long escape the notice of Acton Kathenor.

He went to a long, narrow table, which stood along one wall, and took from a drawer several sticks of incense: myrrh for memory, cinnamon for expanding awareness, rose because it was favored by Boccob himself. Kathenor carried these to the torch and ignited them, and sweet smoke quickly began to curl about the room. To each of the cardinal points he went and shook the sticks, mingling their odors as he offered short prayers. That done, he went to the mirror and circled it three times, offering more prayers. Finally, he stood still, turned the sticks upside down, and began to draw circles above the glass, faster and faster, as if he were stirring the images reflected there.

The glass began to cloud once more, and the images spun as if the whole thing had turned to water. A vortex formed at its center, sucking the smoke down into it. Acton Kathenor gave a high-pitched scream and dropped the sticks. They quickly vanished, drawn down into whatever was forming in his cauldron. The mirror-water turned black and glistened.

From nowhere the sounds of crying birds rose, thousands of birds, and winged shadows beat upon the chamber walls and darted about the room. Kathenor flung up an arm to protect his face, but the things had no substance. Gathering his courage, he bent once more over the cauldron. It belonged to him, after all. He was its master. He had to regain control of it.

He braced his hands on both sides of the cauldron and exerted his will, ignoring the shadow-birds that flew at him and beat intangible wings against his face and filled his ears with their shrill calls. Sweat broke out on his brow as he concentrated, and the trembling that filled him now was from exertion, not fear.

The waters stilled suddenly, and the mirror became a mirror once more. Acton Kathenor gave a gasp and sagged forward a bit. But he had succeeded. He peered into the mirror, and his image smiled wearily back. Then, another image began to form. Yes, the old priest thought with a sigh. Now the scrying glass would show him what he needed to know. He bent closer, full of growing excitement.

Dark wings spread upon the precious, far-seeing glass, and a terrible cry filled Kathenor's mind. It was his dream; he recognized it now! Yes, this was it.

Only this was not a dream at all.

A pair of red-glowing eyes turned his way, eyes that burned with evil and malicious purpose. Acton Kathenor knew in that instant that he had been lured here, drawn to the mirror itself by a power greater than his own, a force of which he could not conceive.

He gave a choked scream as he felt the creature's laughter. A web-work of cracks raced over the surface of the mirror. Before Kathenor could move, the Eye of Boccob exploded in a deadly glittering shower.

* * * * *

Garett Starlen woke with a start as his landlady gently shook his bed. Dumbly he stared at her wrinkled old face. Recognition came slowly as the details of the real world settled into place. He looked around the room, then back at his landlady. Gray and white strands of hair rose about her head like wisps of smoke, and the once bright topaz of her eyes had faded to milky blue. There was a hint of worry in her face.

"I called from the doorway," she said softly, "but you didn't stir."

"That's all right, Almi," he answered vaguely. He was long past the time when a sudden wake-up could be dangerous for the person disturbing his sleep. He no longer even kept a knife under his pillow, though his sword was close at hand where it leaned against the wall.

"You work too hard, Garett," Almi continued, shaking her head. She went to the small table that occupied the center of his single room, where she'd placed a tray containing several thick slices of buttered bread and a bowl of dark brown gravy made from beef drippings. There were two apples, also, and a cup of hot broth to drink.

Garett sat up, wrapping his sheet closer around his waist, as she brought the tray to him. The sheet was damp with his sweat, and it reminded him again of the dream that he couldn't quite recall. He took the tray from her and balanced it on his thighs, lifted one of the slices of bread, and dipped it in the gravy. "You're too good to me, Almi," he said as he brought the bread to his mouth. "Planning to raise my rent?" He chewed off a mouthful. The gravy was delicious, as always.

"Don't you know?" Almi answered with a shrug as she backed toward the door. "You already pay twice what I charge my other tenants." She opened the door and stepped out onto the landing just beyond. The stars shone around her head, and the outline of several darkened buildings framed her. "By the way," she said, hesitating. "It's been dark for several hours. Can't be long before midnight." She left then, closing the door behind her.

Garett Starlen finished his meal, except for the apples, and set the tray aside. He paused a moment, then wiped the grease from his hands over the black mat of hair on his chest. Rising naked from his bed, he strode stiffly to a trunk on the far side of the room, opened it, and pulled out a pair of finely crafted trousers of black leather and a fresh red sleeveless tunic with a brightly sewn and highly stylized yellow star across the chest and back, which was the uniform of the City Watch. From beside the trunk he took up his boots and stamped his feet into them.

Back by his bed, he lifted the still half-full mug of broth and took a sip. He let go a little sigh of pleasure as the steam curled around his nose, and he put the mug down again. Almi's cooking was one of the reasons he'd never married, he told himself. He'd never find a woman who could cook like his landlady.

It was time to arm himself. He reached for his sword by the bed. The scabbard was of clean white sheepskin, but was crisscrossed with bands of black leather and decorated with silver coins from different lands. Pretty, but not too ostentatious. He slid the sword half out of the sheath. The blade was short, well honed. It gleamed with a fine sheen of oil in the light of the room's hanging cresset, which Almi had considerately lit for him. It was a plain-looking sword, but it had served him well. The imprint of his hand was plain to see on the wrappings of the grip.

He fastened the sword belt around his waist and moved to another trunk not far from the foot of the bed. He opened it and reached inside for his favorite dagger. Its blade was nearly the length of his forearm, and in a pinch it had served him nearly as well as a sword. A plain leather sheath with a matching belt housed the weapon. He fastened it over his sword belt, and then, picking up his purse with his few coins, fastened that to the dagger's belt.

A smaller sheathed dagger hung on a peg inside the trunk. That he slid down into his left boot.

Finally he lifted out a pair of broad leather bands and fitted them one at a time around his biceps. Small, square brass studs in the ends slipped through appropriate holes in the other ends, though there were not enough to hold the bracers in place long by themselves. Garett reached back into the trunk and selected two bronze throwing stars. Square holes in each of those corresponded with the size of the studs. He mounted them on the bands and gave them a twist, locking them in place. He half smiled to himself. The stars looked like little more than ornamentation, as he'd intended when he designed them.

Closing his weapons trunk, he returned to the first, which held his few garments, and selected the lightest red cloak he owned. It was approaching the summer solstice, and even the nights were warm in Greyhawk. The cloak, though, was part of the uniform, and it fastened with the gold brooch that bore the sign of his captain's rank.

He looked around the room for his helm and picked it up from the corner of the floor, where he'd dropped it when he came home. He tucked it under one arm. Then, as an afterthought, he turned it upside down and deposited his two apples within its padded interior.

It was nearly time to go, he reckoned. He closed the shutters of his two windows and carefully barred them. Without the thin breeze, the room quickly became an oven. Garett went to a hook on the south wall and unwound a cord there, lowering the cresset. He blew out the small flame, plunging the room into darkness. For just an instant, some element of a dream flashed back into his head, but it was too elusive and quickly gone. He hesitated, then shook off the chill sensation it had brought with it, and stepped out into the night.

He paused again on the landing, took an iron key from his purse, and locked his door. Putting the key away again, he turned and surveyed the city from his second story vantage. A few lanterns sputtered from posts in the empty street immediately below him. The Lamplighters' Guild in Greyhawk was nothing if not efficient. But most of the shops and dwellings around him were dark. The peaks and pinnacles of rooftops rose around him, stark silhouettes in the encompassing blackness. The air was quiet, almost still. But that was because he'd chosen a quiet neighborhood in which to rent his small apartment.

There were other parts of Greyhawk, he reminded himself, where, like Capt. Garett Starlen, the residents never stirred until nightfall. Those streets and those people were his special province.

His apartment dwelling was only two stories high. He ran one hand along the stucco wall as he descended the narrow stairs to street-level. Almi was in her window, as she always was, and waved him off. Her quiet little tavern would stay open most of the night. She'd keep an eye on his place, and none of her customers would cause trouble, because it was generally known that the captain of the City Watch's night shift lived above her business and would take any harm to her person or her furnishings most personally. Most personally, indeed.

With a nod to Almi, he stepped out into Moonshadow Lane and walked south a short distance to Cargo Street. West would take him to the river wharves, and he should probably check that area out later. There had been reports of theft along some of the docks lately. Instead, though, he turned east toward the Processional, which was Greyhawk's main street. In no time, he arrived at the Garden Gate, which separated the Garden Quarter and the High Quarter, the patrician sections of the city, from the rest of Greyhawk's "great unwashed." The four guards on duty at the gate recognized him at once and saluted as he passed through.

The Processional led directly into the High Market Square. For the first time, as Garett walked across the broad expanse, he noticed the waxing moon as it shed its silvery light upon the hard-packed ground and threw his shadow far before him. Again he noted the surprising quietness of the city. It was most unusual. Even in the High Quarter, of which the High Market Square was officially a part, he normally encountered a few folks wandering about.

At the end of the Processional loomed the Grand Citadel. It was a tall, intimidating structure, apparently windowless to outside appearances due to the way the stones had been cut. Officially it housed offices for the mayor and members of the Directorate, as well as some of Greyhawk's military leaders, but these days it primarily headquartered the City Watch.

A flock of birds calling to each other as they flew overhead made Garett look up. Briefly they crossed the moon and were gone. The cries faded shortly after, and the night was still once more.

Garett sighed and wondered what it would be like to be curled up on the bank of the Selintan with a soft woman in his arms, listening to the purl of the river as it flowed between its banks from the great lake called Nyr Dyv southward to the Azure Sea, with nothing over them but the stars and the moonlight. That would be nice, he figured.

But he had given up such pleasures. He was captain of the City Watch's night shift. Night after night, he walked this same route, to this same building. He dealt with the same kinds of scum and solved the same kinds of crime. Or didn't solve them, as often as not. It was easy for a man to murder in the darker streets, or along the wharves, and disappear in Greyhawk. And it was just as easy to steal in a city where half the politicians were openly members of the Thieves' Guild.

Still, someone had to try to keep order. That was his job, to try. Not to solve every crime or catch every criminal. Just to try. Though he was damned to explain why, he bore a strange affection for this cesspool of humanity, this city of his birth, and figured as long as any honest men walked its streets, the gods would let it stand one day longer.

Sometimes, though, he felt as if he were the last one.

Four more guards stood duty watch at the Citadel's entrance. They snapped a smart salute as he approached. He paused to exchange a few words with them. Drawing out his two apples and his dagger, he divided the fruits and gave a half to each man. They relaxed a bit and accepted his offering gratefully.

"I assume His Lordship Korbian Arthuran has departed?" Garett commented as the four munched their apples.

"Has the sun gone down?" one of the soldiers rejoined, casting innocent-faced glances over both his shoulders, as if looking for the shining orb.

Garett didn't bother to rebuke the man for his mockery. No one cared much for Korbian. The captain-general was never about his post, leaving his duties instead to junior officers. As a minor noble, he considered his title purely ceremonial. Each afternoon, he put in an appearance at the Citadel and hung around until sundown, playing at his office and attempting to "chat the men up," as he put it, claiming it raised their morale, while in reality every soldier on the watch sniggered behind the old man's back.

Maybe it was good for morale after all.

After a few more pleasantries, two of the soldiers opened the great doors, and Garett passed inside. Torches sputtered in sconces mounted on the walls and poured a black, oily smoke into the air. The main hallways of the Citadel had never been fitted with proper lamps or cressets, and the city was too cheap to pay the Wizards' Guild for any of the ensorcelled globes of light that lit the better offices and richer streets of the High Quarter. Thus, the air constantly reeked of burning rags and stale smoke.

Garett wrinkled his nose. It was always worst when he came in from the outside air, but he knew from experience that his delicate senses would quickly adjust and push any awareness of the foul stench to the back of his mind.

He made his way to his office, returning without enthusiasm the salutes of soldiers who passed him in the halls. He mounted a set of stairs and climbed them wearily. He just wasn't in the mood for this place tonight. Its thick walls oppressed him as much as the smell. He seemed to feel their ponderous weight on his shoulders.

He pushed open the door to his office. At least here the light was better. He paid for new lamps himself, out of his own pocket, and he kept the oil wells filled personally. It was a ritual with him to fill them each night, just as some merchants watered flowers and plants in their shops. He went straight to his desk, opened the bottom drawer, and removed the pot that contained his precious supply of galda oil. It was an expensive luxury. The oil had to be squeezed from the pulp of the fruity galda tree in the Cairn Hills. But it produced a sweet smell that invigorated the otherwise drab atmosphere of his small space.

"Evenin', Cap'n."

Garett didn't jump. He knew the voice. Burge spent as much time in his captain's office as he did his own, no doubt because he, too, preferred the better light. Garett straightened, his pot in hand, and turned toward his lieutenant. Burge was draped languidly over the chair behind the door. His violet eyes, which betrayed his elven blood, were dulled with boredom, as was his entire expression.

"Welcome home, Burge," Garett answered, not because his friend had been on any trip. It was their not-so-private joke that the Citadel was really the only home either of them had ever known. They frequently greeted each other so at the beginning of a shift.

Burge rose, stretched his lanky form, and took a new seat on the corner of Garett's desk. Garett turned to refill the first of his five precious lamps. "Anything interesting on our docket tonight?" he asked. Burge was always the first night-shifter to arrive, and he always had the day's gossip for his captain.

"The day's been reasonably quiet," Burge reported as he picked up a stylus and began to play with it. "No leads yet on the dock robberies. Korbian says he'll try to get to it just as soon as the new mayor and magister are installed in office."

Garett looked up briefly from his refilling and mentally counted the days until the summer solstice. On that day, Ellon Thigpen would be made mayor by the Directorate. In turn, Thigpen would invest Kentellen Mar, his personal choice for magister, to run the city's judiciary.

"Has Kentellen returned yet?" Garett asked offhandedly as he returned to his task. The soon-to-be magister had decided to take a vacation before assuming his new duties. Rumor put him somewhere in the north of Furyondy.

"Not yet," Burge answered. The half-elf crossed his long legs, leaned back on the desk, and studied the ceiling. It was then that Garett realized his friend's boredom was only an act. Well, he'd just laid it on too thickly.

"You're holding something back," Garett said, setting his pot down, turning to face Burge. "You want to tell me, or you want to walk double-shift with Blossom?"

Burge leaped up in mock alarm and held his hands out before him pleadingly. "No, Cap'n, sir. Please not that, sir." The half-elf put on quite a show, pretending to swallow hard as he wrung his hands. Then he dropped the act and turned serious again. "The day watch found another body floatin' in the stream down by the Old Town wall this mornin'."

Garett frowned as he bent over his desk. That made five in the last two weeks. "Same as the others?" he asked.

Burge leaned against the wall and picked at a nail as he nodded. "Not a pretty sight at all. A woman this time. Nice lookin', too. And there's been reports of several more disappearances in the Slum Quarter."

Garett pulled out his chair and sat down, digesting the information. A piece of his dream fluttered through his brain again, but it was gone as soon as he tried to grasp it. For some reason, he thought of the birds he'd seen above the High Market Square.

"Was it a patrol that found her?" he asked sternly.

Burge shook his head, and a flicker of irritation showed on his face. "A couple of merchants on their way to set up shop in the Petit Bazaar. You can't keep this quiet, sir. Rumors are already beginnin' to spread. People in the lower quarters are gettin' nervous."

"Exactly what we don't need with a big citywide celebration coming up," Garett said, his mind working. "Double the patrols in the Artisans' Quarter, the Slum Quarter, and the River Quarter. The Foreign Quarter, too. And alert all the watch houses to keep a sharp eye out." He leaned back in his chair, put his feet up on his desk as he thought, and turned his gaze up to the ceiling. "I've got this strange feeling."

"A woman would take care of that," Burge quipped, rolling his eyes. "I've told you, a night down on the Strip is what you need. I could show you some places that would straighten your chest hair."

Before Garett could make his usual excuse, his door opened. Blossom ducked her head as she passed under the jamb, and a cascade of blond hair spilled forward. The woman stood nearly seven feet tall. That was the first thing a man noticed about her. The second was her startling beauty. The third was the hard gleam in her cobalt eyes, which said she didn't take dung from anybody.

"Trouble, Captain," she reported crisply. "We've got a patrolman downstairs. He says Acton Kathenor has been murdered."

Garett and Burge exchanged looks. Garett hissed an unintelligible curse and rose from his chair.

TWO

A swift walk down the Processional brought Garett, Burge, and Blossom to the Street of Temples in the sector of Greyhawk known as the Halls. It was in this part of town that most government offices were located and where most of the day-to-day bureaucratic activities took place. Greyhawk University was also located here, as well as most of the city's major religious institutions. It was a refuge for intellectuals and scholars, clerics and priests.

Rudi, the fourth member of what Garett considered his personally selected, elite team, was already on the site, blocking entrance to Acton Kathenor's inner sanctum. He was short, a mere five feet, two inches, and sensitive about it. He was as cute as the proverbial bug, too, almost cherubic, being a mere seventeen years old. His size and his looks had made him the victim of a lot of teasing in his earlier years. No one teased him anymore, though. Not unless they were damned good with a sword.

Two men from the patrol that Rudi led had a big, rough-looking character at sword-point between them. A score of acolytes and novitiates crowded the narrow corridor from the main hall to Kathenor's sanctum, demanding access to the chamber, shouting questions and accusations and demands in very unpriestly language.

"Shut up!" Garett yelled at the top of his lungs, and to his surprise, the priests fell silent. "All of you, back out into the main hall. Boccob alone knows what evidence you might have trampled on, pressing back here like this. No one gets into Kathenor's sanctum until I say so!"

One of the priests stepped forward. Garett didn't know him, but from the red sash the man wore around his waist, the captain guessed he was a priest of some rank. "This is our temple," the man said gruffly. "Your orders have no weight here."

Without a word, Blossom stepped next to the priest and glared down at him. He looked up, finding himself suddenly eye-to-cleavage, and his cheeks began to redden, but whether from embarrassment or anger, Garett couldn't guess. Nor did he care.

"If it's weight that concerns you," he said dryly, "I can order her to sit on your chest. That ought to keep you out of the way."

The priest sputtered and threw up his hands. Turning, he pushed the acolytes out of his way as he stormed back into the main hall. Most of them followed. A few others lingered, but Rudi drove them off with a scowl.

"Who's this?" Garett said, indicating the tough Rudi's patrol had nabbed.

"Not sure, Captain," Rudi answered, returning to Garett's side. "We found him wandering around outside. Definitely foreign. He had a sword, but couldn't produce a license. We haven't had time to question him further."

Garett stepped closer to Rudi's prisoner and looked him up and down. "Ratikkan, I'd say, by the look of him." He pursed his lips and nodded, content with his assessment. "Mercenary?" he asked, expecting no answer other than the stubborn glare he got. Ratikkans were like that: too stupid to know when trouble was worth getting into.

Garett shrugged and turned his back. "Bring him along," he said, pushing open the door to Kathenor's sanctum.

Boccob's high priest was bent over the cauldron, which was slowly filling with blood that leaked from countless deep lacerations on the old man's face and throat. Blood had also spilled down the outside of the cauldron. A pool had formed on the floor around the iron tripod's legs. Something crunched under Garett's boot, causing him to look down. Shards of glass were scattered everywhere.

"Has anything been touched?" Garett asked Rudi.

The diminutive patrolman shook his head. "Not since I got here, sir," he said. "My patrol was working up the street when one of the novitiates came screaming out, calling for help. We got here pretty quick." He rubbed his chin as he spoke. "One of the other priests might have touched something, though."

"This torch was burning?" Garett probed.

Rudi nodded. "Yes, sir."

"Bring it closer."

Burge took the torch from the sconce and carried it to the cauldron. Garett bent down to see better and frowned. Steeling himself, he grabbed a handful of the old priest's white hair and lifted the corpse's head. Bits of glass, embedded in the skin, caught the torchlight and sparkled. Kathenor's throat had been multiply sliced along the strategic arteries. His eyes were bloody holes, and his face looked like tenderized meat. Even so, it wore a look of horror that sent a chill up Garett's spine.

Garett let the head fall forward against the inside of the cauldron, and straightened, resisting the urge to vomit. It was a holy place, after all, and he wouldn't defile its floor— or the cauldron, either—with Almi's bread and gravy.

He moved away and examined the walls, finding bits of glass embedded there as well. "I think we can let your prisoner go, Rudi," he said, turning slowly, running a thumb thoughtfully over his lower lip. "He had nothing to do with this."

"How do you know without questioning him?" Rudi asked, too surprised to add his usual "sir." "We found him right outside the temple." He cast a sidewise sneer at the Ratikkan. "And he's obviously the type."

Garett continued to rub the ball of his thumb over his lip as he walked back toward Kathenor's body and bent near the cauldron. With the toe of his boot he pushed at three half-burned sticks of incense, which lay on the floor. "First of all," he said, peering down into the bloody cauldron, "the outer door was locked until one of the priests called for help. Even if the Ratikkan could have gotten inside the temple, how would he have found this room? The main hall was absolutely dark, and the entrance is hidden behind arras." Garett straightened, circled the cauldron, and took up a position behind Kathenor's doubled body. Slowly he looked over both his shoulders.

"Assuming he did manage to get in somehow, if you wish to press the point," Garett said, continuing, "do you think he killed Kathenor by smashing his head down through the glass?" He winked at Rudi and shook his head. "No. In fact, this is the most fascinating part." He beckoned to Burge, who held the torch. "Stand in front of me with the light," he directed.

Burge took up a position on the opposite side of the cauldron and held the torch steady.

"Look at the wall!" Blossom exclaimed, pointing.

Tiny spears of mirrored glass glittered, embedded deeply in the wood paneling of the east wall and a portion of the ceiling. Yet there was a space where no glass at all sparkled.

"Kathenor must have bent over like this," Garett said, imitating the position he surmised the old priest had taken just before his death. "That's why you see him slumped so. The mirror exploded outward. The area on the wall without glass roughly corresponds to the shape of Kathenor's body. His flesh intercepted those fragments."

"But if the mirror exploded outward as you say," Burge interrupted, "then the fragments would be randomly dispersed about the room." He looked at Garett with a puzzled expression. "From the looks of things, though, the force of this explosion took a specific direction." He pointed at the south wall.

"How about that?" Garett said with a vague smile.

Rudi harrumphed. "That's impossible."

"Not for magic," Blossom responded, low-voiced.

The room fell silent. Even the torch seemed to cease its sputtering. At last, Garett spoke again, turning to the Ratikkan. He should have gotten rid of the man earlier. He had no doubt the adventurer would soon spread the story of Kathenor's murder through every tavern in the city. "There's a tax on mercenaries in Greyhawk," he told the man. "No foreigner carries a sword unless he's paid three gold orbs for the license. You have three gold orbs?"

"He was probably coming here to steal them," Rudi commented rudely.

The Ratikkan sneered down at the little soldier. Then he looked at Garett and shook his head.

Garett sighed inwardly. At least he could delay the spread of this tale for a few hours. Maybe he could find something out in that time, though he had precious little to go on and little appetite for stepping into something involving magic—and, inevitably, wizards.

"You'll be our guest for the night, then," Garett told the Ratikkan. "We'll confiscate your sword, of course." He waved to the pair of Rudi's men who held the mercenary at sword-point. "Take him to the Citadel."

As the man was led away, Garett turned again and studied the room, imprinting every last detail in his mind.

"Who could have the power," Burge whispered, coming to Garett's side, "to strike at Boccob's high priest through his own scryin' glass in his own private sanctum?"

"Magic," Rudi muttered to Blossom. "I hate magic."

"But it does lend itself to interesting crimes," Garett said with a touch of sarcasm. Actually, he hated magic as much as his small sergeant. He shook his head as he turned slowly, studying the room one last time. "Tell the priests they can clean up here if they want. We're done."

Garett left Blossom and Rudi to deal with the priests while he exited the sanctum and pushed his way through the crowd of white-robes now gathered in the temple's main hall. He made his way quickly to the outer door and stepped into the warm night air. From the top of the temple stairs, he gazed down into the empty street.

Murder by magic.

His thoughts churned. It was the worst kind of case. It was a rare occurrence, thank the gods, but when it happened, it was inevitably on the night shift. Why? he cursed. Why, for once, couldn't it happen in the daytime? It would be fun to watch Korbian Arthuran stew in his own ineptitude if he ever actually tried to solve a real crime. Of course, Garett's pompous superior would never really sully his hands with a case. He'd delegate the task to someone. Most likely to Garett.

He walked halfway down the steps, stopped, and stared up and down the Street of Temples. The dim light from street lamps hung high on slender poles cast shadows everywhere. A wind swept suddenly up the street, blowing a thin curtain of swirling dust before it. The flames in the lamps flickered only slightly, just enough to set the shadows dancing.

Across the street rose the graceful and beautifully designed Temple of Celestian, the Star Wanderer, which was really more of an observatory and an educational center for astronomers, astrologers, navigators, and philosophers than an institution for religious worship. Its principal tower rose higher than the roof of any other temple or building in the quarter, giving a clear, unobstructed view of the night sky.

The teachers and priests of Celestian were not watching the sky tonight, however. The temple's porticoes and porches were unlit, but Garett Starlen noticed the figures milling about curiously in the darkness, their gazes turned toward the Boccob temple. Obviously, the Celestianites knew something was up. Probably, someone had heard the cries that had alerted Rudi's patrol. Certainly, they had seen the Ratikkan escorted away.

He looked to the temple on his right. The adherents of St. Cuthbert were equally intrigued. The chief priest, a stout fellow with flowing white hair, dressed in a fluttering green robe, stared firmly in Garett's direction and lifted a hand in greeting or salute, while shaking the mace he clutched in the other hand. Garett recognized the salute for what it truly was, an offer to help if help was needed.

The followers of St. Cuthbert were like that, helpful to the point of being meddlesome. Garett returned the salute, then turned his back to the old man as a gesture of "thanks, but no thanks."

Why Acton Kathenor? Garett asked himself slowly. Why the high priest of Boccob and not the priests of Celestian or St. Cuthbert? Some personal grudge? An old enemy of Kathenor's?

Garett glanced toward the Temple of Istus, a two-level sprawling complex just to the left and down the road. No lights burned in any of its windows, and as far as he could see, no one stirred upon its open grounds.

Footsteps sounded on the marble steps behind him. Garett turned as Burge, minus the torch, descended to his side and gave an exaggerated sigh that did little to mask the impatience and irritation that radiated from him. "It's times like this, Cap'n," he muttered, "when I wish I'd never left the elven highlands and my father's people."

"Death can be disturbing," Garett agreed, "particularly the grisly ones like this."

"Give me a break, Cap'n." Burge answered disdainfully. He shot a look over his shoulder at the half-open temple door. "It's priests, I'm talkin' about. Mealymouthed psalm-sayers. One of 'em tried to convert me while we were finishin' up. 'Get a life,' I told him." The violet of Burge's eyes flashed suddenly in the street light as he rubbed a hand over the dark stubble of his cheek, frowned further, and continued shaking his head. "Soft as a slug's belly, he was, under that robe. Never so much as held a sword in his life. You could tell by lookin' at him."

Garett smiled inwardly. Normally, he couldn't stand elves or folks with elven blood. Too damned ethereal and otherworldly for his tastes. It was almost impossible to hold a decent conversation with one, unless it was on some matter of philosophy, and that usually degenerated into a lecture if a human dared hold another point of view. Oh, they were great hunters and artists and builders and all that. But there was a chauvinism in most of them that he found more than vaguely annoying.

Not Burge, though. It seemed his mother had managed to get herself pregnant by some passing elf prince who'd promised her the world, shown her the hayloft, and vanished shortly after. With an almost vengeful determination, she'd grounded her son in the agrarian values of small-town farming life, attempting to stifle any trace of otherworldliness he might harbor in his father's blood. In time, of course, Burge rebelled and ran away to seek his father. But his mother's training had taken root too deeply. After a short stay with his father's people in the highlands, he left and took a job as a riverboatman working the Nyr Dyv and the Selintan. That life, with all its crudities and hardships, had driven the last drop of elven influence from his blood. At least that's what Burge had once confided to Garett.

Every now and then, though, Garett thought with an inward grin, the elf part still slipped out.

Blossom, Rudi, and the two remaining men of Rudi's patrol emerged from the temple. They descended the steps to the point where Garett and Burge stood, then they went down to the street together. Garett glanced up at the priests of St. Cuthbert, who were beginning to file back into their own temple, as if realizing that whatever excitement had brought the City Watch running was at last over. Only the old white-haired priest kept vigil as Garett and his companions passed by on their way back to the Citadel.

"We're going to have to go to the Wizards' Guild with this one," Blossom said quietly.

Garett agreed. He'd have to make a full report to Korbian, of course, and the Directorate would have to approve any involvement by the Wizards' Guild. Seeing Korbian meant staying up at least until early afternoon when the old fool usually showed up. Then he'd probably have to go straight over to the guildhall. It would cost a pretty coin to involve the Wizards' Guild. Magicians placed a high value on their services, especially when the funds were coming from the city coffers. The new mayor wouldn't like it at all.

There was nothing to be done about it, though. Politics be damned. Garett had worked enough of these kinds of cases to know he was helpless unless the guild could give him some kind of clue about how to proceed.

As they reached the end of the Street of Temples and stepped out onto the better lighted Processional, Burge touched Garett's arm and stopped. A group of six men was approaching, coming up the Processional from the direction of Old Town, walking purposefully, and they carried their lanterns high. As they drew closer, Garett noted the cudgels that two of them carried and the blue tabards with embroidered crossed cudgels that the same pair wore. On their heads they wore light blue caps with long white feathers stuck in the bands.

"Ho, night watchmen!" Garett called, stepping into the center of the street where he could plainly be seen.

The Guild of Night Watchmen was a group separate and distinct from the City Watch. For one thing, they were all volunteers. Each night, they walked the streets in teams of two or four. If trouble occurred, they tried quietly to calm the situation, or one would run for the City Watch while the other observed the situation. They could be hired as escorts for citizens who needed to be abroad after dark and wished the extra security, or they could be hired to guard warehouses, shops, or even estates in the High Quarter. They were scrupulously honest and maintained a good relationship with the City Watch, whose burden they helped ease.

The man in the lead stopped suddenly and squinted. "Captain Starlen, is it?" he said with a trace of surprise. "Now there's a bit of luck. We were just on our way to see you, sir. There's been a murder in the Foreign Quarter."

"A murder?" Garett said. He looked past the night watch leader. Four of the men with him were not night watchmen at all. They were Attloi. By their brightly colored dress Garett recognized them. Gypsy people at heart, they knew no nation or homeland. There was always a contingent of Attloi, though, in the Foreign Quarter. Garett frowned. One murder a night was enough for him. But there was no way around this. It was his job. "Who was murdered?"

"Exebur," one of the Attloi growled angrily. "What are you going to do about it?"

"Exebur the Seer," the night watch leader explained calmly, deferentially. "Most unusual, it was, too. His throat was cut with one of his own tarot cards. Apparently while he was laying them out for a reading."

"You're sure it was a card?" Blossom asked doubtfully. He was only a night watchman, after all, her tone of voice seemed to say. Not a true professional.

"A card," the night watchman replied, unoffended. "It's still in his neck, real deep, too, if you care to come and look, my lady."

"If you'll forgive a morbid curiosity," Burge inquired, "which card?"

The angry Attloi man spoke up. "The Raptor," he answered darkly. "It's one of the major arcana. A card of great power. An evil omen." Several of the other Attloi grumbled in agreement and made warding signs in the air, as if even speaking of the card was reason enough to protect themselves.

"Exebur was our greatest seer," the Attloi leader went on bitterly. "He made us much money wherever we went. He had the true vision."

Garett pursed his lips thoughtfully. This Attloi was more concerned about the loss of income to his tribe than about another man's death. He looked the man up and down, studied him, and noted the garish quality of his clothing. He was wealthy by Attloi standards, perhaps a gypsy prince. His bearing conveyed the same impression.

There was more here, though. Something to take note of. It couldn't be coincidence. Garett didn't believe in coincidence, especially when murder was involved. He looked to Burge and turned his back to the others. In a voice too low for anyone else to hear, he said, "Kathenor was a seer."

Burge raised an eyebrow. "Think there's a connection, Cap'n?"

"I think we're not going back to the Citadel yet," Garett answered, his head bobbing up and down slowly, his mind racing. Here was a mystery. The high priest of the wealthiest temple in Greyhawk and an old gypsy fortune-teller, both murdered on the same night, apparently in the same hour. He put his hands together and began to rub circles on his left palm with his right thumb. It was a habit he had when confronted with a puzzle. "I want to see the body," he announced.

"I told you!" the night watch leader beamed suddenly, his face lighting up as he turned to the Attloi at his side. "If your friend had to get murdered, night's the time for it. Captain Starlen there, he knows what's what. We'll have the killer now, that's for sure, and soon!" He turned back to Garett, and flashed a proud smile. "Who do you think did it, Captain, sir?"

Garett put on his best patient expression. "Maybe I'd better see the body first," he reminded.

"Right," the night watchman agreed with a hint of embarrassment. "Right this way." He parted the Attloi men and beckoned, and they all started south on the Processional for the Foreign Quarter.

The gypsies dwelled in the poorest section of the Foreign Quarter. The stone and stucco tenements rose up ominously, shutting out the moonlight, as the party turned off Marsh Street and walked up Chokerat Road. Here there were no street lamps, and Garett was grateful for the night watchmen's lanterns. The air in this part of the city smelled vaguely of the swamps that stretched just beyond Greyhawk's wall. Whenever the wind blew, it brought the marshy odor.

As they turned another corner and started up Mouser's Way, the heart of the Attloi community, they spied torches and a crowd of people all quietly packing wagons, hitching mules, and preparing to leave. No matter that it was the dead of night. Even as Garett and his companions drew nearer, a pair of carts separated from the rest and headed for the Marsh Gate, the closest exit from the city. A man and his son drove the mule. A woman and two small daughters walked alongside. No one was speaking.

The night watch leader brought the group inside Exebur's apartment. The single room was filthy and littered with possessions, knickknacks, and things Garett guessed the old man had scavenged from the alleyways of Greyhawk. A pair of candles burned on the table in the center of the room, and a deck of fortune-telling cards lay scattered all about, as if a powerful wind had swept through the only window.

On the floor beside a chair that had turned over, Exebur's body lay in a pool of its own blood. As the night watchman had assured him, the throat had been cut. A thin red line was plainly visible from one side of the neck to the other, and the edge of a single card was still deeply embedded under the left jaw.

"I've seen paper cuts," Burge muttered, "but this is ridiculous."

Garett took one of the candles and knelt by the body. He

bit his lip. Then, seizing a corner of the deadly card, he drew it out and held it up to better light. Blood streamed down one edge and dripped on the knee of the captain's trousers until he stood up.

The card was saturated with Exebur's life fluid, but it was still possible to see the huge black bird painted upon it, wings displayed, its red eyes burning, a naked man and woman grasped in each of its talons as it swept them into the air.

Garett shivered as he looked at the card. The Raptor, it was called by the Attloi. Or, sometimes, The Bird of Prey. He placed the card down on the table and backed a step without taking his eyes off it. It disturbed him strangely, lying there among the other cards, stained as it was.

He felt the others around him watching him, Burge and Blossom and Rudi, the two patrolmen, the night watchmen, and the four Attloi who had come seeking him. Even Exebur. No one had closed the old seer's eyes yet. They were all watching him. Perhaps they, too, felt the same strange tension, like a fire in the air.

Let them think what they would. Garett couldn't help himself. He picked the card up again and held it to the candle flame. At first, it only sputtered and smoked, too wet to take fire. But the flame found a dry spot near Garett's fingers and began to eat its way into the card's heart. Garett dropped it. Before it touched the floor, most of it was ash. What remained blackened and curled and folded and crumbled in on itself.

A tenuous smoke wafted unpleasantly through the room. Garett looked at his comrades as he took another step away from the table. The sole of his boot was sticky. When he looked down to see why, he discovered that the red pool around the old man had spread to the spot where he'd been standing.

THREE

Three more seers were found dead before morning rose over Greyhawk. In the Garden Quarter, the seeress Katina was found drowned with no more than a scrying bowl full of water on the table above her body. In the River Quarter, Davin Timbriel was discovered by the late-night arrival of his lover, who had summoned the watch at once; his skull had been crushed, and his own crystal ball had been the weapon.

On an impulse, Garett sent Rudi's patrol back into the university section of the Halls to check on old Qester Redmorn, the most renowned seer in the city. The aging Redmorn lived alone and seldom ventured out. His ability to foretell events once had brought him renown throughout the entire Flanaess. Rudi found the old man with the thin gold chain of a pendulum twisted and knotted around his throat. The windowless room in which he died had been locked from the inside.

All the greatest seers in Greyhawk were dead, murdered in one night, possibly in the same hour, each by the instrument of his or her divinatory art.

"I want this kept quiet," Korbian Arthuran insisted, thumping his hand down on the corner of his desk for emphasis. He glared at his night shift commander. "Do you understand? Warn your people they're not to speak of it. The mayor's investiture is just a few days away. We don't want to frighten the citizenry before such an important occasion."

Garett stood at ease in the center of the captain-general's office, unable to hide the look of disdain on his face. It had been a long night and a longer morning. He rightfully should be home in bed now, but there'd been too much for him to attend to for him simply to leave at the end of his shift. Unfortunately, he'd been obligated to inform Korbian of events. Now his superior officer was trying to tell him how to run the show.

Korbian Arthuran, however, had not been able to keep the news to himself, and shortly after his arrival at the Citadel, the new mayor had walked in. For most of an hour, Ellon Thigpen had listened quietly, even intently, to Garett's report. He had asked a few reasonably intelligent questions, then fallen silent again.

Suddenly, though, he stepped away from the shadowed corner where he'd been leaning. "And how do you propose to keep the murder of five notable citizens quiet, Korbian?"

Thigpen was all politeness and manners as he moved about the room. Yet, Garett wondered abruptly if there wasn't just a hint of acid in the mayor's tone of voice as he spoke to the captain-general.

"Particularly these five," Thigpen continued. "Except for the priest, Kathenor, and old Qester, the others have clients, some of whom are probably showing up for appointments even as we stand here." He rubbed his chin with one hand and inclined his bald head thoughtfully as he paced back and forth between Garett and Korbian. "No, no. There's no way we can keep their deaths secret. What we must do, however, is play down this magical angle. Convince the people these are common murders."

Garett gave a sigh as he listened to Ellon Thigpen. He once had held the man in some regard, considering him one of the few honest individuals to hold a seat on the Directorate. But even in the short time since the announcement that Thigpen would become mayor, Garett thought he noted changes. There was his dress, for one thing. As a wealthy merchant, Thigpen had always been well groomed and fitted. But of late he had taken to wearing robes from cloth-of-gold and blouses of the finest silks. Where before he had worn none at all, now his body fairly dripped with jewelry. Fat chains of gold and silver hung from his neck, and brilliant gems in elaborate settings ringed his fingers.

"I'm making you responsible for this matter, Garett."

It took Garett a moment to realize that Korbian Arthuran had addressed him.

"I'm much too busy with the details of the coming investiture ceremonies to personally handle this matter," Korbian went on as he circled around his desk and moved past Garett to his office door. "Security measures for all the attending officials and the logistics of crowd control have to take precedence." He put his hand on the door handle, but hesitated. He fixed Garett with a hard eye. "I *know* you can take care of this quietly." He opened the door and tilted his head to indicate Garett's next course of action.

Garett paused long enough to glance at Ellon Thigpen. The mayor folded his arms across his chest as he leaned back on Korbian's desk. His expression was cool and unreadable. He lifted his nose ever so slightly, though, as he realized Garett was observing him.

"That's all for now, Captain," Korbian said pointedly to speed Garett on his way.

Garett executed a half-hearted salute and exited his superior's office. The wooden door closed behind him with a sharp thud, and for just a moment, the voice of Ellon Thigpen followed Garett down the empty hall. Garett smiled to himself, not bothering to hide the pleasure he felt as the lord mayor tore into Korbian Arthuran. For just an instant, he entertained the notion of creeping back to the door and setting his ear against it to overhear the tongue-lashing.

Then he admitted to himself that, frankly, he didn't care what the two men said to each other. The matter had been dropped into his lap, whether he liked it or not, as most such matters usually were. It didn't surprise him. He'd been prepared for it. He only hoped that with the coming celebration to occupy them, Ellon and Korbian would stay out of his way and let him run a proper investigation.

He worked his way through the labyrinthine Citadel and down to the next level. There were more people in the halls here as officers and soldiers checked in before reporting to their assigned watch houses in each of the quarters, as minor bureaucrats from the Halls rushed about with forms, as various other personnel went about their duties.

Garett returned salutes and muttered distracted greetings without stopping for anyone as he made straight for his own office. Not until he kicked open his door without even bothering to try the handle did he realize how angry he felt. The door smashed back against the stone wall and rebounded. Garett blocked it with an elbow, went inside, and closed it quietly. In the privacy of his office, he stood stock-still for a moment and drew a deep breath.

"It's only because they know in their heart of hearts you're still prettier than they are."

Garett hadn't even noticed Burge lounging in his chair with his feet propped up on his captain's desk on the other side of the room. The half-elf regarded him with a crooked grin while he drummed the fingers of his left hand absently upon his chest.

"You should be in bed," Garett said, his tone of voice betraying his own weariness as he took a seat on the corner of the desk and ran a thumb over the pile of reports that came in each morning from the watch houses.

Burge shifted one foot so that the heel of his boot rested on the reports. At the same time, he reached down on the floor beside the chair and brought up a ceramic bottle and two silver cups. He pulled out the cork with his teeth as he slid one of the vessels toward Garett. "I was headed there," he said, spitting the cork across the room. It hit the far wall and rolled about on the floor. Burge could spit a cork farther than any man Garett had ever seen, even knock an object off a table from ten paces. His skill and accuracy was legendary in half the taverns in the River Quarter. "Then I saw Korbian come in with blood in his eye and Ellon Thigpen right behind him," he continued calmly. "I figured it would take 'em about an hour to decide to cover it all up, then you'd need some of this." Without taking his feet from the desk, he leaned forward and filled the cup in front of Garett, then his own. "Go on, it's the best Celanese in the city."

Garett frowned, then picked up the cup and sipped. The fine, sweet wine flowed sensuously down his throat, and he closed his eyes, the better to savor its flavor. "Nice," he murmured as he raised the cup and sniffed the wine's heady aroma. "Very nice."

Burge tossed the contents of his own cup down in a single gulp and refilled it from the bottle. "Let's finish it," he suggested, holding the bottle out to top off Garett's cup.

"Let's not," Garett answered firmly, pushing the bottle back and setting his own cup down. "We're going to need rest and clear heads tonight, not hangovers." He hesitated and stared out the narrow window, the only one in the room. Its shutters had been thrown back to admit the breeze and the bright morning light from the east. The sky beyond was a perfect, clear blue. Yet Garett's thoughts were on the night to come. "This isn't over," he told his friend quietly. "I feel it in my bones."

Burge took his feet down slowly, rose, and went to stand by the window with his cup in his hand. "Maybe you need some time off, Cap'n," he suggested, his voice pitched low with concern. Pausing, he sipped from his cup and regarded Garett over the rim before he continued. "You haven't had a night away from here in over a year. You take your duties too seriously."

Garett frowned again and waved him off.

"A tired man makes mistakes," Burge persisted, throwing one of Garett's own favorite aphorisms back at him.

"Then we should both get some sleep," Garett said, rising to his feet. In fact, he was quite tired and looking forward to his bed. Maybe Almi could prepare him a simple breakfast before he retired. "Tell Blossom and Rudi to come in early tonight, though. You, too. Say, just after dark."

"Slave driver," Burge muttered with a sidelong glance. He tipped his cup and drained it again. He gestured toward the bottle on the table. "A good Celanese shouldn't be recorked, you know. Loses its flavor, it does."

"Then I suggest you take it back to the barracks and share a drop of it with your comrades there," Garett answered good-naturedly. Unfortunately, he didn't have the benefit of an elf's alcohol-resistant constitution. Not even a half-elf's. He picked up his cup and poured the remains back into the bottle. The one taste had been paradise. But one taste was enough. "I appreciate the thought, though, Burge," he added as he bent over to pick up the cork. He wiped it with the hem of his scarlet tunic and tossed it across the room. "You're a good friend."

Burge caught it with an easy sweep of his hand and pushed it back into the bottle. "If I didn't know you, Cap'n, sir," he said, collecting both the silver cups in one hand, "I'd think you were a stiff." He shrugged as he headed for the door, opened it, and paused there. "All right, then. We'll all check in early this evenin' to please our cap'n." He stepped across the threshold into the hall and turned back again. "You comin'?"

Garett nodded and answered, "Shortly."

Burge made a face. "Uh-huh. I know what that means."

He gave another shrug and, without looking back, walked away down the long hall that led from Garett's door.

Garett watched his friend's back until Burge was gone. Then he moved around his desk, settled himself in his chair, and reached for the stack of reports. He let go a small sigh as he read through the first one. The Slum Quarter, at least, had had a quiet night.

The sun was far above the upper edge of his only window when the captain tossed the last report back onto the desk, leaned back in his chair, and stretched. The breeze blew on his neck as he folded his hands behind his head and closed his eyes. It was a warm breeze, but still welcome. Any breeze that managed to find a way into the Citadel was always welcome. He rose and went to the window. Leaning there, he looked down and south into the expanse of the High Market Square. A number of people with time to spare meandered about the grounds while clerks and soldiers made their way purposefully in a straight line between the High Market Square and the Citadel's main entrance.

How had he come to this? Garett wondered suddenly as he looked out at the city of his birth. Its buildings and streets glittered in the sunlight. The splendid estates of nobles sprawled around him in this section of the High Quarter, all carefully and beautifully kept, and the tall, majestic grove of trees that surrounded the Lord's Tomb swayed gracefully under the gentle brush of the wind.

Necropolis, the City of Night, was gone. Greyhawk in the daytime was a matchless pearl.

Yet he knew that was only the view from the High Quarter. In the Artisans' Quarter, where his parents had reared him—or, worse, in the Slum Quarter or Thieves' Quarter—the views were quite different. There, even in the daytime, some of the streets remained dark where the tall, crumbling tenement buildings pressed close together.

He thought fondly of his parents. His father, Dranh Garett, had been a weaver and merchant of basket goods. Through hard work and long hours, Dranh had managed to provide a good life for his small family and saved enough to give his son an education. Garett had been their only child. Too late in life, his mother, Naria, had attempted to bear a second child, and it had cost both her and the baby their lives. His father never quite recovered from the loss, and took to drink. One night, while Dranh wandered home drunk from the River Quarter, two thugs accosted him on Horseshoe Road, took his purse, and shoved a dagger into his belly. It took Dranh four days to die.

Garett had been twelve years old. With the help of a family friend, he managed to liquidate all his parent's assets and belongings and put the money in trust with a reputable moneylender. Keeping only a small sum, he purchased a sword and a horse, a few supplies, and left Greyhawk. At the time, he thought it would be forever.

He still remembered the feeling that had surged through him on that day when he rode east through the Druid's Gate into the wide world. He had never in his life been outside the walls of Greyhawk. Despite the grief he felt, a sense of wonder washed over him as the entire world spread before his feet. He rode eastward through the Cairn Hills, stopping long enough to see the incredible gem mines nestled there before pushing on to the Duchy of Urnst.

In Urnst, he killed his first man, a road agent who tried to steal his horse one night. The man had come upon him in his sleep, tried to slip the line, and ride away. But Garett hadn't been asleep, just stretched out quietly by his fire.

Dranh had trained his son to weave baskets, not to fight with a sword. But Garett found, almost to his surprise, that he had an affinity for the weapon. He had not been proud of the killing, but it had pleased him to know that he could defend himself.

He had spent the next few years after that merely adventuring around, wandering without purpose, seeing the sights. He had sailed on the Azure Sea in the southlands and traveled the edges of the deadly Sea of Dust in far-flung Bakluni. From the rocky shores of the Dramidj Ocean he had seen the Pinnacles of Azor'alq, rising slate-gray and as sharp as daggers from the tossing white-capped waves, and he had seen the circling dragons that made their nests there. To the fantastic lands of Oerth he had journeyed, providing for himself a better education than Greyhawk University, with all its teachers and philosophers, could ever have given him.

His tutors had taught him to look into books, to look at the stars, to watch the flights of birds, to note the march of history. But now he learned more practical skills, how to fight, how to survive, how to look into the hearts and souls of men. He fought wars for countries whose names he couldn't remember. He killed more times than he wanted to remember. The scars on his body were too many to count. He couldn't remember the exact day when wandering took a darker turn toward the mercenary side of life.

Nor could he quite remember the day when he woke up and realized how tired of it all he had become. But he rose that same day, rode to the nearest port, and booked passage on the first ship that would take him closer to Greyhawk. The journey took months of sea and overland travel. Finally, a boat carried him up the Selintan River from the Azure Sea and deposited him, weary and down to his last silver noble, on the docks of his hometown. That was in his twenty-fifth year.

The moneylender with whom he had left his small inheritance was, of course, dead. The weasel-faced cousin who had assumed the business had no record of any such transaction. Garett only grinned and took it all in good humor. Then he proceeded calmly to smash the man's place of business. As soon as the City Watch arrived, he asked for a job, and when he demonstrated that he could read and write, they made him an officer.

That had been five years ago, and he had risen fast through the ranks. But, he realized, now he had risen as high as he ever would, and sometimes the memories of those distant, wonderful places he had visited called to him. He had never seen the Burning Cliffs far up north by the Icy Sea. He had always wanted to see the Burning Cliffs.

Garett gave another stretch and straightened the reports on his desk. There was no point in dwelling on the past, he told himself. He had come home to Greyhawk, and here he intended to stay. He'd traveled enough to learn that he couldn't make the world a better place, but maybe he could make one or two streets just a little safer.

He closed his door behind him as he left his office and made his way out of the Citadel into the bright day. A strong western breeze blew over him, bringing with it just a whiff of the Selintan River. He accepted it gratefully. The day was already scorching; without the breeze, the heat would quickly become unbearable. Reaching up to his neck, he unfastened the brooch that held his cloak and slung the garment over his right arm.

At the eastern edge of the High Market Square stood the Hall of Justice. It was a long, low building fronted by twin rows of columns carved from white stone that sparkled in the sunlight. Within, Greyhawk's eight magistrates sat in judgment over those accused of crime, or weighed arguments between litigants in civil matters. Even without a magister to oversee the eight, the courts still continued to function, though it was up to the judges themselves to work out who heard which cases until Kentellen Mar took office.

Adjacent to the hall stood the jail, a much smaller building to appearances, though actually there were two subterranean levels. Only very special prisoners or prisoners awaiting trial were kept there. Most of those convicted of major crimes were either executed, banished, or sent to workhouses in each of the quarters for a period of hard labor. For minor crimes, usually a heavy fine, or perhaps the loss of a hand, finger, or ear, was the expected punishment. In that way the city saved itself the cost of feeding and housing the perpetrator.

As Garett passed by, a group of prisoners were led out of the jail and into the light by a patrol of seven men and hustled toward the Hall of Justice. He watched them go, studying the sullen faces, then continued on.

The Processional skirted the eastern edge of the High Market, where only the most accomplished artisans and vendors of the finest wares were allowed to set up shops. The square was crowded today. Scores of patrician ladies with their husbands and servants squeezed among the narrow rows of open-fronted tents for a better look at the merchandise. It amused Garett to watch these most upstanding of Greyhawk's citizens elbow and nudge and curse each other as they vied for an expensive vase or a bolt of material the way poorer men might fight over a melon in the Petit Bazaar. His father had sometimes brought him here to sell baskets, and almost always, it was with a sense of relief that Dranh returned home at the end of the day.

"Good day, Captain Starlen!" A bald-headed halfling, draped in soft blue silk, whose belly hung over his belt, waved cheerfully to Garett from a throng of shoppers. Garett didn't recognize him at all, but he forced a smile and returned the wave as he passed on.

"Ho, Cap'n!"

From the corner of his eye, Garett saw something hurtling at his head. An apple, he realized at the last instant, and instead of ducking, he snatched it out of the air, took a bite, and turned to greet the prettiest merchant this side of the Nyr Dyv.

"Hello, Vendredi," he said, pushing his way as politely as he could through the crowd that was gathered around Vendredi's baskets of fruit. Several customers gave him vile looks until they realized who he was. He worked his way around to the side of the counter board where he would be out of the press.

Vendredi stepped from the shade of her tent into the sunlight and smiled up at Garett. Her red hair shimmered, as did the flesh of her ample breasts above the low cut of her dress. "Nice catch," she commented dryly as she reached up and took a bite of his apple before returning it to him.

"One day, I'm going to bounce one of these off your noggin, though." She shot a look suddenly toward a customer at the far end of the counter board.

"Now isn't that really stupid?" she scolded the man sharply. "What with a City Watch commander standing right here?" She gestured toward Garett while all the other customers grew suddenly quiet and backed up a bit.

The would-be thief paled as he stared at the gold-embroidered insignia so prominently displayed on Garett's chest. Garett merely folded his arms and glared. The thief swallowed and slowly lowered his arm. A fat pear rolled out of the loose sleeve, back into the basket it had come from.

"I swear," the thief protested. "It got there by accident." He forced a weak smile and tilted his head.

Vendredi put on a stern face. "Then I'd better see a pair of commons accidentally appear on my palm before my friend here," she said, again gesturing toward Garett, "becomes angry and decides to rush to my defense!" She held her hand under the man's nose.

"A pair of commons!" the thief sputtered. "For a pear?"

Garett took a bite of his apple, letting a trace of juice run from the corner of his mouth. He wiped it away with the back of his hand. "It's cheaper than the fine a magistrate would levy," he said quietly as he chewed.

The thief swallowed again and reached into a small leather purse that hung from his belt. That alone told Garett the man was no professional. The lowest apprentice in the Thieves' Guild would laugh at a man who wore his purse so visibly. Frowning, the man extracted two copper commons and placed them on Vendredi's waiting hand. Then he glanced surreptitiously at Garett and sped away.

"Hey!" Vendredi shouted, waving another customer out of her way as she snatched a pear from the basket and drew back to throw. "You forgot your purchase!"

The pear struck the poor man squarely in the back of the head, splattering in his hair as it flew into several pieces, knocking him flat. In no time, though, he was on his feet and disappeared into the crowd.

Vendredi's customers cheered, grateful for a little entertainment, and resumed their shopping. For a moment, Vendredi became too busy to talk to Garett. The action had actually helped her business as the curious stopped to watch. Now they pressed closer for a better look at Vendredi herself, and inevitably, they bought.

"If you ever want to work security," Vendredi told Garett over her shoulder, "I bet I could pay you better than the city."

Garett didn't answer. He finished his apple, nibbling it right down to the core while he watched her work. Vendredi was a bright point in his day. Almost every morning she tossed an apple at him, and almost every morning he stopped for a brief chat. She had a small farm and an orchard just outside the city walls and grew the best fruit in the district. It was a rare thing for a single woman to make her own way in the world, Garett knew, and he held a deep respect for her for managing it.

"I'd better be getting on," he said when the apple was gone.

Vendredi stooped down, pulled out a tin box, and set it on a low stool. She opened it, with a watchful eye over one shoulder. It was half-full of coins of all kinds: copper commons, silver nobles, electrum luckies, even a few gold orbs. Bending a bit lower over the box, she pressed a hand against her bosom and more coins came rushing up from her cleavage and fell tinkling into the box. When the cascade ceased, she straightened and gave herself a shake. Still a few more coppers and a noble appeared on the ground under the hem of her dress. She snatched them up quickly, dropped them in the box, and shut the lid. She pushed the box back under a basket and turned another of her dazzling smiles up at Garett.

"I like the way you do business," he said, unable to hide his grin.

She gave the neck of her dress a tug and twitched a bit as

she came to his side. "I think I've got a lucky stuck down here," she said with a pout. "Would you like to get lucky?"

Garett's grin widened, but he held up both hands and shook his head.

Vendredi lowered her eyelids playfully. "How about a pair of nice melons to take home?" she offered, running the finger of one hand lightly downward from her throat.

An old orc with bad teeth and gold earrings who had stood by listening, suddenly leaned closer. "I like melons," he said with a dry rasp characteristic of his race, licking his lips. Without sparing him so much as a glance, Vendredi picked up a lettuce and hit him over the head with it. The creature slunk away.

"Sorry," Garett said with genuine regret, knowing Vendredi wouldn't be offended. They played this game with each other quite often. Sometimes she was the aggressor and he the prey. Sometimes it was the other way around. But one of them always politely, but regretfully, begged off, and nothing had ever happened between them. Garett doubted if it ever would. "It's been a long night," he added, suddenly weary, "and tonight's going to be longer."

Vendredi abandoned the game at once. "Is it true?" she whispered, dropping her voice so her customers wouldn't overhear. "Acton Kathenor was murdered last night?"

Garett resisted the urge to laugh and gave a little sigh instead. The mayor and Korbian were fools. Already the story was spreading through the streets. By noon, there would be a dozen versions, each more fantastic than the last.

But Garett was supposed to keep it quiet. "Don't you worry, my little redhead," he answered with mocking paternalism. "Our new mayor and our captain-general have everything under control. They told me so personally."

"Thanks a lot," Vendredi deadpanned. "I feel safer than ever."

Garett said good-bye once more and started down the Processional. The street was crowded and dusty, and he was bumped and jostled more times than he could count. Each time, he paused and took a mental inventory to make sure he hadn't been pinched by some pickpocket.

The guards at the Garden Gate saluted smartly as he passed through, but he didn't stop to talk. His apartment on Moonshadow Lane seemed a long way off, and he only wanted his bed. Already his garments were sweat-drenched. It would be good to get out of his clothes and lave some cool water over his body.

A cart loaded with crates nearly ran him over as he turned up Cargo Street. "Open yer damned eyes!" the driver yelled at him, raising a whip as if to strike. Then he recognized Garett. "Oops. Sorry, Cap'n! Good day to ye!" The man cowered back down on his seat and drove on.

Garett shook his head and walked on up the street. Carts and wagons continued to trundle by. Cargo Street was the city's main route to the docks and the river, and goods came down it bound for their various markets. Still, it was less crowded than the Processional, and he made better time.

Idly he wondered what would happen if he or Vendredi ever stopped playing games, and one of them said "yes," and meant it. He had to admit she had a knack for making him smile, and he didn't know of a lovelier lady in all of Greyhawk.

From Cargo Street he turned right up Moonshadow Lane and arrived at Almi's tavern. The old woman had not risen from bed yet. The tavern required her to keep hours like Garett's. But she had thoughtfully left a plate of beef strips, a chunk of bread, and a pitcher of watered wine on the table in his apartment.

He stripped off his weapons and his clothing as he ate, then stretched out naked on his bed. He would wash later. Right now, all he wanted to do was sleep.

FOUR

Garett woke. His room was pitch black and stifling, and for a frightening instant, he didn't know quite where he was. Then he threw back the sheet and swung his legs over the side. He hung his head in his hands and just sat there for a moment, feeling as if he'd been in a good fight and lost. His heart hammered, and he ached in a score of places. Gods, he was drenched with sweat, and so was his bed.

He rose shakily, disoriented, and fumbled toward the table in the center of the room. Overhead he felt for the cresset on its slender chain. It was cold. He groped his way to the window and threw back the shutter. Immediately a soft breeze blew into the apartment and a little light spilled in from the street below.

Beyond the window, night had fallen. Garett listened to a pair of voices, a young couple who made their way up Moonshadow Lane and entered Almi's tavern. Damn! He'd forgotten to tell Almi to wake him early. That's why there was no fire in his lamp. She usually lit it before waking him.

He cursed himself as he pulled on the same tunic he'd worn the night before. He didn't have time to dig around for a clean one. Burge, Blossom, and Rudi would be waiting for him. What time was it, anyway? Almi hadn't come up yet, so it had to be well before midnight. And if couples still felt safe in the streets of the River Quarter, it couldn't be that long after dusk.

He pulled on his leather trousers and stamped into his boots. His cloak was around somewhere, and so were his weapons. Damn, he thought. He was usually so orderly about such things! He opened his door, and a thin ribbon of illumination fell across his floor. It wasn't much light, but enough to help him move about and find the things he had so carelessly discarded. In no time at all, Garett was dressed and armed.

He paused long enough to pour himself a cup of the leftover watered wine, then took a long sip as he glanced out his apartment door. A trio of characters came up the lane, locked arm in arm, laughing and staggering. They had the look of bargemen about them, kind of rough, but good-natured. Garett watched them until they passed out of sight and quiet reigned in the street once more.

He wiped the back of his hand over his forehead where a bead of sweat trickled from his hairline toward his left eye. Was it the heat or was it that damn dream again? He glanced toward his bed. The strewn sheets were clear evidence of his tossing and turning. His body was stiff, as if he'd gotten no real rest at all.

And yet, for the life of him, he couldn't remember anything about the dream. All that remained was a deep foreboding, a restless sense that something loomed out there in the night, waiting.

He swallowed the last of his wine and set the cup back on the table. Using the key in his purse, he locked his door and descended his stairs into the street.

Almi was in her window as she usually was. After all, she had hired girls to see to her customers. Minding the business of the street was her main occupation. "You're up early," she said by way of greeting.

"I'm late," Garett answered curtly, frowning at himself.

Almi ran a hand through the wild knot of hair that crowned her head. "Well, saves an old lady from climbing those steps," she said. "Got time for a bite? Take something with you?"

Garett ran a hand over his stomach, but he shook his head.

"Well, you be careful tonight, Garett Starlen," Almi said strangely. She rolled her eyes up toward the dark roofs on the other side of the street as if searching them, then craned her old neck back farther to see the narrow strip of star-speckled sky. "There's trouble in the air."

Garett followed her gaze. "I know," he answered before he could stop himself. His frown deepened. It was an odd, pointless thing to say.

Almi's gaze settled on Garett again, and she sighed heavily. "I'd have a tough time getting as much as I get from you if I have to rent that room to someone else."

Garett spared the old woman a brief smile. "Two bowls of gravy tomorrow night," he told her, "and half a loaf of bread to go with it. And you can rub my back, too, before I get up."

"Hard beans and water." Almi scowled teasingly as she waved him on. "That's what you deserve!"

There was a bit more spring in his step as he turned east onto Cargo Street, where a string of citizens meandered his way. The raucous sounds from the Strip a few blocks away drifted to him, and the people he passed were obviously headed there. He almost envied them. Burge was right. He was forgetting what pleasure was. When was the last time he'd gone out for a good time?

As he stepped out onto the Processional, he watched a crimson and gilt palanquin with drawn curtains come his way, borne on the shoulders of four stout servants and guarded by four more blue-shirted, cudgel-bearing night watchmen. They turned up Cargo Street, no doubt also bound for the Strip. Some noble out slumming, Garett thought with a disparaging sneer. Blue-shirts or no, that one would be going home without his purse. The thieves would have it, or the gaming houses.

He proceeded north toward the Citadel and through the Garden Gate. The High Market Square, so full of activity during the day, was abandoned now. The gray, hard-packed ground shone silvery in the light of Oerth's two moons. Garett thought briefly of Vendredi, home now in her bed, or perhaps reading by the light of a fire. A smile flickered over his lips. Perhaps someday he would call on her.

There were fewer people on the streets of the High Quarter. A few lamplights gleamed in the unshuttered windows of the nobles' estates, and here and there a figure or two shifted on a rooftop veranda. A small carriage, drawn by a single horse, approached and passed him. He listened to the sound of hoofbeats until they faded in the distance. The other parts of Greyhawk sometimes ran like a circus with no closing hour, but the High Quarter was usually quiet.

A couple of off-duty guards leaned against the wall to the jail. They nodded toward Garett as he walked across the High Market Square. He responded with a curt wave and went straight to the entrance to the Citadel. Two of the four sentries there, however, moved suddenly and blocked his way with their lances.

"Soldiers!" Garett snapped, stepping back and peering at the men.

One of the soldiers saluted crisply. "Begging Captain's pardon, sir," he said with a straight face. "Where's our apple, tonight, sir?"

Garett realized these were the same men who had stood duty at the entrance last night, and he hid a grin. After all, he appreciated a sense of humor, as well as a man with courage enough to use it on his superior officer. Still . . .

Garett put his face close to the face of the soldier who had spoken. "Are you asking for a bribe, man?" he accused in his sternest voice. "I give you something, and you let me in? Is that it?"

The soldier paled a bit and shook his head vigorously. "No, sir! That wasn't . . . !"

Garett turned toward the others. "Are any of you taking bribes? Speak up!"

All four shook their heads as they shot nervous glances at each other. The two who had crossed their lances to bar the captain's path snapped to attention, bringing their weapons to their sides, opening the way for him.

"That's good," Garett growled as he peered at each of them in turn. "I'd hate to think ill of any member of Greyhawk's constabulary." He made a face and drew his thumb slowly across his throat before he went inside.

He grabbed the first man he encountered in the hallway, a young lieutenant whose name he didn't remember. "Go to the barracks at once," he ordered the man. "Get four apples from the kitchen and give them to the guards outside."

The lieutenant sputtered as he adjusted the weight of an armload of papers. "Sir, I hardly think . . . ,"

"I'm sure that's right," Garett interrupted. "Don't argue. Just do it."

"But, sir," the lieutenant persisted. "The cook will be asleep!"

Garett caught the young man by his arm, pulled him close, and pressed one finger to his lips. "Shhhh," he whispered conspiratorially. "Don't alert the cook or anybody," he said. "You take care of it personally. Sneak in. Be quiet. Can you handle it?"

The lieutenant drew himself erect. "Of course I can handle it," he said, suddenly cooperative and eager to prove himself.

"Then go!" Garett turned him around and pointed him to the door.

Halfway there, the lieutenant turned and called back in a loud whisper. "Sir, is it all right if I take one for myself?"

Garett grinned and nodded, then headed for the stairs that would take him to his second-level office. Even from down the hall he saw the fine line of light that seeped under the edge of his door, and he drew a breath and let it out, knowing that his friends were already waiting for him.

He pushed open the door, spying Burge at once. The half-elf was sprawled atop his desk, propped up on one elbow, with one knee bent. Garett pointed a finger at him. "Don't give me a hard time," he ordered, hoping to defuse any criticism.

Burge, of course, ignored him. "See?" he said to Blossom, who leaned against the wall to his right. "I told you he'd be here on time. The sun just sets a little slower in the River Quarter, that's all."

Blossom said nothing. She merely frowned and turned blue eyes, heavy with boredom, on Garett.

"Welcome home, Captain," Rudi said patiently from where he sat in the chair right behind the door. "I took the liberty of refilling your oil lamps, sir."

"Thank you," Garett answered, setting his helmet down on a corner of his desk as Burge swung around and sat up. "I'm sorry I'm late. Anything from the watch houses?" He pulled out his chair, but instead of sitting down, he planted his hands on the desk and leaned over it.

Burge rose with a fluid grace and went to stand by the opposite wall, facing Blossom. "Every Attloi in Greyhawk has packed up and fled the city," he answered quietly.

"All of them?" Garett said, incredulous. "In one night?"

Burge pursed his lips. "All of 'em," he affirmed.

"That's not all," Blossom said. "A number of dwarves, or folks with dwarvish blood, have reportedly slipped out, too. Sentries also reported a pair of half-orcs left through the Highway Gate at the far south end of town."

Garett raised an eyebrow. "Dwarves? Orcs? None of them have been murdered. The Attloi I can understand after seeing Exebur's body. But why them?"

Blossom folded her hands behind her back and began to pace in a small area. She'd tied her blond hair back in a tight braid, and it swung as she moved. "I think we should ask Burge how he feels right now." She shot him a look from the corner of her eye and leered down at him. "How about it, sugar boy? Any queasies?"

Burge drew himself straighter and flashed her a bright smile. "I feel fine," he answered at once.

"Burge?" Rudi said at the same time. "Why?"

"Think," Blossom said with smug superiority. "Gypsies, dwarves, orcs. All people or races who are sensitive to the presence of magic. There's a pattern. Why not elves?"

"I'm not an elf," Burge snorted, looking insulted.

Garett rubbed a hand over his chin, wishing he'd had time to scrape his cheeks and bathe himself. "You think they're getting out because of the murders last night?" he said to Blossom. She was irritating sometimes, but she had a keen mind.

"While the 'getting' is good," she answered seriously.

Garett paced behind his desk, ignoring his friends while he thought out a course of action. The murder victims of last night had been the best seers in Greyhawk. That was the only connection they all shared. Due to the nature of the murders, the criminal was undoubtedly a wizard. Presumably then, there was some thing or some event this unknown magic-user didn't want them to "see" in advance.

But, surely, in Greyhawk, a city some called Necropolis, those were not the only five seers. They were the best, maybe, but there had to be others.

"I thought we were goin' to turn to the Wizards' Guild for a little advice," Burge said with the penchant he had for sometimes knowing what was on his captain's mind.

Garett stopped near the window and gazed down into the darkness that filled the Great Square. Beyond, the lights of the High Quarter shone like little earthbound stars. "I suggested that this morning," he answered. "But our new mayor, Thigpen, rejected it this early in the investigation. 'An unwarranted expenditure of city monies,' he called it."

Burge snorted derisively.

Rudi put on a small frown, being generally more supportive and respectful of Greyhawk's leaders than either Burge or Blossom. "Well, look at it from Thigpen's point of view," he said irritably. "You know what those mages charge every time the city asks them for the smallest favor. They've got no sense of civic responsibility at all. Ask any common constable in the watch how much a guild wizard wants for the simplest capture spell. They're worse than the Thieves' Guild, I tell you!"

Burge waved a hand before his face, as if swatting Rudi's words aside. "When five citizens die in one night," he countered coolly, "you'd think Thigpen would at least ask their fee."

"Why?" Blossom said with sudden indignation. She tossed her long braid over one shoulder and stared stony-faced at Burge. "Because these five all lived on the north side of Black Gate?" Her voice was sharp and ice-edged. "Five bodies have also been found recently in Old Town, too, or did you overlook that coincidence?"

"That's Old Town," Rudi interjected disinterestedly. "Bodies turn up there all the time. It's the Thieves' Quarter, for all the gods' sakes, and the Slum Quarter. Those people will kill for a scrap of food."

Garett turned a sharp eye toward Blossom. "Five in the New City and five in Old Town. Are you suggesting there's a connection?"

Blossom frowned again and slumped back against the wall, resuming her former relaxed posture. "I'm not suggesting anything, Captain," she said wearily. "But that kind of attitude really yanks me off. Five poor souls wind up floaters in the south stream, and it's a normal night in Old Town, nothing to get excited about. But a few wealthy fortune-tellers get capped, and the city wets all over itself."

Burge balanced his right ankle on his left knee and held

it there as he leaned forward. "You've got that look, Cap'n," he said quietly.

Garett looked at each of them. "I wonder if Blossom's on to something," he answered with a look of calculation. "Five and five. It *could* be coincidental." He gave a shrug. "Then again, I don't believe in coincidence." He faced Blossom. "This was your idea. You locate the watchmen who found those bodies. I want to hear their reports personally before I leave here in the morning."

"Some of them were daylighters," Blossom responded. "I'll have to wake them up."

"Wake them up," Garett ordered. Most watchmen of enlisted rank lived and slept in the barracks just off the High Market Square grounds. Only officers and those granted special permission had private apartments. Blossom could rouse the sleepers just before their shifts began. "Have them here in my office just before dawn."

Blossom nodded. "Anything else?"

"Yes," Garett said. "Any of you. By reputation or report, these were the five best seers in the city. Their visions were the clearest. They saw farthest into the future. Even the Attloi, Exebur, if he was as good as his people claim. Now with them out of the way, who else would you go to if you wanted to know what the future held?"

"Duncan, in the River Quarter on Queer Eye Street," Rudi answered, then hastily amended, "but most people say he's a fake."

"The Cat," Burge suggested thoughtfully. "He's an old man who lives in the slums. On Bladder Lane, I think. He's supposed to have the power."

Rudi snorted. "How much power can he have," he queried, "if he can't make enough money to get out of the Slum Quarter? Or maybe he likes living with the mice?"

Burge turned one eye toward Rudi without altering his posture in the least. "Perhaps he prefers the mice of Old Town," he suggested evenly, "to the rats who live in better places."

"Well said, elf." Blossom nodded appreciatively to Burge before she looked at Rudi and addressed him steely-voiced. "You insist on reminding us of your youth at every opportunity."

"I'm *not* an elf," Burge muttered, running his gaze calmly up her seven-foot frame, "you unfortunate, mixed-up mass of glandular confusion."

"What do you mean by that?" Rudi asked Blossom indignantly.

Garett interrupted before an argument broke out. These were his chosen officers, as well as his friends, but they didn't always get along with each other. Rudi was the youngest and sometimes said thoughtless things, and both Burge and Blossom had tongues that could cut stone or tickle silk, however they chose to employ them.

"That's enough." Garett rapped once on his desk with his knuckles to draw their attention. "Rudi, you take a patrol to Queer Eye Street. Find Duncan and ask him to come to the Citadel. Tell him I need my palm read, or my tea leaves studied, whatever it is he does."

"It may take a little time," Rudi said, rising to his feet. "He doesn't have a shop front. He works the streets and the street corners."

"Just find him," Garett repeated. "Blossom already has her assignment. I want to know everything about these Old Town murders. You're right; we haven't really done enough to check them out. You get me the details, and get me those watchmen."

Burge uncrossed his legs and stood up. "What about me, Cap'n?"

Garett put on his best false smile. "It's a beautiful night," he said slyly. "You and I are going to take a little walk down to the Slum Quarter."

Burge put a hand dramatically to his chest. "I haven't a thing to wear."

"Rip something," Blossom suggested helpfully.

"Like a stomach muscle," Rudi added with a caustic note

as he opened the door and exited.

"Nice kid," Burge commented as his eyes met Garett's. "Were his mother and father by any chance brother and sister?"

FIVE

A high wall, so ancient it was blackened with stone-rot from the heat of old fires, separated Old Town from the New City, and the Black Gate, as it was called, was the only entrance or egress. Beyond the Black Gate lay the Slum Quarter and the Thieves' Quarter, and the guards kept a careful record and a sharp eye on those who traveled back and forth, for no one did so on honorable business.

Garett and Burge took a single lantern from the gatehouse, and after exchanging a few pleasantries with the guards on duty, they passed under the gate's imposing arch and into the Thieves' Quarter, the most dangerous part of Greyhawk.

There were no street lamps in Old Town, and the darkness was oppressive. The Processional became an ill-kept road, full of ruts and holes, littered with refuse. Even the buildings in Old Town looked tired and weary. They leaned at odd angles on settled foundations. Shutters hung on broken hinges, and chimneys pitched precipitously, as if at any moment they might crumble and slide into the street below.

A few taverns were still open. This close to the gate, few businesses flourished. A bored young noble with a taste for adventure—but not too much adventure—might wander this way for a drink and brag about it afterward to his friends. Some of the lower quarter's citizens sometimes preferred to take their pleasures on the south side of the Black Gate, rather than venture into the River Quarter, where their poorer clothes might subject them to scorn and prejudice.

And of course there was the usual assortment of thugs and ruffians and low-life characters one would expect to find in the most impoverished section of the city. Men could hide in the labyrinth that was the Thieves' Quarter and never be found again. Indeed, most of Greyhawk's criminal element did just that. This quarter was home not only to the city's powerful and devious Thieves' Guild, but to the Assassins' Guild and the Beggars' Union as well.

The sound of raucous laughter spilled suddenly into the street. A door crashed open unexpectedly, and somebody sprawled face down in the road at Burge's feet. A large man, his bald head gleaming in the lamplight, suddenly appeared in the doorway, his hands curled into fists. Several others crowded quickly behind him, expecting the fight to continue.

The man at Burge's feet gave a moan and rolled over. He stared upward in confusion for a moment, his panicked gaze swiftly raking over the two men above him before he shot a glance toward the door. Then he gave another moan, scrambled to his feet, and disappeared up a narrow alley.

The large man and his comrades directed hard stares at the two City Watch officers before returning to their drinks and gaming tables. Someone closed the door, shutting in the light that had spilled onto the street. Garett and Burge both felt the surreptitious eyes that watched through the cracked shutters as they started down the Processional again.

"Wonder what that was all about?" Burge said conversationally.

Garett shrugged. "I'll wait if you care to make inquiries."

But neither had any intention of returning to the tavern. Their scarlet cloaks and star-embroidered tunics meant little in the Thieves' Quarter after dark. They were not afraid. They just weren't looking for that kind of trouble tonight.

Just ahead, three more men stepped out of another tavern and halted when they saw the gleam of Burge's lantern. For an instant, they stared at the pair of watchmen, their expressions surly, and Garett thought there would yet be trouble. One man's hand drifted toward his sword, and he tossed the corner of his cloak back over one shoulder to make sure the trio saw that he was armed. After a moment more, the three exchanged dark glances and wandered down the street and around a corner.

"Lower the hood a bit," Garett told Burge. His lieutenant fingered a small lever on the side of the lantern, and a thin metal panel slid down a few inches over the glass front, narrowing the aperture through which the light shined. The amber pool surrounding them drew in by half, and Garett nodded approval as his eyes adjusted to the new darkness.

As they walked farther on, the blackness and the silence deepened. Ramshackle tenements rose on either side of them, old wooden structures barely fit for habitation. In a good wind, they swayed and groaned, and timbers could be heard as they cracked under the stress. In Garett's memory, two such tenements had collapsed without warning. Seven bodies had been found in the ruins of the first. No one had bothered to excavate the other.

"We're bein' watched," Burge announced in a whisper. Though he continued to face straight ahead, his eyes raked from side to side.

"Of course," Garett answered without hesitation.

The old wooden boards of Kastern's Bridge creaked

softly underfoot as they passed above the shallow waters of the South Stream. The bridge, named for its architect, was one of the oldest surviving structures in all of Greyhawk, dating from the city's earliest village days. The square-cut stones that made its supporting arches had been quarried and brought all the way from the Cairn Hills by cart and set in place by hand.

South Stream made a pleasant enough sound in the quiet night, but a mild odor caused Garett to rub his nose. The stream was a narrow, meandering ribbon that actually began at the upper end of the High Quarter, where it was called, logically enough, North Stream. But as it flowed southward, it collected most of the city's waste and refuse. By the time it passed under the Black Wall, it was quite unsanitary.

A few of the poorest citizens still drew their water from the stream's banks and sometimes fished in it for their suppers, a thought that made Garett shudder, since so much of the city's sewage also emptied into it. Still, he had seen hungry men do worse. He wondered, though, if Greyhawk hadn't grown too large for its own good, when it couldn't take better care of its citizens.

Once across the bridge, they left the Processional and turned up the Serpent's Back, a twisting, shadowed street that ran diagonally through the Thieves' Quarter into the Slum Quarter. Ancient warehouses, long unused, rose on either side of them. Dark holes could be seen in the faint moonlight where the roofs had fallen through.

"Damn!" Burge muttered suddenly, stopping, and lifting one foot. The lantern revealed the look of disgust on his face as he hopped aside and scraped his boot several times on the ground. A noxious odor wafted up from the spot where he had stood a moment before. "Stepped in somethin'," he added needlessly.

"Smells like a couple of fools to me," a gruff voice said from overhead.

"Come on down," Garett invited calmly, not bothering

to look toward the source. "I was getting tired of listening to you breathe up there."

A lithe shadow dropped to the ground in front of him. In its hands it clutched a stout club. Three more figures landed noisily in the street behind them, blocking that way. Garett turned only enough to ascertain they carried similar weapons.

"You might have told me they were there," Burge whispered as he moved to Garett's side and turned to face the three. His sword was already in his hand.

"I didn't want to upset you," Garett answered with quiet sarcasm. "There's only four of them."

Actually, Burge's hearing and eyesight were considerably superior to Garett's, thanks to his father's elven blood. "Afraid not, Cap'n," Burge muttered.

"Four, did you say?" the leader interrupted, proving the quality of his own hearing. He snapped his fingers. Just up the street, another pair of figures stepped out of the shadows. As far as Garett could tell, they still only carried clubs, though it was possible they had daggers tucked into their belts.

"You're on our turf," the leader commented, clearly thinking himself in command of the situation. He was a wiry little fellow, perhaps a third of Garett's age, though most of his teeth were already missing. A gleam of desperation burned in his eye, despite his mocking tone. He tapped his club against the palm of one hand in an intimidating manner. "You want to use the Serpent's Back, you got to pay a toll. You haven't paid the toll yet, General."

Garett frowned. "It's captain," he responded dryly as he studied the figure before him.

He'd encountered such gangs in Old Town before, rover packs of desperate youths who usually preyed on the weaker, poorer members of the neighborhood. Lacking talent to win a place in the Thieves' Guild, too proud to join the Beggars' Union, and too stupid to learn a fair trade, they ran wild, depending on their numbers for survival. It was unusual for a gang to come this far north, though. They usually stayed to the southern part of the Slum Quarter.

This group, then, probably counted itself as one of the more important and daring of the Slum Quarter gangs. The possessions of a couple of city watchmen would make nice trophies they could show off. No doubt they would win a lot of respect from rival gangs.

Too bad for them it wasn't going to be that way.

"We can do this politely," Garett suggested reasonably, addressing the leader. "Let's just go our separate ways and pretend we never saw each other. No embarrassment for either of us. My men at headquarters won't laugh at me for walking into your very clever trap . . ." Garett shrugged and turned his palms outward in a gesture of offering. "And you don't get your guts handed to you by my nasty-tempered friend here." He put an arm around Burge's shoulder, and the half-elf gave a low growl.

The gang leader put on a smirk. "He don't look so nasty to the *six* of us," he proclaimed, emphasizing their greater numbers. "Now the toll on the Serpent's Back is kind of expensive this time of night. First, it'll cost you your swords. Then, we'll see what else you got."

"Don't he know, Cap'n," Burge said in a mocking voice as he waved the sword he'd already drawn easily before him, "that it's illegal for a citizen to carry a sword on the streets without a proper license?"

The leader watched Burge's sword warily. The blade gleamed with a mesmeric quality in the amber light that seeped through the lantern's narrowed aperture.

"That's true," Garett replied. "You don't have a license, do you?" he said to the leader.

An impatient voice from behind them hissed sharply. "Enough of this, Burko! Let's just bash 'em and take their stuff before somebody else comes!"

"Now that would be really stupid, Burko," Garett warned quickly before the gang leader could think it over. "There are six of you, yes, but you've only got clubs." At least, he hoped they only had clubs. At most, some might have daggers or knives, but if they did, surely they'd have them out by now. With a hasty glance around, he still counted only clubs.

"On the other hand," he continued, "we've not only got swords, but these long, ugly stickers, here." He gestured toward the long-bladed daggers both he and Burge wore on their belts. "Now, even if we weren't watch officers, even if we hadn't had a bit of training in our lives, it's still a safe bet one or two of you would die before you bludgeon us."

"All you have to do, little boy," Burge said, openly taunting them now, "is figure out which of you is gonna get it." He laid the flat of his blade back on his shoulder, as if it were a shovel or an axe being carried home at the end of a long day's work.

Garett watched Burko carefully, noting the doubt that crept over the young man's face. It might still be possible to bring this to an end without killing one of them. "Let's give them a sporting chance, my friend," Garett said with a wink to Burge.

Burge frowned and shook his head with great drama. "I don't know, Cap'n. They might be tougher'n they look." With a show of reluctance, though, he sheathed his sword.

"Look at 'em, Burko!" hissed the voice behind them again. "They're laughing at you! A couple of soft-bellied New Towners in their prissy uniforms, and they're laughing at you!"

"Shut up, Whisper!" Burko yelled suddenly, loud enough to be heard several blocks away in the stillness of the Slum Quarter. It was an amazingly careless thing to do. There were always rival gangs in the quarter who might decide to drop in on Burko and try to take his captives away from him and stomp Burko in the bargain. Burko knew it, too. It showed in the way his gaze suddenly raked along the rooftops above them.

"Last chance, lobbers!" Burko said with frantic intensity, obviously feeling the pressure from his gang to do something, at the same time realizing he might have bitten off more than his small mouth could chew. He tried to bluff his way through now. "You gonna give up them weapons? We might let you walk out of here alive!"

Garett was running out of patience. He might have tried to bargain with this poor idiot earlier and found some way to let Burko save face before his followers. He was simply no longer in the mood. If there was going to be a fight, it was time to get on with it.

He crossed his arms in a defiant pose. "No," he said flatly.

"That's tellin' 'em," Burge muttered out the side of his mouth. "You silver-tongued devil, you."

"Well . . . !" Burko fumed and stamped his foot, looking desperately for a way out and finding none as his men began to shuffle closer. His sigh was almost explosive. "Aw, bash 'em!" he shouted.

Garett moved as Burko raised his club. A silver star flashed through the darkness and thunked solidly into the wood in the narrow space between the gang leader's two hands. Burko gave a loud yelp and froze in midcharge, staring at the star. Garett moved again, and with the instep of his left boot, he swept the boy's feet out from under him. Burko hit the ground hard as the point of Garett's long dagger came to rest at his throat.

Almost at the same time, behind Garett, the hood on the lantern shot wide open. Someone moaned at the sudden brightness, and the thick sound of a fist sinking into flesh followed. "Come on!" Burge bellowed. "I won't even use a weapon!"

But the only other sounds were of feet flying in the darkness. Garett glanced over his shoulder to see Burge with his foot in the small of someone's back. The half-elf had a smug, pleased look on his face as he swung the lantern gleefully back and forth. "Go on, struggle!" he told the squirming figure under his boot.

Without taking his dagger far from Burko's throat,

Garett leaned over and picked up the gang leader's club. A well-balanced and honed throwing star was too fine a weapon to waste. He backed up a step, sheathed the dagger, and began to worry the star loose.

"You missed," Burge said with a grin.

"No, he didn't," Burko croaked before Garett could answer. The look of humiliation on his face was gratifying as he sat slowly up and felt his throat where the dagger point had touched him. He knew Garett could have killed him with either the star or the blade, and instead had chosen not to. He glared at the watch captain, but it was the dull glare of resignation.

There was a watch house in each quarter of the city with cells to hold a few prisoners until they could be transferred to the jail at the Citadel. Garett knew he should haul these two over to the Thieves' Quarter watch house, but the thought didn't appeal to him. He'd come to find an old man on Bladder Lane, not to clean up the town or do social work.

He bent down and casually seized the front of Burko's tunic and pulled him to his feet. "Have you ever seen the inside of a prison workhouse?" he asked the boy. Burko shook his head sullenly. "Let me tell you what it would be like for you," Garett continued. "You'd spend your days repairing streets or breaking rocks, and your nights upside down." He smiled his best menacing smile. "Yes, they'd like you in the workhouse. They'd feed you the best rat-bone soup. Of course, you'd have to catch your own rat and hide it from everyone else. You know how to make rat-bone soup?" Again, Burko shook his head. "Well, first you catch a rat and kill it. Then you wait a few days until it goes stiff and begins to rot. Now, every morning the guards at the workhouse will bring you a cup of water. It won't taste very good, because they never wash the mugs, but that's no matter. Anyway, when the rat is good and rotten, you dunk it in the mug and swirl it around. If the corpse is ripe enough, little bits and pieces come off. Real nourishing, but not too tasty. Still, they say you can make a big rat last several weeks."

Garett ran a hand lightly over the front of Burko's tunic, smoothing the wrinkles, and he dusted a speck from his shoulder. "You think you'd like that, Burko?" he asked quietly.

"No, sir."

Garett smiled to himself. Burko was a fast learner, it seemed. "Your friend over there." He nodded toward the gang member under Burge's boot. That one, too, had grown silent and still as he heard about life in the workhouse. "Is that the one you called Whisper?" Burko nodded hesitantly, earning a nasty scowl from his cohort. "Well, I'm going to give both your names to the local watch officers," Garett continued. "And I'm going to keep an ear out down this way. If I ever hear your names mentioned in anything less than a complimentary context, we're going to have this little talk again." He put on a big smile as he patted Burko's shoulder in a not-quite-fatherly manner. "Now, do you mind if my friend and I continue on? We're here on official business, you know."

Burko nodded again without managing to lift his gaze from the dirt at Garett's feet, and stepped out of the way.

"Thank you," the watch captain said politely, and he looked over his shoulder. "Let that one up, Burge."

Burge barely moved his foot. Whisper rolled away, scrambled up, and dashed up the road as fast as he could run. The darkness quickly swallowed him. When Garett looked back, Burko was gone, too.

"That was fun," Burge muttered, grinning as he adjusted the hood on the lantern once more. "I liked the part about the soup."

Garett set his throwing star back on the stud on his biceps band and gave it a twist. "When I was a kid, I loved the storytellers who worked the streets. I thought that was what I wanted to be when I grew up."

"Cheer up, then," Burge answered with sage sarcasm.

"You've still got time."

They walked the rest of the way down the Serpent's Back until they were deep in the heart of the Slum Quarter. Here the buildings were crowded together, each seeming to hold up another. They leaned at treacherous angles, many without doors, without shutters on the windows. Some had no roofs. Some were only the frames of buildings whose interiors had long ago fallen into rubble.

Black, narrow alleys twisted like poisoned veins among the ruined tenements, connecting roads that had no names or whose names had been forgotten. The gutters were full of refuse and slop. The air reeked.

Yet what depressed Garett most was knowing that these buildings were full of people. He and Burge might have been the last two men on Oerth, for all the signs of life he saw about him, but behind these walls were huddled the poorest of Greyhawk's citizens, the very old with no children to support them and no place left to go; the disabled, whose handicaps barred them from society; and the mad, who were exiled forever from the New City.

If the air reeked, it was with the smell of hopelessness, and the only wind that ever swept these streets was the breath of despair.

At the end of the Serpent's Back, they turned up Killcat Lane and followed that for a short distance. The black outline of Greyhawk's western wall loomed briefly against the starlit sky before they turned again and walked along a nameless street.

"We're bein' followed again," Burge commented.

Garett nodded. "I don't think they'll bother us."

The half-elf snapped his fingers. "Drat," he said.

Two more turns brought them to the street commonly known as Bladder Lane. It was not really a lane. Little more than an alley, in fact. In the old days, several popular taverns had sat very close by. It was due to this fact that a mere alley, conveniently positioned, had earned such a grand name, and one that yet lingered in the memory of

Greyhawk's citizens.

Burge lifted the lantern high as they started up the alley. With his other hand, he pinched his nostrils shut. "The taverns may be gone," he complained, "but apparently a beloved tradition is still venerated."

Halfway up the alley, the lantern revealed an old door. The wood was so old it had started to crack and splinter. The hinges were neither metal nor leather, but thick folds of half-rotten cloth that someone had nailed in place with slender pegs. Garett reached out and knocked.

"Maybe he's shoppin'," Burge suggested when they got no answer.

"I think the stores are closed," Garett rejoined. He pushed, and the door edged open an inch. "Cat?" he called.

Still no answer came. Garett eased the door open farther until the lantern's light spilled past the threshold. A table stood in the near corner, and the stub of a candle rested on the worn and scarred surface. Garett stepped inside and felt the wick. It was cold.

Burge shone the light around the tiny room. A pile of rags against the north wall had made the old man's bed. Other than the table with the candle, two chairs and a footstool were the only other pieces of furniture. There was a lot of clutter, though, dirty old bottles and pieces of clay pottery, rocks and bits of driftwood, broken tools and broken toys. The Cat had been quite a scavenger. But then, so was anybody who lived in the Slum Quarter.

"He's gone," Burge commented needlessly.

Garett turned back toward the table. The wall above it was scratched and scarred with strange markings. Lacking any writing tool, the old man had used a knife or some other sharp instrument to make his records a permanent part of his home. Some of the symbols were zodiacal, Garett knew that much. The rest were a mystery to him—all but one.

"Bring the light closer," he instructed Burge as he ran his

finger over one particular marking, feeling the rough-cut edge. The scratch was fresher than the others, the edges still splintered and pale against the darker wood. In the light, it was plain to see—a skull with horns and a pair of snakes intertwined beneath it.

It was the blazon of the Horned Society.

For many years now, the society had been the major threat to Greyhawk's peace. Not satisfied with their conquests in the Shield Lands on the northwestern shores of the Nyr Dyv, they sought to extend their influence, and eventually their dominance, through all the nations surrounding the great lake. Only Greyhawk's economic might and a not-so-secret alliance with Furyondy, the strongest naval power on the lake, stood between the Hierarchs of the Horned Society and their ambitions.

"What do you know about the Cat?" Garett asked Burge as he straightened and began to move about the room.

"Not much," Burge admitted. "He was a strange one. Kept completely to himself. Some claimed his power as a seer was great enough to make him a livin' fit for any part of the Garden Quarter. But they also said he was afraid of it, wouldn't use it, except when he had to, and certainly never to make money." Burge shrugged as he followed his captain around the room. "Like I said, a strange one. Maybe a fake. Think he's dead like the others?"

Garett shook his head. "No body," he answered. "I think he's left Greyhawk. There are certain things missing that suggest a journey, probably a permanent one."

"Maybe he was robbed," Burge suggested.

"No," Garett replied thoughtfully. "A thief in these parts would have taken everything. Certainly they wouldn't have left something so useful and easy to escape with as the candle. No, he wasn't robbed. But an old man would have had a cup to drink from and a dish to eat on, and I don't see them. Nor is there a knife to eat with. And he had something that in this quarter would have been considered a treasure." Garett stooped and pointed to a ball of thin gray hair that was speckled with dust where it lay on the floor by the bed of rags. "A hair brush," he said. "That's gone, too. And where are his scrying tools? Gone."

Burge rubbed his chin as he held up the light. "The Attloi left last night, and the dwarves and orcs today. Maybe the Cat was among them. Nobody really knew where he came from."

"Maybe," Garett said, rising, "but I think it's something more subtle. Let's go find Rudi. He was supposed to locate the other seer, Duncan. But I'm willing to bet Duncan's gone, too."

Garett headed for the door and stepped out into the darkness, intent on making his way to the River Quarter and Queer Eye Street as fast as he could. Questions burned in his brain, and a renewed urgency filled him.

"Bet?" Burge called with amused excitement as he followed with the lantern. He paused long enough to pull the door closed. The neighborhood thieves would learn soon enough that the old man's things were theirs for the taking. He hurried after his captain. "Did I hear someone say, 'bet'?"

SIX

On any given night, the River Quarter was the liveliest part of Greyhawk and the Strip was the liveliest place in the River Quarter. Even so late, the street was crowded with pleasure-seekers drawn by the taverns and gaming houses that never closed, by the whorehouses and businesses that catered to more unusual joys. It was said that anything could be bought or sold on the Strip, and if it couldn't be bought, it could at least be rented for an evening or so.

Garett shouldered past a couple of bargemen, who still stank of the river, as he fought his way through the milling throngs that filled the street. The larger of the pair gave him a hard look and curled one meaty hand into a fist until he noted Garett's scarlet cloak and tunic and quickly grew calm again. Garett paid the man no mind. His gaze swept over the faces in the crowd, and his thoughts raced inside his head.

He genuinely didn't know if it was excitement or fear that had set the blood to pounding in his ears and his heart to thundering, but it was hard to keep a stony face as he pushed and shoved through the strollers and gawkers. He glared around impatiently, seeking Rudi or the fortune-teller, Duncan, who was said to work the crowds here to earn his living. It might have been easier if he'd had some idea of what Duncan looked like. As it was, he watched for anyone who looked the part.

"A common, wealthy sir?" An old man leaned against a lamppost, carefully balanced on a crude wooden crutch. He shook a bowl as Garett walked by. "A plain copper common for an unfortunate veteran?"

That brought Garett to an abrupt halt. He had fought in too many campaigns in his younger mercenary days not to feel sympathy for the aged wretch he saw before him. The poor man's left leg was badly twisted, and a thick scar ran down the front of the thigh and over the kneecap. He had lost his right eye, too, and a dirty bandage covered it. His clothes were filthy rags. The bones of his face showed through his pale, undernourished flesh.

Garett frowned at his own softheartedness even as he reached for the small purse he had tucked inside his wide belt. As he did so, the old veteran leaned forward, and the light from the lamp above his head shifted subtly.

Garett's frown deepened. With one hand, he pushed his purse back in place. With his other, he reached out and seized the front of the old man's tunic and jerked him forward. Reacting by instinct, the fellow caught his balance on his injured leg without so much as wincing or wobbling. Garett shook his head, irritated with himself, as he put one hand down the front of the old man's tunic and drew out the small wooden hand on the chain around his neck.

The hand was the sign and license of the Beggars' Union. All members wore it when they worked.

Realizing he had betrayed himself, the beggar shrugged off his act, straightened his posture, and pushed up the eye bandage. He wasn't blinded at all, nor was he old. The scar on the leg, that was real, probably self-inflicted, but the cut had never gone deep enough to permanently injure bone or muscle. "What gave me away, sir?" he said with humble politeness. "I'd appreciate advice from a man with so sharp an eye."

Garett let him go. "The makeup is good," he answered grudgingly. "And the shadows from the light overhead heightens the general effect of gauntness. But you were too eager for my coin. When you leaned forward, the light shifted, and I saw the faint smudge of kohl you'd used to bring out the cheek bones and deepen the sockets of your eyes."

The beggar bowed. "Thank you, sir. Now, I must move along to a new spot. This one's no good, now that you've exposed me." He pulled his bandage back down and drew his crutch under his left arm. Instantly he resumed his role, turning back into an old man again. Garett watched as he hobbled off into the crowd.

"You just can't pass up the chance to instruct, can you?"

Garett turned at the sound of Burge's voice. "Did you find Rudi?" he asked, remembering their purpose in coming here.

"I've been all the way to the north end," his friend answered.

For an instant, they were separated as a group of merrymakers surged between them, singing and laughing. A woman ran her hand over Garett's chest and batted her eyes at him invitingly, though she clung to the arm of another. Her companion was too involved in the song, though, to notice, and the entire party moved on.

"No sign of the little runt, or Duncan, either," Burge concluded as they came together again and started up the street to continue their search.

"Let's check the watch house," Garett suggested. "Perhaps Rudi has been there. If nothing else, we can alert the patrols in this quarter to keep an eye out for Duncan."

They headed north up the Strip. The sweet, warm smells that issued from some of the restaurants they passed reminded Garett that he hadn't eaten. There was no time to stop, though. Instead, he paid a balding street vendor the exorbitant price of two commons for a honey-soaked melon cake the size of his palm. Garett wolfed the heavy pastry down in a couple of bites, and Burge watched disgustedly as he licked the sticky syrup from his fingers. It was hardly a meal, but at least it filled his stomach.

At the far end of the Strip, they turned up a short street and cut over to Ratwater Way. It was but a short distance up that street to the River Quarter watch house. The crowds here were thinner, mostly men who made their living along the river or on the docks, either on their way to, or just returning from the Strip. They were a raw, rough-looking sort, but Garett knew them generally to be good men. In the River Quarter, it was usually the nobles who started trouble with their superior, condescending attitudes and haughty manners.

A standard patrol of five men, led by a junior sergeant, emerged from the doors of the watch house to begin their rounds just as Garett and Burge arrived. The junior sergeant drew up sharply, signaling his men to halt as he executed a crisp salute. "Captain Starlen!" he exclaimed in surprise. "Is this an inspection, sir? Your visit honors us!"

Garett did his best to hide a frown. It annoyed him when officers behaved like puppy dogs, licking at his boots, hoping for pats on the head. "Save your flattery, Sergeant," he answered smoothly. "If you want to impress me, do it with deeds. Find me the seer named Duncan. He's said to work the streets of the River Quarter. Do you know him?"

The sergeant paled at Garett's tone, but quickly composed himself. "I know him," he replied, somewhat offended as he drew back his shoulders and met Garett's gaze. "He reads fortunes in the throws of the dice."

Garett nodded as he took a second look at the young man before him. If he were bold enough to meet his captain's gaze so defiantly, then perhaps there was something to him after all. "I wish to speak to him," Garett continued.

"Alert the other patrols. I want Duncan here within the hour, Sergeant."

The sergeant saluted again and led his men down Ratwater Way toward the Strip.

Garett and Burge moved up the five shallow stone stairs and into the watch house. Another patrol of six men nearly knocked them over as they prepared to exit on their rounds, and Garett and Burge quickly backed out again until the patrol passed. Garett doubted if the leader, a huge, longhaired Velunan, had even noted his superior rank. There was no puppy dog, seeking promotion or a better assignment. That one was all business.

When it was safe to enter again, Garett and Burge did so. The watch house was lit with smoking cressets, and the interior was stale with the odor of burning oil and men's sweat. Only the narrowest of windows allowed any fresh air inside. The River Quarter watch house was the busiest post in Greyhawk, and scores of men moved about in the dim yellow light. The far side of the watch house was lined with steel-barred cells. Already they were jammed with the night's catch of drunks and pickpockets and troublemakers, and still more were lined up before a desk to have their names inscribed in the arrest book. When that was done, they would join the rest in the cells.

The place was a barely controlled tumult. The prisoners shouted curses at the guards or at each other. Some whined for release, for food or water, or some other privilege. Watchmen hustled prisoners from the arrest line to the cells, or from one cell to another as they separated fighting prisoners. Another patrol formed and departed.

Garett shouldered his way to the arrest desk. "Where's your commanding officer?" he demanded of the wearylooking lieutenant who sat there. He had to raise his voice to be heard over the din. Before the lieutenant could look up, however, someone grabbed Garett's shoulder and spun him around.

"Please, Your Honor!" begged a middle-aged man

whose silken dress marked him as either a merchant or a noble. A dark bruise colored the left side of his face, and his eye was beginning to swell. He folded his hands in supplication under Garett's nose as he screwed up his face and shed fat tears. "Tell them it's a mistake! Don't let them arrest me! Please!"

A pair of guards wrestled the man back into line.

"Well, at least he didn't say he was innocent," muttered the lieutenant behind the desk as he leaned back and looked up at Garett.

Burge continued to watch the poor man with a trace of amusement as the wretch offered a bribe to his guards. "What'd he do?"

The lieutenant set down his stylus and folded his arms behind his head. The arrest line came to a halt. "He beat up one of Quisti's girls down at the Sea Willow," came the answer. The lieutenant didn't bother to hide a smirk. The Sea Willow was one of the finest pleasure houses on the Strip. Quisti, the owner, was renowned throughout the city for the quality of his staff. He hand-picked each girl himself, it was said, and woe to any man who abused one of them.

"My wife will kill me!" the man shrieked suddenly in despair as the guards twisted his arms up behind his back.

The lieutenant gave a sigh and leaned forward again. "What can I do for you, Captain?" he said. "As you can see, we've got a busy night down here. Everybody's celebrating early, you see. Kentellen Mar comes home tomorrow."

Garett raised an eyebrow at that piece of news. No word had been spoken of it at the Citadel. He glanced at Burge, but his friend was obviously as surprised as he was by the lieutenant's pronouncement.

"Who told you this?" Garett demanded.

It was one of the prisoners who answered, leaning into the conversation. "Oh, it's all over the city, it is," he said, flashing a toothless smile. "Kentellen's camped just a few miles outside the Duke's Gate. He'll be here tomorrow, all right." His smile widened from ear to ear, revealing withered gums, but there was a twinkle in his merry eyes as he nodded toward the lieutenant. "You can take his word for it, you can, Cap'n."

"Thanks, Perch," the lieutenant answered with a wry yawn. To Garett, he explained, "Perch is one of our regulars."

Garett waved a hand under his nose as he turned away. Perch's breath was nearly a lethal weapon. But if what he said was true, the celebration in the streets would go on at least until Kentellen Mar entered the city, and not just in the River Quarter, either. It would spread to all the other quarters. The man was immensely popular with the citizens of Greyhawk. More so even than the new mayor.

Garett drew a deep breath, feeling the weight of the city slowly settling onto his shoulders. "Who's the commanding watch officer, lieutenant?" he repeated again.

The lieutenant stuck out a hand without rising from his chair. "I'm afraid I'm it, sir," he said. "Soja's the name." He shook hands with Garett. As he did so, he called out, "Hey, Graybo! Get over here and take charge of this line. Now, man!"

A heavyset sergeant with a permanent scowl carved into his face ambled wordlessly over and took the lieutenant's place behind the desk. With a grunt, he picked up the stylus, dipped it in the inkwell, and looked up unpleasantly. The arrest line began to move again.

"Let's see if we can't find a little quiet, Captain Starlen," Soja suggested, indicating a door just to the right of the row of cells. Garett and Burge followed him as he cleared a path through the crowded watch room.

"Hey, you back there!" a guard shouted suddenly. He raked a heavy cudgel along the bars of one cell in a menacing manner, setting up a considerable clatter as the prisoners snatched their fingers clear. "You mess up my floor, an' I'll come in there an cut that thing off!"

Soja opened the door to his office and beckoned Garett and Burge inside. When he closed it, the sounds from the outer watch room were muffled only a little. Still, that little was a grateful relief.

"I gather it's been some time since you've visited us," Soja said, walking to a cabinet that stood in one corner, opening it, and taking out a bottle of local Greyhawk wine. He offered each of them small, thimble-sized cups and poured.

Usually Garett shied away from wine, but the taste of the honeyed melon cake was still in his mouth, and he welcomed anything that would wash it down. "Most of my duties keep me in the Citadel," he admitted. It had, in fact, been some months since he'd visited any of the watch houses. He intended to correct that quickly. "Recent events, however, have compelled me to take a personal hand in an investigation."

"The murders of the seers?" Soja interrupted over the rim of his cup. He nodded briskly. "Nasty business, especially old Kathenor. I'll bet his followers are foaming at the mouth."

Burge downed his thimble cup in a quick swallow and held it out for a refill. "It's another seer we're interested in tonight," he said.

"His name is Duncan," Garett added. "He works the streets around here." He raised his cup and took a delicate sip. The taste of cinnamon warmed the inside of his mouth. An instant later, the alcohol warmed the inside of his belly. "I want him found."

A knock sounded on the office door. "Come in, damn it!" Soja shouted impatiently.

The door swung open. In walked the junior sergeant Garett had encountered outside the watch house. At his side stood a frightened-looking young woman. Her clothes were an amazing collection of color. Green skirts were layered on red skirts, which were layered on orange. Her blouse was purple and blue and yellow, as if it had once been three garments sewn into one. Her left arm was covered with jingling bracelets from wrist to elbow, and cheap, gaudy rings bedecked each of her fingers and thumbs. A yellow scarf tied back her night-black hair, which spilled almost to her waist. She was not pretty at all, yet there was something appealing about her. Her black eyes sparkled in the light from the cressets.

"Well, don't say we're not efficient in the River Quarter," Soja said with a sardonic gesture. "Come on in, Kael. Bring her with you."

Burge tossed off his drink and set the cup on Soja's desk. "This is Duncan?"

The young woman moved nervously into the center of the room. She clutched her hands together just under her bosom, but her gaze darted to each of their faces. She trembled visibly. "My father had quite a sense of humor," she explained in a meek, apologetic voice.

Garett felt suddenly sorry for her. Obviously, she was terrified, though she struggled to hide the fact. Who knew what the junior sergeant, Kael, had told her when he picked her up? She didn't know what she was doing here, or why the watch would want her. "Don't be frightened, girl," he said, going forward, taking both her hands reassuringly in his. He pulled her around Soja's desk and held the chair for her. "Sit down," he urged. "I just want to talk to you."

"I haven't done anything," she insisted quietly.

Garett put on a gentle smile. "I know that," he said. On an impulse, he poured a dollop of cinnamon wine into Burge's cup and offered it to her. She'd probably never tasted cinnamon wine. "There's no charge against you," he continued. "I just want to talk to you."

Like a timid mouse eyeing the cheese in a trap, she stared at the cinnamon wine. Finally she lifted it in a trembling hand and raised it to drink. Her lower lip was like a flower petal unfolding to catch a drop of dew. When she lowered the cup, she put three fingers of her other hand shyly to her lips, bent her head almost to her chest, and swallowed. It was all an act of great delicacy.

"I'm told that you can see the future," Garett said slowly, keeping his voice low and soothing.

Duncan nodded without saying anything. She glanced at all their faces again, as if searching for some cue to the proper responses.

"I'm also told," Garett continued, "that you're a fake." He studied her expression for some reaction. "Are you?"

Again she studied all their faces. Slowly, she nodded. Then she sipped quickly from the cup, as if she expected the wine to be taken from her as punishment.

Garett didn't want to frighten her. She had a precious quality, something that reached out to him and touched him somehow. He had seen street waifs in many cities and many lands. He knew how hard a life it was, especially for a female. His heart went out to this one. Yet he still needed answers. "Which is it, Duncan?" he persisted quietly. "Can you see the future? Or are you a fake?"

She hung her head, and tears welled up in her eyes. "You are going to arrest me," she whispered.

Garett took the cup of cinnamon wine from her hand, refilled it, and offered it to her again, ignoring the look of consternation on Soja's face. "I'm not going to arrest you," he assured her. "If you wish to, you may walk out of here right now."

Duncan rolled moist eyes up at him. "I can go?" she said with a mixture of hope and surprise.

Garett nodded, looking at the others, who moved away from the door at his silent command.

Her way out was unobstructed, but she hesitated. "It is very difficult," she said at last, clinging to the small cup as if it were a lifeline. "Sometimes, I can see true visions. But sometimes, I must lie or go hungry." She looked up at Garett again, and though there was shame in her face, there was also determination. "I don't like to go hungry," she told him.

Burge came closer to the desk. "How do you do it, girl?" he inquired. "What method?"

Setting aside the cup, Duncan reached down the front of her blouse and pulled a small leather purse from her cleavage. Carefully, she loosened the purse strings and turned it upside down over her hand. Five glimmering amethysts tumbled into her palm, each cut into the shape of an octahedron.

"They're beautiful!" Kael exclaimed, coming closer to see the stones. "She couldn't afford those! She must have stolen them!"

Duncan recoiled, clutching the amethysts to her breasts with both hands. "I didn't," she whispered tensely. "They're mine! My father gave them to me!"

Kael snorted derisively. "Father! She probably doesn't even know who he was!"

Garett whirled on the young officer. "Get out!" he ordered savagely. "You found her, and I'm grateful. But my gratitude has its limits, and so does my patience!"

Anger and hurt flared in Kael's eyes for an instant. Then he saluted smartly, turned, and exited the office. The noise from the outer area surged in for a brief moment before the door slammed shut again.

Garett turned back to the cowering young woman in the chair. "It's all right, Duncan," he told her. "It's all right." He got up and paced back and forth before the desk. Burge went to lean against the door. Soja moved into a corner near his liquor cabinet, out of the way.

Duncan relaxed a bit. After a moment, she leaned forward and took up the cup of cinnamon wine and sipped it again. She opened her left fist slowly, and the amethysts gently slid onto the desk. The lamplight glittered and glimmered upon them. Splinters of purple lanced across the desktop.

"How do they work?" Garett asked, stopping to stare at the stones. They were no bigger than dice, but with eight smooth sides.

Duncan leaned over them. Setting her cup down again, she set her hands on either side of the dice, swept them together, and covered them with her cupped palms. "These are amethysts," she began with greater enthusiasm. "If they were garnets, then my visions would always be true, and they would come easier, for garnets are my birthstone." She took her hands away, and the lamplight reflected upon the dice again, and the splinters of purple took on a new pattern. "But I cannot afford such stones. These belonged to my grandmother. Amethysts were her birthstone. Still, there is a blood connection between us, and I can use these somewhat."

"I've heard somethin' of this custom, Cap'n," Burge said from the doorway. "It's practiced in the Bone March, far from here."

"Go on," Garett said, turning back to Duncan.

She picked up the amethyst dice and cast them over the desktop. "I roll them," she explained, "and sometimes, fragments of the future reveal themselves in the facets. But it takes great concentration. It does not always work."

Garett extracted his purse from its resting place under his belt, opened it, and took out a silver noble. He laid the coin before the young girl. "I want you to try," he said. "I want you to try to see who killed Acton Kathenor. If you succeed, I'll give you another noble."

Duncan stared at the coin. She reached out and touched it with the tip of one finger and ran the tip in small circles around its circumference. Finally, she drew her hand back and looked up. "I will try," she said. Then she smiled for the first time, a very shy, nervous smile. "If I may have one more cup of that wonderful beverage."

Garett looked at Soja, who trudged over to the desk and lifted the bottle. "Well, then we might as well all have one," he muttered. He refilled Duncan's cup, then Garett's, and gave his own to Burge. There might have been another cup in the cabinet, Garett thought. Three was an odd number. But Soja instead claimed the bottle and tilted it toward his mouth, swallowing noisily. "It's been a wretched night, anyhow," he said, capping the bottle and returning it to a shelf in the cabinet. It was a not too subtle way of saving what was left.

Duncan took a sip of the cinnamon wine and set her cup aside. A tiny drop of the red liquid clung to her lip as she leaned forward and gathered the amethyst dice between her hands. She licked the drop away with a delicate flick of her tongue and let the crystals fall. They scattered upon the desk and came to rest in small pools of reflected purple. Duncan studied them carefully, then gathered them up and cast them once more.

Garett went to the far side of the room to watch and wait. Over and over, Duncan cast the dice. The clatter they made on the wooden desk began to grate, and he felt his patience wearing away. Outside, the noise in the watch room grew louder than ever. Garett paced toward the desk, picked up his own cup of wine, which he had left sitting there, and downed it in a gulp. Burge slipped out for a moment. When he returned, the racket from the watch room had lessened somewhat, and he nodded toward Garett.

The dice clattered on the desk again. "I told you," Duncan said without being addressed. "It's difficult." She picked up the dice and cupped them to her breasts. "Perhaps, if you ask a specific question?" she suggested, looking to Garett. "It's easier to see for someone else."

Garett went to the desk. Inwardly he cursed Ellon Thigpen. If the common-pinching fool had just allowed him to approach the Wizards' Guild, this lengthy business might not be necessary. He might have some answers already. "What do I do?" he said.

She handed him the dice. "Hold them," she instructed. "Warm them with your body heat and concentrate on your question."

Garett cast a glance at Burge, who watched wordlessly, and wrapped his hands around the amethysts. He closed his eyes and drew a picture of Acton Kathenor into his mind, recalling the copper cauldron and the blood, the bits of broken mirror, all the details of the room in which the priest had died. Then he did the same for each of the other murdered seers, one by one, lingering on the visions as he rolled the dice between his cupped palms. Who killed them? he questioned silently. Who is the murderer? He called up an image of a figure, a face cloaked in shadow, and willed features to appear—a nose, a mouth, eyes that would become the face of the killer. The shadows persisted, though. It was not truly his job to lift them. He wasn't the seer. It was only for him to shape the question.

Duncan took the dice from his hands, and Garett opened his eyes. She blew on the crystals, turning them over and over, shaking them, her own eyes shut tight with concentration. The crystals scattered over the desktop. Her eyes snapped open, and she stared expectantly. The breath hissed angrily between her teeth. She snatched them up and cast them again.

Impatiently, Garett went to Burge. Lieutenant Soja also crept nearer from his place by the cabinet. "This is getting us nowhere, Captain Starlen," he whispered.

Burge looked at his commander, gave a sigh, and went to the desk. He knelt down opposite Duncan and watched as she cast the crystals again. Then his voice sounded barely over the clatter of the dice. "Feel your grandmother's blood," he whispered tersely. "Feel it flowing in your veins. She's here, in you. You're one. These dice are yours. They belong to both of you. Her vision is your vision. See as she would see."

Duncan's face screwed up. She said nothing, just gathered and tossed the dice, gathered and tossed. Beads of sweat appeared on her brow and ran toward her eyes. Without thinking, she wiped them away and cast again.

"Her vision is your vision," Burge continued in a low drone. "She is in you, part of you."

Faster and faster, Duncan's hands flew, casting the dice and sweeping them up. The lamplight danced on the amethysts. They sparkled with flashes of purple and violet fire, and Duncan's eyes sparkled with a black brightness.

Suddenly, she cried out. Her hand froze, on the verge of sweeping the stones up once more, and trembled above them instead. Slowly, she withdrew it and bent closer. "I see!" she gasped. "I see!"

"What?" Garett demanded as he leaned over the desk. The amethysts shimmered impossibly, almost as if they quivered, alive, under the light. He could see nothing in the facets. "What is it?" he shouted.

Before Duncan could answer, a wind whistled sharply through the office. Duncan's wine cup overturned, and the blood-red liquid spilled out. It flowed around the five dice. Overhead, the cressets swung wildly. Garett shot a look around the room. There was a single, unshuttered window, but the wind didn't seem to come from there. The desk began to shiver and vibrate and move across the floor. Duncan gave a shrill scream.

Above the dice, a violet, nebulous light formed and swirled, and the crystals rose slowly into the heart of the smoky radiance. Like tiny stars, they spun and whirled, throwing flashes about the room. Garett felt a pressure on his ears, behind his eyes. A great invisible hand seemed to press on his chest. The crystals spun faster and faster until they could no longer be seen individually, but formed a single orbit around some unseen center. The violet light burned hotter.

Then something smashed Garett to the floor. A scream rang in his ears. A light exploded in his head and burst into thousands of colors.

The pressure, though, was gone. With a groan, he rolled over and stared at Burge, who was still half on top of him. "Sorry, Cap'n," the half-elf muttered. "Had to do that. I saw it comin'."

Garett struggled to his feet as the office door slammed open. A dozen faces, prisoners as well as guards, stopped at the threshold and stared. Graybo, the officer at the arrest desk, shouldered his way past the others, and the prisoner, Perch, came behind him, wide-eyed.

"What in the hells?" Graybo demanded, glaring at the body of Lieutenant Soja, which was crumpled next to his precious cabinet.

A pool of blood was forming under Duncan's head where she'd fallen behind the desk. Garett bent down beside her, his own head still swimming, and carefully turned her over. The fortune-teller's eyes were gone, replaced with empty holes that bubbled blood. "My gods," Garett muttered, though he honored no deities.

"The lieutenant took it through the head," Graybo reported, bending down beside his superior. "What in the hells hit him?"

Burge pointed to the door, where he'd been standing just an instant before he'd hurled himself at Garett. One of the purple dice was deeply embedded there. Another was embedded in the far wall. "That one was for you, Cap'n," he commented. "I'd say there's someone or somethin' out there that doesn't *want* to be seen."

Garett didn't answer. He pushed a blood-drenched lock of hair back from Duncan's face and tried to master the rage that swelled inside him.

SEVEN

Garett put Graybo in charge of the watch house and grudgingly named Kael the new second-in-command. Their appointments, of course, were only temporary. Korbian Arthuran, as captain-general, would no doubt wish to name permanent replacements for a post as busy and important as the River Quarter.

A rickety old cart pulled up outside, drawn by a single black horse and bearing a cheap wooden coffin on its flatbed. Led by Burge, two dark-robed representatives from the Guild of Embalmers and Gravediggers strode with somber grace, their hands folded before them, into Soja's office. They nodded wordlessly in Garett's direction, then looked around.

"Oh, my," said one of them suddenly as he looked from the still form of Duncan to Soja's corpse. "There are two." He turned to his comrade with a look of paternal consternation. "We were not properly informed," he continued to Garett. "I'm afraid they shall have to share a box for now. We can separate them before burial, however." He made a wave of dismissal, and his comrade went back outside.

Garett turned away. He had little love for gravediggers, and this one reeked of embalming fluid and the smells of the death house. His smooth, calm voice only irritated Garett, who drew his dagger from its sheath and set about gouging free from the wall and the door the amethyst dice that had missed Burge and himself.

The second gravedigger returned, bearing the wooden coffin on his back and shoulders. He bumped roughly against the sides of the doors as he struggled under the burden, but the first gravedigger made no effort to help him with it. At last, he set it down on the floor and lifted the lid.

"Forgive me for bringing up unpleasant matters at a time like this," the first one said with an oily voice, and Garett slowly turned back to face him. "Who will pay?" He batted his lashes unconsciously. It was the only part of him that seemed to move as he waited for an answer.

Garett resisted the urge to toss his dagger at the man's toes. There would be a mean pleasure in making the pompous fool jump, watching his placid demeanor fall apart. He knew, though, deep down, that his anger was not truly directed at the gravedigger, but at himself. He felt responsible for Duncan's death. He had sought her out and compelled her to use her dice and try to find a murderer. But the murderer had taken her right out of Garett's hands, and Garett had been helpless to prevent it.

He shoved his dagger back into its sheath and made a fist around the two amethyst crystals. "The lieutenant has family, I believe," he said through clenched teeth. "Ask them what arrangements they wish to make. As for the girl . . ." Garett shrugged, gave a great sigh, and shook his head. "She was a street waif. Give her the usual funeral and bill the city." That meant, of course, a soggy grave somewhere out in the marsh west of the city wall. And the guild would cut itself a small profit by charging for a coffin that would never be used.

The first gravedigger nodded, then made a gesture to his partner. The second man bent and lifted the lieutenant's body while the first merely watched. He dropped it into the open coffin, banging an arm against the side, bumping Soja's head in the process. When he went to Duncan's body, Burge stepped quickly in to help, lifting the seeress's arms while the gravedigger took her feet. Together, they placed her with greater gentleness on top of the lieutenant.

The first gravedigger watched expressionlessly as the lid was settled in place. "Would you ask some of your watchmen to please carry this to the wagon?" he said dispassionately when the job was done.

Garett frowned to himself. Not once had the man unfolded the hands he held clasped together so regally upon his robe. His attitude, his posture, everything about him offended Garett. Still, he nodded to Burge, and the half-elf summoned Graybo, Kael, and two other men. Even old Perch stepped in to lend a hand. It was a measure of how disorganized things had become that the fellow had not yet been jailed.

When the coffin, with its double burden, was loaded on the wagon, the first gravedigger at last prepared to leave. Garett followed him out of the office, out of the watch house, and down the steps. The gravedigger climbed aboard and settled himself down beside his lesser partner, who already had the reins in hand.

"Wait," Garett commanded, and the first gravedigger stared down at him. Did Garett imagine it, or was that really a look of contempt in the guildsman's eyes. Well, by the gods, they would profit enough by cheating the city in their usual manner. They were not going to gain further by tonight's misfortune. He held up the pair of amethysts. "There are two more of these," he said, and though the gravedigger tried to hide it, a new gleam of greed shone suddenly in his gaze. "In the girl's brain. They're what penetrated her eyes. There's another in the lieutenant's body. Dig them out and bring them to me at the Citadel within an hour. Is that understood?"

The gravedigger hesitated, and the barest hint of disappointment flickered across his lips.

"Let me make this clear, guildsman," Garett added sternly. "These stones are evidence in a murder investigation. If they do not arrive in my office within an hour, I'll hold you personally responsible. Is *that* understood?"

Abruptly, Kael appeared at Garett's side. "Sir, if you wish, I'll accompany the coffin to the death house, and see that your stones are safely delivered."

Garett gave the junior sergeant another look of renewed interest. He was brash, yes, but he had a head on his shoulders. He would bear watching. "That's an admirable idea, Sergeant," he said, clapping the young man on the shoulder. With a lithe move, Kael sprang up onto the wagon's flatbed and knelt down by the coffin.

The gravedigger could no longer hide his displeasure. His face soured, and he nudged his partner with a sharp elbow. A moment later, the wagon trundled off down Ratwater Way, ringing the iron bell that warned pedestrians and sleeping citizens alike that death was passing in the streets.

"A hard business, Cap'n," Burge said from the top of the steps.

Garett went up to join him. "You saved my life in there," he said. "I'm grateful."

Burge snorted. "Faster-than-human reflexes," he muttered. "It's one of the few things I can thank my elven dad for." He looked away abruptly, unable to conceal even briefly the bitterness that crept into his voice whenever he mentioned his father. "Anyway," he continued, putting on a grin, resorting to mirth as he usually did to smother the deeper emotion. "I couldn't let your little apple-seller, Vendredi, be deprived of the night of her life."

It was Garett's turn to snort. "Afraid you've got the wrong idea, there, Lieutenant," he said.

"No, sir," Burge countered, cocking an eyebrow. "It's

just a matter of time before the two of you are squealin' like pigs in springtime."

They went back inside the watch house long enough to help Graybo put things in order and get the prisoners under control again. The arrest line had shortened considerably, as some of those arrested but not yet placed in cells had availed themselves of the confusion and escaped into the night.

It was with some amusement, however, that Garett noticed Perch sitting patiently on a stool in the corner. If anyone had had a chance to make a getaway, it was Perch. Curious, he went over to the old man. "What did they pinch you for, Perch?" he asked.

"Spittin' on a lady, Yer Honor," Perch answered without blinking.

Garett rubbed a hand over his chin and considered. "Well, you've been a help to us here," he continued finally. "Let's just overlook it this time. Go on home."

Perch's ears turned a bright red, and the old man slammed a fist down on his bony thigh. "Home?" he shouted, enraged. "I was arrested proper and legal, I was! I did the crime, an' I admit it! Now you got to lock me up!"

Garett looked down at the thin, rag-tattered figure. Of course, Perch didn't want to go home. He probably didn't have a home to go to. Spitting on a lady? What kind of a crime was that? No doubt, Perch had intended to get arrested. At least, in jail, he'd get a bowl of crude gruel to eat.

Garett left Perch fuming and went to Graybo. "How often do you see him here?" he asked the huge sergeant in a soft whisper.

"Perch?" Graybo almost laughed, but Garett's stern visage warned him to lower his voice. Graybo folded his arms across his chest. "We put the pinch on him just about every other night, I guess. Always minor things. We toss him in for the evening, and let him go come sunrise. He never gives us any problems. I think he comes mostly for the breakfast meal. Gods know why. I sure wouldn't eat it."

"This place is filthy," Garett said, glancing around and putting on his most officious manner. "It stinks, too. I think you could use someone around here, Sergeant, to run a broom and mop occasionally. You understand me?"

Graybo looked bewildered for a moment, then he began to nod. "That's real kind of you, Captain," he said quietly.

"Just give him a copper or two every time he sweeps," Garett continued conspiratorially. "Take it out of general operating expenses. And if Korbian Arthuran names a permanent commander later to take your place, you just tell him Perch has always worked here. If there's a further problem, you let me know, and I'll handle it. Got it?"

"That's real kind of you," Graybo repeated. The gentle expression he suddenly wore seemed wholly out of place on his huge body as he stared into Garett's eyes and bobbed his head up and down.

Garett felt abruptly uncomfortable. He looked around for Burge and spied his friend standing by the open doorway. As he headed across the room to join him and leave, however, Perch leaped up and caught his arm. When Garett stopped, the old man took advantage of it and spit on his boots.

"I didn't want to do that!" Perch scolded angrily, still clinging to Garett's sleeve. "Ye made me! Now, am I under arrest, or what?"

Garett did his best to put on a scowl as he called to Graybo. "Lieutenant, lock this man up!" Then he gave Graybo a wink and gently pulled his arm free of Perch's grip. The old man smiled as if he'd just been invited to the governor's feast as Graybo personally led him away.

The night breeze bore the odors of the river as Garett and Burge left the watch house and started north up Ratwater Way. Even here, north of the Strip and west of the Processional, people wandered in the street, half-drunk, singing and making merry, getting a head start on the celebration that would greet Kentellen Mar's return to Greyhawk.

If the River Quarter watch house was any indication, Garett's night shift officers would have their hands full tomorrow evening. The drinking would begin early as merchants and dockers and workers throughout the city declared a holiday and took to the streets. Only the taverns and inns would be operating, and their doors would be wide open. The pickpockets of the Thieves' Guild would have a field day, of course. The whole population would turn out to watch the fireworks display the Wizards' Guild had promised. That meant more people in the streets.

Then, sometime after darkness settled, the fights and assaults would commence. It would start in the River Quarter. It always did. Then it would spread. The fights would lead to knifings, and the knifings to killings. Garett's watchmen would be going crazy, and the jails would be overflowing. Civilized Greyhawk would fade away. By midnight, Necropolis, in full ugly flower, would take its place.

Garett hated holidays and celebrations.

Ratwater Way took them over to Horseshoe Road. There were fewer people out, but candles and lamps still burned in the windows of many of the dwellings and apartments that lined the street as the citizens within made their preparations for the morning and Kentellen's arrival.

Kentellen Mar was much loved by the common people of Greyhawk. After all, he was one of them. Born and raised in the lowest corner of the city's Artisan's Quarter, in a shack near the Black Wall, he was the success story that inspired all poor citizens. His father had been a sewer scraper—one of those who managed repairs and kept the sewers and ducts of Greyhawk free from blockages. Such men were generally considered pariahs, because they voluntarily worked in filth under conditions that were usually reserved for the prison work gangs. His mother had been a sometime midwife to the poor, which meant she brought in little money.

Somehow, from this bleak beginning, Kentellen Mar developed a taste for learning. At an early age, while most other youths were roaming the streets looking to do mischief, he started spending time in the small gardens and groves of the Halls, that section of the city where professors and students and priests, as well as the city's army of bureaucrats, were wont to dwell. He'd sit at a respectful distance and listen to their lunch-time discourses, or hide in trees to overhear the open-air philosophy classes and theology lectures.

Ultimately, of course, he came to the attention of those professors who were flattered by his hunger to learn. When he was old enough, with their help, he worked his way into Greyhawk University and, finally, into the College of Law, where he excelled beyond any of his fellow students.

In the years that followed, he made a name for himself as a defender of the city's poor. A man without a common in his pocket could turn to Kentellen Mar and hope for representation if he could convince Kentellen of his innocence. The poor people came to trust and love him, and even Greyhawk's nobles respected him for his honesty. Kentellen Mar could have made himself rich by serving those nobles. He could have lived in a fine house in the Garden Quarter, or even the High Quarter. But, instead, he had lived his life quietly and never moved from the small house he purchased near his parents' original home.

A near riot had been the result when Ellon Thigpen, himself newly appointed to the office of mayor, named Kentellen Mar to become the new magister, the city's highest judiciary official and the supreme interpreter of justice. Kentellen had claimed surprise, and no one doubted him. Everyone had expected the post to go to Elmon Kohl, the headmaster of the Guild of Lawyers and Scribes, who already had a seat among the city's all-powerful directors. In fact, many speculated openly about the politics behind Thigpen's decision. There was no doubt, however, as to the popularity of his choice, and that alone may have been the reason behind it. After all, no one really liked or cared much for the high-born and haughty Elmon Kohl, except Elmon Kohl himself.

It was as a small reward to himself for years of hard work that Kentellen Mar then decided to take a vacation before assuming the office of magister. His youth and middle age had slipped by, and he had never been farther than the lands surrounding Greyhawk. He had outfitted a small caravan, and in the company of a close band of friends, set out to hunt and explore the lands that surrounded the greatest of all lakes, the Nyr Dyv. A voyage of discovery and self-discovery, he had called it cheerfully in his farewell address to the people who saw him off at Druid's Gate.

Now Kentellen was camped just a few miles from Duke's Gate to the northeast of the city, about to return home after an absence of three months. Already the city was going crazy with anticipation. What, Garett wondered worriedly, would the actual day of investiture be like?

Garett spared a glance toward Burge as they came to the end of Horseshoe Road and turned out onto the Processional, where the crowds were thick again. His friend had said not a word since leaving the watch house. His thin, half-elven features were creased with a deep frown, and unconsciously he hugged himself, as if against some chill as he walked.

"You're awfully quiet," Garett said as they weaved their way among a line of torch-waving celebrants, who were twining back and forth through the street in a serpentine dance. "Because of Soja and Duncan?"

"Partly that," Burge admitted after a moment's pause. He glanced up toward the sky and hugged himself again without seeming to realize he did it. "I don't know, Cap'n. It's like I got an itch I can't quite scratch. Like there's somethin' in the air. I don't know what. But it's trouble, and it's big, and somethin' in me's whisperin', 'Get out, Burge. Get out while you can.'" He shut up, looking embarrassed by his admission, and again he rolled his eyes skyward. "You noticed how many birds are flyin' around here lately?" he asked, changing the subject. "Big black ones, all at night."

Garett followed his gaze upward. High above, crows and ravens and all manner of black birds gyred and danced, their wings shining in the reflected light of the street lamps that lined the Processional. Burge was right. There had been a lot of birds lately. But the summer had been hot, and the marshes just beyond the east wall were a fertile breeding ground for insects. It was only natural for the insects to be drawn to the Processional's brighter street lights, and only natural for the birds to feast upon them.

Still, an odd shiver rippled down his spine as he watched them and listened to their shrill, muted calls. "Let's get back to the Citadel," he said suddenly, quickening his step.

But before they got much farther, all the hells broke loose. The air shook with a sound like thunder, and the black heavens transformed. For an instant, Garett thought the sky itself had caught fire, and a true religious terror gripped his heart. It was Burge who spun him around and pointed back in the direction of the Halls.

The last wisps of a huge geyser of fire rocketed into the sky and faded. For a brief moment, the black of night reasserted itself. Then a second geyser shot skyward, as high as a mountain, and another blast of thunder rocked the street as the air super-heated and the night once more burned.

A hot wind rushed unexpectedly over Garett. From somewhere came the groan and crash of timbers as a building or buildings crumpled under its force. Someone screamed, and someone else took it up. The celebrants along the Processional suddenly ran like panicked animals. A woman, her eyes on the fire geyser, blundered into Garett. It was enough to snap him from his own fear and spur him into motion.

"Come on!" he cried, and began running toward the Halls.

"You are seriously out of your mind!" Burge shouted when he realized they were heading for the disturbance, not away from it like all the saner folks around him. Nevertheless, he followed.

The second geyser faded like the first, rocketing into the clouds, and the world turned dark once more. A third time, though, fire fountained upward, crackling. Thunder roared, and a scorching wind whipped savagely over the city. This time, though, a new sound joined the din. It was a cry, a monstrous, bestial trumpeting, a bellow that only one creature on Oerth made.

"It's a dragon!" Burge cried, catching Garett's arm and drawing him up short in the middle of the street. "A dragon!" His grip tightened suddenly, painfully on his captain's arm. "Look! It's rising!"

Over the dark outline of the Halls, immense wings slowly spread and flexed, and again the creature bellowed. Up, up into the sky, its long neck gracefully stretched, and its head swept back and forth. The light from a dozen fires flickered and rippled upon its red-scaled hide, upon its splendid, horrifyingly powerful wings. One great pinion twitched and brushed against the stark silhouette of a tall building, sending it toppling. The beast screamed, as if in pain, arched its neck and shot fire at the moon.

The dragon rose into the night. For an instant, it hovered above the city, writhing and shrieking, exhaling blasts of fire, as if in fierce battle with some invisible foe. Finally, with an extended cry of torment, it flew off into the night, northward, leaving Greyhawk behind.

Leaving it to burn! Garett thought suddenly, forcing aside the images of beauty and terror that still filled his head. The dragon was gone, but the danger to the city was greater than ever. Fire! There was no greater threat to any city.

"They're usually peaceful creatures!" Burge shouted, wondering aloud as he stared after the rapidly vanishing dragon. Bursts of flame punctuated its departure, lighting up the distant clouds. "Who was it, do you think, Cap'n? What made it go mad?"

But Garett wasn't listening. He glanced hastily around to get his bearings. They were on University Street. He grabbed Burge's arm and began to run toward the blazes. Already the houses and apartments were emptying as people spilled into the streets. Cries of "fire!" filled the night. To the credit of Greyhawk's citizens, most did not run away. With buckets and pans and jars, men and women alike, even some children, surged out into the roads. Like a human wave, they rushed toward the crackling glow, knowing full well what they all stood to lose if the fire spread.

At the edge of the devastation, Garett stopped short again and stared in horror. Two blocks of Bard Street had been leveled. Not a house remained standing. Flames rose from the broken ruins, and from another row of buildings on the next block. An old dormitory for students attending the university was already completely swathed in flame. As Garett watched, it crashed to the ground, sending streamers and sparks in all directions to spread greater destruction.

Already, though, water lines were forming. Hand to hand, buckets and containers were passed down lines extending from the two Clerkburg wells to the south, from the well at University Park to the west, and from the well near the Garden Gate. Men gleamed with sweat from their furious, determined labor, and their bodies reflected the heat and the fire's glow. Women worked the lines as well, those who were strong enough, passing the heavy buckets with noisy grunts and shouts of encouragement. The weaker ones worked with children, using heavy rags and pieces of scavenged carpet to beat out the smaller fires and sparks before they could blossom into deadlier form.

Nearby, an old man danced and whooped excitedly, beating his arms up and down, hopping from one foot to another. He spied Garett's red cloak and the gold embroidery on his tunic that marked him as a watchman and capered nearer.

"Biggest one I ever saw!" the old man sang, his eyes bright with shock or madness. "Biggest one ever! Knew they was here! Everybody said they was one here right amongst us! Whooeee!" He grabbed Garett's sleeve.

"Did'ja see it, General? Didja?"

"Just how many dragons have you seen before, Grandpa?" Burge asked sarcastically, staring past the old man at the fires. Reflected in his violet eyes, the flames leaped and danced, giving him the appearance of a demon until he turned his head.

"First one!" the old timer cackled. "Always wanted to see one, too! An' I got to see the biggest!"

Garett pulled his arm free and walked away from the old man. Another man, bald, with the flames reflected on his shiny scalp, caught his eye, a professor, judging from his scholar's robes. The man was on his knees, weeping, holding his empty hands before him as he stared into the heart of the raging destruction. The captain bent down and put an arm around the bald man's shoulders.

"Are you all right, sir?" he said as gently as he could over the desperate shoutings that filled the night. "Are you burned? Can I help you?"

The professor turned disbelieving, tear-filled eyes up at him. "My books!" came the barely audible reply. "Oh, my books! My books!"

Garett bent down and embraced him as tightly as he could. He shared the man's despair and shook his head in sadness. He could read, too, and loved books, loved the feel of them, the smell of them, though he'd never been able to afford to own one. But there was more to think about now.

"Your books are lost," he whispered sympathetically. "And we can't save them. But, look, the university's near. There are books yet to save. The university itself. We need your help, teacher." Slowly, he urged the weeping man to rise. "Will you help us? We all need each other tonight."

The professor wiped at his eyes and leaned weakly into Garett as he let himself be lifted to his feet. Still the tears came, but he cast a glance toward the university, and a new determination settled over his features as Garett showed him a place in the water line. The first few buckets came to him, and he accepted them with slumped shoulders and a weariness of spirit. But by the third or fourth, curses were spewing surprisingly from his mouth and demands for the buckets and the water to come faster.

Garett glanced around again as he dipped his hand in one of the buckets and rubbed it over his face. His skin stung from the heat, and his eyes burned from the clouds of smoke that hung in the air. Burge had disappeared. He couldn't see his half-elven friend anywhere.

By now, though, every watchman in the city was here. Red cloaks worked the water lines, and red cloaks beat at the smaller fires. The blue-shirted members of the private Guild of Night Watchmen worked right alongside them. From every corner of the city, more help came. Known thieves worked hand-in-hand with dockers and merchantmen. Pimps and prostitutes, still decked out in the gaudy costumes of their trade, labored good-naturedly beside priests and acolytes from every temple in town.

But, still, through all of it came the whimperings of the burned and the cries of those who had lost loved ones. On the ground not far away, the injured were being laid out on blankets or scraps of cloth in neat lines. The beggars of the city seemed to have taken it on themselves to care for these, though there was precious little comfort they could offer. They wetted thirsty lips, peeled away burned clothing from burned flesh, held in their arms children made suddenly orphans.

"Where are the damned wizards!" a wild-eyed woman shrieked, grabbing Garett's arm and spinning him about with a strength that belied her tiny size. Her face was a mask of anger and outrage. "We need rain! They could make it rain! Where are the wizards?" Then she let go of him, stomped a few paces away, and shrieked again. Her fingers curled into claws as she whirled about, screaming at the mob, "Where are the wizards?"

Where *were* the wizards, Garett thought suddenly. Why weren't they here to help with their spells and magic? They *could* make it rain. And even if that weren't enough to extinguish the fires, their enchantments could at least ease the suffering of the injured. He almost found himself shouting, Where are the wizards?

A hand settled on his shoulder, and he turned to find Quisti, the half-giant owner of the Sea Willow pleasure palace standing at his side. Both of the brothel keeper's huge, meaty hands were reddened with burns, as was his left earlobe, where the big gold loop he wore there had overheated. His bare scalp also looked tender, and the hairs of his mighty mustache were singed. His great body gleamed with sweat and stank of smoke.

"We're in luck tonight," Quisti said, and he licked his lower lip.

Garett stared stupidly at him. "How do you figure that?"

"The wind," Quisti answered reasonably. He licked a finger and held it up. "It's blowing the fire toward the city wall instead of back into the Halls or down into the Artisans' Quarter. If it doesn't shift, we can beat this." He licked his lip again, and in the shimmer of firelight on the wetness, Garett saw he had been burned there, too. "It's going to be a long night, though," Quisti added.

"The dragon," Garett muttered, realizing he'd never said two words to this man before. He had thought Quisti was just a pimp, albeit a wealthy pimp with high-class ladies and higher-class customers. But, now, Garett saw that he was more, much more. He looked at those burned hands again, and the word "hero" sprang to mind. The night would be full of such heroes. "The dragon," he repeated, his mind seething with images of the beast. "Have you heard? Does anyone know? Who was it?"

Quisti rubbed a hand under his nose. "Chancreon," he answered. Despite everything, there was a hint of amusement in his voice.

"The poet?" Garett said in disbelief. "The one who lectured at Greyhawk College? That little old man?"

Quisti tilted his head, and one side of his mouth curled

upward in a half-grin. "That's what they're all saying. And he lived right in the heart of this mess. And you know dragons. Always so intellectual and artsy. What better disguise to take if one of them decides to live among humans? I mean, who would have suspected Chancreon?"

"What I want to know," Garett said through clenched teeth as he stared back at the fires, "is what forced him out of that disguise?" As if it were in pain, he remembered thinking as it rose above the city. As if it were in battle against an invisible foe.

"Well, we'd better get back to it," Quisti said with a sudden shrug. The brothel keeper went toward the line of injuries, surveyed them, and bent down beside a woman who was cradling her left arm but sitting up. They exchanged a few unheard words, then the woman nodded and gave him her blanket. He watched as Quisti carried it to a bucket of water, immersed it, and lifted it out dripping, then went to join a team of workers beating out smaller fires.

Garett let go a sigh and thanked the gods that Greyhawk was flanked by two rivers. It was unlikely the city wells would go dry, and if the wind, indeed, forced the fire up against the city wall, they would be fortunate. *Fortunate*, he thought with a bitter inward smirk. What a word to use when measuring the size of a disaster.

With a curse and a sigh, Garett unfastened his red cloak and carried it to the nearest bucket to wet it down.

EIGHT

The sun had been up for an hour when Garett dragged himself back to the Citadel. His hands were scorched and reddened from fighting the fire, and his eyes were irritated from the smoke. He itched all over from the dried sweat and soot that clung to his skin. He knew he stank; he could smell himself.

He dreamed of a bath and a bed, but there was still work to do and reports to make. Korbian would want details of the dragon and the fire. And there would be questions about the deaths of the fortune-teller, Duncan, and the River Quarter's watch house commander, Soja. He put a hand to his forehead and wiped at the sweaty grit stuck to his brow, leaving a filthy smear. The skin was tender from constant exposure to heat, but he ignored that.

Hells, he thought, remembering suddenly that this was also the morning that Kentellen Mar was due to enter the city. He cast a quick glance around as he entered Grand Plaza. The streets were still relatively empty, at least in the High Quarter. The fire had quelled a good deal of the city's enthusiasm for any celebration, but that wouldn't last for long, he knew. As soon as people had a little rest and a bite of food, they'd be back in the streets again.

Over against the barracks, a group of weary watchmen huddled. Some leaned against the barracks wall while others slumped down to sit on the ground. Their uniforms were tattered and filthy with black ash, and their faces were streaked. Everyone had turned out to save the Halls.

Well, almost everyone, the captain reflected as he went inside and promptly ran into Korbian Arthuran, who was stalking the corridors with a scowl on his face. Garett couldn't prevent the frown that formed on his face as the man glared at him.

"Come with me," Korbian ordered without so much as an attempt at a greeting or pleasantry.

Garett shook his head wearily as his superior turned his back, but he followed Korbian up several levels. It took him by surprise, however, when Korbian did not stop at his own office, but continued on to the seldom-used chambers provided in the Citadel for the mayor and the city directors.

Garett nodded a greeting at Ellon Thigpen as Korbian ushered him into the room. Thigpen leaned over a large rectangular table and eyed Garett silently as the door closed. Korbian moved away and went to stand at the mayor's side. The scowl had not left the officer's face.

Garett glanced around at the other fourteen directors present. He knew them all, these representatives from the most powerful and influential guilds, unions, and temples of Greyhawk. There was ruddy-faced Sorvesh Kharn, the head of the Thieves' Guild, whom most of Greyhawk had expected to become mayor, before unexpected political maneuverings among the directors gave the post to Thigpen. There was Dak Kasinskaia, the youthful patriarch of the Temple of Rao, and Axen Kilgaren, the silent, brooding master of the Assassins' Guild. Beside Axen sat Greyhawk's plump, bejeweled inspector of taxes, Rankin Fasterace, or, as the general citizenry called him, "Fester-face," for indeed he had the worst complexion of any man Garett had ever seen.

Garett quickly scanned the faces of the rest, recalling names and positions, and noted at once the two glaring absences. As the high priest of Boccob, Acton Kathenor should have been present. Under the circumstances, however, Garett could see why he was not. It was the second absence that most puzzled him. One of the most powerful men on the Directorate was Prestelan Sun. It seemed extremely unlikely that he would miss such a gathering. But there was no sign of the master of the Wizards' Guild.

Garett felt the weight of all their eyes upon him. He gave a barely perceptible shrug and sighed. It was going to be a long and unpleasant morning. "Good morning to you, gentlemen," he said with a lightness of spirit he didn't feel, regretting as soon as the words left his mouth the hint of mockery that edged them.

"You're a mess, man!" Rankin Fasterace sneered, wrinkling his nose in disgust. "I can smell you from here!"

"Forgive me for offending your sensibilities," Garett answered with a bow. More mockery, he realized. He was just too tired to care. He wiped a hand again over his forehead. "You may have heard: we had a small fire last night."

"Is the fire out?" Thigpen asked, still standing over the table. There was an impatience in his gaze that put Garett on his guard and commanded a tautness in his posture. The livid veins in the little mayor's neck stood out against his pale skin. His hands gripped the edge of the table tightly.

Garett drew another breath and nodded. "The worst flames are beaten," he reported. "We still have teams stirring in the coals and ashes. Many of the buildings in that section were built with timber, and you know how wood can burn inside and cause a new fire if it's not watched."

"We were lucky." Axen Kilgaren regarded Garett with a quiet respect. Garett had had few encounters with Kilgaren, but he held a measure of respect for the man. Even though Kilgaren was an assassin, Garett had the feeling sometimes that he was the only one on the Directorate who truly had the city's interests at heart—and not just his own.

"Yes," Garett agreed, "because the wind blew the flames toward the city wall instead of into the heart of Greyhawk."

"Was the wall damaged?" Fasterace interrupted. The fat little man reached up to his chin with a heavily ringed finger, manipulated a pimple, and wiped a small trace of white puss on his expensive blue silk robe. "The city coffers can ill afford repairs," he added.

Garett bit back a sarcastic remark. Greyhawk's coffers were fat with the taxes levied against the trading vessels and cargo ships that daily anchored at the city's docks. The city was, in fact, one of the richest along the Nyr Dyv, the Selintan River, or anywhere. If that wasn't reflected in outward opulence, it was due to the notorious stinginess of the city leaders. "Tight as a Greyhawk director" was a running joke in the streets.

"Don't let it trouble your sleep, sir," Garett intoned. "We were able to get large barrels of water atop the wall to pour down upon the flames. It served the double purpose of wetting down the stone and preventing heat-cracking."

As slow-witted as he was, even Rankin Fasterace realized he was being mocked. "You have an insolent tone, Captain!" he charged angrily.

Garett lashed back, too tired to stop himself. "I have an empty belly, a parched throat, and your weight in soot clinging to me!" he shouted. "If you're so concerned about the wall, hire a carriage and go check it yourself. You might also check on the hundreds of people down there who will be rebuilding their own walls from their own coffers!"

"Captain Starlen!" Korbian Arthuran stormed around the table and came face to face with Garett. "You're in the presence of the full Directorate, and you'll keep a subordinate tongue in your head. Is that clear?"

Axen Kilgaren interrupted with a stern voice. "Sit down, Korbian. The captain is right to be upset. He's labored at the fires all night while we've been safe in our beds, and we haven't even offered him a drink to quench his thirst."

Korbian glared at the master of the Assassins' Guild but backed down and said no more. He went to stand beside the mayor again. Axen Kilgaren himself rose from his chair, went to a side table, and poured wine from a glass bottle into a delicate crystal goblet, which he carried to Garett.

"Thank you," Garett said, accepting the precious vessel gratefully. His throat was indeed dry. He inhaled the bouquet of the amber liquid as he swirled it around the interior of the glass. His eyebrows went up in appreciation. He sampled a small quantity. The taste was as rich and smooth as new silk. "Veluna," he said wryly, noting the wine's origin, "Shamarit Province, from its northernmost vineyards." He tasted the wine again and smiled.

Axen Kilgaren moved quietly around the table and threw open the shutters on the chamber's two large windows. New light flooded in, and a refreshing breeze swept about the room. Everyone waited patiently until Kilgaren took his seat again.

Then Sorvesh Kharn rose with a languid grace that belied his impressive size and went to pour himself some of the fine Velunan wine. "Now, then, Captain," he said without looking at Garett. The neck of the glass bottle clinked gently against a goblet that matched the one Garett held, and the sound of pouring liquid was heard as he paused briefly in his speech. "For those of us who are cursed to spend our nighttime hours in sleep, please give us the benefit of a complete report." He turned, raised his glass to his lips, and leaned patiently against the sideboard.

Garett took a sip from his own glass, eyeing the master of thieves, knowing full well the man had more spies than any other director in the room. Every petty thief in the city who held guild status—and that was any thief who valued his life—reported to his guild superior each morning. They, in turn, reported to Sorvesh. Garett had no doubt the man knew as much about the fire as he did.

Garett stared down briefly into the amber depths of his wine, summoning his faculties before he spoke. He began with the unnatural murders of Duncan and Soja, told all he knew about the dragon and the poet Chancreon, and plunged into detail about the fire and the devastation it had caused in the Halls. No one interrupted him while he made his report. The directors sat stony-faced in their chairs, except for Sorvesh, who maintained his place by the sideboard and placidly sipped his wine.

"Very good, Captain," Sorvesh said with a complimentary nod when Garett had finished. "Have you left anything out?"

Garett sensed a trap immediately. He gazed around at the faces turned toward him. Yes, he saw it in their eyes. They knew something he didn't. But what? He gazed toward one of the empty chairs and remembered.

"I've heard reports that Kentellen Mar is camped somewhere outside the Duke's Gate, prepared to enter the city today. I assume the reports are true. There was quite a lot of celebrating in the streets last night."

At the far end of the table, Ellon Thigpen at last slumped into his chair. "It's true that Kentellen is camped outside the city," he admitted, waving a hand to drive away a fly that buzzed around his head, "but he will not enter the city today. In light of all that's been happening, we've asked him to put off his entrance until tomorrow. We've already sent a messenger."

Garett walked to the sideboard and set his glass down unfinished. His thirst, at least, was quenched. But his stomach was still empty, and he didn't need any blurring of his senses now. There was a charge in the room, and all eyes were on him. "Because of the fire?" he said.

"That and more." Dak Kasinskaia leaned forward, one elbow on the table, as he answered in a high, nervous voice. Then he paused and watched Sorvesh Kharn warily as the master of thieves moved away from Garett and returned to his own seat. The patriarch of Rao continued. "I don't think either you or our esteemed Korbian realize, Captain Starlen, that Greyhawk has suddenly become a city on the edge of turmoil."

"Young Dak does not exaggerate," Ellon Thigpen interrupted, drawing a glare from his fellow director at his use of the word "young."

No one was quite sure by what politics one as youthful as Dak Kasinskaia had become the leader of his temple sect. Some thought it was out of respect for his father, a former patriarch, while others charged more devious dealings. However Dak had seized the position and the directorship that came with it, he plainly intended to hold his own among his more seasoned colleagues. For the moment, though, he yielded to the mayor, albeit grudgingly.

"The priests of Boccob are on the verge of declaring war on the Temple of Ralishaz, claiming it had something to do with Kathenor's murder," Thigpen explained wearily. Korbian Arthuran moved to the sideboard and returned to place a glass of wine by the mayor's right hand while Thigpen continued. "The residents of Old Town are making ugly noises about the recent series of murders there." He waved a hand at the fly again, ignoring the wine Korbian had brought to him. "There's a lot of grumbling about these other murders, too, I'm sure you know. Now, on top of it, if this fire is as serious as you say—and I don't doubt you, Captain—there are going to be a lot of injured people with no place to go."

It was Garett's turn to interrupt. "I ordered the university's dormitories opened to them," he said.

Fester-face rose half out of his chair. The look of shock on his face was profound. "You did *what?*" he shrieked. "Have you any idea of the cost?"

"Damn the cost," Garett muttered with an open sneer. "The dorms were half-empty, and those people had to have someplace to go. The students themselves suggested it."

"Actually," said Dak Kasinskaia, rolling his eyes upward in typically priestly fashion, "that's quite a charitable solution, at least for the time being. It's far better than having a disgruntled mob living on the streets with the investiture and the solstice celebrations approaching."

Fasterace sighed and sat back in his chair with a doubtful expression. "Well," he mumbled in a barely audible voice, "perhaps we can charge a rent . . ." No one paid that suggestion any heed.

Sorvesh Kharn rapped his knuckles gently on the table to draw their attention. "We are digressing, gentlemen," he said. There was a silken lilt to his words and a look in his eyes that once again put Garett on his guard. "My original question to our captain still stands. I'm curious to know if there's anything he's neglected to mention in his report."

Garett drew a breath and let it out slowly. He leaned back against the sideboard just as Sorvesh himself had earlier, and folded his arms across his chest. "If you're accusing me of something, Director," he said patiently, "then accuse me outright. If you know something that I don't, then enlighten me. But don't annoy me with games."

Sorvesh held up a hand to silence a purple-faced Korbian Arthuran before the captain-general could speak. "Forgive me, Captain Starlen," Sorvesh continued, almost with a purr. "I realize you're quite tired. I accuse you of nothing. I only meant to prod your memory. Was there anything out of the ordinary about last night?"

Garett felt his temper flare again and barely controlled it before a shout burst from his lips. "Out of the ordinary?" he answered with a tilt of his head, his voice dripping honey. "I'd say the whole damn night was out of the ordinary, Director." He put on a weak smile.

Sorvesh pursed his lips and rose from his chair. With a look of infinite patience, he went to stand behind another of the empty chairs and leaned over it. "As I said, Captain, I realize you're tired." He straightened and rocked the empty chair back on its rear legs as he did so. "What I'm getting at is this: With all this help and fellowship you speak so warmly of regarding the efforts to defeat the fire last night, where were the wizards? I mean, wouldn't their skills have been of particular value?"

Garett forced himself to be calm. "Of great value," he admitted, meeting Sorvesh's steady gaze. "Had they been there."

It was almost with a sense of relief that he noted the faint smile that curled the corners of Sorvesh's lips, and the dark gleam that came into the eyes of the master of thieves. He was setting a trap, but not for him, Garett realized, for Prestelan Sun. Here was some piece of politics, some struggle on the Directorate itself that had nothing to do with him or his job. Sorvesh had merely used him to score some point.

The master of thieves let the empty chair fall forward. It banged against the table with a harsh, wooden thunk, causing a dollop of the mayor's wine to spill over the side of the crystal glass. "So there's the love that Prestelan Sun holds for Greyhawk," Sorvesh suddenly thundered. "Our city burns, but the Lord High Wizard is too busy to descend from his tower and lend a hand. Nor does he send any of his guildsmen to offer their skills."

Sorvesh leaned forward and slammed his open palm down on the table. "And where is he now, gentlemen? Too busy once more to attend this meeting? I myself sent messengers to summon him, but they were turned away by the porters who man his guildhall gates. I say a vote of censure is in order!"

Dak Kasinskaia rose to his feet in protest. "That's preposterous!" the young patriarch shouted. "Your own overweening ambition is showing, Sorvesh. You're still angry because Prestelan voted to make Ellon mayor instead of you!"

An uncontrolled shouting match ensued, fourteen voices all hurling charges and accusations, while Ellon Thigpen attempted uselessly to restore order. Garett stood forgotten, watching it all with thinly veiled contempt, wondering whether he dared to simply slip out.

Beyond the two large windows, the sky suddenly flickered. Then it flickered again. The arguing ceased.

Unnoticed, Greyhawk's sky had turned a leaden gray. Thick clouds obscured the sun, and a wind blew sharply through the chamber. Once more the sky flickered, and a distant rumble of thunder shortly followed.

"Oh, my!" Rankin Fasterace exclaimed, leaping up. "I must get home at once. I'm wearing my best velvet slippers, and they'll be ruined in a storm!" Without another word, he gathered his robes about himself and waddled from the room, not bothering to close the door.

Several of the lesser directors who had not spoken at all also seized the excuse to depart over Sorvesh's angry objections. In no time, he found himself without a quorum and no chance of a vote on his motion to censure. In a mighty rage, he, too, left.

The first droplets of rain blew in through the windows and splattered on the stone floor. Ellon Thigpen went to one window and drew its shutters closed. Korbian Arthuran, following his mayor's lead, went to the other. As he reached out for the shutters, however, the clouds burst open, and a sudden blast of wind struck him like a tide. Sputtering and drenched, he leaped back.

"Damn it all!" Korbian Arthuran shouted, wiping away a faceful of rain.

Ellon Thigpen sighed heavily. From across the room, he waved a hand at Garett. "That's all for now, Captain," he said by way of dismissal.

Garett offered a curt salute and made his exit. The hallway was full with the day-shift staff going about their duties, and he weaved among them as he made his way to his own office a level lower. He couldn't remember when he'd last been in the Citadel at this hour of the day. It surprised him just how crowded the place was.

He reached his office at last and opened the door. A horrid stench assailed his nostrils. Rudi rose from the chair behind the door and turned to face his commander.

"Good morning, sir," he said smartly, executing a proper salute. "I've been waiting for you. I took the liberty of lighting a few lamps."

Garett didn't care about the lamps today. He wrinkled his nose and moved several paces away from the young sergeant, taking refuge at last behind his desk. "Where the hell have you been?" he complained, noting the filthy condition of Rudi's uniform, the slime that still clung wetly to his boots. "No, don't tell me," he said before his sergeant could explain. "The sewers. That's obvious enough."

"We all marvel at your deductive powers, sir," Rudi answered with a straight face. "By the way." He reached into his pocket and drew out three familiar amethyst crystals. "A junior sergeant from the River Quarter watch house came by and said to give these to you." He deposited them on the desk.

A blast of thunder shook the shutters of Garett's only window, and lightning flashed through the cracks. Rain smashed the thin, old wood with the force of driven nails.

Garett reached into the purse he kept tucked under his belt and withdrew the remaining two amethysts and placed them with the others. The five dicelike stones glittered in the lamplight. "I'm surprised he was willing to leave them with you," Garett admitted, recalling Kael's brashness.

"I pulled rank," Rudi answered bluntly, "and sent him away. I figured you'd have your hands full with that bunch upstairs. He can do his sucking up some other time."

Garett grinned. "He tried it with you, too, huh? You have my appreciation and respect, Sergeant," Garett conceded politely. Then he pointed to the chair by the door and wrinkled his nose again. "But please stay over there. You could be the only post in town, and a dog with a bladder infection wouldn't come near you."

Rudi took the chair and folded his arms behind his head. "If I may be so bold, sir," he scolded, making a face of his own, "you could be that same post. Smells like we've both made a hard night of it."

"I'll probably have to have this room cleaned," Garett agreed readily enough as he settled into his own chair and propped his feet up on the desk. He glanced toward the short pile of reports from the various watch houses, which were stacked in one corner, and decided they could wait. "Now, then, Sergeant," he said. "It seems to me I gave you an assignment in the River Quarter last night."

"Duncan's dead, sir," Rudi interrupted.

Garett looked at the boy for a moment, trying to decide if he was being mocked. But Rudi kept the same straight face. "I know," Garett answered with strained sweetness. He pushed at the amethysts with a fingertip. "These belonged to her."

Before Rudi could respond, the door to Garett's office burst open, nearly knocking Rudi from the chair behind it. Korbian Arthuran pushed his head inside. His face was a bloated mask of anger. "This fire has proven a fortunate little diversion for you, Starlen," he raged, "but you'd better have some results on all these murders by tomorrow—or else, damn it!" The door slammed closed with a force that reverberated through the stone walls.

Rudi stared in surprise, holding an arm up protectively, in case Korbian returned and the door sprang open again. Finally he relaxed and rubbed a knee where the door had struck him. "What was all that about?" he asked.

"Never mind him," Garett answered offhandedly. "What were you doing in the sewers when I sent you to find Duncan?"

Rudi swallowed and sat straighter in his chair. "I did look for her," he explained. "But I ran into a patrol coming up the Processional from Old Town. They were on their way to the Citadel." He hesitated and cleared his throat before looking at his commander again. "They found another floater in the old stream last night, cut up like the others. Only this time, they had a witness, sort of. At least, the old man claimed he saw them dump the body."

Garett leaned forward. "He didn't see the killing?"

"No," Rudi affirmed. "Just two figures in black robes down on Pilfer Street in the Thieves' Quarter. He says they came up out of the old sewer grate there and dropped the girl in the water."

Garett frowned at the news. "A girl?"

"Pretty one, too," Rudi answered. "Or she would have been when she grew up." He blinked and looked away. "This one's young, sir, younger than the others and carved up bad."

Garett's frown deepened as he began to thumb through the reports, searching for the one from the Thieves' Quarter watch house.

"I took charge of a patrol and led them down the same grate into the sewers below," Rudi continued while Garett rifled the papers. "We explored several of the tunnels, but didn't find anything. That doesn't mean much, though. There's miles of tunnels down there."

Garett gave up his search. The watch house apparently had not turned in its report yet. That didn't surprise him. Any men that weren't with Rudi in the sewers were, no doubt, busy fighting the fire in the Halls all night. In fact, the stack of reports on his desk was quite thin. Several watch houses had neglected that particular duty.

"You believe this old man?" Garett asked Rudi.

"I do, sir," Rudi answered firmly. "First of all, he seems a decent sort. One of the few people down there with steady, if low-paying, employment of a respectable nature. He's a street sweeper. Secondly, folks down there are simply too upset about these murders to lie about something like this."

"All right, then," Garett said, rising to his feet. "Don't bother to change clothes tonight. We're going back down into the sewers. Assemble four patrols. We'll go in at different points and comb every inch of those tunnels. If there's something down there, we'll find it. Let Blossom and Burge know. They'll be coming with us."

"I'll tell them to dress appropriately," Rudi assured him.

"Then go grab a bath and some sleep," Garett ordered. "We'll all need to be fresh."

Rudi pulled open the door. "Don't worry," he muttered over his shoulder. "An hour down there, and we'll be fresh enough."

Garett watched the door close, then slowly sat back in his chair and let his lids slide over his weary eyes. It was a pleasant moment of solitude that he badly needed. The noise of the rain beating at his window shutters was the only sound, and it lulled him gently. He shook it off, though, and rose again. He needed food before he slept, and he needed a bath as well. He left his office and left the Citadel without a word to anybody.

The rain fell in a solid silver sheet. Overhead, the sky was the color of unpolished steel. The air shivered with the force of repeated thunder blasts, and the wind whistled. Lightning crackled.

Instantly drenched, Garett lifted his face to the rain and felt the grit and ash wash away from him and run down into his clothing. At least the rain had a clean smell to it. He strode across the High Market Square, which looked more like a High Lake. The water was halfway up to his ankles. Beyond the square's entrance, the Processional was a ribbon of dark mud.

If this was wizard-weather, Garett thought smugly, they were a little bit too late. A rain like this might have saved half the homes that the fire had destroyed.

But in his heart, Garett suspected that Prestelan Sun had nothing to do with this storm. He stared toward the tip of the tall black tower that loomed in the distance above the far northern edge of the city. It was barely visible through the curtain of rain, quiet and suddenly ominous.

Forked lightning shattered the sky, and Garett felt his hair stand on end. For an instant, the world turned stark white. Afterimages danced in Garett's eyes, and he rubbed at them with his fists until his vision cleared. In some part of his brain, he wondered if Rankin Fasterace had made it home in time to save his precious velvet slippers.

Then, abruptly, he realized he was the only soul in the street as far as he could see. There's a metaphor in that, he thought wretchedly, hugging himself, for the wind had taken an unseasonably cold edge.

Soaked to the bone, he trudged his way home through lonely streets, and when he finally reached Moonshadow Lane and climbed the stairs to his small apartment, he thought the place had never felt quite so welcome.

Let the storm rage, he thought. It can't get in.

NINE

After the rainstorm, the summer heat once more asserted itself. The night air was thick and humid, and a carpet of mist blanketed most of the city. Overhead, black clouds, like monstrously distorted birds, raced across the sky. Only rarely did either of Oerth's two moons dare to peek through.

The weather had put a pall on the city. In most quarters, the streets were empty. Even in the River Quarter, only a few of the boldest dockers and the most determined celebrants dared to challenge the ankle-deep mud and the winding, fog-bound roads to quaff a couple of beers. The taverns were strangely quiet. The women of the Sea Willow hung languidly out their windows, watching the night pass with bored eyes, or leaned in the doorway, allowing the scant breeze to blow upon their bodies as they restlessly wiped sweat-soaked locks back from their foreheads and thought their private thoughts. The air, usually rich with aromas from the many restaurants, bore only the fetor of the rain, mist, and muck.

Greyhawk seemed poised, Garett thought silently to himself, as if the whole city were waiting for something to happen. He felt it, too, though he couldn't say how or why. He had slept through the entire afternoon, and his belly was full with Almi's food. Physically, he felt great. But the quiet unnerved him.

The calls of those ever-present blackbirds in the sky caused him to look up. Kule, Oerth's brighter moon, winked ever so shyly through the clouds and vanished again. Of the birds he saw nothing, but he heard them, heard their shrills, heard the soft beating of their wings.

"Still no word from the Wizards' Guild?"

Garett started at the sound of his own voice. Had he really spoken so loudly? The words, though muffled by the fog, ricocheted in his ears. He was sure he had only whispered. Still, it was as good as blasphemy, the way it broke the unnatural quiet.

Burge's boots made a sick, squishing sound as he slipped a bit in the mud and recovered his balance. "Nothin' at all, Cap'n," he answered lowly. His eyes combed the fog as he and Garett walked, searching the swirls and eddies, as if the lieutenant expected shapes to form or foes to attack them from out of the mist. His hand never left the hilt of his sword. Such behavior surprised Garett. He thought he had never seen his half-elven friend so on edge before. Burge jerked his head to the left as they passed the darkened mouth of an alley, and watched it until they were well beyond. Only then did he continue. "Their porters aren't even answerin' knocks at the gate. No one's even sure if they're there."

Garett looked up as they passed under a street lamp. It hung like a pale, washed-out ball in the gray haze, the post on which it was mounted little more than a tenuous shadow. Without stopping, he reached out to touch it to assure himself it was there.

"You think they've used their magic to teleport away?" he asked uneasily. He didn't want to think about what it meant if all the wizards—if Prestelan Sun himself—had fled Greyhawk. But why not? First the gypsy Attloi had departed. Then the magical races, the dwarves, elves, orcs, and others, had slipped quietly away. Next a dragon that had lived in quiet secrecy for years as a human poet in the Halls had panicked and fled. Why not the wizards?

Garett repressed a shudder and thought unpleasantly of animals fleeing the path of a deadly storm. Even more unpleasantly, he had the feeling he was about to get caught out in the rain again.

He and Burge approached the Black Gate that led into Old Town. The guard there had been doubled at his order, and he'd tripled the patrols on the streets, though it had meant juggling shift assignments at the barracks and caused some unhappy grumbling. But he'd made himself clear. All watchmen were to be on the streets in teams of four throughout the night. No hiding out in the watch house. There'd be no more little girls stolen from their families and murdered in the night if he could prevent it.

From the guards at the gate, Garett and Burge took a pair of torches and continued on along the Processional. Old Town was just as eerily quiet as New Town, and the night seemed to hold its breath. The taverns were all closed early. Not a candle burned in any window. All was darkness, save for the glimmering of their own two torches.

Up ahead, though, as they rounded a bend in the Processional, they spied the collective gleams of many torches. The fires shimmered weakly in the silver mists, and spectral figures stirred, muttering and coughing, by Kastern's Bridge.

"Hail, watchmen," Garett called, uncomfortable with the way he kept his voice pitched low. He couldn't escape the feeling that there was something out there in the night, something ominous that might be sleeping, as most things did in the night. If no one spoke too loudly, perhaps it wouldn't waken.

"Hail yourself, Captain," Blossom said, stepping away

from the rest as she raised a hand in salute. She, too, kept her voice down unconsciously, and though she addressed Garett Starlen, her eyes wandered warily beyond him into the fog. "All assembled, as you ordered, sir."

Garett cast a half-interested glance at the twenty torches dotting the night, barely noting the men who held them. Blossom and Rudi would have picked the best men; he had no worry on that account. He walked a few paces out onto Kastern's Bridge. The ancient boards creaked under his bootsteps, but with a strangely wet and muted quality. He leaned on the side and peered over. The waters of the South Stream, swollen by the rain, rushed beneath, white-capped and swirling. It might have made a roaring torrent as it swept between its muddy banks, but even the stream seemed oddly muffled.

Garett tried to shake free the lethargy that filled his mind. Almost without his noticing, Burge, Blossom, and Rudi had slipped up beside him on the old bridge. They were his team, his most trusted friends.

"I haven't forgotten the assignment I gave you, Lieutenant Blossom," he said in a near whisper. "I still want to talk to the watchmen who found the bodies down here. But it'll have to wait until morning. I want these sewers searched thoroughly. I mean, for the slightest clue or shred of evidence."

"Question them when you will, Captain," she answered. A breeze blew a strand of blond hair across her face. She reached up and swept it back with a gesture as she stared down into the water under the bridge. There was an uneasy look upon her face. "I brought them along. They're part of our search party."

Garett straightened, turned away from the stream, and regarded the gathered watchmen with new interest. "Which ones?" he asked, and Blossom pointed out six men. "Does that include whoever discovered the new girl?"

"A civilian did that," she reminded him curtly, intending no impertinence. "But, yes, the officer who took the report and pulled the body out of the water is there." She pointed the man out with an extended finger. The man looked their way, realizing he had become the object of discussion.

Garett only nodded. Later, he might want to personally question the old man who had found the girl's body, but he didn't want a citizen along on the search they were undertaking tonight. It was enough that Blossom or that officer knew the location of the drainage grate the old man claimed the murderers had emerged from before they dumped their victim's body.

He looked up suddenly and scrutinized the nearest rooftops, those he could see in the fog. "Burge," he said in a grumble, knowing the half-elf's eyesight was better than his own. "Anything up there?"

Burge scanned the roofs, turning in a slow circle as he did so. At last, he pursed his lips and shook his head. "Just some birds," he muttered.

Garett sensed eyes upon him as surely as if a hand were touching him on the neck. The tiny hairs there rippled and stood on end. He tried to brush the feeling aside. Maybe it was one of the Old Town gangs watching from a rooftop or a shadowed alley. Or maybe it was a Thieves' Guild member, carefully hidden, waiting to report his observations to Sorvesh Kharn.

But a worse thought occurred to Garett. At least one of the murderers they were after was a magician of great power, able to strike down from a distance Greyhawk's most gifted seers, possibly powerful enough to drive away a rare dragon and spread a muted panic through the magical races and magic-sensitive people of the city.

Every step in his investigation brought Garett closer to that unknown wizard. He suddenly felt the weight of the five amethyst crystals in the purse beneath his belt and realized just how vulnerable he was. It might very well be that same magician who watched him now.

Garett felt cold. The mist slithered around his feet, and the wind blew feather-soft on his cheek. He stared down at the drainage grate. "Get it up," he said.

Blossom directed a pair of brawny watchmen to lift the heavy grate. As they bent to the task, Garett turned toward the South Stream. Perhaps fifteen paces to its banks, he estimated. He envisioned two black-cloaked men emerging from the drain, disposing of a body, and vanishing again. With night to hide them, it would have been swift work and easy. It was only luck that anyone had seen them.

The grate made a loud shriek and clang, metal against metal and stone, as the two watchmen lifted it from its grooved joints, moved it aside, and set it down. Garett noted the noise instantly. His gaze swept along the dark buildings on either side of the stream's bank. The windows were dark. Not a lamp or candle burned. Such a racket would surely draw attention. He wondered suddenly why Rudi's witness, the old man, hadn't mentioned it.

With the grate removed, he leaned over and shone his torchlight down the black hole. The light didn't penetrate far. He set his foot on the first of the iron rungs, which were set deep into the moss-covered stonework, and began his descent into the sewers.

Brackish water rushed below him. In the stone-lined tunnel, it made a potent roar that filled his ears. The smell of it, a fetid, sour pungency, was almost enough to drive him back up again. He stepped down, seeking the flooring. The water surged around his ankles, up his shins, almost to his knee before he finally found footing. He let go of the rungs, careful to keep his torch dry, and with his free hand tugged the tops of his boots higher over his thighs. Then he unfastened his sword from around his waist, buckled the weapon's belt again, and slung it over his shoulder so that it hung upon his back. He had no intention of dragging a fine blade or its scabbard through that water.

Burge came down next, and Garett moved out of the way. The light of a second torch did little to repel the oppressive gloom. The water swirled, darkly gleaming, swollen by the torrential rain. Garett moved closer to examine the bricked wall. Mold and lichen had grown thick in the cracks where the ancient mortar had crumbled away. He put his hand out about shoulder height. It was easy to see on the wet stonework how high the drainage had reached during the peak of the storm.

"Ugh!" Burge exclaimed, clamping his nostrils shut with his free hand and making a face as he turned around. "You wanna find the murderers, Cap'n?" he said sarcastically. "We don't need to go through this. Let's just walk through town and sniff. If they been runnin' around down here long, they'll be easy to spot."

Another pair of men descended, and the sewer began to brighten with the added light. Garett wasn't sure that was an advantage, though, as he regarded the garbage and waste that floated by. Something brown and unpleasant brushed against his boot and stuck to the leather until he shook his leg to dislodge the foul mass.

The rest of the party reassembled below, leaving two men above to guard the opened grate. Soon, the patch of tunnel in which they found themselves was as bright as day. Still, Garett wondered if they would find any clues to the Old Town murders, or if the storm had completely washed any evidence away.

The last watchman down hesitated on the final rung and glared around. He made a wrinkled face and muttered. "I'm missing a decent night's sleep for this?"

Apparently he was one of the daytimers that Blossom had conscripted for this particular duty. "Think of sleep as dying," she told the man, slapping him rudely on his rump. "Then you won't miss it so much."

"She's one of my favorite people," Rudi whispered with a snide wink to Burge and Garett.

"Yeah," Burge agreed, keeping his voice low, though Blossom surely heard every word being said. "But your sense of humor will be the death of you someday. If she'd actually shown up in dress uniform, as you tried to convince her was our fair captain's order, you'd be her favorite snack food by now."

Rudi's lips curled upward in a leer, as if he were actually considering such a fate. There might, in fact, be worse ways to go, Garett had to admit as he regarded his tall, blond lieutenant from the corner of his eye.

"All right," he called to his watchmen. "Everyone choose a partner. Stay in twos and watch out for each other. Look for anything that seems out of place, anything unusual. Let's go."

At this particular juncture, the sewer flowed southward only a short distance before depositing its waste into the South Stream. Garett led his team north instead. He no longer had the feeling that he was being watched, and that allowed him to concentrate on the matter at hand. At the fore, with Burge by his side, his gaze roamed over every brick and stone, seeking anything that would confirm the story of Rudi's witness that the murderers had come this way.

The smell in the tunnel's close confines grew worse the farther into the sewer they penetrated, and the filthy water seeped into their boots in no time. Garett was grateful he'd thought to leave his cloak at home. The garment would have been hopelessly ruined. He'd already made up his mind to burn everything else he was wearing.

Up in a corner, where an arch of stone buttressed the tunnel's ceiling, a faint movement caught Garett's eye, and he stopped suddenly. A fat black spider, as big as Garett's thumb, eyed them coolly from the center of its web. The web itself was dotted with the silk-wrapped corpses of luckless insects that had blundered into its sticky strands.

"Oh, great!" Blossom muttered. The tallest of their party, she crouched a little lower, her gaze nervously wandering around the ceiling. "All I need are those things dropping down on me. I hate spiders."

Burge brought his torch close to the web, the better to

see. Then, suddenly, he thrust it at the huge arachnid. Strands of webbing flared and popped, and the flames consumed the creature instantly. "Me, too, Blossom," he agreed. "Never could stand 'em. Saw a man die from a spider bite once. Not pleasant."

"That's enough, Burge," Garett ordered. He turned long enough to give his watchmen a once-over, and saw how their tension level had gone up. Like Blossom, they were all scanning the upper corners and shadows for spiders. He didn't need Burge feeding their imaginations with tales. Then he added for the benefit of his men, "Most spiders aren't deadly, anyhow."

"Fine, Cap'n," Burge answered as Garett started forward again, and he followed close at his heels. "Next one we meet, you shake hands with 'im and ask if he's seen anyone pass this way carryin' a dead girl. Then, when you're done talkin', I'll wait 'til you move on down the tunnel a little bit before I fry 'im, so's not to offend your sensibilities."

Before long, they came to a fork in the tunnel. Garett held up his torch and peered both ways. The water in the new shaft seemed more shallow, and a bit less swift. It was also somewhat narrower. He called Rudi up beside him and pointed. "Take five men," he said, "and follow that. When you come to the first grate, raise it, take a peek, and see where you are. If the tunnel splits, send two men, and two men again the next time. Never less than two. Got that?"

Rudi nodded and beckoned to the five nearest watchmen. "Keep your torches dry," Garett cautioned them as they separated from the main party and waded into the new tunnel. He watched until the smaller group rounded a bend and its torches' light slowly faded. With a wave of his hand, then, he led his own men ahead.

Not much farther on, they encountered the first evidence that someone else had passed this way. Iron bars, like those in a cell door, blocked their way. Only the center bars had been bent far outward, wide enough for any man to squeeze through.

Garett knew his party was precisely under the Black Wall, which separated Old Town from the New City. The bars had been placed here, and at all such junctures in the tunnels, to prevent the residents of the Slum Quarter and the Thieves' Quarter from using the sewers as a secret means of passage between the two parts of Greyhawk. It didn't surprise him, however, to find the bars in such a condition. He had long known that the thieves of Sorvesh Kharn's guild had some way of traversing the wall without passing through the Black Gate, where the guards would log and record their passage. The sewers were the most logical means, and bars such as these, heavy with rust, would have been a small obstacle to men like Sorvesh Kharn or his predecessors.

Nevertheless, Garett paused to examine them carefully before he squeezed through to the other side and waited while each of his men did the same.

"I fear the rain has washed away anything useful," Blossom said as she stepped to her captain's side and peered at the iron bars with him.

But Garett touched her arm and drew her closer. "Maybe not," he said softly. "Look here." He pointed at a small yellowish smear about head high on one of the bent bars and pressed his thumbnail into it, leaving an impression. "That is tallow wax, and we all have torches. Someone else has come this way, and recently. If the wax was old, it would be brittle. My nail would have broken it."

Blossom shrugged. "Then under all this water, there's probably a trail of tallow droppings that could tell us which way the murderers went." She leaned her head to the side as she frowned, and a thick blond braid slipped over one shoulder and shimmered in the light of her torch.

"We don't know who came this way," Garett cautioned her. "Maybe the murderers, but, then again, maybe not." He quickly explained to her his suspicions about the Thieves' Guild and Sorvesh Kharn. "All we know for certain," he concluded, "is that someone passed this way recently."

"Could Sorvesh be the one behind these killings?" she wondered.

"I don't see how it would profit him," Burge said, interrupting, as he brushed one hand through the damp locks of his long black hair. "An' Sorvesh Kharn is the kind of man who does nothin' unless it turns a profit."

"Unless he thought he could sow enough unrest in Old Town to cause the Directorate to turn against Ellon Thigpen," Garett suggested, recalling the animosity he had seen on the thief master's face in the directors' meeting earlier that day, when he had attempted to turn his fellow directors against Prestelan Sun. And all because Prestelan Sun had supported Ellon Thigpen for mayor. "No," Garett said, thoughtfully scratching his chin. "I don't think we can rule Sorvesh Kharn out so easily."

"If it is Kharn," Burge whispered, leaning close, "then you'd best take care, Cap'n. As either a city director or a master of the Thieves' Guild, he'd make a nasty foe. But Sorvesh Kharn holds the resources of both offices. He'll be a tough nut to crack."

A little farther on, the tunnel forked again. This time, Garett chose six men and sent them off with the same instructions he'd given Rudi's team. He waited as they splashed their way up the sewer. When their torches were no more than a distant ruddy glow on the brickwork, he turned away.

Blossom gave a choked scream. Her sword whistled out of the sheath on her back and flashed downward, striking only water. Again she raised it, and again she struck downward as the nearest watchmen fell back away from her, shouting curses, trying to dodge her blows and protect their faces from the foul water she was slinging everywhere.

Garett and Burge reached her at the same time and caught her arm. She looked at them for an instant with an expression of utter repulsion before she began to blush. "It was a rat," she explained, breathless, "swimming right by me. I almost touched it."

"First spiders, now rats." Burge snorted with good-natured mirth. His violet eyes sparkled in the torchlight. "You're turnin' squeamish in your old age, Lieutenant."

Blossom dipped the tip of her sword and flipped water upward into Burge's face. When he twisted aside to avoid taking it in the eyes, she used the flat of the blade to deal his backside a sharp swat. "Mind your manners, elf," she said petulantly. "It's not polite to tease a lady."

Burge grinned as he rubbed his rump where her blow had landed. "My wee and delicate Blossom," he answered with a mocking bow. "Forgive me. I sometimes forget that you are, indeed, a lady. From time to time, I have to strain my neck to look up an' remind myself of that fact. Duck, now, cause we're comin' to another arch."

She had been watching Burge, expecting some retaliation. Barely in time, she reacted to avoid bumping her head on the stone support.

"Look out," Burge warned, pointing to the dark corner where the arch met the ceiling. "There's another spider there."

Unable to stop herself, Blossom shuddered and jumped sideways, splashing water, her eyes darting fearfully up into the empty corner. With a small yelp, she started to slip until Burge caught her arm and steadied her. "Guess I was mistaken, milady," he said with a broad smile.

Blossom glared at him as she sheathed her sword, straightened her damp tunic, and tossed her wandering braid back over her shoulder. "When we get back up into the real world," she scolded, "I'm going to severely punish you."

Burge held up his hands and shook his head. "Not me, milady," he answered. "But thank you for the offer."

Garett knew his two lieutenants well enough not to worry. Their banter was always in fun, no matter how they insulted each other. Probably no one else but Blossom could continually call Burge an elf with such scorn and escape a beating. And certainly any other man would be a fool to make fun of Blossom's size.

The water in this part of the sewers no longer ran swiftly. In places, it was almost still and came no higher than their ankles. But Garett could feel the slime underneath the water through his boots, and the smell was still nearly unbearable. He couldn't help wondering at the desperation that drove some men to seek employment as sewer sweepers, those poor citizens who, day after day, crawled down here to clear the sludge and sewage. He remembered Kentellen Mar's father had been such a man.

They came to yet another fork in the tunnels and stopped. Garett realized suddenly how the light had dwindled. From twenty torches, they were now eight, and if he sent men up this new shaft, there would be fewer still. There was nothing else to do, though. Lieutenant Burge and three men moved off, and Garett watched them go, as he had the others, until the light of their torches was gone.

He stared ahead into the darkness that closed around him as he led Blossom and the two remaining watchmen in his group up the original tunnel. Despite their four sputtering torches, the gloom had a suffocating quality. More than ever, he was aware of the weight of stone and brick and earth over his head, of the closeness of the damp walls on either side.

There was little water on the tunnel floor now, just puddles and a thin stream of fetid sludge. A pair of rats looked up hesitantly from a meal they were making on the corpse of a poor drowned cat, and scampered quickly out of their path. Garett stared at the cat as he passed it. It was pretty chewed, but what riveted his attention were the dark, moist sockets where the animal's eyes had been.

Why the seers? a part of his brain asked suddenly. Just as suddenly, the answer came to him. *Because there's something someone doesn't want them to see.*

A scream reverberated with frightening intensity through the tunnel. Garett spun about as one of his men dropped a torch from fear-numbed fingers. The flame popped and sizzled in a puddle and went out. Shamed, the soldier recovered himself. "Sorry, Captain," he muttered apologetically, one hand still clenched tightly on the hilt of his sword.

"Understandable," Garett responded even as he drew his own sword and started back down the tunnel at a run. In truth, he'd nearly dropped his own torch. The hair was still standing on the back of his neck.

"It came from that last fork," Blossom shouted, running alongside her captain. "Burge's party!"

They splashed noisily back through the tunnel as the sewage deepened, found the fork, and raced up it. The torches crackled and smoked in the wind of their passage. Behind Garett, one of his watchmen slipped and fell with a sharp scream of his own, and another light went out.

Then, out of the blackness came a terrible screech. For the briefest instant, Garett had the impression of something huge, a winged form with monstrous talons rushing at them out of the dark. A wind blew upon his face. With a shout, he threw himself against Blossom, knocking her aside. His torch sizzled in the water and went out as another human scream, from the watchman behind him, ripped through the tunnel and ceased with a horrifying finality.

Garett rose on his elbows out of the putrescent water and stared the way the creature had gone. His heart thundered in his chest as he pulled himself to his feet. Amazingly, Blossom had managed to save her torch. Though she was drenched, as he was, she was unharmed. He left her and hurried back to the fallen watchman. The man was dead, his neck broken as if by a powerful blow from the monster's outspread wing.

A splashing alerted Garett, and the remaining watchman, the one who had slipped, came rushing up, his weapon in hand. "What in the hells was that?" he shouted. The look on his face was the result of both anger and fear, as it so often was on men at the edge of hysteria. "It passed right over me before I could get up!"

"Who knows what it was?" Garett snapped too loudly. He drew a deep breath. There was still the first scream to investigate. That had to have come from Burge's party. "Take care of him," Garett ordered, indicating the fallen watchman. He turned to rejoin Blossom, who was on her feet.

"You're not leaving me here in the dark!" the soldier cried desperately. He slammed his naked blade against the stone wall, striking sparks, and Garett saw that he had, indeed, crossed the delicate edge. The man would fight rather than lose the light of Blossom's torch.

"Then pick him up and bring him, gods damn it!" Garett turned his back as the soldier hurried eagerly to obey. Once the burden was shouldered, they all splashed ahead.

A new side tunnel intersected at a right angle, and someone shouted out even before Garett and Blossom reached it, alerted, no doubt, by the torch's light. "Down here!" they called. "Help!"

The side tunnel was a dead end. A wide drainpipe near the ceiling gave a steady trickle from the upper world, and a green mossy stain trailed down the far wall. Two watchmen from Burge's team rose unsteadily from where they were crouched. A third floated face down in the foot or so of water that filled the tunnel. Burge himself sat propped against one wall. His head lolled to one side, and his eyes were closed. Blossom's torch revealed three sharply defined streaks of crimson that began on the side of his neck and ended just above his left nipple. The front of his tunic was entirely ripped away.

Garett went to him at once and felt for a heartbeat. "He's alive!" he declared.

"I thought I was never gonna see light again in my life!" one of the watchmen exclaimed.

"It was a bird, Captain!" the other watchman hissed excitedly. "I mean, sort of! I mean, it was a man first when we came upon him. But then he changed. I mean, just changed! Right in front of us! The lieutenant there tried to grab 'im, but you see what that got!" He pointed to Burge's wounds. "The thing just swiped at him and knocked him aside like he was a doll. Then it rushed at us. Me and Henget here—" He indicated his partner. "We ducked. But all of us, everyone, lost our damn torches!"

"What happened to the other one?" Blossom asked, moving toward the floating corpse, taking the light with her.

"Damned if I know," the one called Henget answered. "He went down, too. Then it was dark. We didn't move."

Blossom turned the floater over and winced. The man's throat was ripped away. As she let him go and rose again, the light of her torch fell fully on the far end of the tunnel, and she let out a short exclamation.

Garett heard her and turned to see what her light had revealed. Together they approached the low, stone altar while the other watchmen hung back silently. It was fashioned from large, unmortared blocks, recently assembled, and the cracks between the blocks were stained red where blood, and lots of it, had flowed down into them.

At one end of the altar, Garett found several strands of blond hair caught in those cracks. The little girl from Old Town whose body had been found yesterday—her hair had been blond. He put the palm of his hand down where her small head must have lain, and a tremor of anger went through him.

"Look," Blossom said, touching his shoulder as she raised her torch a bit higher.

On both walls, at either end of the makeshift altar, was a sign, crudely painted in red, that Garett knew. It could not be coincidence that he had seen it most recently carved in the wall of the apartment belonging to the old seer called the Cat.

It was the horned skull above two coupling serpents, the symbol of the Horned Society, the most despised of all Greyhawk's enemies. For years, the sorcerous Hierarchs that ruled the society had glared enviously across the Nyr Dyv, coveting Greyhawk's power and wealth. But their own conquests and expansions had overextended their military strength. The Hierarchs lacked the navy to reach across the lake. And thanks to the political machinations of Greyhawk's wiliest politicians, a precarious series of alliances with other nations around the Nyr Dyv ensured they would never develop one.

Then, suddenly, Garett took a closer look at the symbol. He grabbed the torch from Blossom to see better and held it right under the paintings, which were not done in paint at all, but in the life fluid of some victim, and it was still wet, still fresh.

Garett repressed a shudder and forced himself to study it closely. They were not horns that adorned the skull this time. They were slender wings.

"Let's get out of here," he announced abruptly. "Tomorrow, I want this thing taken apart stone by stone and the pieces thrown into the Selintan River. And have the sewer sweepers scrub these walls."

He gave the torch back to Blossom. "One of you carry that man," he ordered, pointing to the floater. "None of my men get left down here." Then he bent and picked up Burge and cradled the half-elf's head on his shoulder.

Not another word was said until they found the other teams, located the nearest grate, and reached the upper world.

TEN

Garett watched the sun rise from a window in the barracks infirmary. It proved no more than a pale white ball in the overcast sky. The fog lingered. Tendrils of mist wafted eerily through the air. The wind, when it blew, carried a chill that was completely out of character with Greyhawk summers.

With Blossom and Rudi worriedly looking on, he watched the physician take the final stitch in Burge's wounds. A small spell of healer's magic kept his friend unconscious during the process, and there was an expression of peace on the half-elf's face that seemed completely at odds with the rest of the world.

Despite that, Garett worried. As ugly as they were, the cuts on Burge's neck and chest were simple matters. It was the wound on the back of his friend's head that was the true cause for alarm. Apparently he had struck the sewer wall with considerable force, and Garett knew how dangerous such head injuries could be. The physician, however, could do no more than stitch the cut on the scalp, smear some salve upon it, and apply a bandage. Sometimes that was enough. But Garett once had seen a man awaken blind from such an injury.

The physician, Dav Govaker, worked for the garrison on permanent retainer and enjoyed a considerable reputation among many of the watchmen. He set aside his needle and thread, rose from the cot where Burge lay sleeping, and stretched. Govaker was a tall, thin fellow with a nose as sharp as his instruments and a wit to match. His fatigue, however, was plain to see as he rubbed his eyes and the bridge of his nose with a thumb and forefinger.

"He'll sleep the day away," Dav reported in a strained voice. "I suggest the three of you do the same. And I might mention I intend to charge twice my usual fee for this night's work. It's rude enough to be called from a sound sleep and a warm bed, but to have to perform careful work with the four of you smelling like a Nyrondian outhouse is simply too much for a man of my delicacy and breeding." He wrinkled his nose and made a face as he waved a hand to clear the air. "In fact," he added, "I may charge triple."

"Delicacy and breeding?" Rudi mumbled from where he leaned by the doorway. There was a gleam in his eye that had nothing to do with the glare from the oil lamps as he regarded the lanky physician. "The way I hear it, you got your start castrating reindeer in the Northlands and worked your way up from there."

Dav Govaker's eyebrows shot up disdainfully as he looked down the length of his nose. "They were not reindeer," he answered with an exaggerated sneer, "but gerbils. And I still like to keep in practice, so I may call on you sometime." He ran his gaze up and down Rudi.

"He must have seen you at the baths," Blossom interjected with a wink and a grin, never able to resist hurling a barb.

Rudi turned his own nose up at that in a mawkish imitation of Govaker. "He probably peeks through the knotholes," he said.

Dav Govaker gave an exasperated sigh and swept all his bandages and needles and instruments into a large, embroidered bag. Half the bandages were from the infirmary's own supply, and Govaker had no claim on them, but Garett said nothing. The man took too good care of his watchmen.

"Well, it's been fun, Captain Starlen," Govaker said, coming over to shake Garett's hand. "Always nice to see you, and this fine lady, too." He nodded courteously toward Blossom. "Next time, though," he continued, casting a spare glance toward Rudi, "perhaps you can find a sitter and leave the little one at home."

"They can be such a bother, can't they?" Garett agreed as he steered the physician toward the door.

Dav Govaker gave each of them a final nod and passed wordlessly out the door.

Blossom yawned and headed for her quarters in the barracks. Garett left, too, but, though he longed for his bed back on Moonshadow Lane, there was still business to finish in his office. One of the men who had died in the sewers had a wife—a widow now—and the city paid a special bereavement bonus to the families of watchmen killed in the performance of their duties. Some other officers had taken it upon themselves to inform the woman of her loss, but it was up to Garett to push through that extra payment, and he didn't intend to wait.

It surprised him when he exited the barracks to find a crowd milling about the High Market Square. Then a furious racket drew his attention to the dais under construction in the square's center, where a squad of bronzed and barechested workmen wielded heavy hammers.

A minstrel appeared suddenly in Garett's path. Wearing a plaintive and soulful expression, he sang and played on his stringed instrument, but the hammering nearly drowned him out. Garett ignored the man and walked on toward the Citadel.

"What's going on?" he asked the guards at the main entrance, though he already had a pretty good idea.

All four guards snapped to formal attention and executed proper salutes. Their crimson uniforms were clean and neatly worn, their cloaks draped perfectly over the shoulders, their boots polished. "It's official, sir," one of the four reported crisply without meeting Garett's eyes. "Magister Kentellen Mar will enter the city through the Duke's Gate at exactly noon today, sir."

Garett had to give Korbian Arthuran credit. His daytime watchmen certainly looked and sounded elegant. The captain wondered what they thought of his fouled uniform and the rank smell he exuded. If they gave it any notice at all—and how could they not?—they kept it carefully hidden behind perfectly straight faces.

He bid them good morning and entered the gloomy depths of the Citadel. No matter what time of day, the corridors of the mammoth structure were always dark and lit with lamps and lanterns. He made his way straight to the Office of the Paymaster and there gave the sergeant in charge the name of the dead watchman and the widow's name and address, with instructions that the bereavement bonus be sent at once by a special watchmen's representative.

After that, he headed for Korbian's office three levels higher. The upper halls were full of people he didn't know—low-ranking bureaucrats, minor dignitaries, and secretaries. A steady stream of these functionaries flowed in and out of the Directorate chambers. When Garett failed to find Korbian in his offices, he also headed there.

Korbian and Ellon Thigpen sat side by side at the large meeting table, a stack of papers before each, a map spread between them. Various aides bent over the directors' shoulders, observing a red line marked on the map as Korbian trailed his finger along it and explained the route by which Kentellen Mar would enter the city.

Garett pushed his way to the table and leaned both his hands upon it, deliberately interrupting Korbian in the middle of his instructions. "We need to talk," he stated quietly, including the mayor in his gaze. Then he added pointedly, "In private."

Korbian put on a frown of annoyance and waved him away with a beringed hand. "Not now, Captain," he declared bluntly. "We are in the middle of important preparations. Kentellen Mar arrives at noon, and we still have not determined exactly who will sit on the dais when the mayor presents his welcome. Such matters of precedence. . . ."

Ellon Thigpen reached out a hand and laid it palm down on the map. It was gesture enough to silence Korbian Arthuran. The mayor paused a moment to lean back in his chair and turn his penetrating gaze up to Garett. Then Ellon folded his arms across his chest, and his hands disappeared inside the perfect folds of the sleeves of the finest blue silk robe Garett had ever seen.

"I believe our Captain has something on his mind," Ellon said with quiet patience. He rose slowly from his chair. Without a further spoken command, the room emptied of all but Korbian, Garett, and Ellon himself. "I assume you have something to report. Does it concern Acton Kathenor's murder?"

Garett shook his head. "I took a squad of men to Old Town last night," he began.

Korbian Arthuran pushed his chair back noisily and stood up. "We hardly have time right now to worry about a few low-lifes getting their throats cut before being dumped in the river." He leaned on the table and glared impatiently. "It happens all the time in Old Town, Captain. That's why there's a wall down there to separate Old Town from the civilized part of the city."

Garett glared at his superior. At that moment, it was hard to contain the contempt he felt for Greyhawk's captain-general. "If you bothered to read the reports that I have left on your desk every morning, you'd know the latest of those low-lifes was a young child, kidnapped from the streets while she was playing."

"So?" Korbian began to fiddle with the pile of papers

and maps spread before him. "Her family probably did the deed because they couldn't afford to feed her anymore. As I said, it happens in Old Town."

"Please, Korbian!" Ellon Thigpen slammed a hand forcefully down on the table, his face reddening with sudden anger. "Don't make yourself sound any more like a fool than we already know you are!" The mayor turned away from a stunned Korbian and back to Garett. He let out a long sigh and straightened his resplendent robe. "Now, then, Captain. For better or worse, I am mayor of all Greyhawk, Old Town and New. What about these murders?"

Garett ignored the deadly looks Korbian Arthuran gave him over Ellon Thigpen's shoulder. With a few harsh words, the mayor of Greyhawk had accomplished what Garett had tried hard to avoid for the past year, and driven an unremovable wedge between his superior and himself. From that moment, he knew he had best never turn his back on the captain-general.

He fixed his gaze on Ellon Thigpen and began a calm, methodical report on the latest murder, the events described by Rudi's witness, and how it had led them deep into the city sewers last night. The mayor paced around the room as he listened. His expression grew grave, and he stroked his chin with one hand. When Garett began to describe the creature that killed two of his men and injured another, the mayor stopped his pacing and glared at Korbian Arthuran.

"You said nothing to me about two watchmen dying last night," Ellon accused angrily.

Korbian stiffened. "Captain Garett is late with his report, as usual!" he countered. He whirled to face the night watch commander and slammed his hand down upon the table for emphasis, just as the mayor had done. "Why was there nothing on my desk this morning about this?"

There was nothing Garett could say. For once, Korbian was right. He *was* late with his report. The business with

Burge and the physician, Govaker, had consumed his time. Since he had no excuse, he offered none. He simply ignored Korbian and went on, instead, to describe the altar and the temple they had found, in all its crudity, in the sewer depths, hesitating only before describing in detail the symbols painted on the walls. He stopped then and waited.

Ellon Thigpen let out a long sigh and resumed his pacing. "And what conclusion do you draw from all of this, Captain?" he asked finally, his hands disappearing once more into those finely crafted sleeves.

It was Garett's turn to draw a breath and give a long sigh. He rubbed his nose and looked askance for an instant before saying bluntly what he knew neither of the men before him would want to hear. "These murders are the work of the Horned Society," he stated, "or one of its cults."

Korbian Arthuran slammed his hand down again. "That's preposterous!" he shouted.

"*These murders*," Ellon Thigpen repeated, turning his back to Korbian. "You mean just the Old Town murders?"

Garett hesitated, then shook his head. "I think they're linked," he admitted. "The Old Town killings, Acton Kathenor, all the seers." Without realizing he'd been doing so, he found himself with one hand tucked deep into his belt, his fingers playing with the amethyst crystals contained with a few coins in his purse. He pulled his hand out at once.

"You *think*," the mayor said pointedly. "Do you have any evidence they're connected?"

Garett thought. He had to admit it was still mostly just a gut feeling. But there was one piece of evidence. "We tried to find an old seer in the Slum Quarter, a man called the Cat. He was gone, and investigation indicates that he fled the city. But in his quarters we found the symbol of the Horned Society—the horned skull above intertwined serpents—carved into his wall."

"Well, then he must have been the murderer!" Korbian declared. "He knew we were closing in and ran before he could be apprehended. If he's gotten away, that's probably the end of it."

Garett couldn't hide the look of scorn that danced across his face. "The little girl was murdered *after* the Cat vanished," he said with an open sneer in his voice. "And Rudi's witness claims *two* men dumped the body in the South Stream."

Ellon Thigpen was barely listening. He paced back and forth with his head in one hand, deep in thought, his blue silk robe swirling about his feet. "You know what it means if the Horned Society actually is involved, don't you?"

"Why would they be killing Greyhawk citizens?" Korbian asked in a more reasonable voice. "Especially Old Towners? How would it possibly profit them? When you deal with the Horned Society, you have to think in terms of profit!"

Garett frowned. "We obviously don't have the complete picture yet," he admitted. "But it must be part of some bigger plan. I think that's why they went after the seers who might have divined their schemes and given warning."

Korbian Arthuran came around the table and stood between Garett and the mayor. "This is sheerest conjecture!" he declared, glaring from one man to the other. He whirled on Garett, sternly tapping one index finger against the palm of the other hand. "When you described the symbols on the sewer wall, you said the skull had wings, not horns. That alone is enough to cast doubt on this ridiculous theory."

Ellon Thigpen looked suddenly peevish. He went to the table, gathered up all the notes and maps piled there, and pushed them into the captain-general's arms. "None of this must spoil Kentellen Mar's arrival," he stated brusquely as he seized Korbian Arthuran's elbow and ushered him toward the door. "And I'm sure you still have security arrangements to oversee, friend Korbian. We mustn't keep you from those duties any longer. I'll finish up here with the captain."

"But, Ellon!" Korbian shouted with a look of hurtful surprise as the mayor moved to push the door closed in his face. "We still haven't decided who will stand with you on the dais!"

"I trust your judgment, Korbian," Ellon Thigpen answered with a sweet smile that vanished instantly the moment the door clicked shut. He leaned his back against it and drew a breath before striding back to the center of the chamber, where he resumed his pacing.

From outside the chamber windows the noise of the gathering crowd drifted up to Ellon and Garett. It was still hours before Kentellen Mar was due to arrive, and the hammering that rose from outside told that the dais was not yet even completed, but already people were staking out the best places from which to watch the welcoming ceremonies.

Ellon Thigpen went to one of the windows and stared down. "Captain," he said quietly, "how certain are you of any of this?"

Garett could only shrug as he, too, moved closer to the window. Below, the High Market Square was half-full of colorfully dressed citizens, all milling about, waiting for something wonderful to happen. More and more people streamed up the Processional. Soon the square would be full. Some citizens had opted for the roofs of buildings that lined the parade route. They would not be able to hear the speeches, but they still wanted a glimpse of Kentellen Mar.

"I'm not certain of any of it," Garett confessed as he watched the mayor out of the corner of his eye. "These are not ordinary crimes, sir. We're dealing with magic. Of that, I'm certain. And crime and magic are a very subtle mix. I request again that the city directors allow me to consult with the Wizards' Guild."

Ellon Thigpen rolled his eyes melodramatically. "You know what old Fester-face thinks about that," he said, waving a hand in the air. He raised his voice an octave and whined in an almost perfect imitation of the fat tax collector. "The cost, the cost!"

Garett was too tired for such games. "What of the cost to Greyhawk if the Horned Society is really involved?" he stated flatly. "There's a powerful wizard behind these murders. And have no doubt—he is an enemy to this city. I say, consult with the guild and worry about the fee afterward. After all, Prestelan Sun lives here, too. He has a stake in this."

Ellon Thigpen moved suddenly away from the window and resumed his pacing. He glanced at Garett with a troubled expression, then glanced quickly away again. "Yes, well," he started. "That was my attitude, also, Captain." The mayor drew a deep breath and let it out in a gush, his shoulders suddenly sagging in the folds of his fine silk garment.

"I trust you, Captain Starlen," Ellon said abruptly. There was an intent gleam of determination and worry in his eyes as he fixed Garett with his gaze. "I think you care about this city in a way that Korbian does not. To him, the watch is just one step on a ladder to a better social position. But you actually care about the job you do." He took another breath and paced to the window, where he looked out over his people. "So I'm going to tell you something that must not leave this room."

The mayor turned around and faced Garett. His expression was completely serious. His hands came together, and the fingers interlocked. The thumbs rubbed nervously against each other. "No word has come in or out of the wizards' guildhall for two days," he said, unable to disguise a raspy note of fear in his voice. "I've sent messengers," he said. "I even went myself. The porters do not even answer at the gates, and the gates themselves are sealed fast."

Garett was incredulous. "There is no word from Prestelan Sun?" Even as he spoke, though, he recalled the archmage and guildmaster had not attended the meeting of directors the morning before, something that was unheard of.

"None," the mayor affirmed.

Garett scratched his chin. "No one has tried to get inside?"

Ellon Thigpen scoffed. "Come now, Captain. You know the dangers in that as well as I."

The mayor had a point there. It was a known fact that the walls and gates of the wizards' guildhall were protected by formidable spells and wards. More than one petty burglar, usually a foreign adventurer not familiar with the ways of Greyhawk, but with more ego than brains, had learned that at the expense of his life, and possibly his soul.

"I'm afraid you're on your own, Garett Starlen," the mayor said. "It's up to you. Greyhawk is in your hands."

Garett regarded the mayor through suddenly narrowed eyelids. He didn't particularly like Ellon Thigpen's choice of pronouns.

"But if you can stop these murders and find out clearly what is going on," Thigpen continued smoothly, "then Greyhawk may have itself a new captain-general."

Garett bristled, though he tried to hide his reaction. "You'd dump Korbian, just like that?"

"Dump him?" Ellon Thigpen frowned and shook his head. "Of course not. He has his uses. But I'm sure I could arrange to move him up his ladder," he hesitated, and the faintest trace of a smile turned up the corners of his mouth, "and out of our way."

Garett raised an eyebrow. "*Our* way?" he queried.

The mayor nodded firmly. "You must keep me completely informed. I want to know everything you learn as soon as you learn it, every phase of your investigation."

The noise of the crowd in the square rose again, louder than before, and the hammers rang furiously. Outside the window, all in the city waited for their hero, Kentellen Mar.

Garett knew he must step carefully. He had little desire to take Korbian's place as captain-general, and less to let Ellon Thigpen use him as a lackey. The seat on the Directorate that would come with such a promotion was no lure to him, either. Politics in general, and Greyhawk's politics in particular, held no attraction for him. He sensed it would be unwise to say so at this moment, however.

"As soon as I have anything to report, you'll know about it," Garett answered diplomatically.

"Good," Ellon Thigpen said with a sigh. "Now, I must return to the business at hand, I'm afraid. And, please, Captain. This is the second time you've come before me smelling of the Abyss." He made an unpleasant face and added paternally, "Try to clean yourself up a bit, as befits your station. Otherwise, our newfound friendship might not stand the strain."

Garett only inclined his head before he turned and left the mayor's chamber. He didn't even stop at his office. As quickly as he could, he exited the Citadel and hurried down into the crowded square. He drew a deep breath and let it out slowly. Never in his life, he thought, had he needed fresh air so desperately.

ELEVEN

Garett worked his way wearily through the throngs that filled the High Market Square. No one moved aside for him, and he had to push and elbow his way along, muttering curses as he went. He was in no mood for festivities. More than anything, he wished for the relative peace of his apartment on Moonshadow Lane. He wanted nothing more than his bed and a good sleep.

What was there to celebrate, anyway? he thought, glancing at all the happy, cheering faces. Kentellen Mar was coming home. So what? The magister-to-be might be a decent fellow now, but after a few months on the Directorate, no doubt he'd become just as devious and petty as the rest of the directors. He'd have to, just to survive in the position. If the people truly loved him, they'd do everything they could to discourage him from the office.

A pretty young girl with blond hair that hung in curls over her shoulders and big, wide eyes the color of robins' eggs, danced into Garett's path. She was barefooted. Her dress was a clean but threadbare scrap, and the blue ribbon in her hair was pressed but faded with age. He guessed it was a hand-me-down from her mother or an older sibling. In the crook of her right arm she carried bunches of flowers. Smiling, she thrust a small bouquet up at him. "Buy some flowers, lord?" she sang sweetly. "Just two commons!"

Garett scowled, but still he found himself reaching into his belt and drawing out his purse. He took the bouquet and dropped the coins into her small hand. "I'm not a lord," he told her gently.

"Thank you! Thank you!" she responded gleefully, dropping the coppers in a pocket. "Everyone's a lord who buys my flowers!" Instantly she turned away to thrust another bouquet at someone else and make her exuberant pitch.

"You've got a soft heart," a familiar voice said close to his ear.

Garett turned and gave Blossom a sidelong look. She'd changed out of the smelly uniform she'd worn in the sewers and taken time to bathe. It reminded him of how badly he stank and how filthy he felt. She looked fresh in a plain blue tunic and black trousers tucked into leather knee-high boots. The sword at her hip was the only indication of her status with the City Watch. In fact, she might have been any adventurer who had paid the city's licensing fee to carry the blade.

"I thought you were going to bed," Garett commented, eyeing her with new interest. He'd never really thought of Blossom as beautiful before. She was one of his officers. But out of uniform, with her usually braided hair flying loose in the wind, standing head and shoulders above almost everyone else in the crowd, she was quite a stunning woman.

Blossom shrugged as she looked around. "Who can sleep with all this going on?" she answered, surveying the nearest faces. "They're pressed right up against the barracks walls."

Garett understood her point. The High Market Square could hold as many as five thousand people. It had to be nearing that limit already. Garett frowned to himself as he stared over the heads of the mob toward the Garden Gate. The Processional would be full of people, too, he realized. It was going to be tough getting home.

"Why don't you let me buy you a drink, Captain," Blossom offered, as if realizing the reason behind his frown. "No point in trying to make it back to the River Quarter now. You'll just be swimming against the current."

Garett thought about it and agreed. "We'll still have to make it out the gate, though," he reminded her doubtfully.

"Not necessarily," she answered quickly. "You just follow me."

With her intimidating size, Blossom had no problem turning northward and clearing a path through the crowd. People saw her coming and did their best to make way, and if she had to push a soul or two out of her way, nobody complained loudly enough for her to hear. She was known to the citizens of Greyhawk, even without her uniform.

Garett followed in her wake, both amused and amazed by the reactions of the people she passed. The men gave her looks, sometimes of lust and sometimes of anger, depending on how quickly they stepped out of her way and how roughly she shoved them. A few even dared to mutter curses, though not too loudly.

It was the women and girls in the crowd, though, that fascinated Garett most. They watched Blossom with open admiration in their eyes. To them, she was a kind of heroine. No husband would ever beat her, they realized. No brother or father would bully and order her to fetch their beer or fix their meals. He could almost hear their silent cheers every time a man stepped aside for her or every time she pushed one out of her path. And Blossom didn't say anything to anyone. Either they moved or she moved them.

In no time, they were out of the High Market Square and headed back toward the Citadel. As Garett had predicted, the Processional was crowded as far as he could see. Banners had been draped across the road, and pennons were flying from every window and rooftop. From all directions came the music of street performers and minstrels. It was as if a great carnival had come to Greyhawk and taken over the streets.

"How about The Tomb?" Blossom asked, naming a nearby tavern where many of the watchmen spent their off-duty hours. She rubbed her throat as she looked around disapprovingly. Despite the slate-gray sky that threatened rain at any moment, the celebration was only building.

"Fine with me," Garett answered halfheartedly. Part of him still would have preferred to fight his way through the crowds to his apartment and fall into bed, but it had been a long time since he'd had a quiet drink with one of his officers, and longer since he'd visited The Tomb, where he'd spent many of his early hours with the watch before he'd risen through the ranks.

Side by side, they turned off the Processional and took a narrow side alley called Leaf Street, which ran through a carefully tended grove of trees, one of several such gardens in the Garden Quarter. Even here, the noise from the Processional and the High Market Square could be heard. Unless everybody stopped for a drink, Garett figured, Greyhawk would be very hoarse before Kentellen Mar ever poked his face through the Duke's Gate.

At the end of Leaf Street stood a squat, windowless brick building, whose sign out front proclaimed it The Tomb. It stood opposite another, far more graceful structure, one of the most famous in Greyhawk, called the Lord's Tomb, which contained the remains of the city's founder, whose name was lost in antiquity. Some considered it sacrilege that a tavern called itself after such an important landmark. Garett didn't care. And after a few beers, no one he knew cared, either.

Blossom held the door while he led the way inside. For good reason was it called The Tomb. He paused for a moment on the threshold while his eyes adjusted to the darkness.

"Come in or get out!" someone shouted gruffly. "But close the damn door!"

Garett hesitated the merest instant, and a piece of crockery shattered against the wall near his head. Hastily, he stepped inside and pulled Blossom after. He hadn't forgotten the legendary temper of The Tomb's owner, an amazingly fat half-orc named Kestertrot. Garett pulled the heavy door closed. Immediately, all the noise from outside stopped. Barely able to see in the smoky gloom, he took the three short steps down to the floor. A pair of dim lamps, suspended from the ceiling by old chains, provided the only illumination. Whether it was intended to or not, the place gave the impression of the caves where Kestertrot's ancestors dwelled.

"I can hardly see!" Garett muttered good-naturedly as the owner waddled toward him.

Kestertrot harrumphed as he took Garett's hand and shook it vigorously. Kestertrot was only half-orc, but he had all the features of his father's race. Tiny eyes peered up brightly from a face that was mostly black, wiry hair, and his nose was almost the size of a fist. "Don't blame me for your pathetic human eyes," he answered gruffly. "I can see just fine. Been a long time, Starlen. Thought you didn't like old Kestertrot anymore."

The owner guided Garett and Blossom to a table in the far corner near the kitchen door. Half a dozen other men from the watch bent over their drinks and nodded quiet greetings as they passed. At another table, a mercenary, whose oily, double-pointed beard and tightly bound hair revealed him as Nyrondian, looked in Garett's direction, lifted his nose, and glanced pointedly away. Garett refused to feel irritated. He'd been to Nyrond once. Never had he seen a nation with so little reason for believing itself superior to the rest of the world.

"Here, I think you should probably have these," Garett said pleasantly, passing the bouquet of flowers to Blossom when Kestertrot had taken their orders for barley beer and left them alone.

Blossom leaned her elbows on the table, cupped the bouquet between her hands, and inhaled the fragrance of the flowers. "Blossoms for Blossom," she answered sweetly with just a hint of teasing in her voice. "But don't get any ideas, Captain Starlen. We can never be more than just good friends." She put on a small, coy smile, a delicate upturning of her lips that lent her a very feminine beauty. For a second time, Garett realized he just wasn't used to thinking of his lieutenant as a woman, and it disconcerted him.

"If you couldn't sleep," he said quickly to divert the unexpected course of his thoughts, "why didn't you join the celebration in the streets like everyone else? You might have caught a glimpse of Kentellen Mar."

The smile faded, and a definite frown took its place. "Give me a break, Captain," Blossom said in a low voice. "There's not a man or woman with eyes in this city that hasn't seen Kentellen Mar walking the streets on his way to court or wandering the grounds of the university or quaffing a drink in the River Quarter from time to time." She rolled her eyes and leaned back in her chair. "I swear, the man gets handed an office, and suddenly he's a god."

"It's an important office," Garett replied, also leaning back in his chair, willing to let a bit of friendly debate pass the time. "The people of Greyhawk think that, as magister, he'll bring back an element of fairness that's been missing from the judicial system."

Blossom stared at him. A corner of her mouth turned upward in cynical amusement as she crossed one leg over the other and tilted her chair back on its two rearmost legs. "We both know the only reason Kentellen Mar was given the appointment is because Ellon Thigpen is a shrewd politician. He thinks he can use Kentellen's popularity to consolidate his own standing with the citizens. And since Kentellen has no experience at all as a director, he'll be grateful for his appointment, but out of his element, thus easy to manipulate."

Garett regarded her. He knew well Blossom's skill with her weapons and her dedication to her job as watchman. But his lieutenant also had a keen mind. "Perhaps not as easy as you think," he suggested quietly.

"It doesn't matter what I think," she returned with characteristic bluntness. "It's what Ellon Thigpen thinks."

The kitchen door swung open, and Kestertrot appeared bearing a tray with two tall mugs of pungent barley beer. He set one down before Blossom, frowning at her wordlessly until she straightened up and placed her chair down on all four legs. Then he moved around to Garett and set the second mug before him. "You stink," the half-orc stated loudly enough for all in the room to hear. "You'd think a captain of the watch could afford to bathe before visiting a *decent* establishment."

Garett picked up his beer and blew away the foamy head. He was getting a little tired of people commenting on his personal odor. "I do bathe," he answered with light sarcasm, "when I visit decent establishments."

Kestertrot made another of his throat-clearing harrumphs as he tucked the tray under one arm and wiped his hands on his dirty apron. Then he turned and went back through the kitchen door. As soon as the half-orc was gone again, Blossom leaned her chair back on its rear legs and looked thoughtful. Slowly, she lifted her beer and brought it to her lips. The froth left a tiny white mustache, which she licked away.

The door to the outside opened. Bright sunlight streamed inside briefly, and another pair of watchmen came into The Tomb and found seats at a table. They had a familiar look of weary dishevelment. Garett recognized them in the poor light. Night-shifters assigned to the watch house in the Artisans' Quarter. With an inward groan, he realized the likelihood that none of his men were going to get any sleep today for the noise of the celebrations.

"It's going to be dicey tonight," he muttered over his beer. "Half the city drunk and half the night watch asleep on its feet."

Blossom only nodded as she sipped from her mug and cast a glance around at her fellow watchmen. "I wish it were all over," she said at last. She wore a strangely troubled expression. "I've had a bad feeling for days."

Garett looked at her, puzzled by the sudden change in her voice. Abruptly, The Tomb seemed even darker than he knew it was, as if the wicks on the lamps had been turned down, though no one had gone near them. Even the air felt thicker.

"As if you were being watched?" he asked in a whisper, trying to sound casual. He remembered the sensation he'd felt on Kastern's Bridge and in the sewers. He felt it again now, no matter how he told himself it was only in his mind.

"I don't know," she answered, looking away self-consciously, refusing to meet his gaze. "But there've been moments the last couple of days," she confessed, "when I felt almost on the verge of panic, like I just wanted to run as far away as I could." She shook her head and took a long drink of her beer. "It's completely irrational," she added firmly, as if trying to convince herself.

Garett leaned forward and peered at her intently. "Blossom, you don't, by any chance, have the blood of any magical races in your veins, do you?"

Blossom turned toward him, obviously startled by his question. Then she barked a short laugh, set her beer down, and lowered her chair to its four legs. "No, Captain," she answered with a patient grin. "There's no truth at all to the stories that I'm part giant. I'm completely human."

Garett's mouth drew into a tight line as he settled back again. It had been a dumb question, and he hoped she hadn't taken offense. He was completely human, too, but there was still that odd, creeping sensation on the back of his neck. But when Blossom said she'd thought of running away, it had suddenly reminded him of Burge's report that the elves and dwarves and orcs had all left town.

But Kestertrot was still here. He was only half-orc, though. For that matter, Burge was still here. Garett frowned, suddenly worried about his half-elven friend. What if there was something in his elven blood that was trying to warn him of danger? Would Burge recognize such a warning? Someday, he was going to have to reconcile himself with his magical heritage. No one could live with such self-denial forever.

Garett took a drink from his mug, feeling like a man with all the pieces of a puzzle spread on the table but no clear idea of where to begin. It was an irritating admission. He gripped his mug tightly between his hands and stared down into it. With a start, he realized he was trembling.

I need some sleep, he told himself. He gazed up uneasily, wondering if Blossom had noticed, but his lieutenant appeared lost in her own deep thoughts, her eyes turned toward the darkest corners of the tavern. He stayed long enough to knock back the rest of his beer, then rose. "I must be going," he said with a vague sense of disappointment. He had thought to have a long, pleasant conversation with a friend and fellow officer over a couple of drinks, but something—he didn't know exactly what—had spoiled it. The mood was suddenly as oppressive as The Tomb itself. "I'll pay for the beers," he added.

Blossom snapped to alertness and fumbled for the purse on her belt. "No, no!" she insisted, embarrassed. "I invited you!"

Garett laid a hand gently on her arm as he came around the table and smiled at her, trying his best to shake off his burdensome solemnity. "Captain's prerogative," he told her firmly, "and captain's privilege."

Blossom acknowledged the compliment with a grin and a sharp salute. Then she rocked her chair back again, propped her booted feet up on the table, crossing them at the ankles, and raised her beer in a silent toast to his health.

Garett looked around for Kestertrot, to pay him his coins. The fat old owner wasn't to be seen, though, and

Garett remembered the kitchen. He pushed through the door. The room, lit by a single lamp, was crammed with kegs and barrels and crates, old blackened pots and pans, jugs and mugs and wooden spoons, all scattered everywhere. Garett wondered how even a half-orc with an orc's eyesight distinguished the clean vessels from the dirty ones, or if he bothered.

A table stood against the far wall, its top cluttered with all manner of utensils. A dark shape lurked beneath it. Garett crept a little closer. Bending down, he called, "Kestertrot?"

A bulbous nose poked up out of the gloom. A moment later, the rest of Kestertrot followed. The old fellow rose stiffly and made a show of brushing the knees of his trousers.

"What were you doing under there?" Garett asked in puzzlement.

"Dropped something," the half-orc answered too quickly. He moved away from Garett to a fat keg balanced on its side upon a rickety old crate. He grabbed three mugs from another table and began filling them. "What do you want back here, anyway?" he demanded.

"The beers," Garett answered quietly, frowning at the tavern owner's broad back. "How much?"

"Four commons," Kestertrot snapped. "That's two coppers each. Just leave it." He didn't turn around. Garett fished the coins from his purse and set them on a packing box by the kitchen door. He started to back out when the half-orc turned a little and muttered over his shoulder. "You watch your back, Starlen," he said, trying to sound a bit more pleasant.

Watch your back. It was a common expression in the orc nations, like "so long" among humans, or "be seeing you." But there was an edge in Kestertrot's voice. And Garett could not shake the impression that the old owner had actually been huddled under the table when he came into the kitchen, as if he'd been hiding from something.

But Kestertrot turned away again and concentrated on filling his mugs, plainly intending to say no more.

"You, too," Garett told him. He left the kitchen then and nodded to Blossom as he strode toward the door to the street. She raised her mug to him once more and watched as he went out.

He gave a sneeze in the bright sunlight and blinked until his eyes adjusted. The noise from the High Market Square and from the Processional assailed him. The intensity of it surprised him. The thick stone construction of The Tomb had shut it out almost completely. Not far away, a great cheer went up and seemed to last forever. It spread and built and fed on itself, and suddenly he knew that just a few short blocks away, Kentellen Mar was passing by.

Garett thought of heading for the Processional. The parade and the pageantry would be spectacular as Kentellen's entourage wound its way to the square. Garett had never quite gotten over his boyhood admiration for the tumblers and acrobats and dancers that he knew would be there. But right now, he dreaded the thought of the crowds and decided to work his way through the Garden Quarter by the back roads. He glanced up at the sky. It was still the same slate-gray color, full of dark, threatening clouds.

It took him twice as long as normal to get home. By following the Garden Road, he went all the way to the wharves, where the great trade ships that plied the Nyr Dyv and the Selintan River rocked gently in their berths, abandoned, for the most part, by sailors and dock workers who had gone to join the celebration. Most of those he saw there were the blue-shirted private guild watchmen, hired to guard the vessels and stacks of cargo goods. He entered the River Quarter by way of the Cargo Gate and made his way wearily to Moonshadow Lane.

Almi was sitting in her window, watching the street, as he approached. He went up to her and leaned on the sill.

"You stink!" she said, wrinkling her nose in disgust.

"I've been told that by better men than you," he answered with mock sweetness, and he blew her a kiss. "Would you mind having your girls draw me a bath if they're not off celebrating?"

"My girls?" Almi answered indignantly. "Let them run loose among all that rabble?" She snook her head. "I'll send up some lunch, too. You look as bad as you smell, you know."

Garett thanked her and started up the steps to his apartment. Before he went inside, though, he happened to turn. A sound caught his ear, not the sound of the crowd or the noise of celebration, but something else, something that had now become almost familiar. He gazed up toward the sky.

Hundreds of black birds wheeled and gyred in the ashen sky, riding the wind on outspread wings. Garett stared across the street, over the rooftops to the west. He leaned out and raised as high on his toes as he could to gaze eastward over his own roof as he listened to them, calling, calling.

They were everywhere.

TWELVE

Wearing only a loose white robe of thin material, Garett climbed the stairs to his apartment and went inside. His hair still dripped rivulets of water, and his face felt raw from the close scraping he had given it. At least he felt clean again. Now all he wanted was some sleep.

He opened the shutters on his windows. On such a gray day the sunlight would not keep him awake. He welcomed the gentle breeze, though. Later, when the revelers spread away from the High Market Square and the Processional into the River Quarter, the noise might wake him. On the other hand, he thought he had a fifty-fifty chance of sleeping through *anything*.

He pulled the soft robe over his head, carefully folded it, and placed it on the table next to the coin purse and sword he'd put there earlier. Naked, he fell face down onto the cool sheets of his bed and scrunched the pillow under his head. The light wind whispered upon his bare flesh, a soothing sensation that relaxed him. As an afterthought, he drew a corner of the sheet over his body, remembering that he'd left Almi with instructions to wake him at dusk.

He wasn't sure how long he lay there. It surprised him that he didn't fall asleep at once. Outside, the birds continued their incessant screeching, though it sounded a bit farther off. A pair of women walked by in the street below, giggling like giddy virgins. A fly set up a steady drone as it explored the apartment. The door to Almi's tavern slammed. Garett closed his eyes. *Please*, he begged, straining toward sleep. His body ached so, and a heaviness weighed down his thoughts. In the street below, someone laughed. At last, though, sleep did claim him.

An odd light penetrating his lids woke Garett. Wearily he cracked open one eye. A soft violet light filled the room. All his senses snapped alert, though he kept perfectly still. It was no natural illumination, he knew. With careful deliberation, Garett rolled over onto his right side. Silently he cursed himself. His sword was not where it should be at the head of his bed. He had left it on the table across the room, out of reach. He slowly sat up and turned toward the source of the strange purple illumination.

The five amethyst octahedrons hung in the air, burning with a steady glow as they spun in a circle, like jewels on an invisible ring, on the far side of the room. They had been in his coin purse, but some force had freed them and set them dancing. The same force, he assumed, had closed and sealed the window shutters.

He rose cautiously, crept to the table, and freed his sword from the scabbard. The purple light rippled up the silvery length of the blade as he drew it clear. He touched the coin purse. The strings were loose; a few silver nobles and gold orbs lay scattered on the table, likewise shimmering as if touched by violet fire.

Around and around the crystals whirled, faster and faster, as he stepped away from the table and into the center of the room. The purple glow began to throw off streaks of whiter intensity, but in the center of the circle described by the spinning gems, a spot of blackness took form.

Now Garett felt that same sensation he had known on Kastern's Bridge and in the sewers. Someone was watching him, observing from out of the center of that black spot. He felt that unknown gaze like a lightning charge on his skin. The hair rose on the back of his neck, and his every nerve trembled. Suddenly a wind ripped through that tiny black void and swept about Garett. It overturned his table, scattering coins everywhere. It snatched the sheets off his bed and set them snapping and dancing about like costume ghosts. The white robe he had set aside earlier, and a few other pieces of clothing, whipped violently through the air. Garett flung up a hand to protect his eyes from the stinging force of the unnatural gale.

Then the black spot began to grow. It filled the circle described by the jewels. Next it swallowed them. Still the purple light shone, as if from behind the swelling blackness. Garett took an uncertain step away and felt the foot of his bed brush against the backs of his legs. He brought his sword up and gripped it tightly in both hands. Now the circle of darkness began to stretch and reshape itself, and he watched, mesmerized, as it became rectangular and its growth abruptly stopped. The wind, too, stopped, and an eerie silence filled the apartment.

A door, Garett realized, staring at the black rectangle. Within its darkness he could just make out the dim shadows and outlines of a world cloaked by night. There were mountains, he thought, and a shifting expanse of something darkly silvered. The smell of salt air brushed his nose, and he knew it was a sea. But what sea? What world?

It would do him no good to stand here and wonder. Whatever or whoever had such power to reach into his apartment and create this portal could have, no doubt, slain him just as easily in his sleep. Instead, it had sent him an invitation, and as he stood there, staring into that vague otherworld, he knew his curiosity would not let him decline.

Sword in hand, he padded barefoot across his floor and

experienced a frightening instant of icy coldness and utter dark as he stepped through. Then it was dew-damp grass that cushioned his footsteps, and a peppering of bright stars twinkled overhead. It took but a moment for him to observe several familiar constellations. They were somewhat skewed, as if he had traveled a great distance. But still, he knew their shapes. Wherever he was, he was still on Oerth, and he found a measure of relief in that.

He turned, half-expecting to gaze back into his old apartment above Almi's tavern. The magical door and the purple glow from the amethyst crystals, however, were gone. He stared, instead, at the highest point of a ring of mountain peaks, barely visible against the night sky.

Not far away he heard the sound of breakers, and again he inhaled the fragrance of the sea, much stronger now. A gentle salt breeze brushed his skin, reminding him that he was naked. He experienced a moment of annoyance with himself for not snatching up a garment, but he pushed the feeling aside as a more important consideration occupied his thoughts. His sword had not made it through. Whoever had brought him here had brought him unarmed.

He waited for guidance, not knowing which way to go or what to do. He still felt that arcane gaze upon him. His host knew he was here. Well, what now? he wondered, and at last he shrugged his shoulders and began walking, not toward the mountains, but toward the sound and smell of the sea.

He had no idea how long he walked. Behind him, a fat crescent moon, Kule, the first and larger of Oerth's two, climbed slowly above the peaks and poured a pale radiance across the land, and the beads of dew glimmered mysteriously upon the blades of grass, seeming almost to wink as numerous little insects hopped or fluttered out of Garett's path. He perceived, in the moon's milky glow, that he was approaching a great cliff, for far beyond, at the rim of his vision, the darkness turned liquid and a vast stretch of ocean rolled and shifted, gleaming where its waves and whitecaps strained up toward the heavens.

The night breeze sang in his ears, and the sound of the surf rushing upon rocks that he could not yet see kept a steady rhythm. Despite the danger and the nature of his coming here, he began to feel a rare sense of peace. He glanced skyward again, finding those familiar constellations to reassure himself that, yes, this really was his own world.

I'm dreaming, he decided. I'm back home in my bed, and this is a dream.

The sound of the breakers was much nearer now, and Garett could see the sharp edge of the cliff jutting out over the sea. He quickened his pace in unconscious anticipation. Ahead he could clearly see the black line where the land met the sea, and beyond that, another line where the sea touched the star-flecked sky. *Boom*, went the breakers, and the surf answered, *sshhhh*, as if it were the guardian of the world's tranquility.

Then he was at the cliff's rim, staring outward. It was more than he expected, and his breath caught in his throat. The sea rolled on into infinity, its liquid surface an undulating chiaroscuro, alive with the light of moon and stars and the shadows of great rippling waves. Below, the water dashed upon jagged rocks that jutted up like the grasping claws of some giant, drowning beast, and the wind carried up the salty spray and dampened Garett's hair and skin as he flung out his arms and tipped his head back to receive it. A small moan of pleasure issued from his lips at its chill embrace.

Gone was all thought of Greyhawk. Garett looked around for a path that would take him down to the narrow strip of beach below and found a steep, thin trail. With boots or sandals, he would not have hesitated, and even barefooted he lingered only for a moment before starting his descent. It surprised him that the trail was so well marked. He didn't need a torch or lantern to make his way as long as the moon was overhead. Still, he went carefully, for the sea spray had slicked the stones.

Once down, he stood upon the white sand shore and stared outward again. The mist and spray quickly soaked his hair. Great waves broke right before him on the piles of massive rocks that rose out of the water no more than a hundred feet from the beach. Now the waves had a greenish cast, as well as a black and silvery one, and the sea rocked with much more violence than it had appeared to from above.

A seashell gleamed white on the ground at his feet. He picked it up, brushed the sand away with a finger, and peered at it. He didn't know what kind it was. Someone else might have kept the shell and made an ornament out of it, a necklace, perhaps, or a bracelet, or something more useful, like a button or even a needle. Garett drew back and flung it with all his might. It sailed into the moonlight and struck the water, skipping upon the waves three times before it sank. Garett smiled.

Then he spied something from the upper corner of his eye. He turned and gazed upward. His descent along the trail had taken him up the beach a bit as it angled down the cliff face. At least that was why he told himself he must not have seen the tower that loomed high atop the cliff before. Or perhaps he had seen it but mistaken it for one of the mountain peaks. Or perhaps the peaks themselves had formed a backdrop that camouflaged it from his vision.

Down here, on the beach, though, he saw it, and its shadow spread out upon the ocean. Suddenly, Garett remembered why he had come. The moonlight that touched the tower had an almost violet glow.

He knew with an inner certainty that it was his ultimate destination. There was nothing to be gained by reticence. He started back up the narrow path, making the steep climb, not at a rush or with hesitation, but with a calming deliberateness of motion. He leaned forward, using his hands to steady himself on the slippery rocks, but always he looked up, keeping his gaze on the tower.

Near the top of the cliff, he paused long enough to tear one fist-sized rock from its earthen bed. He tested its weight on his palm before he finished his climb. It wasn't much of a weapon, a mere rock, but he felt better with something. He reached the top of the trail and started off toward the tower. By some trick of light, it had seemed closer when he stood below on the beach than it did now.

Oerth's second moon, Raenei, almost full, a round topaz jewel in the night sky, had risen just above the horizon in pursuit of its brighter companion. Though still in their waxing stages, the combined light of both moons was enough to show him the way safely. Garett's twin shadows floated over the ground as he went along, briefly eclipsing the brilliantly sparkling dewdrops in the plush grass.

The air had turned crisp. Or perhaps it was just the beads and droplets of sea spray evaporating on his skin that chilled the captain so. In any case, he wished that he was not naked. He gritted his teeth to keep them from chattering and increased his pace, hoping to warm himself as he followed the edge of the cliff. The tower simply couldn't be that far away. He could see it clearly, limned by a sourceless radiance, and he doubled again his pace.

A flight of dark little gnats surrounded Garett suddenly, then was gone, leaving only the few he unwittingly managed to snag in his mouth and nose. He sputtered and spit, doing his best to rid himself of an unpleasant taste, and still he kept his gaze on the tower for fear that it would vanish if he looked away. The slick, wet grass and the tiny stones, pieces of twigs, and myriad unseen things it hid, began to take a toll on his bare feet. He could feel the bruises forming on his heels and the strain in his toes. Nevertheless, he pushed on, refusing to slow or rest.

Both moons rode high in the night by the time he reached the outer edge of an ancient, ruined estate. Garett didn't understand how it could have taken him so long to reach it, but he didn't question. Magic, by its nature, was impervious to any assault by logic. He just gripped his rock in a tighter fist and let his senses and instincts take over.

A triple row of once-grand marble columns surrounded the solitary tower. Though spotted with the black stone-rot of age, still they glittered in the moonlight. A few, here and there, had toppled off their pedestals and lay in shattered sections on the grass. A few others still stood, but with great, dark cracks running like captured lightning bolts upon their surfaces. Garett thought he might only brush them with a hand and send them crashing down. He restrained himself, however, out of respect for something so old and once graceful.

Between the innermost circle of columns and the tower, he found three pathlike rings upon the ground. The rings were made of smooth white pebbles that he fancied had somehow been reclaimed from the ocean, for only its constant tides could have worn away the roughness. Two men could have walked upon them side by side in idle conversation, so wide was each of the rings. As far as he could tell, like the columns, they encircled the dark tower.

Garett clutched his rock as he stepped over the innermost ring and started across an expanse of ground toward what he perceived in the tower's strange glow was the entrance. Before going far, he walked into a single line of spider's web, invisible in the darkness. It draped lazily around his face. Utterly repulsed, he wiped at it furiously with his free hand, trying to rid himself of the sticky strand. With a shudder, he continued ahead. Only a few paces on, he blundered into a second line. It wafted over his nose and cheeks, and this time he gave a soft, involuntary cry at the silken touch, and dropped his rock, so desperate was he to wipe it away with both hands.

It embarrassed him to behave so squeamishly, and he was grateful there was no one to see. No one, he reminded himself, except that unseen watcher whose patient gaze had never left him, the one who had brought him here. Garett picked up his rock, swelled out his chest as he lifted his chin, and determined not to react so poorly when he encountered the third web that he knew would certainly be there, and because he looked very carefully, he managed to catch just a glint of moonlight on that final thread. He drew his hand through it, severing it. At least it was only his hand that suffered its contact and not his face. He shuddered anyway.

The entrance was a pair of huge iron-banded doors made of rare but weather-scarred roanwood. Great rings of twisted iron hung upon each door as well. The hinges and bolts were also of iron. Garett gazed at the doors, each twice his height, and up at the tower itself. Immense squares of some dark stone, unknown to Garett, made its walls. The mortar between some of those blocks had crumbled away, and moss and lichen filled the niches. There were no windows that he could see, nor any crenellations at all. It was more than a fortress, he thought. It was a vault. But to keep someone out, or to keep something in?

He reached out, intending to grasp one of the iron rings and try his strength upon the doors, but no sooner did he move his arm than both doors swung slowly and silently open of their own accord. Garett stood at the threshold with his rock in his hand, staring into the torchlit interior. Suddenly, his stone seemed a pitiful weapon indeed. He relaxed his grip and let it fall to the ground. Then he passed between those great doors and went inside. It did not surprise him at all when the doors closed again without ever making the slightest creak or sound.

A ring of ten torches burned in sconces at equal intervals around the room. Garett counted them, noting their regularity, before he glanced up. If he had expected several levels within this tower, he was disappointed. The only ceiling appeared to be the roof itself, in the gloom far above his head. And that was where he knew he must go, the tower's roof, for the interior was quite empty of anything except the torches and a narrow wooden staircase that twined concentrically up the walls to that high place.

Garett took a torch from one of the sconces and moved

toward the stairs. His footsteps left perfect prints in the thick carpet of gray dust on the old stone floor. He wondered how the torches had been lit, for there were no other prints at all, not even around the sconces. Plainly, no one had been here for a very long time. But then he reminded himself of the shortcomings of logic. He had no doubt that someone was at home. He could feel them watching.

He set his foot on the first step. The old wood groaned under his weight. The wooden railing was damp under his palm, slick with wood mold. He moved cautiously up. Two steps. Ten steps. Twenty-five steps. The entire staircase vibrated and shook. The railing trembled like something alive. The higher he went, the greater the danger became. A treacherous groaning and creaking filled the air. The stairs began to buck and sway violently, as if trying to hurl him off. Garett dropped to his knees and clung to one of the steps with his free hand. Pieces of wood came away under his fingers, but he found new purchase and clung on, holding his torch like a shield of light, gritting his teeth and staring at the floor a dizzying distance below, doing his best to keep perfectly still.

Finally the shaking slowed and ceased, and Garret rose from his crouched position. At his smallest movement, the vibration began again, the merest causing shivers deep in the old wood. He sucked his lower lip and lifted himself as gently as possible onto the next step and felt it crack under his weight. He skipped to the next one as quickly as possible, and the shaking began again.

Garett's heart hammered in his chest. Feeling as desperate as a trapped animal, he shot a glance groundward and another toward the gloom above his head, where the top of the stairs disappeared. With one hand on the railing and the other on the wall for balance, he rose up the steps. The wood under his feet grew soft and spongy. The heavy iron bolts that supported the stairs sawed back and forth in the stone walls and hurled a fine powder downward. The structure's groaning became a cacophony that fed on its own echo until its shrieking filled his ears.

Wood snapped suddenly, and Garett's foot crashed through the next step. With a fearful cry, he snatched at the railing, and his torch went tumbling over the side with a hiss and flutter of flame while the nails of his other hand raked the wall, seeking purchase. For an instant, he seemed to hang over empty space, and the world reeled around him. Then he had his balance again and was racing up the stairs as fast as he could run, uncaring of the danger or the darkness, his breath coming in ragged gasps, his eyes locked steadfastly on the roof, his destination.

The stairs ended on a small, narrow landing. Without even pausing for breath, Garett smashed his hands against what had to be a trapdoor. To his immense relief, a door did indeed fling open, and it crashed backward with a resounding slam. Three more swift steps, and Garett rose into the cool air of the night. A breeze brushed against him, chilling him. For the first time, he noticed how thickly he was sweating.

The roof was not quite what he had expected. It was not precisely even the roof. Another ring of slender white columns, each twice as tall as a man, rose around the top of the tower, supporting the true roof, a shallow, smooth-sided dome full of gloom that began to glow with a soft golden color as the captain gazed up at it.

With a start, Garett realized that a tall, heat-blackened brazier near his left side had taken fire. The smell of hot coals and incense wafted into the air. Four more such braziers, placed strategically around the strange, open-aired chamber also began to burn. It was the light they shed that filled the dome above his head.

Quietly he bent and lowered the trapdoor back into place. Then he began to move about. The floor was covered with thick old carpets, woven with odd designs, some of which Garett believed to be magical. They had that look about them. In the center of the chamber was a small table draped with velvet. A crystal ball rested in its center. It reflected his own face when he leaned down and peered into it. There was another table nearby, littered with glass beakers and tubes. Some were half full of strangely colored liquids. One, in particular, caught his attention. Unstoppered, it gave off a thin wisp of smoke, though there was no source of heat, and the beaker, when he touched it gingerly with a fingertip, proved cool. He sniffed. There was no odor to the smoke it exuded.

He moved to the edge of the roof between a pair of columns and leaned upon the low encircling wall. Far below, the sea waves curled and crashed upon the rocks, but the sound of it was no more than a gentle, distant rush, and the whitecaps might have been small white doves, drowning on the water.

He moved again and found a table against another part of the wall. His fingers brushed over an old astrolabe and sextant. Garett gazed up at the sky. The stars glimmered warmly in the night. Once, when he was younger, he had known all the constellations by name.

Garett turned away from the wall and moved back toward the center of the room. There was a soft couch and a plush, stuffed chair with a footstool, and between them a low, round table. A gold goblet shimmered in the firelight from the braziers, and a bottle of red wine stood beside it, casting a ruby reflection.

"Please, drink if you wish."

Garett turned sharply, startled by the rich, deep voice. But there was no one behind him. There was no one that he could see anywhere. "I would prefer water," he stated calmly, though his gaze darted to every shadow.

"Then it is water," the voice answered with the merest hint of amusement.

Garett failed to spot the speaker, so he turned, and the bottle contained a clear, sparkling liquid that he didn't doubt was water. He tipped the vessel delicately and filled the goblet. He took a sip and found it the freshest, coldest spring water.

"It's delicious," Garett commented. "Will my host drink with me?"

Another brazier slowly began to burn on a side of the roof that Garett had not yet explored. It revealed a high-backed chair and a figure reclining there. Garett could not see, though, its still-shadowed face. He saw mostly a lap—where rested a pair of folded, gnarled hands—the hem of a black robe, edged with silver thread embroidery, and soft felt boots, crossed at the ankles.

At the same time that Garett spied the speaker, he realized why the voice had confused him so. The dome that made the second roof played strange tricks with sound.

When the figure didn't answer, Garett shrugged and sipped his water again. "You have an interesting place here," he said conversationally.

There was a pause before the man in the chair answered. "I don't come here as often as I used to." There was a vitality in the voice that impressed Garett. He stared at those ancient hands, trying to reconcile his impressions.

"You have another home?" Garett asked over the gold rim of the goblet.

The shadowed figure seemed to nod. "In the Yaril Mountains," he answered. Then, stiffly, the figure began to rise, pressing with both hands on the arms of his chair until he finally stood. Once on his feet, though, he seemed to gain vigor. An old man, tall, almost willowy, he stepped out of the shadow. His close-cropped hair and beard, once black, were heavily streaked with gray. The wind set his black robe to fluttering as he moved toward Garett, and the captain of Greyhawk's night watch could not say for sure if the old man's feet even touched the floor.

His host stopped beside the couch and peered at Garett. Even in the ruddy glow of the firelight, his old eyes were the keenest, clearest blue.

"You've been watching me for days," Garett said matter-of-factly. He didn't doubt that statement at all. He knew the intensity of that blue-eyed gaze. He had felt the weight of it on his back for too long. "Why?"

The gaze locked with his, and the two regarded each other unyieldingly for a brief moment. "Allow me to provide you with a garment," his host said finally. Going to an old trunk, he pulled out a soft robe of white silk, which fit Garett perfectly.

"Thank you," Garett said, feeling the cool slide of the fabric over his skin as he tied the belt. The slightest breeze caused the material to stir and flutter. It almost tickled. His host moved to the wall, leaned his back against a column, and stared out toward the moonlit sea. Garett followed.

Again his host fixed him with that blue-eyed gaze. "I am Mordenkainen," he said.

Garett's throat went suddenly dry, and he thought briefly of the goblet of water, which he had left sitting on the low table by the couch. Maybe he could have it changed back to wine again.

He knew the name, of course. Mordenkainen was the legendary leader of the Circle of Eight, a cabal of the most powerful wizards on Oerth. Once, according to many stories, the Circle had held a subtle sway over most of the affairs of the world, carefully balancing matters so that no one force or nation or power ever rose to a position of total dominance. They were neither good nor evil. Or perhaps they were both. Such things always depended on point of view. But they saw that a balance was maintained. No one, however, had heard from the Circle in over fifty years, and Mordenkainen himself had not been seen for longer than that.

Garett regarded the man he saw before him and remembered all the stories he had heard. Then with characteristic bluntness, he asked, "Was it you who killed the seers of Greyhawk?"

The corners of Mordenkainen's mouth twitched, but whether it was a frown or a grin he put on, Garett couldn't tell. "You accept my drink and my garment," Mordenkainen said with a droll lilt, "then you accuse me of murder." He shook his head. "No, I didn't kill the seers."

"But you know who did," Garett pushed. Now that he finally had a chance to get some answers, he wanted them all at once. "And the Old Towners. I bet you know what's going on there, too. Is the Horned Society involved?"

Mordenkainen shook his head again, leaned on the wall, and gazed toward the distant waves below. "I can't help you," he answered quietly.

That took Garett aback. He stared at the old wizard, whose shoulders seemed to stoop suddenly under the fluttering black robe. "What do you mean you can't help? You must have brought me here for some reason!"

"I did not bring you here," Mordenkainen answered stubbornly. He straightened abruptly and thrust a finger, pointing far down the coastline. "I brought you *there*. You made your own way *here*."

Garett couldn't believe what he was hearing. "What?"

The old wizard shrugged and turned away from the wall. "A small distinction, I admit," he said, almost plaintively. "But small distinctions can be important in the cosmic scheme of things." Mordenkainen strode toward the low table, picked up Garett's goblet, and handed it to him. As Garett had silently wished, this time it contained wine.

"Stop that!" Garett snapped as he accepted the vessel and caught a whiff of the fruity aroma.

The wizard shrugged again as Garett, nevertheless, prepared to drink. With his mouth prepared for wine, he found water trickling into his throat and sputtered at the unexpected taste. He set the cup aside, rapidly growing tired of games, and paced around the table.

"You say you can't help me, though you've had me under observation for days. You must know what's going on in Greyhawk. Damn, if even half the stories about you are true, you know what's going on all over Oerth." He dropped down suddenly into the stuffed chair and glared at his host. "All right, then. Why *did* you bring me here?"

"I cannot help you in this matter," Mordenkainen answered firmly. "Nor can any member of the Circle of Eight.

I cannot tell you what or who you face. I cannot even tell you what the danger is."

"But there is a danger?" Garett interrupted eagerly. "A danger to Greyhawk itself?"

"I cannot tell you that," Mordenkainen snapped, his features turning stern. "Ask me no questions about your city or your killer. I am enjoined by powers and contracts you do not understand from answering such queries. The members of the Circle do not yet feel it is time to take an active part in the affairs of the world again."

Garett sighed, feeling the heat of anger in his cheeks. So it was politics interfering with his job again. Politics among the directors; politics among the Circle; always politics. He ground his teeth in frustration. "Once more, then, wizard," he said. "Why am I here? I have honest work to do."

"And it is work you do honestly and well," Mordenkainen complimented with an almost paternal patience as he turned to regard Garett. "*That* is why I brought you here. To reward you."

Garett looked suspicious, but he listened and watched as the old wizard paced back and forth.

"There are twelve Great Swords," Mordenkainen explained. The wind swirled about him as he spoke, and the sleeves of his robe rose out like the wings of a bird. "The Pillars of Heaven, they were called in the ancient days. No one knows who forged them or where they came from, but they are blades of tremendous power. That power was used well by many, but also misused, and at a chaotic time in Oerth's history, the decision was made to hide them. For the most part, they are forgotten now." He paused and tapped his temple with a gnarly index finger. "But not by me."

Despite himself, Garett leaned forward with interest.

Mordenkainen motioned him to rise and follow, and together they went to the crystal ball on the velvet-covered table. "One of these twelve swords is but a half-day's ride from Greyhawk." He waved a hand over the crystal. "It lies in the Mist Marsh," he continued, "at the very heart of the swamp."

A thick fog filled the gleaming ball, and through it formed images of water reeds and dripping fronds, of moss-hung trees and lush vines. Then the images turned more sinister. One of the vines stirred and undulated and became a thick, green serpent. A creature with an impossibly long snout and rows of sharp teeth thrust up from under the water and clacked its jaws. Insects buzzed everywhere.

But, next, those images faded. A fog filled the ball again, and when it cleared, a sword floated at its center. At first glance, it was a perfectly plain sword. It bore no special adornment, nothing to distinguish its legendary craftsmanship.

"Now look again," Mordenkainen said. He brushed Garett's eyelids with the tips of two fingers and stepped back as the captain bent closer to the crystal.

It was the same sword, Garett knew on some instinctive level, but now the silver blade bore a line of black runes down both its sides, and the tangs on either side of the two-handed grip were fashioned to resemble the necks and heads of fanged tigers. As he watched, the weapon began to glow from point to pommel stone with an emerald radiance so intense that the crystal ball, tabletop, and the chamber itself shimmered with its light.

Mordenkainen leaned close to Garett's ear as he, too, peered into the crystal ball. "This sword is called 'Guardian,' " the wizard whispered with a note of awe in his deep voice. "According to the oldest legends of Oerth, it was the seventh sword of the twelve to be forged." He put an arm around Garett's shoulders as they regarded the blade side by side. "Know you, Garett Starlen, that its razor edges can sever any magic spell, no matter how powerful, no matter who the caster. And if you have been uncomfortable with my observing you, know also that while you carry Guardian, you cannot be seen by magic."

Garett straightened, but the image of the sword continued to hold his attention. "You're giving this to me?" he asked.

"I cannot give it to you," Mordenkainen answered sternly. "That would be help, and I am forbidden to help. If you want it, you will have to go get it yourself. I have merely told you where to find it." Then his voice softened a bit, and his gaze took on a kindly glint. "But you are sensitive, Garett Starlen, though you don't realize it. That is why you felt me observing you from afar. That is why you feel the force that threatens your city. If you have the courage to go and claim it, you and this sword will serve each other well."

"I've never been to the Mist Marsh," Garett said quietly, rubbing his chin. Already he was making a list of the things he would need for the journey. He turned to ask a question of Mordenkainen, but the wizard was beside him no more. Garett looked around and spied his host by the wall facing the sea. As he moved to join the old man, Mordenkainen climbed up on the wall, spread his arms, and issued a sharp whistle.

"Stay back," Mordenkainen warned as Garett came to the wall. "I've done all I can. You must help yourself now, and help Greyhawk."

A dark, solitary cloud hanging in the sky far down the coastline suddenly changed shape, elongated, and sprouted wings, a long, sweeping tail, and a sinewy neck. It turned toward the tower as Mordenkainen whistled again.

"A cloud dragon!" Garett muttered in disbelief. Such creatures were almost never seen by the eyes of men, preferring as they did, to spend their time in their favorite disguise. A herd of them might fill the sky on a warm summer day, and humans would never know it. But now Garett had seen one. It turned its head only briefly and regarded the watch commander with a disinterested, faceted gaze as Mordenkainen stepped from the top of the tower and settled himself comfortably upon the beast's neck.

"Good luck to you, Garett Starlen," Mordenkainen

called. Then he touched the cloud dragon's neck. It turned and swept off across the sea, cut a wide arc across the star-dazzled sky, and flew down the coastline.

One by one, the braziers burned out until the emerald glow from Guardian's image in the crystal ball was the only light. Even that began to fade, and Garett found himself standing in darkness. He looked around nervously, thinking of the wooden steps he had to take to leave the tower, wishing for a torch, a lantern, anything.

One by one, Oerth's two moons faded, and, impossibly, one by one, the stars did as well, until the darkness was complete and utter.

Garett turned around and around, confused, uncertain where to go.

THIRTEEN

Garett woke with a start, sweating and disoriented, back in his apartment. He sat up in his bed, the sheet slithering down about his waist. A cooling breeze blew across his chest through the open shutters. His heart still hammered against his ribs, and his breaths were short and rapid.

"That must have been some dream."

Garett turned toward the voice. Sorvesh Kharn, well-dressed in leather trousers and a black lace-up tunic of fine linen weave, sat in a chair by the door, his booted feet propped up on one of Garett's trunks. The master of thieves had a small, jeweled dagger out, and he cleaned his nails idly by the light of a candle, which he must have lit. The light glistened in his oiled beard and in his hair, which was blacker than night itself and pulled back in a braid so tight that Garett thought it had to hurt his face.

"How did you get in here?" Garett muttered angrily, wrapping the sheet about his waist as he rose from the bed. He glanced toward the place by his pillow where he usually kept his sword. It wasn't there. Then, remembering, he glanced toward his table, where he'd left it.

Sorvesh Kharn put on a smirk as he continued to clean and pare his nails. "Oh, come now, Captain. Let's not begin with insults."

Garett admitted to himself it was a stupid question. Sorvesh Kharn hadn't risen to the leadership of his guild by letting little things like locks stand in his way. The point of that small dagger had probably fitted quite easily into the keyhole on his apartment door. It would have been no obstacle at all to Kharn. And the fact that he had done it so silently and made himself at home while Garett slept was further testament to his skills.

"How long have you been here?" Garett asked suspiciously as he went to his table and took up the white robe he had placed there after his bath. He unwound the sheet from his waist, tossed it back on the bed, and slipped into the robe, using its folds to mask his movements as he surreptitiously loosened his sword in its sheath. Just in case.

Then his hand brushed against his coin purse. Its strings were pulled tight. Frowning, he opened it and poured the contents into his palm. All his money was there. So were the five amethyst crystals. He glanced around the room. Nothing was disturbed.

Sorvesh Kharn rose to his feet. "Really, Captain," he scolded. "I haven't rifled a mere purse in years."

"I wasn't thinking of that," Garett answered distractedly as he returned the crystals and coins to his purse. He slowly turned and surveyed the room. Everything was as it should have been. He went to his window and leaned out. Sounds of celebration could be heard in the distance, from the direction of the Strip. The weak sun, a pale white ball that barely penetrated the heavy cloud cover, hung just above the western rooftops. But it had been deep night at Mordenkainen's tower.

"It was a dream, then," he muttered to himself. He ran a hand through his hair and scratched the back of his head.

He turned back to Sorvesh Kharn. "How long did you say you've been here?"

The master of thieves shrugged as he put away the dagger, slamming it into a small sheath on his wrist and tugging the sleeve down to conceal it. "Perhaps half an hour," he answered. "I thought it best to let you sleep."

Garett tried to put the dream from his mind. He scrutinized Sorvesh Kharn with a frown. If the man had one dagger up his sleeve, how many other weapons was he carrying? There was the large knife on his belt; that one was obvious. At least one more, probably two, in those high boots. Kharn was a large man, especially for a thief, but his speed and reflexes were legendary through Greyhawk, as were his rages and temper tantrums.

"You seem in a much better mood than the last time we met," Garett observed cynically as he folded his arms upon his chest and leaned back casually against his table.

Sorvesh Kharn waved a hand nonchalantly. "Directorate meetings," he answered disdainfully. "They can tax one's patience, can't they?" He put on a weak smile and added with an apologetic air, "I was overwrought." The smile vanished just as quickly as it had formed, and Kharn's gaze took on a harder edge. "But only because of the incompetence demonstrated by Thigpen and his lapdog supporters. I noticed that you, Captain, seemed as irritated with them as I."

Garett closed his eyes briefly and hung his head. He was in no mood for this, but he knew he had to move carefully. Kharn was an ambitious man, and such were always dangerous. There could only be one reason why he had come to Moonshadow Lane. Somehow, he had decided that Garett fit into his ambitions. The watch captain saw it in his eyes, recognized it in the buddy-buddy tone of his voice.

"I'm only the night watch captain," Garett answered cautiously. "I have a job to do."

Sorvesh Kharn nodded. "And they are impeding your progress," the master of thieves agreed sympathetically with just the right amount of anger added for effect. "Do you realize that just this afternoon, Rankin Fasterace insisted on a rent of one common per head per day for those who were burned out of their homes in the Halls and are living in the college dormitories and gymnasiums?"

Garett's frown deepened. "I didn't even know there was a Directorate meeting today."

Sorvesh Kharn sat back down in the chair and propped his feet up on the trunk again. "It was a mere formality, a party, actually, to welcome Kentellen Mar. But to everyone's annoyance, Kentellen didn't show up. And things—" Sorvesh looked thoughtful, then shrugged. "—shall we say, *degenerated* into business."

"Excuse me," Garett interrupted. "What do you mean Kentellen didn't show up? He didn't enter the city?"

Sorvesh Kharn rocked the chair back on its rear legs and rolled his eyes toward the ceiling. "Entered the city—now there's an interesting expression. Occupied it, some would say. Rode right up the Processional with his entire caravan, about fifty followers and some little orphan boy at his side. He made quite a show of it, too. You'd have thought Greyhawk had crowned him king."

Garett ignored Sorvesh's sarcasm. Kentellen Mar was finally home. The streets would be chaotic tonight with revelers and party-goers. For the next five nights, until the investiture on the day of the summer solstice, the streets would be full of celebrants.

Sorvesh Kharn folded his arms over his chest and gazed out the window, where the sun was slowly going down. "Personally," he grumbled. "I find it appalling that so much attention is being paid to Kentellen Mar and so little to all these murders."

"And that would be different if you were mayor," Garett said bluntly.

Sorvesh Kharn gave him a sharp look, realizing he'd been seen through. He set the chair down on all four legs and rose stiffly. "I see you are no fool, Captain Starlen," he said coldly. "Forgive me for mistaking you for one. Yes, things would be different. The best mayors this city has ever had have all come from the Thieves' Guild." He jabbed the air with a finger. "I tell you this. I would not be charging rent for floor space in public buildings to homeless, burned-out families. Apparently, it takes a *professional* thief to know the stupidity of robbing a poor man who has nothing."

Garett was surprised by Kharn's sensitivity to that particular issue, and he could not deny that he shared Kharn's contempt for the idea. But he didn't trust the master of thieves, and he wondered if it was honest outrage or just a plank in a new campaign platform. It would make a powerful issue with which to attack Ellon Thigpen if Kharn took the matter before the masses.

"Tell me," Garett said, abruptly changing the subject. "You have eyes and ears all over this city, especially in Old Town. What do you know about these murders?"

Sorvesh Kharn gritted his teeth, and his right hand curled into a fist. "If I knew any more than you, Captain, I would tell it." His eyes flashed angrily as he turned toward the light of the candle. The room was growing darker as the weak sun vanished and night closed in. "I am feeling a certain—pressure, shall we say—from Old Towners. They look to me and to the guild to take care of them."

Sorvesh Kharn swallowed and relaxed a bit as he stroked his beard with the fingers of one hand. "But perhaps I can help you with another matter." He gave Garett a long look from the corner of his eyes. "Two of my men tried to break into the wizards' guildhall last night."

Garett leaned forward with interest, reading the tension in Kharn's body. No one, in his knowledge, had attempted such a thing. It was impossible to successfully break into the guildhall of the wizards. The magical wards and protections were too many and too powerful.

"They have not been seen or heard from since," Kharn added pointedly.

"Prestelan would have turned them over to the City

Watch," Garett explained. Kharn knew that as well as he did, though.

The master of thieves leaned against the door and tilted his head. "As you said, I have eyes and ears everywhere. The thieves were not turned over to the watch. They went over that black wall and—" He made a little gesture in the air, pinching his fingers together and opening them suddenly. "*Poof*. Vanished. You should know that I sent them myself. No one has gone into or come out of the guildhall for several days. There isn't a wizard in the streets. Not even their dwarvish porters answer the gates if anyone knocks. Prestelan Sun himself has not been seen."

"So you decided to take the opportunity to see what you could pilfer," Garett concluded sarcastically.

Sorvesh glared disdainfully, his dark features looking almost demonic in the ruddy candle glow. "I asked forgiveness for treating you like a fool earlier, Captain," he said coolly. "Don't mistake me for one." His words hung momentarily in the air like a threat before he continued. "I sent them in *expecting* them to be caught and turned over to the watch. I would have bribed their way out of any jail time, believe me. But I thought there was a chance they would see something or someone that would provide a clue as to what was going on there." He paused then moved away from the candle, into the shadows. "You're a competent man, Starlen. It can't have escaped your attention that our best seers are dead, our wizards are vanished, and the nonhuman races have skipped town faster than mice at a cat convention. There has to be a connection."

Garett regarded Sorvesh Kharn with the first glimmerings of new respect. The man was shrewd as well as observant. "Have any of the other directors figured that out yet?" he asked.

Sorvesh Kharn smiled. "Why, Captain, is that a sneer I hear in your voice?"

Garett kept his face impassive and gave no answer. He wasn't ready to play Kharn's game yet. He would say nothing overt against the directors.

Kharn gave an amused shrug. "Axen Kilgaren is an intelligent man," he said meaningfully. "As for the others, they can't see their feet for Kentellen Mar's backside."

Garett drew a slow breath, his mind working furiously, wondering how much he could trust Sorvesh Kharn. And yet he seemed to have a genuine interest in solving this rash of murders, even if it was only to gain a political edge. Garett wondered if he could turn that to his own advantage.

"Are you willing to work with me on this?" he found himself tentatively asking the master of thieves.

Sorvesh Kharn didn't nod or say anything, but he regarded Garett intently.

"With all these celebrations," Garett continued, low voiced, "my men are going to be overextended the next few nights. Something is happening in the sewers under Greyhawk, something connected with all these murders. Something that I think involves the Horned Society."

"Yes, yes," Kharn said impatiently, frowning. "You made that pitch at yesterday's meeting."

"And you were less than attentive," Garett reminded him sharply. "But now you have your own evidence that something odd is happening at the wizards' guildhall. How much more farfetched is this?"

Kharn looked askance and shrugged. "What are you suggesting?" he asked.

"You have men at your command, men with skill at stealth and concealment."

Kharn gave him a doubtful look. "You want me to send them into the sewers?"

Garett shook his head. "I want you to plant them at every sewer grate and opening in the city. And I want them out of sight. Tell them to watch and listen only. These Old Town murders—these *sacrifices*—have all taken place in the sewers. I want to know who goes down there and who comes up, and I want to know where they go afterward." Garett stood up and regarded Sorvesh Kharn evenly. "Will you do that?"

Kharn thought about it, then nodded. "That much I'll do." He glanced away and stared at the candle flame. Its orange glow lit his face, shadowing the deep sockets of his eyes, creating a masking effect. "But what will you do for me, Captain?"

Garett didn't hesitate with his answer. "I'll make sure you get proper credit when we catch the murderer. I'm sure you'll find a way to turn that to your advantage."

Sorvesh Kharn smiled. "You know, of course, that when I'm mayor I'll need a new captain-general?"

Garett didn't get a chance to decline. Before he could express his distaste for the idea, a knock sounded on his door. Sorvesh Kharn turned suddenly, jerked it open, caught Almi by her old wrist, and pulled her close. In the same smooth motion, he planted a big kiss squarely on her lips. "It's all right, madam," he said when he released her. "As you can see, Captain Garett is awake." He stepped back with a gallant bow so Almi could see her tenant.

A bright smile of surprise lit up the old woman's face. "Who cares?" she answered. "If you need a room, sir, I'm sure I can arrange to throw him out. He's quite a bother to an old woman like me, you know."

"I'm sure, madam," Kharn answered sympathetically. "But I'm quite well entrenched in other quarters."

"Well, I guess I'd better bring him some supper then and send him on his way," Almi replied with melodramatic disappointment. "Bread and gravy, again, Captain?" she called to Garett.

"Thank you," Garett said, and Almi, smart enough to realize she'd interrupted, made a polite exit.

"I will be in touch, Captain Starlen," Sorvesh Kharn said. Then he, too, slipped out the door, closing it without a sound.

Alone, Garett gave a small sigh and tried to collect his thoughts. Had he made a mistake, involving Sorvesh Kharn in this? He was sure Korbian Arthuran would have a fit if he found out. Neither would Ellon Thigpen be pleased.

He leaned back on the table again, and his hand brushed his coin purse. He'd almost forgotten it, but now the dream came rushing back upon him. He poured the amethysts out onto his palm again. They glittered in the candlelight, casting little pools of purple reflection on his skin. Just a dream, he told himself. Mordenkainen, the tower, the cloud dragon, all of it. The sword. Just a dream.

He put the crystals back in the purse and picked up the candle and used it to light the lamp that hung overhead. The room brightened considerably, and he began to dress.

* * * * *

The clouds had not broken by nightfall. No stars shone in the sky. Both of Oerth's moons were obscured. None of the revelers seemed to care. They danced in the streets, drank in the alleys. Like moths attracted by the streetlights, they filled the Processional from one end of Greyhawk to the other.

It took Garett twice as long as usual to reach the High Market Square. The square had been cleared of people, but refuse lay scattered everywhere. Relatively speaking, it was almost quiet in the marketplace. The platform where the day's speeches had been made stood like a lonely ghost in the empty center. Garett turned away from it and headed for the barracks infirmary in the Grand Citadel.

Six sentries stood guard duty at the Citadel's gate, preventing anyone who was not on official business from entering. The guards saluted when they saw him approaching and opened the doors just wide enough for him to enter.

He found Burge awake and chatting with an off-duty watchman in the infirmary. As Garett walked through the door, Burge saw him and quickly shoved a metal wine flask out of sight. The covers slid down a bit as he did so. The white bandages around his chest showed just over the top of his sheets. "How are you feeling?" the captain inquired of his friend.

Burge put on a grin, lifted his arms, and clapped his hands together over his head. The movement put an obvious strain on his chest muscles, but Burge didn't flinch. "Fine, Cap'n," he answered jovially. "Come on in an' sit."

"Can't," Garett answered. "Just going on duty. But I wanted to see how you were first."

"Fine, Cap'n," Burge assured him, repeating himself. His grin turned into a full-fledged smile as he nodded his head. "Just great. Don't worry about me."

Garett put on a grin himself as he turned to leave, but he hesitated just long enough to watch from the corner of his eyes as Burge pulled out the wine flask, took a quick sip, and passed it to his partner.

Why did Burge hate his elven blood so much? Garett wondered as he left his friend. A human could almost envy such a heritage. Better sight, better hearing, and a much faster rate of healing. All those things came to him through his nonhuman father. Garett couldn't remember the last time he had worked a case or walked a patrol without Burge by his side, but in all those nights, all those conversations, Burge had never so much as mentioned his father's name. Did he even know it?

Blossom and Rudi were waiting for Garett in his office. One of them had lit his lamps, but left it to him to perform his ritual replenishing of their oil reservoirs. "We've doubled patrols in all quarters," Blossom told him as he went about the task. "So far, we've recorded one hundred seventy-two arrests, mostly on drunk and disorderly or fighting charges. I've ordered update reports from all the watch houses every two hours." She leaned back against the door and swung her blond braid over one shoulder.

"Good," Garett answered as he refilled the last lamp. "But we're going to visit the watch houses ourselves. An unannounced inspection, if you will. I want to see, personally, that everyone's on their toes. That goes for the patrols in the streets as well. I don't want to find any watchmen *celebrating* on duty."

"Where do we start?" Rudi asked, sitting casually in his usual chair beside the door. Sometimes, Garett thought he should have the little sergeant's name engraved on it.

"In the Garden Quarter," Garett answered. "It's closest. Then the High Quarter watch house. After that, we'll work our way southward."

"By the way," Blossom said, without moving from her place by the door, "you should know that not everyone out there is celebrating. There was a near riot this afternoon at Greyhawk University when word began to spread that Rankin Fasterace had some boneheaded rent plan to present before the Directorate."

Garett made a face. Sorvesh Kharn would be delighted by that news, he thought. In fact, now that he considered it, he wondered if it was Sorvesh's thieves who had spread such word. "Any arrests?" he asked.

Blossom shook her head. "In a rare fit of good sense, Korbian Arthuran realized those who were most upset were people who had lost their homes in the fire. He said they'd suffered enough, and once things were calmed down again, he ordered the release, without charge, of anyone we'd picked up."

Garett made another face. That didn't sound like Korbian at all. It did sound like Ellon Thigpen attempting to win the gratitude of his people by demonstrating leniency and understanding toward the rioters.

"Korbian wasn't all sunshine and flowers about it, though," Rudi added, wearing a malicious smirk. "Because of the trouble, His Benevolence missed a party hosted by the Directorate for Kentellen Mar this afternoon."

"Well, Kentellen didn't show up, either," Garett told them offhandedly as he headed to the door and beckoned for them to follow. "Maybe he needed a rest after his long vacation."

"Maybe someone warned him about the directors' boring parties," Blossom muttered.

They moved out of the Citadel, across the square, and into the streets. Together, clad in their bright scarlet cloaks, they made quite an eye-catching trio. Rudi, on Garett's right, was as short as Blossom, on his left, was tall. No doubt they were an odd sight as they walked along, and even the most drunken celebrants made way for them.

The Garden Quarter boasted a higher class of restaurants and taverns than the River Quarter, but, like the River Quarter, all the establishments were overflowing. So, too, were the gambling houses, where the spin of the wheels and the clatter of dice could sometimes be heard between shouts of triumph or despair.

Minstrels and mimes and storytellers worked every corner, and the Beggars' Union was out in force, milking the crowd with their canes and crutches and eye-patches and tales of woe. A good tale of woe from a clever beggar could, after all, be just as entertaining as any minstrel's whiny song. Why not pay a common for it? Tonight, at least, it was all part of the festivities.

A pair of watchmen came up Amaryllis Street. Garett, Blossom, and Rudi waited at the corner of Amaryllis and Rose Avenue as they approached. The two guards dragged a sour-faced man between them. Their prisoner was well dressed. His trousers were blue velvet tucked into expensive leather boots, and his shirt was of gold damask with silver buttons down the front. He clutched a rumpled velvet cap in one fist. The gray plume that extruded from it was bent at an improper angle.

"Evening to you both, Strevit and Deeve," Garett said, greeting the watchmen by name as they reached the intersection. He eyed their captive carefully. There was a familiar look about him. Garett couldn't recall the little man's name, but remembered that he owned a shop over on Ladanum Road, from which he sold fine dishes, table cutlery, and imported pottery. "What have we here?"

"Wedger, a merchant," Strevit answered, frowning down

at his prisoner. As Strevit turned to look at Wedger, the streetlight showed the red mark of a fist on the watchman's cheekbone. "Charged with drunkenness and starting a fight at the Silver Ferret."

"And with striking an officer of the watch," Deeve added, grinning at his partner.

Strevit's frown only deepened. "Little fool caught me off guard," he said defensively. "He's half my size. Who'd have thought he'd try it?"

Wedger looked up sullenly. "They cheated me!" he cried. "Their wheels are crooked!" Then he lapsed into silence again.

"That's wine for you," Blossom answered Strevit with a shrug. "The smaller they are, the more they drink. The more they drink, the bigger they think they are."

"Didn't anyone ever tell you a woman's place was in the kitchen?" Rudi replied, taking personal slight at her remark. "But, then, I guess they don't make kitchens big enough for you, do they?"

"Take him to the watch house," Garett instructed, interrupting Blossom and Rudi before their constant needling could go any farther. "We're headed there ourselves."

They resumed their walk up Rose Avenue, headed for Wharf Street, the only road in the Garden Quarter that wasn't named after a flower or an herb, shrub, or tree. The watch house was located near the Cargo Gate in the heart of the busiest part of the Garden Quarter.

"What's that?" Blossom asked, stopping abruptly to stare northeastward.

Garett had caught it, too, just out of the corner of his eye. "A lightning flash," he answered. "Look at those clouds. We'll have rain again tonight."

Another bolt lit up the sky even as they watched.

"Never seen a lightning bolt shoot upward like that," Strevit muttered doubtfully as he scratched his stubbled chin with his free hand. Even Wedger the merchant looked up to see.

"I don't mean to be an alarmist," Rudi commented in a low voice as a third bolt raked the night. "But notice where it seems to be coming from?"

"Iuz!" Garett cried, employing the chaotic god's name in a rare curse as he started running with Rudi and Blossom at his heels. "The wizards' guildhall!"

"Get out of here, and don't let me see your ugly face again!" Strevit shouted as he pushed Wedger away. Then he and Deeve went running, too, leaving the drunken merchant in the dirt to wonder at his good luck.

A huge throng had gathered, attracted by the display, their numbers choking Wizards' Row, the wide street that led to the front gate of the wizards' keep. Every time a rippling bolt shot upward, the crowd gasped with pleasure and appreciation, clapped their hands, and called for more.

"It's a fireworks show!" Blossom shouted in Garett's ear, trying to make herself heard over the noise. "Just part of the celebration!"

Garett shook his head vigorously. "When did you ever hear of a mage wasting his power on such ostentation?"

The crowd watched, wide-eyed with expectation, a sea of faces all turned upward. Then a collective sigh rose as a searing bolt of red crackled upward. Try as he might, Garett could force his way no closer to the guildhall. Worse, the masses were packing in behind him, too. Soon he would be trapped in the crowd.

Suddenly, a bolt shot *downward*, a blue-white tongue of energy that struck the highest tower of the guildhall and hurled a shower of glowing fragments into the air. The sound of the blast was barely audible over the excited gasps and cries and hand-clapping from the crowd.

"Think it's still a part of the celebration, leaf-brain?" Rudi asked with a smirk to Blossom.

"What the hell is going on up there?" Deeve exclaimed, grabbing Garett's sleeve as he leaned closer. "An explosion like that—people could get hurt!"

But Garett's attention was riveted on the top of the

tower, where a tall, slender figure in flowing white robes was climbing on top of the broken battlements. He glowed with a beatific, sourceless light, and the wind whipped his garments as he drew himself erect and stretched his hands toward the sky.

Garett had no doubt that it was Prestelan Sun himself.

Scarlet lightning flowed from the mage's right hand, and immediately a second bolt followed from his left. For an instant, the sky lit up as bright as day as the two intersected and exploded. In that same instant, a different bolt lanced downward, straight for the lone figure on the top of the tower, but something stopped it. In the explosion, Garett thought he saw a faint green flickering of an arc, seemingly just a piece of light, that shielded Prestelan Sun.

The wind wailed in response. Prestelan Sun's robes became an enemy as he stood upon the tower, and with a shrug he cast them off. The wind seized the garments, and they blew away like white, spastic birds, tossed on the currents.

The image was not lost on Garett. "Listen!" he said sharply to his comrades. "Do you hear them?"

"What?" Blossom said.

"Hear what?" Strevit echoed.

The crowd had quieted somewhat, waiting in anticipation of the next display.

"The birds!" Garett answered, staring overhead. "Listen to them!"

They flew overhead, circling, tiny shadows against the clouds and the darkness. Thousands of crows and other birds, all screeching and calling.

"So what?" Deeve shouted. "The show's up there!"

Another bolt of energy raced up from Prestelan Sun's hands, and again the arcing emerald barrier erupted, protecting him from an answering bolt. The clouds reflected the lightning, and the sky turned a dazzling color as another furious tongue licked upward.

Garett stared hard through the bright glow. The tension

roared in his head and his heart hammered as his gaze swept the sky above Prestelan Sun and he waited for the next answering bolt. He intended to see the wizard's foe this time, even if he had to burn out his eyes to do it!

A bolt of purest blue speared downward. Prestelan Sun did not hesitate this time, but thrust out his arms and spread his fingers, hurling a flurry of lightning bolts against the clouds, and once again the world flashed an eye-aching white. But Garett did not flinch or shield his vision this time, but forced his eyes to remain wide, though the light stabbed his brain. When he cried out, though, it was not from pain.

A huge black bird, ravenlike in form but fantastically large, soared on the air high above Prestelan Sun. Its wingspan was as wide as any cargo ship in the river, and the plumage on its breast glistened with the reflection of the fire its talons hurled. Even as Garett watched, an upward-thrusting bolt singed its left wing, and the feathers smoked. But the beast gyred away. Then, folding its wings in close to its body, it plummeted again, one claw extended. The talon flung lightning, smashing its energy uselessly against the wizard's emerald shield as the bird pulled out of its dive and swept away to circle and attack again.

"Can you see it?" Garett shouted, grasping Blossom by the arm and pulling her face close to his. He pointed upward with a finger. "Watch there, when the lightning flashes. You have to catch it in a flash. Don't blink!"

Blossom strained to see, and so did the other watchmen. At the next exchange, Blossom's mouth fell open. "My gods!" she uttered in stunned amazement.

Strevit made a holy warding sign. "In Celestian's name!"

"We're in the stew for sure," Rudi muttered.

Again lightning shot into the sky, and the crowd roared furiously with appreciation, oblivious to the battle being fought. Garett strained to follow the bird, feeling helpless, but once more, he thought, Prestelan Sun had singed the creature. The wizard's green shield ignited and blocked the answering blast.

The giant bird wheeled about to attack, revealed, if one knew where to look, in the reflection in the clouds. It screamed this time as it plummeted toward Prestelan Sun. But this time, its bolt did not fly at the wizard or his shield. It smote the tower itself at the midpoint, exploding stone, filling the air with dust and stone fragments.

The tower trembled, and Prestelan Sun seemed to hesitate. The bird did not wait to turn. As it climbed away, it hurled another blast, again striking the tower. Prestelan Sun teetered and flung out his arms for balance. His answering bolt missed by a wide mark.

The crowd grew tense and quiet as the explosion echoed over their heads. At last, they seemed to sense that this was not a show for their amusement, not a part of the city's celebration. They stirred uneasily, all eyes staring toward the tower.

"If this mob panics," Blossom whispered worriedly in Garett's ear, "it's going to be hell."

Garett didn't answer. He watched as the great bird began what he knew would be its final dive. It had admitted the strength of Prestelan's shield, but found another avenue of attack. He admired its strategy even as the horror of it gripped him. The creature swept downward in a rush. At the apex of its dive, it released its strongest attack yet. The bolt struck the tower with thundering force. Too late, Prestelan Sun fired back. Stone shattered and showered outward. The tower shivered and groaned and collapsed in a great gush of dust and fragments. Prestelan Sun opened his mouth in a soundless cry of despair and was engulfed.

The crowd, too, trembled. For a fearful instant, Garett thought they would turn in panic and flee, lest the destruction overtake them. Hundreds would be crushed or injured in the flight. But it was only an appreciative, stunned silence that followed. Then the crowd erupted in wild applause.

FOURTEEN

"Blossom, with Burge out of commission, you'll be the officer in charge of tomorrow night's watch."

Garett, Blossom, and Rudi stood in the center of the Grand Citadel's courtyard. Except for a pair of off-duty watchmen unable to sleep, who leaned against the outside of the barracks and chatted in low voices, they were alone. They hadn't completed their inspection tour of the watch houses. After events at the wizards' guildhall, Garett had insisted on returning straight to the Citadel.

"Why, Captain?" Blossom answered in surprise. "You planning to go somewhere?"

She had meant it as a frivolous question, but Garett nodded. "Yes," he said. "And if I'm not back by tomorrow night, you'll have to cover for me again."

"Just where do you intend to go?" Rudi asked quietly. "You haven't missed a night walking watch in all the time I've known you. Not so much as a single night off."

"Then I'm entitled, don't you think?" Garett snapped gruffly. But he wasn't really angry with Rudi. He kept thinking of Prestelan Sun's magical shield, the way it had glowed with a pure emerald light when the great bird's lightning struck it. In his dream, the sword, Guardian, had shimmered with that same glow. Mordenkainen had told him where to find it. He was sure now it wasn't a dream. At least not entirely a dream. "The Mist Marsh," he said, relenting. He clapped Rudi on the shoulder in friendly fashion. "I have to go to the Mist Marsh."

"Then I'm going with you," Rudi replied without asking the why or the wherefore. If his captain was going, he was going, too. For him, it was as simple as that.

"Count me in," Blossom said. "If you're looking for something, three pairs of eyes will be better than two. And if you run into trouble, my sword arm's a damn sight better."

"Yes, the sewer rats tremble when they see you coming," Rudi answered with a roll of his eyes.

Garett considered it. Both Rudi and Blossom were able comrades. He might indeed find the sword more quickly with their help. He stared off toward the barracks. "Do you think Burge is well enough to hold the fort?" he asked, turning to Rudi, who had last visited Burge in the infirmary.

Rudi shrugged. "He's bandaged, but you know how fast he heals. Besides, all he'll have to do is sit around your office and coordinate things. No one ever declared that a *captain* had to walk watch. You took that duty on yourself."

Garett ignored Rudi's latter comments as he weighed his decision. "All right, then," he agreed. "Blossom, you go to the stables and leave an order to have three horses ready at dawn. Rudi, you see that supplies are prepared. Pack light, but take what you think we'll need. If everything goes well, though, we should be back tomorrow night."

"And what if things don't go well?" Blossom interrupted.

Garett chewed his lower lip as he thought about how to answer. "Well, if worse comes to worst," he said finally, "none of us will probably ever have to make another report to Korbian."

Blossom slapped her thigh. "See? There's a bright side to everything."

Rudi wasn't laughing. "It might help me decide what to take," he said reasonably, "if I had some idea what we're after."

Garett glanced up at the overcast sky and wondered just how much he should explain to them. Should he tell them they were off to chase a dream? How much would they believe? Maybe on the journey he would tell them everything. It would pass the time. For now, though, he held back.

"A sword," was all he said. "A sword at the heart of a swamp."

"This have anything to do with what we saw tonight?" Rudi persisted.

Garett saw no reason to hold back there, and he nodded. Both Rudi and Blossom had seen the giant bird's attack on the wizards' guildhall. "It might be the only weapon that can stop that creature."

Rudi clearly wanted to know more, not from any reluctance to go, but out of his own curiosity. Blossom, though, folded her arms across her chest and rubbed one hand over the lower part of her face. "Sounds like my idea of a picnic outing," she said.

"It would," came Rudi's sarcastic rejoinder. "Me, I hate swamps. Too many bugs, and they smell."

"I'm sure you're much more at home in the sewers," Blossom returned.

Garett broke them up again. It was his usual role, after all. "Both of you go get a few hours' sleep. Greyhawk can do without you tonight. We'll meet at the stables just before dawn, then leave by way of the Duke's Gate and ride southeast from there."

"You should grab a nap, too, Captain," Rudi cautioned.

"I will," Garett lied.

* * * * *

It shouldn't have surprised Garett when, no more than a few minutes beyond the Duke's Gate, a fourth rider rushed after them. Garett raised a hand, signaling for Blossom and Rudi to halt until the man caught up. Of course it was Burge.

Garett didn't even bother to argue. "Just tell me one thing," he asked, dreading the answer. "Who did you arrange to put in charge, in case we don't get back tonight?"

"Don't worry, Cap'n," Burge answered, which immediately caused Garett to do so. "The entire night watch is in on it now. They're all coverin' for you. If Ellon or Korbian come looking for you, you're taking care of something in the Slum Quarter. If anyone goes looking for you there, something else required your presence in the High Quarter. If anyone—I mean, *anyone*—wants to see you personally, sorry, but you're the busiest man in Greyhawk tonight." He put on a big grin, obviously pleased with himself and his scheme.

"Of course, every watchman expects a night off soon if all goes well," Blossom said wryly.

Burge inclined his head. "Well, of course."

Garett groaned and tugged on his horse's reins. If there was any chance of making it back by nightfall, they had to make tracks. He led the way, with Burge taking a position on his right side, Blossom and Rudi following. They kept close to Greyhawk's eastern wall until they reached the southernmost point of the city.

A broad, flat expanse of land, the Plain of Greyhawk, stretched before them. They turned away from the city and rode east by southeast along an old, deeply rutted wagon trail, passing farmsteads and fields, where a few men and women were already hard at work tending crops and caring for their animals. They paused in their labors to watch suspiciously as Garett's group rode by, but none made any effort to communicate.

The morning sun, no more than a whitish egg nestled in thick gray clouds, floated just above the distant Cairn Hills.

Despite the clouds, the air was already turning warm, and Garett wondered if he would regret the short coat of chain mail and the quilted jerkin he had donned under his tunic.

He glanced at Burge. The half-elf appeared well enough, unhampered by his wounds. Like Blossom and Rudi, he had opted for plain-colored traveling clothes. Under their tunics, though, they also wore mail. Garett alone stood out in his watchman's scarlet, for he had taken the mail coat and jerkin from the barracks' armory, and not gone back to his apartment to rest, instead preparing a stack of nuisance reports to leave piled on Korbian's desk.

The wagon trail soon ended, and Garett's group rode across open countryside. The deep grass grew halfway up to their horses' bellies. Only a few wretched trees dotted the landscape. Although the watchmen could see great distances ahead, they knew the plain was not truly flat. Rather, it was a gentle swell of low, rolling hills that gradually climbed away from the Selintan River.

"I'd forgotten what fresh air smelled like," Burge commented as they climbed to the top of a gentle ridge.

Garett took a deep breath and savored it. He had almost forgotten how sweet air could taste when it was free of city stenches. The breeze that blew on his face bore no hint of cook-fires or forges, of tanners' hides or potters' clay, of gutters or sewers. It carried no whiff of muddy streets or dank, stuffy dwellings, nothing of slop barrels or scraps or human filth, none of the myriad odors generated by the thousands of souls crammed within the confines of Greyhawk's high stone walls.

As the sun neared its zenith, they ate a quick lunch of hard black biscuits and slices of cheese. They didn't stop to rest. Rudi took these meager goodies from a bag of provisions tied to his saddle and passed them around while they continued to ride.

On the horizon, a low gray cloud seemed to hug the ground, thicker and darker than those that filled the sky and overshadowed the sun. Garett steered their course toward that cloud, grimly mindful of the passage of time. Under that dense cloud lay the Mist Marsh.

Again the doubts began to assail him. Staring toward that blanket of mist hanging so low under a steel-colored sky, his meeting with Mordenkainen seemed more dreamlike than ever. What if it had been only a dream? What if there was no sword called Guardian. And if the sword did exist, how realistic was it to ride into a place like Mist Marsh and expect to find it easily?

The breeze carried a new smell, the cool odor of water. The land dipped suddenly, and they rode down a long, grassy incline to the northern bank of the Ery River, whose backwash was partially responsible for the existence of the Mist Marsh. The Ery was neither swift nor terribly deep, and Garett's party crossed it without difficulty. They paused on the opposite bank just long enough to drink from the river's fresh bounty and refill their water skins, then rode up a steep incline and continued on.

The low, dark cloud was much closer now. Gradually, the ground began to slope downward again. To the north and the east, and to the far southeast, the Cairn Hills rose to ominous heights, creating the huge bowl-shaped depression that, with time, had become the Mist Marsh.

Garett and his friends rode in silence now, aware that they were approaching the outer fringes of their destination. Unexpectedly, a covey of pheasants exploded out of the tall grass and flew off into the gray sky. Rudi's horse started to bolt, but the young sergeant shouted a loud curse in the beast's ear and slugged it with his fist along its sleek neck, and it behaved itself.

The earth underfoot turned soft and muddy, and a squishy sound accompanied each rise and fall of a horse's hoof. The grass, too, grew taller and stiffer, reaching a rider at midcalf. Grasshoppers and butterflies hurried frantically out of the horses' way. Overhead, the pale ball that was the sun still managed to hurl a sweltering heat down through the covering of slate-colored clouds.

A pair of hawks gyred majestically in the sky off to their left. Mates, Garett thought, or soon-to-be mates. He watched them until the birds turned inward toward the heart of the marsh and disappeared.

The ground was now covered by water that reached over their horses' fetlocks. A grassy sea spread out all around them.

"Watch out," Blossom warned suddenly, keeping her voice calm as she pointed to an old log nearly hidden in the deep grass. Coiled upon the highest end, where it could best catch the sunlight, a deadly marsh adder, its green scales shimmering, eyed them as they rode by.

Burge passed nearest to the log. His sword flashed out of the sheath and arced downward. The flat, serpentine head went flying, its fanged mouth still wide with the unuttered sound of its angry hiss. A sharp thunk followed instantly as the sword's edge bit into the wood, then a plop as the rest of the serpent fell wriggling into the water.

"I hate snakes," Burge muttered, grimacing in disgust as he put away his blade.

"You'll find plenty here to hate, then," Blossom answered unenthusiastically.

A low drone of uncertain origin grew gradually louder as the watchmen kept a straight course. Garett swatted at an insect on his neck, then swatted again as another took its place. Blossom swatted at her arm. Then Burge did the same. Rudi, too.

Suddenly, a black cloud of gnats rose just above the top of the grass and hovered menacingly in the air, and the droning grew louder than ever. The four watchmen stopped their mounts and stared. Rudi waved away something that buzzed at his face.

"I say we ride around it," Blossom commented dryly.

"That's got my vote," Burge agreed.

A sharp slap was the only sound that Rudi made, then a short, satisfied sigh as he wiped his right palm on his sleeve. They rode south to avoid the swarm, then turned east again toward the heart of the marsh. The pale sun could no longer be seen, and they traveled in a strange twilight. Tendrils of steam and fog rose from the water and wafted over the tall grass. Little eddies of mist moved through the air on breezes too slight to be felt. Garett's garments became damp, saturated with the moisture in the air and the sweat that ran down his body.

Then came sight of the first huge mangaroo trees.

"Thank the gods!" Rudi called. "Dry land!"

Burge barked a short laugh. "Not so, youngin'," he said. "Nothin' so nice as that."

A grove of mangaroo trees had to be one of the most impressive sights on all of Oerth. Tall and stately, their twisted branches interlaced with each other overhead to weave a vast, leafy canopy while their massive root systems shot deep into the soft marsh or shallow water, sending tendrils ever outward and downward to lift the trees, forming a madly entangled forest on stilts.

"Are you sure there's a sword in there, Captain?" Blossom muttered, gazing upward uncertainly at the mighty trees, whose highest tops were obscured in the misty cloud that gave the marsh its name. "And is it worth going after?"

Garett, who had not spoken for some time, drew a breath and gave a short sigh. It was time to tell them of the dream, if it was a dream. Time to tell of Mordenkainen and all that he had said to Garett. He related it as calmly, as matter-of-factly, as he could, beginning with the spinning circle of amethysts and ending with his waking.

For a long moment, during which none of his friends looked him in the eye, no one spoke. Burge was the first. "An' you believe this to be real, Cap'n?" he said, finally meeting Garett's gaze.

Garett pursed his lips and nodded.

"If we wade in there, through all these bugs, and don't find a sword," Blossom said with a sigh, giving Garett a steely look as she fingered the long leather-wrapped braid that draped across her right shoulder, "I'm going to tie your neck in a knot. Captain, sir." She slid down from her horse. A splash sounded as her feet disappeared, and the grass, which reached to her hips, gave a ripple.

"What are you doing?" Rudi cried out with some alarm.

"Get used to it, youngin'," she answered over her shoulder, mocking the sergeant lightly. She unfastened her sword belt, refastened the buckle, and slung it over her shoulder so that the weapon rode between her shoulder blades, where the water couldn't get at it. "We walk from here on in. Horses can't get through that."

Rudi looked horrified and clung to his reins.

"It's all right," Garett interceded, recognizing the genuine fear in Rudi's eyes. The sergeant was still young, as Burge and Blossom insisted on reminding him at every turn. In fact, Garett realized Rudi probably had never been this far beyond the walls of Greyhawk in his life. "You'll be staying here, Rudi. Someone's got to mind the horses. We can't risk them wandering off."

Rudi shot a look of hurt confusion at Garett, realizing with a red blush why he'd been singled out. "But, Captain!"

"No buts, Sergeant," Garett said sternly as he dismounted. The grass came up to his waist, the water almost to his knees. He addressed Rudi over the top of his saddle. "It's not because I doubt your ability or your courage. But if all four of us went in, how would we find the horses at all on our way back, unless we leave someone behind to signal us?"

Rudi hesitated as he thought that over. Plainly, the thought that he had shown fear and that because of it his captain didn't want him along still rankled. "How am I supposed to give a signal that you can hear in there?" he answered with a rough pout. "Sing a song every fifteen minutes?"

"Please, don't," Blossom said wearily, rolling her eyes as she led her horse by its bridle toward the nearest mangaroo root, where she tied its reins. "If you care nothing for us, then consider the wildlife."

"According to the barracks gossip," Rudi snapped back, fed up with her comments, "you *are* the wildlife!"

"You'll give a signal like this," Burge interrupted quickly, breaking off a piece of grass. He place it on the tip of his tongue, then pressed that to the roof of his mouth and gave a surprisingly sharp, long whistle with a strange, characteristic trill provided by the vibration of the bit of grass. "It's easy," he added, breaking off another piece and handing it up to Rudi. "Go on, try it."

Rudi mastered the technique after a few tries.

"An' when your bit of grass wears thin, just pinch off another," Burge continued encouragingly. "Blow it every few minutes, an', sooner or later, I'll hear it."

Garett tied his horse beside Blossom's, took Burge's reins from the half-elf, and tied his horse while the lieutenant taught Rudi the grass trick. "You won't need to worry about it for a while, though," he called over his shoulder. "It'll take us some time to get farther in. Don't relax too much. There are plenty of threats to watch out for even out here."

"Yeah," Blossom muttered as she climbed up onto a network formed by the knotted mangaroo roots and levered herself out of the water. "Like lizard men."

Garett saw Rudi start at that and silently cursed Blossom. Sometimes, she took her teasing too damned far. The last remains of that ancient and feared reptilian race had for centuries maintained its last known lair in the Mist Marsh. At one time, the entire swamp had been their preserve, and they had guarded it zealously with sword and shield and javelin. Slowly, though, they had retreated deeper and deeper into the marsh. Most people thought they had died out altogether.

"Nobody's seen lizard men in these parts for years," he said tartly. "Anyway, their lair was much deeper in the southern part of the marsh." He turned back to Rudi. "I meant threats from dangerous animals," he explained.

"Predators. Crocodiles, change-cats, giant rats. The marsh is full of them. You keep an eye out."

Rudi made an unpleasant face, but at last he swung down off his horse and waded the short stretch to the mangaroo roots. He tied his own horse next to the others, then chose the closest thing to a dry spot, high among the roots, climbed up, and settled himself. He unfastened his sword and rested the sheathed blade upon his lap. "All right," he grumbled, glancing nervously at his surroundings, brushing away a huge ant with a quick back-sweeping motion of his hand, "but don't take too long. If it starts getting dark, I'm going to be peeved."

"Build a fire if you want, if you can find dry wood," Garett told his sergeant as he passed two water skins up to Blossom and slung his own across his shoulders. Then he, too, repositioned his sword so that it hung upon his back, where it would stay reasonably dry.

"In this place?" Rudi said doubtfully, looking around.

"He meant it as a joke," Burge explained as he climbed up onto the root network beside Blossom and extended a hand down to his captain.

Blossom had taken a large knife from her belt and busied herself by hacking at three of the lowest, stoutest limbs within her reach. By the time Garett was out of the water and at her side, she had cut three lengths and stripped them of subsidiary branches and leaves to make three slender staves. She gave one each to Burge and Garett and kept one for herself. They were not stout enough for fighting, but that was not their purpose. They were to probe the water, to test the footing before them. Quicksand was just one of the dangers ahead.

Garett looked at each of his comrades in turn. Rudi sat sullenly on top of a knot of roots. Blossom waited, outwardly impassive, but, obviously to Garett, impatient to get on with what she regarded as an unpleasant journey. He turned to Burge. His half-elven friend was almost quiet, not his usual quick-tongued self. In fact, most of the smart remarks today had come from Blossom. "How are the wounds?" he asked Burge.

Burge leaned on his fresh-cut staff and peered toward the gloomy heart of the marsh. The mangaroos grew as far as any of them could see, even Burge with his elven eyesight. And as the mist thickened and the branches and leaves wove together overhead, so did the eerie twilight grow into darkness.

"I feel fine," he assured Garett. Then he glanced at his captain and seemed to sense the true reason behind the question. "I've grown so used to the walls of Greyhawk," he went on in a near whisper, "that I'd forgotten how stiflin' they are." He looked straight at Garett with that intense, violet-eyed gaze. "I'm glad I came."

Garett, too, had traveled the world in his younger days and seen much of the Flanaess, many of its wonders. He, too, knew the thrill of a journey's beginning and the joy of new places. Sometimes, Greyhawk felt like a prison, where his soul had been shut up and all his life there had been only the work time of a sentenced prisoner. In those times, he missed the travels and dreamed of his days along the Azure Sea and the adventures he had known there.

But for everyone, those times came to an end. He did not live long who lived by selling his sword. One king or master after another. Different nations, different lands. Despite all the odd customs and strange cultures, too soon they all blurred together. Eventually one had to find a place to make a bed and a hearth to light a fire each night, and honest work, too, to occupy the hands and the mind.

"I'm glad I came," Burge repeated, half under his breath.

It was enough to snap Garett out of his brief reverie. Burge knew the dangers as well as he. It was too soon to wax romantic about the Mist Marsh.

"Save that kind of remark 'til we're home," Garett warned.

FIFTEEN

Cattail reeds and tall saw grass grew in thick clusters among the mangaroo roots. Brightly colored water lillies floated on the still water. Ivy streamed down, sometimes in slender vines, sometimes in curtains, from the high branches. Narrow beams of light speared through the leafy canopy overhead to create dazzling spots on broad, moisture-pimpled leaves, on the murky water, on the lichen-covered bark of old trees, and on the roots themselves.

An angry feline meow caused Garett, Blossom, and Burge to stop and glance overhead. High among the branches sat a common-looking house cat, its ears laid back, its eyes burning steadily as it watched them. An instant later, though, the air shimmered around it, and the small form became a far larger, more powerful, and far more deadly beast. Dark spots covered its tawny, muscled body. Fangs and claws gleamed. It roared, and the sound echoed through the swamp.

"A change-cat!" Burge whispered, keeping his voice low

and calm so as not to startle the creature.

"I don't think it's going to attack," Garett said, leading them quietly, cautiously forward, though his eyes remained on the change-cat. "It's just warning us away from its territory."

"We better find this sword quick," Blossom grumbled as she waved a small swarm of gnats away from her face. Her gaze constantly raked from side to side as she advanced. "I don't want to be here when night falls."

A fat brown frog sat perched on a root, watching as they approached. Suddenly, it plopped into the water. Another sprang from hiding in a floating cluster of dead leaves, flopped under the surface, and disappeared with an awkward kick. A whole series of rapid plops followed, and for a moment, the marsh was quiet again.

A snake rippled through the water not ten feet ahead of the watchmen, and they paused, motionless, until it disappeared under another cluster of mangaroo roots. Carefully, Garett followed it. They had to climb that root cluster to continue on. Garett made it out of the water and to the top first. He reached down to help Blossom out, and they both helped Burge.

When they all were out of the water, and there was no sign of the snake, Garett glanced up and quickly cringed. Not more than a foot above his head, a large web glistened between two low-hanging limbs. Its hairy occupant, nearly the size of his fist, slept impassively at the center, lulled by the gentle breeze that rocked the web. Garett glared at it from a crouch, his heart hammering.

In a few moments, they were over the root cluster and back in the water again, moving toward the next cluster. The mangaroos were beginning to thin, though. The tallest trunks and the most massive root clusters were farther and farther apart. They still dominated the marsh, but they were less dense. The party mounted a small rise of land, trampling a patch of tiny white flowers that had taken root in the brown mud, and rested.

"Gods!" Blossom cried suddenly, dropping her staff and staring at the back of her right hand in horror. A black leech, as long as one of her fingers, clung to her skin. She snatched at its mottled body and flung it away in disgust. A red welt showed where it had been. Almost immediately, she shrieked again. "There's one on my neck!"

"Don't!" Burge ordered, catching her hand before she could grab at the repulsive creature. "I see it. It's not in too deep, though. Let me." He reached into his belt and extracted his coin purse. Opening it, he extracted another, smaller pouch and opened that. A white powder glittered within. Burge pinched some between his fingers and sprinkled it generously upon the leech's body.

Her head tilted to let him work, Blossom still tried to watch from the corner of her eye. "Is that a magic powder?" she asked nervously.

"It is if you eat at The Tomb very often," Burge answered with a grin as he sprinkled another pinch upon the bloodsucker. "I swear that old orc never salts anything."

Garett searched his own body as Burge removed the slimy parasite from Blossom's neck. He found three of them climbing his left boot and quickly brushed them away, suppressing a chill of revulsion as his skin made contact with them. Together, he and Blossom checked Burge, but the half-elf was clean, relatively speaking.

"I guess they can recognize a case of indigestion when they see it," Blossom commented to Burge. She patted his backside lightly, trying to conceal her earlier display of fear with a veneer of humor.

"My lady, you are welcome to their fullest attention," Burge answered in his most genteel manner as he put away his pouch of salt. "And I suspect we'll find more of their brethren dogging our tracks as we go."

Blossom didn't say anything, but she rubbed a hand tentatively over the welt on her neck, and the look on her face said she wished she'd stayed with Rudi, or better yet, not come at all. "I am not having a good time," she muttered, picking up her staff and starting bravely down into the water again.

Burge leaned close to Garett as they followed. "Do you have any idea where in the marsh this sword might be?" he asked. "Or are we just supposed to wander around looking for it?"

Garett had been asking himself a similar question for some time now. "Mordenkainen said it was at the heart of the swamp. That's all I know." Garett shrugged.

"The elves have a saying, you know," Burge told him conspiratorially. " 'Beware of wizards bearing gifts.' "

"Humans have another," Garett said in a low voice. " 'Beware of elvish sayings.' "

A loud slap interrupted them. Blossom frowned in disgust at the huge dead mosquito on her palm before she wiped it on her tunic.

They pushed on in silence, climbing knots of mangaroo roots, wading water and mud, ducking vines and dangling webs, on constant alert for snakes. Overhead, colorfully feathered birds darted back and forth among the rich foliage, filling the air with their calls and chitterings.

Garett stopped suddenly, motioning for his companions to do the same. A thick patch of cattail reeds grew directly in their path, and among the stalks a pair of large eyes gleamed redly, watching them. A sharp warning hiss from the unseen creature caused the two men to reach for their swords. Blossom brought her staff into both hands and balanced it in a defensive grip. For a tense moment, the standoff continued. Then an immense brown-furred rat swam out of the reeds, waddled up onto a knot of roots, and climbed the trunk of a mangaroo, where it perched on the lowest branch and hissed at them again.

Garett let go a small sigh of relief. He and Blossom started on again, but Burge stood his ground. "Do you hear that?" he asked, when, only a few paces on, they stopped and waited for him.

Garett knew how sharp Burge's hearing was. The half-elf

stood stock-still, listening, an odd, puzzled expression on his face. Garett listened, too. All he heard were the birds and the hissing of the rat and the rustling of the leaves in the breeze. "Hear what?" he asked quietly.

Burge frowned. "I don't know," he answered curiously, tilting his head. "It's gone now." He shrugged his shoulders and waved them on. "Maybe I imagined it. This place is getting to me."

But Garett knew Burge better than that. The half-elf advanced through the clump of cattails, his senses more alert than ever. Every little sound made him stop and listen. The smallest motion, even the trembling of a leaf, caught his gaze. His left hand never strayed far from the dagger on his belt.

When they were through the cattails, another knot of mangaroo roots lay in their path. Garett scanned the water quickly for serpents that might be nesting under the roots, then climbed out first and helped the others up.

"It's back," Burge announced as he wiped sweat and moisture from his face with the back of his sleeve. Crouched on a particularly large root, he stared around, trying to pinpoint the direction of the sound's origin.

Garett stood up straight. He could still see the black water down between his feet through a gap in the roots. The footing was slick. He steadied himself by positioning the tip of his staff carefully and leaning on it. He strained to hear over the familiar sounds of the swamp. Just over the calls of the birds, the drone of gnats and mosquitoes, the croaking of frogs, he thought he heard something.

Thump.

It was faint, just loud enough to catch his attention. It came again. *Thump.* Twice more, then it stopped.

"I heard it, too," Blossom affirmed, pointing with her staff. "Straight ahead."

"An animal noise?" Burge questioned doubtfully.

Garett shook his head. "Not like any animal I've ever heard."

"Lizard men," Blossom whispered tensely.

Garett didn't think so. "If the stories are even partially true, you wouldn't hear them until their kill-wires were around your throat."

They traversed the wide knot and slipped carefully back into the water again. It was shallower here, reaching only to their knees, but the muddy bottom sucked stubbornly at their boots. The shadows were growing darker all around them, and the spears of sunlight that penetrated the leafy canopy came in now at smaller angles.

Thump, thump.

They stopped in their tracks and stared at each other. "That was a lot nearer," Burge muttered nervously. Blossom didn't say anything. Instead she drew her large knife from its sheath and swiftly shaved one end of her staff to a sharp point.

When the sound stopped, they waded forward again. A tangled blanket of green leaves and tiny white flowers floated on the water before them. Bees hummed and buzzed happily around the sweet petals, and the trio, deciding wisely not to disturb the insects, detoured around. The silty bottom began to rise abruptly. Soon they found themselves on a muddy bar where only a few bushes and a pair of mangaroo saplings grew.

Then something moved among the bushes. The branches shook, and the leaves rattled. A fat crocodile, its toothy jaws gaping, eyes gleaming with hunger, charged them. With a shout, Garett leaped back, but his boot stuck in the soft, sucking mud, and he fell awkwardly sideways, his arm sinking halfway to the elbow as he tried to catch himself.

He felt the hot rush of the massive predator's breath on his face. Then, with an angry, desperate cry, Burge drove the steel point of his sword down into the beast's thick neck. The toughness of its hide, though, stopped the thrust before the creature was seriously hurt. Turning toward its attacker, it snapped its jaws savagely. Burge jumped clear, but the monster's clawed feet dug into the mud, and it scrambled with agile swiftness after him. Again Burge moved, but the slimy muck played him false, just as it had Garett, and the half-elf fell backward.

Blossom put herself instantly between her comrade and the crocodile. The huge reptile opened its jaws wide. There was nothing womanly or beautiful about the watchman's face as she drew back with her makeshift spear and slammed the sharpened point down through the beast's exposed lower palate. Startlingly, the beast emitted a sharp, hissing growl of pain, the first sound it had made. Its scratching claws hurled mud into the air, and its tail clubbed wildly back and forth. Blossom gave a savage growl of her own. With all her might, she leaned on the spear, pinning the crocodile.

Then its jaws snapped shut, and wood splintered. But Blossom and Burge were up and out of its way. Hissing, the beast turned, blood spraying from its mouth with every exhalation.

Garett drew himself up out of the mud and charged again. He barely had time to get his sword out of the sheath. He leaped sideways, more respectful of his footing this time. With all his bodily strength, he swung his sword downward, not at the crocodile's armored head, but at a more vulnerable foreleg, catching it just above the clawed foot, chopping completely through it.

Again the monster screamed its pain, and the mud roiled as it thrashed around. Burge rushed forward, his sword raised to strike, but in the thrashing, the crocodile's unpredictable tail clubbed him across the shins, sending him tumbling. He rolled awkwardly in the mud, but found his footing and came up with his blade ready.

The crocodile, though, had had enough. With a massive sweep of its tail, it glided over the slick muck and disappeared into the water. A faint trail of red lingered on the black water, then diluted away.

Blossom came forward with the shattered end of her

staff, bent down, and picked up the creature's severed foot. She eyed it with smug satisfaction before she offered it to Garett. "The claws will make a fine adornment," she told him.

Garett shook his head. "You keep it, then," he told her. "I've never been one for jewelry." He wiped the blade of his sword on his mud-splattered tunic and returned it to the sheath on his back. That done, he bent down by the water and rinsed his hands and face.

Blossom crouched down beside him. With her knife out again, she proceeded to whittle another point on her shortened staff. Her face was streaked with dirt and sweat, and the leather-wrapped braid that hung over her right shoulder was half undone. Wisps of blond hair gleamed about her forehead in a stray sunbeam.

"We go back now, Captain." It was not a question, but a statement.

Garett shook his head as he rose. He lifted his sword belt over his head and set the weapon down, then stripped off his tunic. The short coat of chain mail was too heavy and too hot. He shrugged it off and cast it aside. To hell with the expense of replacing it, he thought. The quilted jerkin underneath also was too hot, but at least its thickness offered some protection from the mosquitoes and flies. He slipped it off long enough to wring a heavy stream of sweat and water from it, then put it back on. His tunic was utterly ruined anyway, so he crumpled and tossed it beside the mail coat.

"You can't mean to go on," Blossom protested, slamming her knife back in its sheath. She glared at him, no matter that he was her captain, and she didn't bother to disguise or temper her anger. "Where there's one croc, there's always more; you know that. Look at us! We're not prepared for this! I mean, you're in mail, for pity's sake, and we don't have a lantern between us! It'll be dark soon. What are we supposed to do then?"

"She's right about that," Burge commented as he, too, stripped down to his jerkin and cast his armor aside.

Blossom fell silent and slunk off to the side to remove her own garments and add her own coat of mail to the pile. She gave a low groan of despair when she found two more leeches on her stomach and called for Burge to remove them with his salt.

Garett crouched down again and drank water from a cupped hand. Indeed, he wasn't prepared properly for this kind of journey. The whole idea had begun with a dream, and he had followed it with a dreamlike certainty of success. In doing so, he had put his friends in danger. Blossom had every right to be mad. He was mad at himself.

"All right, we're going back," he announced, standing up and turning toward his comrades.

But Burge held up a finger to hush him. "I don't think so," the half-elf said in an alert whisper that immediately put Garett on his guard. "Something's up." Beside Burge, Blossom also stood tensely alert, listening.

Garett noticed it at once. The silence. He glanced up at the trees. The birds sat there, on the limbs, in the leaves, but unmoving, nervous.

Thump, thump.

As if reacting to a signal, the birds scattered across the swamp, shut off from the safety of the open sky by the dense canopy of vines and ivy and mangaroo limbs that covered the highest treetops. Like colorful streaks, the birds darted off, vanishing into the deepest shadows and recesses. For an instant, the air was aflutter. Then silence again. Not a croak from the frogs, not even the buzz of an insect.

Thump.

Somewhere close by, a thick branch gave a loud crack. The sharpness of the sound lingered in the air before the echoing crash and splash that told of its fall.

"Oh, damn," Burge muttered under his breath. He drew his sword and gripped the hilt in both hands. "It's big."

There was still nothing to see in the marsh gloom, at least nothing that Garett could see with his human eyes. But the tension crawled on his skin like the power from a lightning flash. He drew his own sword and jerked free one of the throwing stars from the band around his right biceps.

It rose up out of the brackish water on the far side of a clump of mangaroo roots, a gray, amorphous shape that continued to rise until it brushed the branches of the trees. Then it fell, sinking below the water until it emerged again and slithered over the knot of roots. It came toward them, sensing them somehow, staring toward them with glowing green eyes, a great, horrible wormlike thing, or a leech of enormous size, with gill-like appendages on either side of its gaping maw.

Thump. The immense gills expanded, like thin, membranous wings that glistened translucently as the late sunbeams touched them. *Thump.* They flattened again, folding against the monster's smooth body as it fell upon the shallow water and glided swiftly toward the mud bar.

Blossom threw her handmade spear at the creature and ran, slipping in the mud and falling with a loud splash, full-length into the water at the bar's edge. She scrambled up and shouted for them to run. Garett waited just long enough to watch the spear dangle in the soft flesh and fall out. Then he slapped Burge on the shoulder, and they followed Blossom as fast as they could.

Plainly, though, that wasn't fast enough. Garett glanced over his shoulder. The worm slid easily over the water, rising above it occasionally with an almost graceful contraction, as if to keep them in clear view, while the silt sucked at their every step and they splashed noisily, crashing through cattails, almost becoming tangled in the net of white flowers they had detoured around earlier.

The worm suddenly towered over them. When it crashed down, its bulk sent a shock wave through the water and the land that nearly toppled them.

"Up there!" Garett cried, pointing to the nearest knot of mangaroo roots. While the others scrambled up, he turned and hurled this throwing star with all his strength. The silver missile bit deeply into the worm's flesh, to no discernible effect at all. Garett hurried up to join his comrades.

The great maw thrust up from the water at them suddenly, and, for an instant, Garett saw into a blackness beyond description. Reflexively, he swung his sword, drawing a deep incision through the gelid, bloodless lips of that horrible mouth. At the same moment, he flung himself against his friends, hurling them all backward off the knot of roots and into the water.

They ran furiously, fearfully, half-swimming through the swamp water, unmindful of any threat from snakes or crocodiles or quicksand. Upon another knot of roots, Burge planted his staff, taking no more than a single thrust to push it deep and set it. The worm crashed down upon it, impaling itself, and thrashed itself free an instant later.

"I wish I had a bow!" the half-elf shouted as he splashed through a patch of tall saw grass.

"You could sink a hundred arrows into that thing," Blossom answered breathlessly, right behind him, "and it wouldn't matter!"

Garett stared back desperately over his shoulder. The saw grass hid them somewhat, and the creature stopped momentarily, raising its great head high to seek them. The eyes! he thought. Green and glowing, glowing like Mordenkainen's sword! "The eyes!" he shouted aloud with sudden certainty. "That's where it's vulnerable!"

"How do you know?" Burge demanded. They were out of the saw grass and heading for another knot of mangaroo roots. A serpent glided over the water between them and the knot, and Blossom used her hand to launch a wall of water at it, sufficient to drive it away.

"I know, that's all!" Garett shouted back.

They scrambled up onto the knot of roots. The worm spotted them instantly and came charging across the saw grass. "Well, the knowledge doesn't do us much good," Burge answered as they scurried precariously across the knot and leaped into the water at a run again. "Anyone's a meal for sure who gets close enough to stick a sword in that thing's eyes!"

"Maybe we don't need to get close!" Blossom cried.

But before she could say more, she gave a sudden yelp and plunged under the surface. Burge did the same. Both rose almost instantly, spitting water and coughing. Burge went under a second time and came back up with a curse on his lips. Garett, trailing just slightly behind so he could keep an eye on the worm, realized they'd found a deep trench. It wasn't more than a few yards, but it was enough to tell him they were lost. They'd encountered nothing like it on the way in. That was the least of his worries, though, he thought, as he planted his feet on the bottom again and glanced back at the worm. The beast was gaining on them again.

Blossom coughed. Apparently, she'd swallowed some water in her unexpected dunking. Still, she beat Burge to the shallow side of the trench. "Find me a rock!" she shouted at Garett as she bent and groped along the bottom. "A stone—anything!" she insisted. Straightening, she held out her fist and opened it. Nothing but silt and mud streamed between her fingers.

The worm was too close. They ran again, the water reaching to their thighs, impeding them. A wide copse of mangaroos loomed on their right, and Garett steered them toward it. Suddenly, the sky was aflutter with hundreds of panicked birds. The worm rose up with astounding speed, opened its maw, and snared four or five of the most unfortunate fowls from midair. It paused only a moment to swallow and to survey the sky, which was now empty, for more birds. Then Garett felt those unnatural eyes turn his way again, and the chase was on.

As soon as they scrambled out of the water and up onto the first clump of roots, Blossom began to struggle with the leather thong that bound her braid. "Help me!" she demanded of Burge. "The knot's gotten wet. Untie it!"

Burge had the thong's small knot untied in no time, and

Blossom yanked it from her hair. It was not just a thong, Garett saw, but a sling. Swiftly her fingers worked, making two loops in either end of the slender pouch. "Find me a stone!" she demanded as they ran deeper into the copse, tripping and stumbling on the mad tangle of interwoven roots that formed the ground under them.

"Can you hit anything with that?" Garett shouted as he glanced back in time to see the worm dive and vanish under the water. It had found the trench, too. It would be at the copse in only moments, but here he hoped the thicker limbs and branches and the closeness of the mighty mangaroo trunks might further slow it down.

"I can castrate a rooster at a hundred paces," Blossom boasted, her sarcasm not diminished by desperation or danger. "But not without a rock!"

Garett caught her arm and jerked her to a stop. "Can you do it here? Right here?"

Blossom looked at him, then gazed around, realizing at once why he'd led them into the copse. "Yeah," she answered, "all this should slow it down enough to make it a sure bet."

Burge stepped up. His breath came in long, ragged gasps. At the top of the bandage around his chest, a trace of red showed through the dirt and the sweat stains. All his exertion had opened his wounds. "I don't mean to be a pessimist," he said, "but this is a swamp. You'll be damn lucky to find a rock you can use in that thing anywhere."

Garett thrust a hand under his wide belt and pulled out his coin purse. It was all coming together, he thought madly as he struggled with the drawstrings. It couldn't be accidental. It couldn't be coincidence. It wasn't a dream at all. Mordenkainen had been real. He had intended for Garett to come here.

Garett poured the contents of the purse onto his palm, letting the copper commons and the silver nobles, even an electrum lucky, spill between his fingers. "Use these," he said. The five amethyst crystals glowed on his palm with a violet light, throbbing with their own inner fire.

"Duncan's dice!" Burge muttered with hoarse surprise. "They're worth a poor man's fortune!"

"My life's worth more!" Blossom answered him practically, snatching one of the small crystals and holding it to the sling's pouch. "They're not very big, but they've got a good weight. Give me room!"

She pushed her companions back with one arm and turned to wait for the worm. With a gush and splash, it rose out of the water at the edge of the copse. Blossom began whirling the sling above her head, holding out her right arm before her to take careful aim. The worm swayed in the air for a moment, then crashed down upon the edge of the root floor and began to slither out.

The impact of its weight set the roots to trembling and shifting. Blossom gave a startled cry and pitched backward into Burge's arms. The stone went plummeting from the sling's pouch and fell between the roots and was lost.

"Another!" she shouted, holding out her hand, regaining her balance as the worm wriggled toward them. She snatched the crystal that Garett held out to her. Again the worm rose up, shattering branches above its head. A cascade of leaves and limbs fell around it. Almost as if possessed of some intelligence, the creature hit the floor again. The entire root floor rocked and shifted, but this time Blossom kept her footing. The sling whirred around her head, faster and faster, until the air fairly sang. Then she let fly.

A streak of violet fire shot through the gloom, straight for the monster's left eye. The beast's maw gaped in a strange, soundless scream as the crystal struck its mark. The eye flashed with green fire, and an unnatural smoke exuded from the wound. A thick ichor streamed out upon its rubbery flesh as its great body lashed back and forth in obvious pain.

"The other eye!" Garett shouted, pushing a crystal into Blossom's hands as she stood, awe-struck, regarding the result of her first missile. Limbs and leaves rained down around them as the swaying hulk bashed the trees and branches. The roots trembled and shook under their feet.

Blossom fit the crystal to the sling and took aim. It would be harder this time since the beast now thrashed mindlessly. Garett watched the determination on her face as she whirled the sling. She gave a gasp as she let go. A second streak of violet fire, arcane in its brightness, sped through the air. Green fire flashed in the worm's right eye. The beast arched at the impact. Again, impossibly, smoke seeped out of the wound in great steaming curls, and a flood of viscous liquid rushed from the blinded orb.

The worm smashed down upon the root floor, thrashing madly. The tangle of roots underfoot began to yawn and gape. Without warning, Burge gave a cry as one foot fell suddenly through a hole that hadn't been there a moment earlier. He might easily have broken his leg. Curling his fist around the remaining two crystals, Garett helped him out. "Get around the tree trunk!" he ordered, grabbing Blossom by the arm. They ran to the nearest mangaroo and, joining hands, wrapped their arms around it and held on until the tremors stopped and the great worm lay dead.

Cautiously Garett let go of his friends and crept toward it. Much of the worm's body trailed away back into the water. He could not guess its length, but lying motionlessly on its side, it was twice again his height in thickness.

The smoking glow in those eyes had not yet faded. It ebbed and dimmed like a candle flame at the end of its wick. Ichor pooled around the monstrous head, sheening with that queer glow, and one of the translucent gills, still open, also reflected the dying emerald luster. As Garett stood watching, it suddenly relaxed and closed with a muffled *thump*.

"Thump," Burge repeated. "It was the sound of its breathing."

"Thump, thump," Garett said quietly, remembering Mordenkainen's words as he returned the remaining two amethyst dice to his coin purse. "The heart of the swamp."

Burge stared up at the creature as he walked around the edge of the pool of ichor that drained from its eyes. The pool did not spread much. It seeped between the roots and into the swamp water beneath. "This is probably why there aren't any lizard men in this part of the marsh anymore," he said.

"Well, if he keeps throwing money around the way he did back there," Blossom said, grinning at Garett as she rewound the leather sling around her freshly braided hair, "I'm sure they'll be back."

Suddenly, the green glow faded completely from the great worm's eyes. The three watchmen stood together in the gloom, abruptly aware of the gathering dark. Night was falling upon the world, and they were still in the marsh, lost.

Then the carcass of the worm gave a tremor. They leaped back, hands going for swords, but the worm did not rise or show any sign of life. A sound echoed suddenly around them and rose up into the trees, a tearing, a ripping. An emerald light of aching intensity shot upward, lighting the landscape with a verdant radiance.

The ripping was the ripping of flesh and tissue. A long fissure opened high on the corpse of the worm. A dark, bilious fluid gushed out, and a mass of entrails spilled from the wound onto the root floor. The fissure opened wider, as if a surgeon were doing work from the inside, and the light grew brighter still, such that Garett raised a hand to shield his eyes. The light came from inside the worm!

From up out of that fissure, out of that horrible corpse, rose a brilliant green star. Its pure fire banished gloom and exiled the shadows. To all corners of the marsh it poured its light, and darkness fled away. Burge and Blossom stumbled back, their eyes and mouths wide with awe that bordered on fear, but Garett walked forward, his eyes unshielded as he stared into its white heart and stretched out his hand.

The star came down to meet it. The fire enveloped him, and he flung back his head and cried out as every nerve in his body came alive with ecstasy. Then the light began to ebb, not with a flicker as it had in the eyes of the worm, but with a slow and steady diminishment. A sword became visible through that glow, with Garett's hand wrapped around the hilt. Still the light faded, until only the runes carved into the blade burned with any brightness. Finally, that glow, too, was gone.

Garett drew the blade close to his body and hugged it. "This is Guardian," he said to his friends. "The sword that Mordenkainen sent me for."

"I'm impressed," Burge said simply, coming closer for a better look at the mystic blade.

Blossom, though, seemed inclined to keep her distance. "I'd be more impressed," she said caustically, glancing around at the gloom that once more surrounded them, "if it had kept glowing 'til we'd gotten out of here."

Garett had to admit she had a point.

SIXTEEN

For some time after claiming the sword Guardian, Garett, Blossom, and Burge wandered in what they hoped was the right direction. The larger of Greyhawk's two moons, Kule, had appeared palely through a gap in the forest canopy. For almost an hour they waited, crouched on a knot of mangaroo roots, watching the moon crawl across that gap. Wisps and tendrils of mist drifted ghostlike through the air, obscuring it, threatening to hide it entirely. Yet they were patient, and the mist held back until they were able to judge from the moon's observed motion which way was west.

At last they reached the outer edge of the mangaroos. The grassy wetlands stretched ahead of them like a strange sea. A gentle, constant wind rippled over the tall blades, and the large moon shimmered on a fine, clinging fog that hugged the water. After their ordeal in the interior, it was a welcome—if unnatural—beauty to behold.

There was no sign of Rudi, nor was there any way of knowing if they were north or south of the place where they had left him with their horses. There was, however, a smell of roasting meat in the air. Though it was faint, it was enough to set their mouths to watering, a more than adequate reminder that they had eaten nothing but a bit of cheese and biscuits all day. They followed their noses northward and spied a small campfire far sooner than they had any right to expect.

Burge plucked off the tip of a blade of grass, put it between his lips and gave a sharp whistle.

A shadowy figure stood up suddenly on the campfire's near side. "Forget it!" came Rudi's voice, and the sound rolled over the grasses. "I blew that damn stuff 'til my lips were blistered. And I think I'm allergic to it, too! You want me, I'm over here!"

Their friend was just where they'd left him, perched on a knot of mangaroos. Somehow, he'd not only found dry wood for a fire, but caught a bird to roast and eat. Feathers lay scattered all around, along with the shells of what appeared to be three goose eggs. Half the fowl was already gone, but half remained.

Blossom went straight to the spit and knelt. "You're burning it, damn it!" she snapped, without so much as a good-to-see-you. "Where'd you ever learn to cook, anyway?" She snatched up one end of the spit in her bare fingers, then snatched them away with a quick curse.

Rudi pointed to his wide leather belt, which lay by the fire. It was greasy with his handprints and marred with a scorch mark. Blossom understood immediately. She picked it up and folded it over the hot end of the stick. Now she had something to grip with.

"The same place I learned to throw a dagger," Rudi answered proudly, if somewhat defensively. "Help yourself, by the way." He settled down again with his back to the trunk of the mangaroo and patted his stomach. "I've already had my fill."

Burge looked down at the young sergeant with a new appreciation. "You killed a bird with a dagger throw?"

Garett grinned as he knelt by the fire and balanced Guardian across his knees. He leaned forward to strip off a piece of the goose before Blossom devoured it all. "Why do you think I let him hang around?" he said. "I told you the kid's good."

Rudi feigned modesty. "It wasn't that hard," he explained. "I saw the nest up in the tree. That's where I got the dry wood, too, by the way. Plenty of old dead stuff up there that hasn't fallen down. Anyway, I thought I'd just eat the eggs." He waved a hand at the broken shells, indicating he'd already done so. "Then I thought, No, wait. The mother bird will be back soon. And when she came back, I picked her off. With her sitting still, it was easy. Even Blossom could have done it."

Blossom glanced up from the steaming piece of bird she clutched in her fingers, long enough to give him a wide, remind-me-to-kill-you-later kind of smile. Then, grease dripping down her chin, she returned to her meal.

Rudi eyed the sword across Garett's knees. The flames glittered red on the naked blade. "Is that it?" he asked simply, pointing.

Garett glanced up and nodded, unable to answer with his mouth full.

"Hey, leave me some," Burge said, squatting between Garett and Blossom. He reached out and stripped off a large, stringy portion of breast and smacked his lips. "Wild goose. What we need now is a good wine!"

"You'll have to make do with water," Rudi answered with an expansive gesture. "But there's plenty of that."

When there was nothing left of the goose but bones, Garett, Blossom, and Burge stripped off their clothes. None of them even bothered to feign modesty. The discovery of another leech on the back of Garett's right shoulder was enough to break down any reluctance. Naked, they explored each other in the firelight while Rudi stood ready with Burge's diminishing packet of salt.

Two of the parasites clung stubbornly on the back of the

half-elf's left thigh. When they finally came away, salted, red oozing weals showed lividly on his flesh. He gave a sudden short scream as a few grains of salt fell down into the wounds, and performed a short, urgent dance. Garett's other concern for his friend proved less of a worry. Though a trace of blood on Burge's bandages when they removed them had indicated his cuts had opened, they had sealed again and scabbed over.

Another leech had made itself a comfortable home under the fold of Blossom's right breast. She gave a little groan at the discovery, then turned her head aside and squeezed her eyes tightly shut and bit down on her lower lip.

"Wait until I tell the boys at the barracks about this!" Rudi laughed as he cupped her breast in one hand, applied the salt, and pealed the viscid creature away.

Blossom didn't protest, didn't open her eyes, didn't say anything at all. She just held herself rigid until the job was done. When Rudi flicked the leech into the fire, where it swiftly sizzled and popped, she wiped a hand over the spot. It came away smeared red.

"Thank you," she said weakly to Rudi, unable or unwilling to meet his gaze. She went straight to her clothing, ran a quick check to make sure nothing else had crawled inside them, and dressed. She shook her boots, too, and ran a hand all the way to the toes before she pulled them on.

There was no reason to stay any longer. Rudi used the instep of his boot to push the remains of the campfire into the water, leaving a blackened, scorched spot on the mangaroo roots, which were far too wet to burn. Garett drew out his old sword and put Guardian in its sheath. He tied the naked blade securely to his saddle and climbed up. The horses looked pathetic and unhappy after standing in water all day with only the short length of their reins to move around on. They were plainly ready to go as their riders turned them and splashed away toward the northwest.

The wetlands took on an almost silvery glow. Both moons floated in the misty sky now, big Kule, so bright, approaching fullness, and smaller blue Raenei, a perfectly round jewel in the heavens. The dew and mist that clung to the grasses reflected the light, and the fog that hovered over the water sparkled.

Riding beside Rudi, Blossom abruptly spoke, breaking the silence that hung like a pall over the surreal landscape. "If you tell anyone that you touched me here," she said, placing a hand on her breast, "I'll kill you." She looked fixedly straight ahead. There was no doubt at all that she meant it.

"It was only a joke," Rudi assured her apologetically.

She didn't answer. Indeed, she didn't speak at all until they reached the edge of the wetlands and stopped to give the area a final look. Then, as they turned their mounts again toward Greyhawk, she brightened somewhat and began to brag about the slingshots that had brought down the monster worm—no matter that Garett and Burge had already filled Rudi in on their adventures. And though their dangers had truly been great, they became even grander in her version.

* * * * *

The walls of Greyhawk loomed starkly in the moonlight. A few watchfires dotted the top of the wall, and a shadow or two shifted here and there as soldiers from the garrison walked their lackadaisical patrols. The wall and all the outer gates were manned, not by watchmen, but by regular soldiers from the garrison. It was considered a soft assignment, since the city hadn't suffered an invasion in any living person's memory.

Garett and his companions rode up to the Duke's Gate. It was long past midnight, and the gates were closed, as were all the outer gates two hours after sundown. It took some shouting before they were able to alert any of the guards above to let them in. Then they were surrounded and held at lance-point and lanterns shined into their faces until a youthful lieutenant finally arrived and vouched that Garett was indeed who he claimed to be.

"Sorry, Captain Starlen," the lieutenant apologized, gazing up at Garett, who was still mounted, with a firm, controlled gaze. "My men intended no offense. But none of you are in uniform, and there've been too many strange goings-on lately. You might have been imposters."

As tired as he was, Garett was generous. It reassured him that someone with a sense of duty and half a head on his shoulders was keeping an eye on things, at least at this one gate. "No offense taken," he told the young officer curtly. "And if you ever want a real job, I'd be happy to have someone like you on the night watch."

The lieutenant knew a compliment when he heard one, even if it was a bit backhanded, and he grinned. "Thank you, sir," he answered with a polite nod. "But if I ever take a *real* job, it's going to have real daytime hours. I've got a wife."

Garett bid all the guards a quiet evening. Then he, Burge, Blossom, and Rudi rode up High Street. He noticed one thing immediately. The streetlights were very dim. Some were extinguished completely. It took no great guesswork to know the reason why. In the High Quarter and much of the Garden Quarter, the Wizards' Guild maintained the lights with their magic. But something had happened to the wizards, and many of the ornate glass globes were failing without the spells that gave them their glow.

"Welcome home to Necropolis," Garett muttered.

"I bet the lamplighters are chortling up their sleeves," Burge commented in a low whisper after Garett explained his remark.

The Lamplighters' Guild maintained all the normal street lights in the middle quarters of the New City, those that had to be lit by hand with real fire. The guild's members hadn't been very happy when the Directorate, at the urging of many of Greyhawk's nobles, awarded a contract to the wizards to illuminate the more luxurious sections.

They considered it money stolen from their own coffers.

On the other hand, many residents were pleased to see the lamplighters get a comeuppance for their refusal to extend their services to any but the most major streets of the Lower Quarter, the Foreign Quarter, and the Artisans' Quarter, and not at all to the Slum Quarter or the Thieves' Quarter. There they bluntly refused to go.

"There are going to be a lot of questions, though," Blossom warned, staring upward as they passed under one of the dead globes.

Rudi agreed. "Some people might realize that Prestelan's fireworks last night were more than just a show for the city's amusement."

They fell silent again as they rode past the Sanctum of Heironeous. A low, dark structure set back off the road, it was sometimes called the Temple of the Righteous Warrior. Two burning braziers on either side of a dimly lit entrance invited anyone in, no matter the lateness of the hour. Many of the party's fellow watchmen worshiped there, as did the garrison soldiers and mercenaries from various lands. Although Garett never worshiped—in fact, paid little attention to any god—he, too, regarded the sanctum as a place of reverence.

Just down the road, the Temple of Zilchus loomed, a squat pyramid, its ugly architecture prettied somewhat by the groves of orange and lemon trees that surrounded it. The trees poured a constant fragrance into the air that Garett had to admit he found pleasing. He had never set foot in the temple, which was favored by moneychangers and merchants, but it was rumored to be the most lavishly decorated and furnished church in all of the western Flanaess.

Beyond the temple, on the north side of the street, stood the Lord Mayor's Palace. At least that was what people called it. Palace was perhaps stretching the word a bit, but it was indisputably one of the finest residences in the city. Most of the building was dark. Not even a guard stood on the fine marble porch. But in the top window of a high tower at the rear of the house, a lamplight burned. That was the mayor's private office, and it pleased Garett to see that Ellon Thigpen was getting no more sleep than he or his friends.

He wondered idly if Thigpen would have sought the mayor's position so eagerly two months ago if he had foreseen the trouble ahead. But he should have foreseen it. Thigpen had already served on the Directorate for several years. He knew well how the game of politics was played in Greyhawk—for keeps. He had had no better chance to learn that lesson than under his predecessor, the former mayor, Nerof Gasgal. Nerof had come to the office as the assistant master of thieves, another in a long line of mayors to come from that guild, and, like his predecessors, he had ruled with subtlety, constantly playing factions against each other, even scheming to create feuds, to maintain his authority.

No one had been too upset when Nerof died suddenly under questionable circumstances. No one except the Thieves' Guild, which suddenly found its grip on the office broken.

"Cap'n," Burge whispered suddenly, drawing back on his reins as he reached out to brush Garett's arm. The watch captain heard the note of warning in his friend's voice and stopped his horse. Behind Burge, Rudi also stopped, but Blossom rode up to her captain's left side, putting him between her and the half-elf.

Burge stared intently toward a thick grove of trees, one of several public gardens in this quarter, that grew on the south side of the street, directly opposite the Lord Mayor's Palace. The lights on that side of the street were dead. Nothing stirred in the darkness that filled the grove.

"Guess it was nothin'," Burge said a moment later.

Yet, before they could start their horses forward again, six men ran silently out from the trees to block the road. Six more rushed out from a different part of the grove to block the road behind and cut off any retreat. All twelve carried swords, but they held them crudely and hesitated, obviously nervous, before they charged the four watchmen.

Garett saw at once it was no professional killing squad they faced. For one thing, they were young. Surprisingly so. They were dirty, and their clothes were little more than rags. Their rush was that of a mob, not of trained fighters. Still, they had weapons in hand and murder in their eyes, and if they wanted to do their work in silence, Garett was loathe to please them.

With a shout, he drew his old sword from the loop on his saddle and leaped to the ground. He was no mounted fighter. He preferred solid earth under his feet. He clung to his reins just long enough to let the attacker's front line get close, then he slapped his horse's rump and sent the beast smashing through them. A pair of shouts sounded behind him, and he took a quick glance over his shoulder as Rudi and Blossom rode straight at the rear line.

Garett slashed at the nearest foe. The boy—for he was no more than that—gripped his blade in both hands and raised it high to block a killing blow. As he did so, Garett kicked him between the legs with all his force. The boy gave a high-pitched scream. The sword fell from his hands as he clutched his ruined groin, and he sagged forward as the night watch captain dealt him a second savage blow to the head with the pommel of his sword. Garett felt bone crack under the impact.

Another youth ran forward, shrieking in anger, but Burge intercepted him. The half-elf had also abandoned his horse to fight on foot beside his captain. He raised his sword like a Slum Quarter stickball player and swung. So swiftly did he strike, his foe never had time to get his sword up, and a shower of blood fountained from a nearly severed neck.

Two more came around on Garett's right. Swinging wildly, they rushed at him. He jumped quickly to the right, putting one attacker in the other's way, and lashed out with a backhanded sword stroke. This attacker, though, had better sense or better reflexes than his comrades. He blocked Garett's strike and managed one of his own that came dangerously near Garett's face. The watch captain leaned back with an inch to spare, feeling the wind of the attack on his nose. Encouraged, the youth grinned.

Quickly, Garett faced two again, and once more shifted his position so that only one could come at him. At the same time, he freed Guardian from the sheath on his back. As he brought his right-hand sword up to defend his head, he swung the one in his left. The nearest boy gave a scream and sagged to his knees, clutching his guts.

The second youth, watching his partner fall, backed away with fear-widened eyes. The sword became lax in his grip. Of a sudden, he turned and started to run, deserting the fight. A black-hilted dagger abruptly sprouted from his back. The force of the throw lifted the lad off his feet and sent him sprawling into the ditch at the side of the road. Garett turned long enough to observe Rudi take his sword once more in his right hand and rush to Blossom's side. The tall, blond watchman didn't need any help, though. She had backed her man across the street and forced him against a tree trunk. Suddenly she opened him, employing an elusive, upward stroke that split him from crotch to sternum.

A sudden quiet fell over the street, broken only by the rough sounds of breathing. Garett whirled, seeking foes. Blossom looked at him from across the street as she wiped an arm across her brow. Rudi spun back toward him, crouched, still ready to fight, not yet perceiving that the battle was all over.

Burge came to Garett's side. "Two of 'em ran off," he reported. "What do you think it was all about?"

Garett gazed around in disgust as he wiped the blood from Guardian and sheathed the blade. Ten still forms lay crumpled in the bloody road. It had been butchery. But he couldn't blame Blossom or Burge or Rudi. They were warriors, and they had been attacked. He couldn't even blame himself, though he felt a vague guilt gnawing at his middle. What in hell would make twelve unskilled youths attack trained watchmen?

Garett leaned on his old sword for a moment, then thrust it point down into the road and left it there as he bent down beside the nearest corpse. He gazed at the dead boy with some sadness and a sense of regret. There were times he didn't like his job very much. After a moment, he rolled the body onto its back. Blood spilled all over his hands. Frowning, he wiped them on the youth's worn and faded tunic, at the same time brushing his knuckles against the youth's ribs. He lifted up the hem of the tunic. Not even the blood could disguise the signs of slow starvation.

He began to search the body, ripping the tunic away completely. Then he ran his hands down each of the body's legs. With a grunt, he lifted one bare foot, grabbed the bottom of a pant leg, and turned it inside out. From a small, hidden pocket, he extracted a single silver noble.

"Search them all," he instructed, holding up the coin, barely able to contain a smoldering rage. There was no place to direct it anyway. Certainly not at his comrades.

On each body they found a silver noble. But on one body Burge found a purse that contained a noble and a gold orb. He crooked a finger and called Garett to come look. He showed his captain the coins and pointed to the face.

"Remember him, Cap'n?" Burge asked as he turned the face to better catch the dim streetlight.

"Whisper," Garett answered as Blossom and Rudi crouched down to look. "One of the members of the gang we met near the Slum Quarter." He went to each of the bodies again and peered carefully at the faces. Burko, the gang's leader, wasn't among them.

"This has a smell to it, Captain, if you know what I mean," Blossom commented unpleasantly. "What's a gang from that end of town doing all the way up here on High Street? How'd they get past the guards at the Black Gate, not to mention the Garden Gate?"

"What I want to know," Rudi interjected, pulling the sword from a dead youth's grip, "is where, in Boccob's sacred name, they got these." He held the sword out to his captain.

Garett didn't need to take the sword. Greyhawk citizens weren't allowed to carry such weapons, and youths such as these would not have been able to afford table daggers, let alone decent fighting blades. Especially these blades. He had already noted them while he searched the bodies.

"Someone provided them," Garett explained grimly. "Take a closer look. They're standard issue blades from the barracks armory."

Rudi looked up sharply. He had grown used to a sergeant's salary and to buying his own weapons, but he suddenly recognized the plain leather hilt wrapping, dyed red like everything belonging to the watchmen. There was no mistaking the weapon. The simplicity of its manufacture and lack of adornment of any kind, whether on tangs or pommel or the blade itself, characterized it. The city was far too tight-fisted to pay a craftsman for such useless extras on a blade that would be passed from man to man.

"Someone paid these guys to kill us," Rudi hissed, his face reddening with anger, "and gave them the weapons to do it."

"He's a little slow on the draw sometimes," Blossom said to Garett and Burge, putting a calculated sneer in her voice, "but he always finds the target."

"Not *us*," Garett said solemnly, jingling the ten silver nobles and the gold orb in his hand as he turned to stare across the street at the Lord Mayor's house. Apparently, the sounds of fighting had not disturbed anyone within. Of course, it *was* set back a way from the road. "It's *me* someone wants out of the way.

"Because of all these other killings?" Rudi asked, but he shook his head before his own question was out of his mouth. "No, this was too crude for a man who uses magic to murder."

"There's the Old Town murders," Blossom interjected. "Those don't have anything to do with magic."

"Don't they, darlin'?" Burge asked, raising an eyebrow as he turned toward her. He rubbed a hand over the lacerations on his chest. "What do you think is lurkin' down there in the sewers then?" He turned away from her and said to Garett, "We didn't even mention to these two that we ran into a street gang the other night, but I can think of one man who made it his business to know. I bet you even put Burko's an' Whisper's names in the report, didn't you?"

Blossom's eyes widened for an instant, then narrowed, and her voice dropped to a tense whisper. "You're talking about Korbian Arthuran."

Garett pursed his lips as he continued to jingle the coins. Korbian could have found out that he'd left town, and knowing that, he could have found out by which gate as easily. It was a safe enough gamble that Garett would check in at the same gate on returning. Korbian was also rich enough to pay the coins and cheap enough to look somewhere outside the usual Assassins' Guild, with its high rates. That wouldn't please Axen Kilgaren. The watch's captain-general could have gotten the weapons from the barracks, too. He might even have smuggled the street gang through the Black Gate and the Garden Gate without leaving a record of their passage.

And yet, Garett wondered, did Korbian Arthuran have nerve enough to try to kill him right outside the mayor's front door?

Garett drew a deep breath and turned to his officers. "Blossom, Rudi, you'll go to the High Quarter watch house and return with a patrol to take care of this mess. But say nothing of what we've just discussed."

Rudi protested. "But, sir, if Korbian—!"

"Say nothing, Sergeant!" Garett repeated sternly, snatching his old sword from where he'd left it sticking in the road. "We were attacked. That's all you know. I'll handle the rest of the report."

They recovered their horses. War-trained, the animals hadn't wandered far from the conflict. Garett tied his sword to the saddle, as he had before, and mounted up. While the others mounted, he wrapped his hand around the familiar hilt. He reflected that in the street fight the sword now sheathed on his back, Guardian, had served him like any other sword.

They rode on along High Street, past the Grand Theater, now closed and dark, and another public garden. Near the corner of High Street and the Processional stood the enclosed compound that was the High Quarter watch house. Blossom and Rudi broke away and rode inside to carry out Garett's instructions.

Across the Processional, Garett gazed at the empty High Market Square. The moons shone down on the tentless space, washing it with a sweet light. He thought of Vendredi and hoped that she was safe at home. Then, with Burge at his side, he turned his horse toward the Citadel.

There still was an hour or more before dawn and much work to do.

SEVENTEEN

"You were absent from your watch last night!" Korbian Arthuran shouted. His face was purple with rage as he slammed a fist down on the table. Plainly, he wasn't in a good mood. "The futile efforts of your men to hide the fact couldn't fool me. I have loyal officers to report such things!"

Garett eyed his superior officer with cool contempt. He had bathed and changed into a standard watch uniform at the barracks in anticipation of the summons that had once more brought him before a full, early morning meeting of the Directorate. Garett had gotten no sleep, but he was wide awake. He let his gaze wander around the table as he studied the other directors' faces.

Ellon Thigpen looked on impatiently, but he allowed the captain-general to rail on a little longer while he leaned back in his chair and sipped from a mug of broth. The mayor's eyes were puffy and ringed with dark circles. He wore the face of a worried man.

But it was the magister himself who interested Garett

most. Kentellen Mar sat at the far end of the table, and Garett felt the constant scrutiny of the man's dark-eyed gaze. Kentellen sat hunched back in his chair, arms folded across his middle, as if feigning a weary, sleepy appearance. But Garett wasn't fooled. From under that long shank of gray hair, those eyes took in everything.

On a chair directly behind the magister sat a young, blond boy, perhaps ten years old. With a discipline uncharacteristic for a child his age, the boy had said not a word, uttered no complaint, nor made any sound at all during the meeting. But he had quick, dark eyes, and the fire of a keen intelligence burned in them. Garett glanced at him time and again, unable to shake the feeling that the child understood everything being said.

". . . tantamount to desertion!" Korbian continued unabated. He was on a roll now. It was no longer a sense of indignation that drove him, but a sense of theatrics. "I could break you for this, Captain! Your arrogance of late has bordered on insubordination. I could make you pay a very high price!"

At last, Ellon Thigpen reached out and touched the captain-general's arm. "Calm down, Korbian," he urged gently. "I don't think . . ."

Garett listened with only half an ear. He didn't bother even to hide a yawn as he reached behind his belt and pulled out a new leather purse. Leaning forward in the chair they had offered him, he loosened the purse's strings and upended the contents on the table. Ten silver nobles and a gold orb spilled out upon the tabletop.

Garett put a hand over the pile of coins as all eyes turned toward it. With a sharp outward thrust, he scattered them. Coins flew across the table. Some fell in directors' laps. Some slid off the table and skittered on the floor. Garett had his own gift for theatrics when he wanted to employ it. The gesture was dramatic enough to shut Korbian up.

"Someone has already paid a high price," he stated icily. "And ten youths paid an even higher price with their lives last night. My investigations required my brief absence, and I returned as quickly as I could." He paused, daring to glare around the room. "One of you paid those boys to take me out. The details of the attack are in my report. You can all read it."

He glanced around the room again, meeting each upturned gaze with cool disdain. They meant nothing to him, this collection of men, these *politicians*. They disgusted him. "And if I were you," he continued, addressing his secret enemy, "next time I'd go to Axen Kilgaren. His price is steep, but he guarantees his work."

Garett finished by setting down the gold orb. He had palmed it when he pushed the other coins across the table. He flicked it with the tip of a finger. It slid over the polished roanwood surface to a smooth stop right before Korbian.

"You go too far," Korbian said in a deadly hiss. He rose out of his chair and leaned forward on the table, planting his hands on either side of the accusing coin. "You are suspended from duty without pay until further notice."

Ellon Thigpen sat back in his chair with a look of pain. "Korbian, don't be a fool!"

Such was the captain-general's anger that he lashed out even at the mayor. "I run the City Watch!" he snapped, curling one fist and clutching it tightly against his side. "I will decide who is to be my second!"

Axen Kilgaren rose slowly to his feet and pushed his chair back. Every eye in the room turned toward the master of assassins. "I do not approve," he said, leveling a smoldering gaze at Korbian. There was no mistaking the veiled threat in his words.

But Korbian didn't knuckle under. "It is not a matter for your approval," the captain-general answered sharply, drawing himself up as if he stood a chance of matching Axen's physically dominating presence.

A small, very subtle scratching sound drew Garett's attention momentarily. A few chairs away sat Sorvesh Kharn with a fingertip on one of the silver nobles that had not fallen on the floor. He pushed it around in a small circle, then back and forth on the wooden surface. From the corner of his eye he glanced at Garett, and the barest hint of a smile teased the corners of his lips.

Exactly what it meant, Garett was not sure. If it was a signal, he didn't understand, so he looked away from the master of thieves and back to Greyhawk's captain-general. "Suit yourself, Korbian," Garett said acidly, employing his superior's first name as if it were an insult. He got up from his chair. "I can use the vacation."

Dak Kasinskaia waved a hand in the air and spoke for the first time. "Wait, wait, Captain Starlen!" he implored in a conciliatory tone. "Just wait, everybody. Korbian, if you suspend the captain, just who do you intend should take charge of the night watch?"

Korbian Arthuran drew back his shoulders and lifted his nose a bit higher in the air. "A young man I've had my eye on for some time, a sergeant down in the River Quarter. He's due for promotion, and with the rank of captain, I'm confident he can do the job."

Ellon Thigpen shook his head and frowned. "And this young man's name?" he demanded.

Korbian folded his arms across his chest and glared defiantly around the room, at Axen Kilgaren, in particular. "His name is Kael."

"Kael?" Garett blurted. "Sergeant Kael in the River Quarter?" He threw back his head and let go a harsh laugh. "Good luck, gentlemen," he said when he recovered. He pushed back his chair and headed for the door as he delivered his parting shot. "It was a nice city until you got a hold on it."

Of course, that wasn't really fair. Greyhawk had never been a nice city.

* * * * *

Garett stormed into his office and kicked the door shut. There was nothing he needed there. He merely sought refuge until he got control of his anger. He went to his window and stared outward as he smacked his palms down on the sill. When was the sun going to shine again? He was sick half to death of all the damned clouds! He slammed the wooden shutters so hard they shook on their hinges.

A knock sounded on his door and a moment later it opened. Kentellen Mar entered, holding the hand of his small, blond companion.

"I hope I'm not interrupting anything, Captain," the magister said politely. The boy at his side clung to Kentellen's robes and stared at Garett with intense dark eyes.

With some embarrassment, Garett shook his head and forced himself to be calm. They couldn't have helped but hear the bang of the shutters. Nor could they help but notice the heat-flush the captain felt still reddening his cheeks, though now it slowly began to ebb. "No, Magister," he answered wearily. "I was just letting off a little steam."

Kentellen Mar pointed to the chair behind Garett's door. It was not heavy, and the little boy moved quickly to push it into the center of the room. The older man sat down somewhat stiffly, and his young charge went to his side. Kentellen slipped an arm affectionately about the boy as he spoke to Garett.

"You certainly have a right to do that," he conceded sympathetically. "Korbian overreacted. In fact, I came here to apologize personally for my silence during the whole unpleasant matter. But until the investiture, I am not truly a member of the Directorate and have no voice in the proceedings. They invited me today out of courtesy."

Garett moved away from his window and leaned on the back of his desk chair as he regarded his visitor. There was a sharpness, a penetrating intelligence, in the older man's nut-brown eyes. The dim lamplight reflected in those black pupils, and the whites gleamed moistly. Garett studied the wrinkles in Kentellen's brow and the deep lines time had carved in his cheeks, lines that disappeared into the thick growth of lush gray beard, and he wondered suddenly at Kentellen's age.

But why did he say he had no voice on the Directorate? Yes, he was the newcomer to that body, but was he truly so ignorant of its workings? Or did he think Garett was the stupid one? The investiture was a formality only, a show put on for the people of Greyhawk. The moment Ellon Thigpen had named him magister-to-be, the mayor had filled Kentellen's hands with power.

"I just want you to know," Kentellen went on, "that I'll do everything I can to reason with Korbian. You are not without friends on the Directorate, Captain. Try to relax and let us do what we can."

"That's very kind of you," Garett answered cautiously. Something is not quite right here, he thought, trying to hide his true reaction. He couldn't put a finger on what was wrong, but he couldn't shake the feeling. He had never met Kentellen Mar personally. He didn't really know the man from a pimple on Boccob's backside. Why was the magister here offering to see Garett reinstated?

Something brushed against Guardian's hilt. As if snapping awake, Garett shot out his hand and caught the wrist of the little blond boy, who looked up suddenly with terrified, wide eyes. Garett hadn't even seen him move! The boy had been standing beside Kentellen Mar. How had he made it all the way around Garett's desk without Garett seeing?

"Cavel!" Kentellen Mar shouted sternly, snapping his fingers and pointing to the floor by his side as he glared at the boy. "Get back here! You know better than to bother adults when they're speaking!"

The boy, Cavel, jerked his arm free from Garett's grip and ran back around the desk to his appointed spot. His two fists clutched at Kentellen's velvet robes as he sidled up to the old man. Safe there, he dared to turn a glare of pure, unchildlike anger on Garett, and his lips curled upward in a soundless snarl. Only then did he hold out his wrist for Kentellen to see where Garett had grabbed him, and clutch it to his chest as he mimed a look of pain.

"There, there," Kentellen said paternally as he patted the boy's shoulder. "It'll be all right. Grown men don't like little boys—or anyone—touching their weapons. Now he didn't hurt you, so be a big boy and don't make such a face about it!"

Garett watched it all with subdued interest. "The boy can't speak?" he ventured.

Kentellen Mar shook his head. "Not a word," he affirmed. "I apologize for his bad manners, but he was fascinated by your sword. It's quite exquisite. I must confess, I don't recognize its workmanship."

Garett glanced down at Guardian's hilt. He had left his old sword in the barracks with the ruins of his old clothes to be claimed later. "It's just a sword," he said with a shrug, peering at the pair as an uncomfortable sensation crept over him.

"May I see it?" Kentellen asked innocently, leaning forward in his chair and holding out his hand. His eyes locked with Garett's.

But Garett hesitated, intrigued and startled by the power in the old man's gaze, before he politely declined. "Forgive me, Magister," he said by way of apology. "But, as you told young Cavel, a man keeps his weapons to himself."

Kentellen Mar blinked and turned away a little. "Of course," he said. "It is I who should ask your forgiveness. It was a stupid request." He rose suddenly with a speed and ease surprising, considering how stiffly he had sat down. "Well, I must be going, but I did want to offer you what assurances of support I could. Greyhawk needs dedicated men like you, Captain. Now, Cavel and I must go home and see about some lunch, even though it's a bit early. I'm afraid I have a full schedule for the day." He did not offer his hand as another man might have, but moved around his chair and headed for the door with Cavel still clutching his robe.

"Where is Cavel from?" Garett called abruptly before they could get away. It was polite inquiry only. At least, he hoped it sounded that way.

Kentellen Mar gave a wry sort of grin that turned up one side of his mouth only. "Why, I found him on the banks of the Ritensa River," he explained, "near where it joins the Nyr Dyv. His parents and family had apparently drowned in a barge accident, so I kept him and brought him to live with me." He reached down and rumpled the boy's blond hair as Cavel twisted around to face Garett once more. His small, round face was expressionless except for those dark, glittering eyes. Garett could feel it. The boy didn't like him much.

"He's going to like it here in Greyhawk," Kentellen Mar went on, smoothing the hair he had just messed up. "Oh, yes, he's going to like it here very much."

The boy's only response was to hug Kentellen and hide his face in the folds of the older man's velvet robe.

Garett watched them go, feeling slightly cold inside. Then he went around to each of his lamps and turned the wicks down until the flames and the light died and left him in darkness. Then he pushed the door closed, pulled out his chair, and sat down. For a long time, he just sat there in the darkness, letting his thoughts lead him down whatever path they would. At last, he got up. The opening and closing of the door as he left his office filled him with a strange melancholy. Somehow, there was such a finality to it.

Once again, the halls were full of faces he didn't know, but that only made them easier to ignore as he worked his way down the levels and out into light and clean air. The sentries at the door saluted him, and without thinking about it, he answered their salute as he passed on.

Halfway across the Citadel's courtyard, though, he paused and craned his neck to gaze upward. The sky above the Citadel was black with circling birds. He watched them until a pain in his palm grew acute enough to make him glance down. He opened his right hand, which had been clenched in a tight fist. A small, crescent-shaped wound, made by the bloodied nail of his middle finger, showed lividly in the center. With a silent curse, he wiped the blood on his trouser leg, gazed once more at the patient birds, and strode off across the courtyard and out the massive Citadel gates.

As usual, Vendredi was at her booth in the High Market. A small crowd was gathered around her baskets of fruit, but as if sensing his approach, she looked up as he came down the Processional.

"Hi, handsome!" she called cheerily, tossing him an apple. "That's not your regular uniform. You get demoted?"

She'd meant it as a joke, so Garett allowed himself to grin as he answered, "You might say that." He took a big bite of the apple and chewed noisily. With his mouth full, he couldn't be expected to explain any further.

Vendredi's brows closed in on each other as she regarded him, and her face took on a serious expression. She put her hands on her hips, and leaned toward him. "I can always use a guard around here," she whispered so no one else could overhear, but she said it with just the right amount of lightheartedness, too. He could take her offer seriously or as just another joke, whatever his ego allowed. She left the option to him.

He looked down at her tenderly. Why couldn't he reach out and stroke that fire-red hair, brush a finger along that rosy cheek? What would the perfume at the nape of her neck smell like if he dared to bend closer? he wondered. What would Vendredi say if she knew he had such thoughts about her? Now, more than ever, though, he dared say nothing, do nothing. Without a job, he had nothing to offer her.

"Pardon me," she said abruptly, saving him the trouble of thinking up a witty remark to answer her with. She picked up a fat orange from a basket and hefted it on her palm. "Clear!" she shouted. As if they'd been trained to her command, the crowd parted. Just beyond the far end of her booth, a man sauntered innocently away. Vendredi drew back and let fly. The orange smashed against the back of the man's head, pitching him unexpectedly forward. As he flung out his arms to catch his balance, half a dozen pears fell out of his sleeves. The man looked fearfully around, rubbed the pulp-smeared spot on his head, and ran off.

Vendredi had eyes in the back of her head when it came to thieves, and Garett was grateful for the distraction as he slipped quietly away. He would apologize to her later.

Walking along the crowded Processional, he finished the apple Vendredi had given him and dropped the core into the dirt. The street was decked with banners that were already beginning to look slightly tattered. Many of the lampposts, however, were garlanded with wreaths of fresh flowers that could only have been put there this morning, and colorful pennons, hanging from many windows, flapped gayly in the breeze. Personally, he was in no mood to celebrate. He wished all the commotion was over.

Garett made his way to Cargo Street, intent on reaching home while he still had ribs left, or before he lost his temper. The throngs were terrible, and he was bumped and jostled at every turn. It wasn't just the citizens of Greyhawk that choked the streets, either. The town was filling up with folks from the outlying communities and provinces, all coming to take part in the celebrations as the day of investiture drew nearer.

As he passed the Low Seas Tavern, a group of six Rhennee bargemen pushed their way inside. A raucous blast of laughter issued into the streets as the door opened and closed, and Garett got a glimpse of the boisterous mob within. The Low Seas was usually a relatively calm place where customers checked their weapons. The tavern had changed owners recently, though, and Garett had no idea if the policy was still in effect.

A cart laden with goods from the wharves, bound for some warehouse, trundled down the street, forcing everyone to the sides. A lot of curses and insults were flung at the driver, and the driver returned them in kind. Garett waited, backed up against a wall, until the cart went past. Not everyone was celebrating, it seemed. For some, work still went on.

He made his way finally to Moonshadow Street. With a look of irritation, he observed a steady flow of traffic even here. As he drew nearer to his apartment, he saw that, for many of them, Almi's tavern was their destination. His landlady had even hung out a new, brightly painted sign. "The Crusty Widow," the sign announced in flaming red letters.

Despite all the hubbub, Almi still sat in her window. There was a big smile on her face, though, as she watched the customers file into her establishment. As Garett walked up to the window, he saw that she had moved a table and her cashbox there so she could work at the same time she watched the street.

Garett leaned on the sill, but before he could say anything, one of Almi's customers, a dock worker, and quite drunk, leaned close and pinched the old lady's bosom. Almi blushed and giggled like a young girl before she picked up an ash pan and banged him over the head with it. The docker reeled backward into the arms of his laughing friends.

"You're open a bit earlier than usual," Garett commented, leaning in through the window to tap her shoulder.

"Why, Captain!" Almi shrieked, pleased to see him. Then she giggled again. To Garett's surprise, her breath bore the powerful odor of wine. Lots of wine. She put a hand to her mouth and gave a little burp. She got control of her giggles and put on a serious expression. "I couldn't turn away business, now could I?" she told him as she burped again.

Garett raised an eyebrow. "You mean, you haven't closed at all yet? This is still last night's crowd?"

She leaned one elbow on the windowsill and rested her chin in her palm as she shook her head. "Oh, it's a different crowd. They come and they go from one tavern to another. And, nope, I haven't closed." Her old eyes glazed over for a second. She raised one hand in a futile effort to smooth down her wild forest of gray hair. For an instant, Garett thought she was going to fall asleep as her eyelids fluttered shut, but she snapped them open again. "I'm exhausted!" she said with sudden brightness. "But look!"

Almi reached out to the iron cashbox on the table beside her and briefly opened the heavy lid for Garett to see. It was near to overflowing with commons and nobles and electrum luckies. He even thought there was the wink of gold among all the coins.

"Damn it, woman! Shut that!" He cast a worried glance around the inside of her tavern. There were plenty of rough-looking, suspicious characters among her customers who might be willing to snatch her box if the opportunity presented itself. This was the River Quarter, where that type hung out. The fact that Almi was being so careless was testament to how much she had drunk. And he had never known Almi to drink at all.

Almi slammed the lid down and smiled at him. "If I closed up now," she cackled, "I might have to raise your rent to make up the difference."

Garett gave a sigh as he left the window and hurried inside. Without another word, he caught Almi by her arm, grabbed her cashbox, and hustled her through the tavern, back to her private rooms.

The old lady spun suddenly away from him, did a little pirouette, and fell on the edge of her bed. Her eyes were wide and shiny, and her lips parted in a silly grin. "Why, Captain Starlen!" she sighed melodramatically. "I had no idea you were so forceful! What about our age difference?"

Garett slammed her door and looked quickly around as

he hugged the cashbox under one arm. "Do you have a safe?" he asked, ignoring her comic attempt at seduction. "A hiding place? Where do you keep your money?"

"Right here, honey!" she answered, jiggling her bosom with one hand. "It's a treasure chest."

Garett groaned as he set the cashbox down on a small table and opened it. There was more money in the box than Almi would make in a normal year. While his landlady watched, he took one of the pillows from her bed, stripped off its linen case, and emptied the coins into it, leaving only what he thought she'd reasonably need for operating capital. Then he tied a knot in the case, got down on his knees, and pushed it under her bed. When he got up again, Almi was stretched out on her back, asleep or passed out.

Garett couldn't suppress a grin as he looked down at her. Almi's daughters would just have to handle things on their own for a while. He picked up the box, slipped out of the room, and started to close the door.

"I don't think you're going to get much sleep upstairs!" Almi called out suddenly. Garett turned around just in time to see her slump back down like a limp doll someone had put aside. His grin only widened, and he shook his head with amusement as he quietly pulled the door shut.

Upstairs in his own room, he sat down on the foot of his bed and tugged off his boots. The sounds from downstairs came up through the floor, and he listened to them with half an ear as he unfastened his sword, drew out the blade, and set it with the scabbard on the coverlet. He would run a polishing cloth over Guardian before he retired.

As he undressed, the soft flutter of wings caused him to turn toward the window. The shutter was open, and a large black bird perched there. It watched him with small, gleaming eyes and gave a chirp as it paced back and forth.

"Yah!" Garett cried, waving his arms to drive the bird away. It spread its dark wings and leaped into the air, and Garett continued with his disrobing. A moment later, the bird returned. Again Garett drove it away, and this time, he closed the shutter, but not before noticing his visitor had left droppings on his sill. "I hope a hawk catches you!" he muttered as he slammed the latch in place.

It was then, in the abrupt gloom that resulted from the shutter's closing, that he turned and noticed the faint green glow from Guardian.

EIGHTEEN

Garett woke with one hand curled lightly around Guardian's hilt. The sword lay sheathed on the sheets beside him. A lamp burned dimly on the table, its wick turned down low. He'd put it there himself, knowing he would sleep past sundown. He stared at the tiny flame and at the shadows it cast around his room as he stretched and slowly sat up.

Almi had been wrong. Despite the noise from the tavern, which even now seeped up through his floor, he had slept better and deeper than he had for days. He felt truly rested and alert for a change. He went to the window and threw open the shutter. Voices rose up from the street below, where a man and woman walked arm in arm. He listened for a moment. They were haggling over some price.

The night was black, and the stars burned like fiery diamonds. He leaned a little farther out, trying to spot either of Oerth's two moons, but his window faced the wrong direction. He wondered what time it was, then told himself it didn't matter. He didn't have to report anywhere tonight.

That didn't mean he intended to sit around. It was past time someone found out what had happened at the wizards' guildhall. Sorvesh Kharn had tried and lost two men in the attempt. No one had ever successfully broken into the guildhall before. The magic wards and protections were far too powerful.

But if what Mordenkainen had told him about Guardian was true, that the blade could cut through magic spells, then Garett stood a good chance.

He went to a trunk and took out trousers of rough black leather and pulled them on. Among the other garments in the trunk lay a black linen tunic, decorated at the lace-up neck and collar with silver embroidery. He pulled it over his head, adjusted the laces, then belted it with his usual wide leather belt. Then he fastened his sword belt over that, arranging Guardian so that the blade rode low on his hip. In the top of his left boot he concealed a sturdy dagger. Lastly, he tied his hair back with a short leather thong.

In the street below his window, a minstrel took up a position near Almi's door and began to strum a lute and sing. The voice was rich and sweet, and the song told the tale of Derider Fanchon, a woman of the old days, a constable and director of the city, who was known for her devotion to justice and to the poor. She was one of the great heroines of Greyhawk, almost a legend. The minstrel sang her song beautifully.

Garett remembered that he had lost all his coins in the Mist Marsh, and he had kept none of the money he had taken from the bodies of the dead youths on High Street. He picked up his purse from the table. It contained only the two remaining amethyst octahedrons. He carried it by the strings to his largest and heaviest trunk and dropped it on the floor while he kneeled down and twisted the trunk's middle catch, then twisted the left catch a different way.

A small concealed tray at the bottom of the trunk sprang outward. Coins of all different values glittered in the lamplight: Garett's savings. He sorted through it swiftly, scattering and stirring with his fingers. Finally, five commons, three silver nobles, and an electrum lucky went into his purse. He tied the strings around his belt and tucked it out of sight under the thick band, as was his usual wont. He pushed the tray back in again and felt the spring latch fall into place. It was almost impossible to see the narrow drawer when it was closed.

He paused for a moment, listening to the minstrel's song, then he turned the lamp's wick down even lower until the barest hint of a flame remained. Garett turned, ready to leave. His shadow loomed upon the wall and reached out to shake hands with him as he reached for the door. He opened it, and a warm night breeze blew upon his face.

"Evenin', Cap'n," Burge said. The half-elven lieutenant craned his neck and looked up from where he sat on the landing outside Garett's door. "I was wonderin' when you'd wake up."

"What are you doing here?" Garett asked with surprise, noticing at once that Burge wasn't in uniform either.

"Funny thing," Burge said, scratching his chin as he stared out over Moonshadow Lane. "Soon as word came down you were bein' replaced, I started thinkin' I was kind of tired of the watch anyway. In fact, I've had this itchin' at the back of my neck to get out of here." He leaned back against the wall, drew his knees up, and rested his arms on them. "Then, when they told me who was replacin' you . . ."

"Kael." Garett snorted in good humor. "That brown-nosing kid. I guess we don't have to wonder who told Korbian about our sneaking out to the Mist Marsh anymore." He nudged his friend in the side of the leg with a toe. "So you quit."

"Yup," Burge nodded. "So did Blossom. She's over at The Tomb now. Decided to join all the celebration."

Garett regretted that his friends had chosen to sacrifice their jobs for him, but he appreciated the loyalty and couldn't resist a wistful grin. "Rudi, too?"

Burge craned around again to look up at Garett, and he cocked an eyebrow. "Now you ask too much," he said disdainfully. Then he softened a bit and shrugged. "But, what in the hells. He's got a new wife to support." Burge stood up and rubbed the back of his neck as he gave his captain a questioning look. "So where we goin'?" he asked.

Garett stepped past his friend and led the way down the narrow stairs to the street. "To Wizards' Row," Garett called back over his shoulder. "It's about time we found out what happened to the magicians in this town."

"You're going to break into the guildhall?" Burge asked doubtfully, and Garett only nodded.

The minstrel still played his lute outside the door to Almi's tavern. Garett stopped long enough to draw a couple of commons from his purse and drop them in the performer's cap, which lay at his feet. The minstrel smiled and executed a deep bow without pausing in his current song.

The Crusty Widow was overflowing with customers. Almi was not in her window. Probably still passed out, Garett decided with an amused snort.

He and Burge walked down to Cargo Street. It was jammed with celebrants. A pair of white-robed, bald-headed acolytes from the Temple of Pholtus rushed up to them, banging tambourines and begging for donations. Burge's lip curled unpleasantly. He gave a feral snarl, and the acolytes found someone else to annoy.

For the first time in years, Garett had to sign a note of passage before the sentries would allow him through the Garden Gate into the Garden and High Quarters. Word had gotten out by now of his fall from grace. The watchmen were quite apologetic, but still they insisted he sign his name. It was a small requirement, merely a way of keeping undesirables out of the wealthier sections of the city, and Garett had not quite fallen that low. He wondered briefly if they would challenge his right to wear a sword, but he had only been suspended, not busted out of the watch entirely, and they said nothing about it.

Grumbling, Burge signed the list also, and the guards admitted them.

They moved swiftly through the Garden Quarter, where the restaurants, the finer taverns, and the elaborate gambling houses were just as full and rowdy and noisy as the River Quarter's, and the streets were just as gay. The only difference, as far as Garett could tell, was that the drunks dressed better in the Garden Quarter and a better class of beggars worked the crowds.

Garett and Burge crossed High Street, which separated the Garden Quarter from the High Quarter. Almost at once, things became quieter. In the High Quarter, where Greyhawk's nobility lived, the parties were more subdued and confined to the estates. It was also much darker. The magic-powered street lamps were almost all out now.

Wizards' Row was deserted. As they turned down the wide street, Garett stopped suddenly.

Burge put a hand on his sword's hilt. "What is it?" he asked nervously.

"Necropolis," Garett answered in a soft voice as he stared ahead.

Kule, the largest of Greyhawk's moons, hung low and red over the broken tower where Prestelan Sun had fought his last battle. The remains of the tower stood like a black splinter thrust at the moon's heart. The moonlight lent a silver-red glow to the sharp edges and to the dark silhouettes of the other buildings within the compound, and a frosty radiance limned the top of the wall. None of the noise from the Garden Quarter reached this far. An icy silence floated over the scene.

Burge stared, too. "It'll be full tomorrow night," he said in a near-whisper.

"So will Raenei," Garett answered. "And that's when the dung will start to rain."

Burge turned toward his captain and raised an eyebrow. "A colorful metaphor," he commented. "What's it mean?"

"Think about it," Garett suggested as he started up the road toward the guildhall's great wooden gates. "Two full moons on the night before the summer solstice. Astronomically speaking, how many times in a lifetime can that happen? It doesn't take a genius to realize such a night would have special significance to a wizard or a sorcerer."

Burge frowned. "You think there'll be another murder?"

They reached the gates and stepped into the deep shadow that cloaked the massive entrance. Garett put out a hand and felt the smoothly polished roanwood. A large sigil was painted on the doors, barely visible in the gloom. Garett didn't know its meaning, but it was rumored to be just part of the protections that sealed the guildhall against intruders.

"This is about more than murder," Garett told his friend. "It's something bigger. The seers were killed to prevent their foretelling it and giving warning. Only the Cat, that old seer in the Slum Quarter, escaped. But he left something carved in the wall over his desk. That horned skull. It was all the warning he had time to leave."

"But what weren't they supposed to see?" Burge muttered, standing back while Garett explored the gates.

"Something powerful," Garett answered without looking around. "Something coming to Greyhawk. I think others sensed it, too. Others who couldn't foretell, but who, nevertheless, knew something was in the air, the way an animal knows a storm is coming. That's why the Attloi left town, then the elves and the dwarves and a lot of the orcs." He thought about Kestertrot, the half-orc owner of The Tomb, and about the way he'd found him curled under a table in his kitchen. "Even some of the half-breeds have felt it," he reported, giving Burge a look.

Burge's frown deepened, and he scratched the back of his head. "Maybe that's why I've been thinkin' so much lately about movin' on and gettin' out of this town," he admitted.

Garett went back to his explorations. "Maybe you don't feel it as strongly because you work so hard at denying your elven heritage."

Burge didn't say anything, and Garett realized he'd taken a step over the bounds of friendship. It was one thing to sometimes joke about his friend's blood. It was another to chide him seriously about it.

"Anyway," he said, continuing, "I think Chancreon, the dragon who'd been living in the Halls as a human poet, sensed it, too, and it drove him crazy. Or maybe something attacked him to drive him out of town. I haven't figured all the details yet.

"What about the other murders?" Burge pressed quietly.

"The murders in Old Town," Garett continued as he ran his hand over the gates and over the huge iron locks. "I think Blossom was right. Those were part of it, too. They were sacrifices. You yourself found the altar down there in the sewers. Whoever this wizard is, he offers blood to his deity. That brings us back to the Horned Society again, where such a thing is common practice."

"You talk as if Greyhawk is under attack," Burge said.

Garett nodded. "It is." He moved back from the gate and drew Guardian from its sheath. A mild emerald radiance washed over the ground and the high gate. Garett held the blade up, marveling. He took a step closer to the gate, and the glow brightened perceptibly.

"It's reactin' to the magical wards," Burge observed.

Garett stepped back, then moved closer again, testing Burge's theory. The glow dimmed and brightened. Mordenkainen hadn't mentioned this aspect of the sword's power. Apparently, there were mysteries unknown even to the Circle of Eight.

"That bird," he said slowly.

Burge moved closer to his side. He held his hand close to the blade, and the light bounced against his palm, turning it green. The half-elf moved his hand through the glow, almost as if he were petting the sword, stroking it. "What bird?" he asked.

Garett told him about the bird on his windowsill. "The sword was glowing very slightly when I turned around. I didn't connect that until now."

"There's somethin' about the birds?" Burge asked, glancing up at the sky, where winged shapes fluttered swiftly across the bright face of Kule and across the star-speckled night. "But there are thousands of them!"

Garett gazed up also as he shook his head. "One bird, or thousands," he answered. "I don't know. But that thing that found Prestelan wore the shape of a bird."

Burge nodded grimly toward the guildhall gates. "I think we'd better take a look in there."

Garett agreed. "Stand back," he instructed as he approached the gates with Guardian held before him.

He touched the point of the arcane blade to the sigil painted on the roanwood. A green-tinged fire erupted at the contact, and a startled Garett sprang back. The strange flame hissed and crackled as it traced the lines of the enchanted seal. A foul-smelling white smoke spewed into the air. Then it was not fire that revealed the lines of the sigil, but a burning white light that grew and grew in brightness.

Abruptly the light began to ebb, turning green as it dimmed and finally fading altogether. Guardian, too, lost its glamour. Darkness returned to Wizards' Row.

Garett crept forward, the sword still drawn, and set his hand tentatively against the gate. Despite the fire and the light, it wasn't even warm. The paint of the sigil, though, had blistered away, and it stood out only as a peculiar scorch mark. "What do you think?" he asked Burge, and when he got no answer, he pushed on one of the massive doors. It opened a crack.

"Maybe they should have relied on more conventional locks," Burge commented, coming closer. His own sword was in his hand now. He put an eye to the crack and peered inside. "Can't see nothin'."

"Let me go first," Garett said, putting his shoulder to the door and opening it wider. Then, with a major effort, he pushed it all the way back.

The moonlight poured a frosty radiance upon the ground. Garett stepped cautiously over the gate's threshold into the vast courtyard that surrounded the wizards' guildhall, and immediately Guardian began to shine with a low-level glow again. Garett's gaze swept around, searching the shadows, alert for any movement. He didn't believe for an instant that the wards on the gate were the only protections on this place.

"Look," Burge said as he came up behind him. He pointed to a slumped form lying against the wall right beside the gate. Together they bent down to examine the body in the moonlight. "It's a dwarf," Burge noted.

"He's been dead for days," Garett pointed out, straightening. He turned and stared toward the pinnacle of the broken tower, still framed by Kule's refulgence. "Dead even before Prestelan's battle, from the condition of his body."

Burge frowned as he stood, but he continued to stare at the dead dwarf. "Then why doesn't he smell, Cap'n? A body like that ought to be quite potent by now."

Garett shook his head. He didn't pretend to understand all the workings of sorcery, and clearly there was some magic at work because Guardian gave off a minutely brighter glow when he passed it near the corpse.

"Touch it with the point," Burge suggested. "See if anything happens."

But Garett refused. "We don't know what's at work here," he explained as he turned away from the body and started walking across the courtyard. "When you visit a wizard's house, you have to expect to see some strange things. And at last count, twelve wizards lived here. If we have to defend ourselves, we will, but let's not disturb anything we don't have to."

Halfway to the entrance, a pair of statues stood on either

side of the walkway. Half human and half lion, they looked ferocious and frightening as the moon shone down upon their marble forms. As Garett and Burge approached, Guardian began to brighten.

"Are you thinkin' what I'm thinkin'?" Burge whispered as they crept down the walkway.

"I'm thinking let's cut a wide circle around them," Garett answered quietly, stepping off the walkway. But the sound of stone grating on stone made them stop. The statues rotated on their bases, turning to face them. Rigid arms and shoulders suddenly relaxed, became supple. The creatures stepped down from the bases and settled into a crouch as they eyed the intruders. One of them gave an animal growl. The moon glinted on long fangs as it shook back its mane and raised mighty taloned hands.

"Maybe you should have gone with Blossom to The Tomb tonight," Garett muttered as he raised Guardian defensively. The blade burned with a beautiful fire.

Burge lifted his own plain sword and prepared to fight. "Some fates are worse than death," he rejoined.

The lion-men rushed them suddenly, raking the air with their deadly claws. Garett gripped Guardian tightly with both hands and leaped in front of Burge to meet both attackers. The sword fairly exploded with light as he swung through the middle of his first foe and chopped with a short stroke at the second. To his surprise, he encountered no resistance as the blade made contact. It passed through both creatures as if they weren't there at all, but immediately they reverted to stone again, frozen in their attack postures. One of them fell over awkwardly on its side, snapping off an arm.

Burge came around Garett and gave the other an easy push. It, too, toppled sideways. "Now they're lyin' men," he said with a smirk.

They moved across the lawn toward the rubble surrounding the broken tower. On the way, they noticed a grove of trees growing near the wall. The moonlight fashioned strange shadows from the limbs and branches and from the thick trunks, but two shadows seemed out of place. Garett motioned to Burge, and they crept nearer. As it had when they approached the stone statues, Guardian began to give a warning glow, and they stopped well back from the grove's edge.

Two black-clad men hung, swaying, from branches that had coiled unnaturally about their throats. The bloated faces still wore wide-eyed looks of terror. One had lost a boot. It lay on the ground under him, as if he had been snatched out of it.

Burge took a step forward, but Garett caught his arm and jerked him back. "Watch," he whispered. He took a couple of steps toward the nearest tree, the sword glowing brighter as he did so. When the lowest limb came alive and snaked down to grab him, he brushed it with the blade. An emerald light flared, and Guardian passed harmlessly through the slender branch. Neither the branch nor any part of the tree moved again.

"Now we know what happened to Sorvesh Kharn's two burglars," Garett said, returning to Burge's side.

Large chunks of brick and stone dotted the lawn as they approached the ruined tower. They climbed over and around the rubble with only the eerie moons to light their way. The tower tilted at a crazy angle on its foundation, testament to the power that had struck it. A gaping fissure showed darkly down one side. Another side had been blown completely away, revealing patches of the shattered interior.

"Over here," Burge said quietly, his voice thick as he pointed at something. Garett hurried to join him.

Prestelan Sun lay crushed under a huge chunk of scorched masonry. Blood covered the right side of his head, where the scalp had been ripped away, and had seeped down to profusely stain the neck of his once fine white robe. The ribs on the right side of his chest simply didn't seem to exist anymore, and his left foot was completely twisted backward at the joint.

Garett turned away, feeling slightly ill. "Let's look around," he said, steering them toward the main guildhall, a pyramid-shaped structure at the center of the grounds. Its smooth marble sides gleamed under Kule's light. Though they found several narrow, metal-faced doors, Garett insisted they try the main entrance.

To his surprise, he found it already open. The great doors hung slackly on broken hinges, as if a great force had struck them. The wind had carried leaves into the main hallway; they rustled and rattled on the tiles as the breeze stirred them. If there had been a magical ward on the door, someone or something had tripped it, because Guardian gave no warning.

"The elves have a sayin'," Burge muttered, peering over the threshold. " 'Never enter a room if it's blacker than your own heart.' "

"Humans have a saying, too," Garett answered, nudging his friend's elbow. "After you."

"Hey!" Burge protested, giving him a look. "You've got the sword."

Garett grinned, then shrugged and stepped inside. Immediately, a small globe mounted on the wall just above their heads began to give off a soft white light. "Just like the street lamps," Garett observed aloud, beckoning Burge to come in. He glanced around the hallway. It was empty of furniture. A slender pedestal stood in the center of the room. When they approached it, they found that it contained a basin of water. Their reflections peered back at them for an instant, then dissolved to reveal the walkway and the moonlit view just beyond the entrance.

"Wizards!" Burge sneered as he discerned the water's purpose. "You'd think they could use an ordinary peephole, like normal folks."

They passed through a doorway, deeper into the bowels of the guildhall. In each room or corridor they found a magic globe, but sometimes the light it gave off was dim, and a few were dark and lightless, as if the enchantment that powered them had faded away. Just like on the streets, Garett thought, taking it as a sign that the wizards had not walked these halls for days.

The library established and maintained by Greyhawk's wizards was reputed to be the finest collection of tomes on magic and religion and philosophy anywhere in the Flanaess, but Garett was unprepared for the sight that greeted him when he pushed back an innocuous pair of hornwood double doors. The far end of the room could not be seen, and row after row of shelves formed a maze that made it impossible to judge the chamber's true size. Nor did there seem to be space anywhere on any of the shelves. They were crammed with books and scrolls and loose-bound manuscripts.

"It's a trick," Burge asserted as he walked past Garett into the library. "There aren't this many books in the world."

Garett shook his head. It was no trick. He ran a finger along the spines of the closest shelf. They were real. He could feel them. He could smell the paper and the glue of the bindings. He could smell the dust that rose at his touch. He drifted into the maze, scanning titles. Some were written in languages he didn't recognize; those he did sounded foreboding.

In one corner, he found a table. A small white globe, resting on a delicate crystal base, shed a pale illumination onto the pages of an open book. Another sheet of paper lay beside the book, half-covered with handwritten notes. Garett bent closer, then called to Burge.

"Look here," he said when his friend finally joined him. "They knew something was up. Someone was doing his research."

Revealed on the left side of the open book, drawn in bright red ink, was the horned-skull-and-serpent symbol that was the blazon of the Hierarchs of the Horned Society. On the opposite page, in the lower corner under a lot of writing, was the winged version they had found painted on the walls of the sewers.

"Can you read that?" Garett asked Burge. The half-elf was as well traveled as he. It was possible he might have encountered the language before.

"Not a word," Burge answered. "But whoever was writin' this could." He picked up the single sheet of paper and held it closer to the light. The notes, though handwritten, were in the same language as the book.

"It also looks as if our scholar left in a rush," Garett observed. He pointed to the final word on the notepaper. "The ink trails off suddenly, as if his hand slipped, and the word looks unfinished." He looked the desk over and pointed again. "See here. The ink jar has been left unsealed. Who would allow precious ink to simply evaporate? And see here." He bent down suddenly and picked up a stylus from the floor. "He dropped this and didn't take time to retrieve it."

Burge backed away from the table, his eyes searching the desk, the floor, the nearest shelves for other clues. "But where did he go?" he asked. "Where did they all go?"

Garett didn't answer. He bent down to the floor again and rose, clutching something between his thumb and forefinger. He wore a puzzled expression on his face as he turned toward Burge and held up a fine black feather.

NINETEEN

Upon leaving the guildhall, Garett and Burge went straight to the High Quarter watch house on High Street. Although Garett was no longer the night shift commander, the officer in charge there accepted his advice and sent a patrol to guard the guildhall entrance now that it was unlocked. It would not have been wise to leave such a place, with its secrets, unprotected.

After that, the two friends returned to the River Quarter and eventually pushed and elbowed their way through the impossible crowds to Moonshadow Lane, where they purchased a bottle of wine from Almi. The old woman was awake and at work again, but her cheeks reddened and she glanced shamefacedly away from Garett when he entered her busy tavern. She muttered something incoherent as she placed the bottle in Garett's hands. When Garett offered his coins, she refused them, shook her head again, and returned to her customers.

Upstairs in his room, Garett found two relatively clean cups and poured wine. Burge accepted his as he settled into the only chair. Garett carried his to the foot of his bed and sat down. The oil cresset above their heads gave off a warm amber light. Apparently, Almi had come up while he was gone and lit it for him, as she sometimes did.

They had only taken their first sips when a knock sounded on the door and it opened. Almi's oldest daughter, Bestra, a plump widow with pleasant eyes and dark hair that was just beginning to gray, entered with a tray containing slender strips of smoked chicken and steaming chunks of fish. There also was a pair of apples, a loaf of bread, a dish of soft, creamy butter, and the appropriate dining utensils.

"Mum's pretty embarrassed about today," Bestra announced wearily as she set the tray on Garett's table and backed toward the door again. "You can probably expect this kind of treatment for a couple of days."

Garett couldn't suppress a grin. "Please, assure her there's no need for embarrassment. Did she find the bag of coins under her bed?"

Bestra bit her lower lip in her effort not to match his grin. "Yes," she said at last, "though there was a brief, but very amusing, moment of hysteria when she woke and discovered her cash box was empty."

She left them alone, closing the door as she departed, and the two men reached toward the tray. Before they could eat anything, though, another knock sounded. Garett turned toward the door with a strip of chicken halfway to his mouth.

It was Blossom.

"Morning, Captain," she said with a suspiciously pleasant tone. There was a moist gleam in her eye, too. Garett assumed she'd been drinking. Burge had said she'd gone to celebrate at The Tomb, and it wasn't *that* close to morning. Then she spied the tray on the table and charged toward it. "Oh, great!" she exclaimed. "Food!"

"I hadn't really planned for a party," Garett mumbled as she rushed past him, seized a piece of fish, and shoved it into her mouth. "I don't even have a third cup."

She waved a hand at him as she chewed and swallowed. "That's all right," she assured. She picked up the bottle, upended it, and took a deep draft. She smiled as she wiped her lips with the back of one hand. Then, one-handed, she unbuckled her sword belt, set it aside, and went to sit on the foot of the bed with the bottle between her knees. "This'll do fine."

Burge took a sip from his cup as he watched the tall blond. His eyes sparkled with amusement. "You must have had a good time at The Tomb with ol' Kestertrot," he said.

"Oh, I did!" Blossom admitted, nodding her head vigorously. She paused to take another swig from the bottle before continuing. "The tavern was packed, and I heard the best news. Kestertrot's gone, by the way. Got an assistant running the place while he takes a vacation up in the Cairn Hills." She raised up long enough to snatch another piece of fish from the tray. "Can you imagine? A vacation, with the investiture coming up and the whole city celebrating?"

Standing beside the table, Garett exchanged looks with Burge at the news about The Tomb's half-orc owner. "Is that what you came to tell us?" Garett asked uncertainly.

Blossom chewed and swallowed her fish. "No, I came to tell you that you'd best get some sleep tonight." A malicious smile crept over her face as she leaned back on the bed and balanced herself on one elbow. "I have a feeling the Directorate's going to want to see you in the morning."

Garett's brows knitted together warily as he raised his cup. "Why do you say that?" he asked over the rim of the vessel.

Blossom's smile turned unpleasant as she lifted her head and gave a little laugh. "Because someone murdered Captain Kael tonight. That's why."

Burge leaped to his feet, slopping wine over the side of his cup. "What?" he shouted, glaring at her with a genuine look of shock. "You didn't . . . !"

"Sit down, elf," Blossom ordered calmly. She lifted the

bottle to her lips, tipped it, and swallowed a mouthful of wine. "Of course I didn't," she continued. "His throat was cut, and the tongue pulled through the bloody gash. Assassins' Guild work. That's their trademark. But that's not the best part." She looked at Garett and gave him a wink. "They left the body on Korbian's doorstep. A warning if there ever was one."

Burge winced and gave a low whistle.

Garett took a drink from his wine cup, remembering the Directorate meeting the previous morning. Axen Kilgaren had risen to protest Garett's firing by Korbian, and Kilgaren was the master of the Assassins' Guild. No member would have dared make such a kill without Axen's approval.

Yet, Garett took no pleasure in the news of Kael's murder. The man had been a pompous, ambitious little yesman, but for all that, he was still a watchman.

The three of them talked a bit more. They told Blossom what they had found at the wizards' guildhall, and Garett explained his suspicions about the coming night of the full moons. After that, the food was nearly gone and the wine bottle empty. Blossom rose and stretched. Now that she'd quit the City Watch, the barracks was off-limits to her, and she'd taken an apartment not far away, down on Horseshoe Road. She buckled on her sword and said her good nights.

Garett escorted her to the door and watched from the landing as she descended the steps and melted into the meandering throngs on Moonshadow Lane. When she was gone, he glanced up over his shoulder. Both Kule and Raenei sailed high in the heavens, and the rooftops of Greyhawk glowed with their radiance. How, Garett asked himself silently, could the days be so cloudy and the nights so perfectly clear?

Burge had neglected to arrange for a room, so Garett put a blanket on the floor for him. Eventually, he turned the wick in the cresset lamp down to only a tiny glow, and they lay down to sleep. The sounds from The Crusty Widow and

Moonshadow Lane drifted up, but the half-elf soon began to snore.

For Garett, sleep would not come. He turned first onto one side, then the other, then onto his back. He thought of skull symbols and the Horned Society. He thought of seers and dead people in Old Town. He thought of amethyst fortune-telling dice and enchanted swords. When he closed his eyes, he saw birds and giant slugs, leeches and a dragon setting fire to the city. The wind outside his window whispered with the sound of Mordenkainen's voice.

Suddenly, Garett sat up and grabbed for Guardian, where it stood against the wall at the head of his bed. He stared at it, gripping it in a trembling hand. Twelve swords, Mordenkainen had claimed, the Pillars of Heaven. Garett turned the weapon slowly. The fanged tigers' heads on the weapon's tangs stared back at him. The eyes were tiny splinters of emeralds, the workmanship exquisite.

"Burge!" Garett shouted. "Wake up!"

The half-elf sat up at once, instantly alert, one hand on the sword that lay on the floor at his side. "What is it?" he asked, quickly perceiving that there was no threat.

Without drawing Guardian from the plain leather sheath, Garett held the sword out. "Tell me what you see," he demanded.

Burge looked at Garett, frowning. His gaze flickered to the sword. An intent expression came over his face. His eyes widened, and he brought a hand to his mouth. "Cap'n!" he exclaimed in an awed whisper. "It's a sword!"

Garett glared angrily. "Damn it, man, don't joke with me! Describe it!"

Burge rolled his eyes impatiently. "What did you expect?" he snapped. He waved a hand at the blade. "It's a sword, isn't it? If it had a red wrappin' on the hilt, it could be standard barracks issue. Except that this sword glows like a firebug in heat and cuts through magic like an axe through butter."

Garett slid Guardian from the sheath and held it up

again. The amber light from the cresset lamp shimmered on the edges. "Now what do you see?" he pressed.

"The blade!" Burge answered sharply, realizing that he was missing something his captain wanted him to see. "It's not even glowing."

Garett pursed his lips and ran his finger down the line of black runes the sword's maker had engraved on the metal.

When he first saw the sword in Mordenkainen's crystal ball, it appeared to be of plain manufacture. But then the old wizard touched his eyes, and when he looked again, he saw the blade in all its arcane glory. The twelve swords called the Pillars of Heaven had been hidden, Mordenkainen had told him. It must have been Mordenkainen's magic then, in that gentle brush on his eyelids, that lifted whatever spell disguised Guardian's true nature and allowed Garett to see it. He touched the runes again, wondering at the language and the unreadable message written there.

Burge couldn't see the runes or the fantastically carved tiger-hilt, or the emerald pommel stone.

But someone else had seen. *It's quite exquisite.* He'd paid little heed when those words were first spoken. He'd been too angry at Korbian and at the directors. Now they thundered in Garett's head.

"I know who the wizard is," he said. He leaned forward and put Guardian into Burge's hands, and when the half-elf's face lit up this time, the awe was genuine.

* * * * *

As Blossom had predicted, Garett was summoned to yet another early morning meeting of the Directorate. A knock at the door woke him and Burge shortly after first light. A patrol escort waited at the bottom of the stairs. Burge rose also, determined to come along. Together, they dressed in plain clothes and strapped on their weapons.

A welcome hush hung over the city. They moved through

the streets at just that median hour when the nighttime celebrants had finally gone home to sleep and the daytime celebrations had not yet begun. The River Quarter was almost empty, except for teams of prison work-gangs, who labored at cleaning the streets and picking up the refuse. It was a welcome calm after all the noise and turmoil.

In the High Market Square, the hastily built dais from which the mayor had welcomed Kentellen Mar home still stood. It had been enlarged, though, and decorated with garlands of flowers and colored streamers. Tomorrow, on that dais, on the day of the summer solstice, at the hour of noon, the Directorate would officially name Ellon Thigpen as Greyhawk's mayor, no matter that he had carried the title and duties of the office for months since the death of his predecessor. Following that ceremony, Ellon would, in turn, officially bestow upon Kentellen Mar the office of the magister.

At the entrance to the Citadel, the patrol stopped. Burge stopped also. "Welcome home," the half-elf muttered.

"It remains to be seen how welcome I am, my friend," Garett answered, pausing before he went inside. "Wait for me here."

A watchman stood guard outside the door to the Directorate's meeting room. As Garett approached, the man threw back the door and announced his arrival, then stepped out of the way. Garett gave him barely a look. Although he was a watchman, he was a daytimer and unknown to Garett.

Again it seemed the entire Directorate was present, despite the early hour. Garett glanced quickly around at their faces, attempting to determine their mood. Ellon Thigpen looked worried and weary. There was the ever-present smirk on Sorvesh Kharn's features. Fasterace the tax-collector fanned himself nervously with a hand fan made of shiny silk cloth and avoided meeting anyone's gaze. Dak Kasinskaia did his youthful best to look perfectly sublime. But it was Axen Kilgaren that intrigued Garett most. Axen did not look like a happy man.

Almost as quickly, Garett noted the only two empty seats. Prestelan Sun, of course, was absent. So was the magister-to-be. That surprised Garett somewhat.

A couple of the less notable members of the Directorate were involved in a heated discussion and unwilling to give up the floor.

"The Lamplighters' Guild refuses to do anything about the streetlights in the High Quarter," stated Patri Cardulo, a representative of the Guild of Lawyers and Scribes, "unless the Directorate completely negates its contract with the Wizards' Guild for lighting services!"

Alek Prestikan, of the Merchants' and Traders' Union, thumped his fist on the table. "That's totally unreasonable!" he blustered, red-faced. "They think they can hold us up, force us to tear up a good contract, just because we need their services for a few stinking nights until we get this all straightened out? Don't they realize some of those streets up there are completely dark? That's unheard of in the High Quarter!"

"I'm sure that's what they're counting on," Patri Cardulo purred. "They want the contract themselves, and at double their usual rate. And I should tell you, a lot of people up there are pressuring us on this. They don't feel safe."

Ellon Thigpen rapped his knuckles on the table, and the room fell quiet. All eyes turned toward Garett as he took an at-ease stance and clasped his hands behind his back to await their pleasure. No greeting was exchanged, and certainly no welcome.

Ellon Thigpen was the first to speak. His voice was flat and matter-of-fact. "I believe you have something to say, Korbian."

Korbian Arthuran rose slowly to his feet. The captain-general looked pale and shaken. Dark circles and thick, puffy eyes suggested he hadn't slept at all. He looked across the room at Garett, then his gaze flickered away.

"Yes, yes," Korbian said haltingly, leaning forward over

the table, almost as if he had to support himself. "I—I was, uh, too hasty yesterday, Captain Starlen," he stated. His gaze flickered to Garett again, then to Axen Kilgaren and to the mayor.

Fasterace gave a tiny, girlish snicker, then quickly brought up his fan to hide his face.

Korbian struggled to continue. "Uh, circumstances have led me to, uh, reconsider your suspension. In fact, to lift it." He shot another glance at Axen, as if looking for some sign of approval. But the master of assassins sat stonily, yielding nothing. Korbian stared down at his own hands. "You are commander of the night watch once more, Captain."

Korbian sat down and said no more while Sorvesh Kharn gave the captain-general a look of utter scorn.

"Thank you, sir," Garett said formally and politely. "I serve at your pleasure, as always."

He had not intended it to sound like a wisecrack, but Korbian lifted his head and shot him a look of pure hatred.

Ellon Thigpen changed the subject. "Is it true you somehow managed to break into the wizards' guildhall last night, Captain?"

It shouldn't have surprised Garett that Ellon had that bit of information. He had little liking for the mayor, but Thigpen was proving to be quite competent. Garett had guessed that for some time he'd been reading the watch reports left for Korbian, or that Korbian had been filling him in on all the details. Of course, the High Quarter watch house would have logged a record of the guards he'd requested to be posted outside the guildhall gates.

"And," said Dak Kasinskaia, rising to stand, "is it true that Prestelan Sun is dead?"

"The answer to both your questions," Garett answered bluntly, "is yes."

Several of the directors rose at once. "However did you get in?" they wanted to know.

"What of the other wizards?"

"Who will take Prestelan's place on the Directorate?"

Too many questions at once. Garett had no intention of telling them about Guardian, but before he could say anything, the door behind him opened.

Kentellen Mar entered with little Cavel at his side. So powerful was Kentellen's presence that the room fell silent as he walked around the table and took his seat. Cavel, never far from Kentellen, took up a position at his side and rested a hand on the old man's arm.

The magister settled back, folded his fingers under his chin, and gave Garett a long, dark-eyed look. "So, Captain," he said quietly, "as I predicted, your absence was not a lengthy one."

Garett felt suddenly cold inside. "It has been a night of surprises," he answered cryptically, "for many of us."

"And a night of loss as well," Dak Kasinskaia stated with appropriate sadness. "We must prepare a suitable funeral and mourning period for poor Prestelan, something that befits a director who has served this city so faithfully."

Fasterace whipped the air with his fan. "Mourning period?" He sneered. "A celebration, you mean!"

"Not that!" someone muttered. "Not another celebration!"

Garett marveled at the capacity of politicians to degenerate from important business into meaningless babble. They confused activity with action and debate with problem-solving. He did not trust them, not one man sitting at that table.

He felt the eyes of Kentellen Mar upon him. Kentellen sat apart, uninvolved in the argument. He did not even bother to hide his interest in Garett. For a moment, the room seemed to swirl, and it was as if the others disappeared and they were alone. Garett's heart quickened, and the rush of the blood in his veins surged in his ears.

Then the moment passed, and Garett discovered his hand curled lightly around Guardian's hilt. He didn't remember even moving. "Excuse me," he said loudly enough to attract everyone's attention, "but I have duties to catch up on. If you have no further questions . . ."

Ellon Thigpen interrupted. "We have plenty of questions, Captain Starlen," he said authoritatively. Then, surveying the expressions of his fellow directors, he relented. "But perhaps we should deal with more pressing matters first. You are excused."

More pressing matters. Funerals and investitures. Fools! Garett thought as he turned and left the chamber. The city could crumble upon their heads, but never without an appropriate ceremony!

Garett went straight to his office. There was no fire in any of his lamps, nor any oil. For light, he flung open the shutter on his only window. Then he grabbed the first watchman he found in the corridor and sent for Burge.

"You've got your job back," he told his friend. "That's not an offer. It's an order. And go find Blossom. I need her, too. All of you. Here, tonight."

"Yes, sir, Cap'n, sir!" Burge answered with exaggerated enthusiasm. Deliberately, he snapped a crisp salute with the wrong hand.

"We're going to do this our damned selves!" Garett swore grimly.

Burge left, and Garett sank down in his chair, turned it toward the window, and propped his feet up on the sill. Once again, he tried to put it all together in his head, to convince himself that he was right. There were so many pieces to the puzzle, and all of them were rough. He told himself he should have been more forceful with the directors. He should have made them listen. But what real proof did he have that his conclusions were the right ones?

How could he hope to convince them that the enemy was their beloved Kentellen Mar?

Garett knew that he couldn't. So he folded his hands over his stomach, leaned back in his chair, and made his plans. The directors would help him whether they wanted to or not. He knew their weaknesses. He intended to use them.

Outside his window, the black birds circled in ever-growing numbers.

* * * * *

By midafternoon, the streets were once more choked with citizens and outlanders come to celebrate the investitures. The High Market was a mass of seething human flesh, and the Processional a colorful river of costumes and banners and flower garlands. People danced on the corners, sometimes in the middle of the road. Men and women leaned out of windows and shrieked at the tops of their voices. Music sounded from everywhere, wild and furious, sometimes played by musicians, and sometimes by folks beating sticks on the lampposts or banging spoons on pots and pans as they marched through the crowds, employing anything that could make a noise.

On horseback, Garett rode through it, taking side streets when he could to avoid the worst crowds. He had never seen the people of Greyhawk like this before, and it disturbed him. *It begins to border on hysteria,* he thought uneasily as he guided his mount southward down the Processional to the Black Gate. Since he was again dressed in uniform, the guards did not bother to stop him. They saluted, and he nodded and passed through into the Thieves' Quarter. He rode up Rat's Road, then turned down Black Lane, and stopped at last before the great hall of the Thieves' Guild.

The hall was the true heart of Old Town. Little transpired south of the Black Wall that was not known, or even sanctioned, here. The hall's windows and rooftop commanded views of every possible approach, and Garett knew that he had been observed for some time by spies who had followed him from the moment he passed through the gate.

A pair of young, rough-looking boys, apprentice thieves, stood guard at the entrance. Garett rode right up to the steps before he stopped and called up to them. "Tell Sorvesh Kharn that—"

The great doors swung inward. "I am here, Garett Starlen," the master of thieves responded as he stepped into the daylight. He came halfway down the steps and stopped, and the pair of guards at the door came down to take up positions just behind him. Still another pair slipped out of the hall and took their posts on either side of the entrance.

Garett nodded to himself with satisfaction. It was a small exercise, but it showed that the thieves were disciplined. "We need to talk," Garett said.

Sorvesh Kharn inclined his head slightly in consideration. "We can do so out here in the heat," came his answer, "or, if you will surrender your weapon and allow yourself to be blindfolded, there is the luxury of my quarters inside."

Garett had expected the blindfold. No one who was not a member of the guild was allowed to enter the hall. And those who were taken inside never saw more than one room. That way, no outsider learned the layout of the place, or where any of the many deadly traps were set. It was the guild's oldest rule and known throughout Greyhawk.

He was, however, reluctant to part with Guardian for any reason.

Sorvesh Kharn saw his hesitation. "You came to me, Captain," he noted. "So you must trust me."

"I will wear your blindfold," Garett answered firmly. "But I didn't demand your weapons when you came to my apartment, and I won't surrender my sword to any man. You must give what you ask for—trust."

Sorvesh Kharn smiled and whispered something to the man at his right side. The apprentice ran back up the stairs and disappeared inside. "I like you, Captain," Sorvesh stated. "You have the courage so many of our city leaders lack."

The apprentice returned to his master's side with a strip of white cloth, and Garett dismounted. Without saying more, he allowed them to cover his eyes. He gave his right hand to the apprentice to lead him, while he wrapped his other around the hilt of Guardian to ensure nobody tried to take it.

"Trust, Captain," he heard Sorvesh whisper with a trace of amusement.

Garett heard someone leading his horse away as the apprentice guided him carefully up the steps. By the dimming of the tiny amount of light that leaked through the cloth on his eyes, and by the smooth tile upon which he suddenly tread, he knew that he was inside. Almost immediately, the apprentice stopped him, then began to turn him around and around. When he stopped again, Garett was thoroughly disoriented.

They led him up a flight of steps, then down another. It might have been the same stairs, for all Garett knew. The floor actually seemed to rise at an incline at one place. They steered him around a corner, and around another corner. Through the blindfold, the light brightened and dimmed.

At last, someone removed his blindfold, and the watch captain found himself in a room whose opulence surpassed anything he had ever seen in Greyhawk. The carpets were blue and red silk, and blue velvet tapestries hung upon the walls. Small sculptures and lavishly decorated vases stood upon slender pedestals and upon tables made of highly polished roanwood. Beautiful paintings stood on display easels in the room's corners, their frames glittering with gold. Two cushioned couches, one of plushest black velvet, the other of rich black leather, faced each other in the center of the room. It was a room to make the nobility of the city envious. And, Garett reminded himself, probably all stolen.

The door closed softly behind him, and the watch captain found himself alone with Sorvesh Kharn. Despite the awe he felt at such richness, Garett forced himself to get to business. "Just how many thieves do you command, Sorvesh?" Garett asked, realizing that the master of thieves would never give him a true answer to that question.

Sorvesh Kharn inclined his head thoughtfully and

steered Garett toward the couches, where they sat, Sorvesh on the leather and Garett on the black velvet. Garett ran his palm over the material, savoring the feel of its incredible texture.

Sorvesh watched him carefully. "Why would you ask?" he queried, a polite dodge.

Garett leaned forward intently, placing his elbows on his knees and interlocking his fingers. "Because I have come," Garett said carefully, applying his hook, "to make you Mayor of Greyhawk."

* * * * *

A short time later, Garett rode up High Street to the palace of the lord mayor. "I have come to make you mayor," he said when a servant led him into Ellon Thigpen's private office.

Ellon gave him a puzzled look. "I am already mayor," he answered.

"Ah," Garett said, holding up a finger. "Not officially until tomorrow at noon. And there is a plot against you tonight."

Ellon Thigpen paled. Then he leaned forward nervously in his chair to listen.

Hooked.

* * * * *

For some time Garett waited in the garden of Axen Kilgaren's home before the master of assassins came to him.

"You should know," Axen said before Garett could speak, "that Kael was not a sanctioned kill. Someone has attempted to make it look like a guild job, but it wasn't. I kept quiet at the meeting this morning only because it got you your job back, Captain, and you are good for Greyhawk." His dark brows furrowed suddenly, and his voice dropped a note. "I won't try to find out who did the deed. However, if the name of the murderer should ever defile my ears, I will be forced to act. I hope it was none of your friends."

Garett studied Axen Kilgaren. Despite the fact that Kilgaren was an assassin—one of the deadliest killers in the city—Garett liked the man. There was an honesty and a directness about him. He wished that he could tell this man the truth about his suspicions, but he didn't dare. Kentellen Mar had too many supporters on the Directorate, and he didn't know where Axen stood.

"I don't know how many men you have," Garett said. "But you must arm them all and put them in the streets tonight. It could make you mayor."

Axen Kilgaren sneered. "I don't want to be mayor."

"Listen to me anyway," Garett continued, unruffled. It didn't surprise him that Axen didn't want the office. That fact only heightened Garett's respect for the man, and he had a different hook to apply. It was only slightly different, but it was the right one for Axen. "And listen closely. There's a plot, and I know how much you love this city."

TWENTY

Raenei and Kule burned like huge white jewels over the city of Greyhawk. Their frosty radiance washed out all but the brightest stars, and the air itself seemed to glow with a milky luminescence.

In the streets, the madness of celebration had reached a peak. There was no place in the city where the noise and music did not reach. Venders hawked quick foods, wines, and beers, for which they charged exorbitant rates. Mimes and minstrels and prestidigitators performed on every corner for huge crowds of gawkers. The watch houses in all quarters were overflowing with petty arrests, and offenders were returned to the streets as soon as their names were logged.

Garett watched it all from horseback in an alley just off Horseshoe Road, which was the boundary between the River Quarter and the Foreign Quarter. Burge, Blossom, and Rudi waited with him. They wore helmets and heavy chain mail under their uniforms. Rudi wore a bow and quiver of arrows slung over one shoulder. It was the order of the night that every watchman was so armored.

Garett scanned the streets for signs of trouble, not knowing from which direction to expect it, but sure that it would come. He watched faces, looking for any suspicious outlander. He noted knives and clubs, which were legal, and kept a sharp eye out for any cloak or loose garment that might conceal a sword.

"The Directorate will have your head if nothing comes of this, Captain," Blossom said in a low voice.

That was certainly true. If he had guessed wrong, his trickery would be obvious to all by morning. The mayor would feel he'd been made a fool of. Garett had convinced Ellon to call out the entire garrison to protect his house and his person, and to search the High Quarter and Garden Quarter for a terrorist team of assassins from the Shield Lands. That put three hundred and fifty men on alert in the two most strategic quarters of the city. The same story had convinced Korbian Arthuran to assign fully half of the day shift watchmen to tonight's duty.

Sorvesh Kharn would be angry, too, and would feel he'd been made a fool of. No matter that Garett had secretly opened the barracks armory to provide his thieves with good swords. Sorvesh wanted to be a hero, to be the man who saved the city from a desperate nighttime attack from a force that had found a way in through the sewers. Every man he commanded was secreted near the gratings, waiting and watching.

Axen Kilgaren might take it in stride. Then again, he might not. It was impossible to predict anything about that man.

There were others whom Garett would have to answer to as well. He had gone to the Temple of Pholtus and given veiled warnings to its patriarch about trouble tonight from the priests of Trithereon, and immediately given the same warnings to Trithereon priests about the Pholtus Temple. The enmity between those two rivals was old and strong, and he knew with certainty that both sides would be well armed and watchful this night.

At the Temple of St. Cuthbert he had taken tea with its patriarch and casually complained about the number of dirty outlanders who were swarming within Greyhawk's walls. An appeal to the old man's prejudice was all it took to win assurances that when Cuthbert's adherents walked the streets tonight they would keep their cudgels handy.

In short, Garett had spent the day making Greyhawk into a tinder box. Now he was waiting for the spark.

Lieutenant Graybo and four watchmen suddenly appeared at the mouth of the alley. Korbian Arthuran had been too busy or to disinterested to name a new permanent commander to take charge of the River Quarter watch house, so Graybo still held the post. He approached Garett and looked up. "The sewer grating on River Street is still locked," he reported quietly, "and the mechanism appears untouched."

"So is the grating back down this alley," Garett answered. "But keep checking them. Check every grating. And if you spot any of Sorvesh's thieves lurking in the shadows, don't give them away. Remember, for this one night, they're working with us."

"Talk about your marriage made in the Abyss," Graybo muttered, turning to look toward the street as a group of celebrants gave a loud whoop and passed by. "What happened back there?" he called sharply to his men at the alley's mouth.

"Couple o' Nyrondians thought they'd step back here an' give themselves a quiet relief," one of the watchmen answered with a snort. "I turned 'em properly around."

Garett looked down as the huge lieutenant turned back to face him. "Keep them on their toes, Graybo," he cautioned.

"They're good men, Captain," Graybo assured him. "Just a little high-spirited, what with all the celebration going on."

Garett nodded understanding, and Graybo rejoined his

men and led them up the street.

"Do you think it was wise to take him into your confidence?" Rudi asked. "I mean, to tell him everything?"

Garett had debated that himself, but the River Quarter was one of the largest in the city, and tonight, one of the most congested. He trusted Graybo, and the old soldier was nobody's fool. More importantly, he had discovered that the other watchmen in the quarter trusted Graybo, too. That would matter if Graybo had to rally them quickly.

Garett beckoned and led his comrades out of the alley. The crowds on Horseshoe Road forced them to go slowly, but not as slowly as if they had been on foot. People just naturally moved out of a horse's way when they would not for a man.

As they left Horseshoe Road and entered the Petit Bazaar, which was a smaller version of the High Market, full of booths and small tent shops that even now were open and catering to the throngs of celebrants, the going became even slower. A pair of blue-cloaked escorts from the private Guild of Night Watchmen accompanied a laughing old lady, a noblewoman or a merchant's wife, who was definitely in the wrong part of town but obviously enjoying herself. She passed close enough to reach out and pat the horses' noses, but didn't.

Rudi leaned from his saddle, frowning. "Captain," he said, trying to keep his voice low and at the same time still be heard over the noise of celebration. "I could swear I saw a sword under that Night Watchman's cloak."

Garett nodded. "That's likely," he admitted. "I armed them, too."

Blossom gave a sigh. "I find myself hoping the Horned Society really does have an army hiding in the sewers," she admitted. "Otherwise, they're going to hang you for sure in the morning."

"I'm not sure it's an army," Garett conceded as they made their way across the bazaar.

"You're not sure of much," Burge reminded him.

They rode a short distance up Craftsman's Way and into the Artisans' Quarter. The smells of tanners' stains and cloth dyes, of potters' clay and sawed wood, lingered in the air. Garett had grown up in the Artisans' Quarter, and the odors brought back old memories. He and his group turned up a dark side street called Weavers' Way. In the middle of the road was another sewer grate.

Burge swung out of the saddle to check the lock on the grate. He slipped his fingers through the narrow bars, grabbed hold, and gave it a tug. "Secure, Cap'n," he called as he returned to his horse.

Garett was convinced that the invaders would come up from the sewers. He had found the altar and the painted symbols of a Horned Society sect down there. Something in those dark depths had killed two of his men and wounded Burge, though the half-elf had recovered quickly. Five Old Town residents had also died down there.

Burge mounted up again, and they made their way to their next destination.

It was quieter in the shadow of the Black Wall, probably because there were fewer taverns and restaurants this far south. They stopped a block away from the house of Kentellen Mar, and a watchman stepped out of the shadows to greet them.

"Hello, Strevit," Garett said quietly. "Any news?"

Strevit shook his head. "I've got men hiding in nooks and crannies all the way to the other end of the street, Captain Starlen," he reported. "But he's not made a move. No one's come in. No one's gone out." He turned around and stared back at the house. A few lamps burned in the upper windows. Otherwise, the place was dark. "Tell me again how you think he's a traitor? I just can't believe it, sir. Not of Kentellen Mar."

"Keep your voice down, watchman," Garett cautioned sternly. Strevit's attitude came as no surprise. Kentellen was the people's hero, the man of the hour. "No charges have been made yet," he reminded Strevit. "But he spent a lot of time during his hunt along the Ritensa River in the Shield Lands. We know that for a fact."

"He may have sold out to the Hierarchs," Rudi interjected.

Strevit shook his head stubbornly. "I still can't believe it," he said. "But I'll do my job and keep a sharp eye out. Maybe I'll be the one to prove you wrong."

Garett nodded. "I'll settle for that, watchman."

The fact that Kentellen's house was being observed, though, didn't reassure Garett. A wizard powerful enough to slay five seers and defeat Prestelan Sun and the entire wizards' guild would surely have spells to teleport himself anywhere he wanted to go.

Where *would* he want to go? Garett asked himself.

"Let's head for the mayor's house," he ordered grimly.

They worked their way northward up side streets, attempting to avoid the largest crowds, and if some citizens were startled by the sight of four fully armored watchmen on horseback, they were too busy with their festivities to make much of it. Through the residential section of the Halls the group went, and past the universities, where Greyhawk's finest students were trying their best to outdo the excesses of the adults in the River Quarter. As if the Halls hadn't known enough of fire recently, someone had set fire to a wagon in College Square, and scores of drunken youths danced wildly around it, shouting and laughing.

When Garett and his friends reached the Garden Wall, they turned westward and headed for the gate. As they followed the wall's shadow, Burge looked up. The night fairly sparkled with the glint of moonlight off the wings of hundreds of northward-flying birds.

"Never seen so many at night before," he marveled.

Garett watched them with an uneasy feeling, recalling the black feather he'd found in the library of the wizards' guildhall. The thing that had killed Prestelan Sun had been some kind of bird or bird-shape, too. So, also, had been the creature in the sewers.

The hairs began to prickle on the back of Garett's neck. He stopped his horse and leaned toward Rudi. "You think you can bring one of those down?" he said.

Rudi looked at him strangely. "Are you serious? If I miss an arrow's most likely going to come down in the middle of a crowd."

But Garett was deadly serious. "Then don't miss, Sergeant."

Rudi stared at him but a moment more, then unslung his bow, braced one end of it against his foot in the stirrup, bent it, and slid the string into place. He took an arrow from the quiver on his back and set it against the string. Drawing a deep breath, he aimed upward, pulled back to the corner of his mouth. He held it there, tensed, waiting for his shot. Then, abruptly, he eased off and lowered the bow, trembling.

"It's too dark," he insisted. "I'm going to hurt somebody."

"You can do it, runt," Blossom urged softly, intending no insult this time. "You picked off a goose with a dagger once. This is easy."

Rudi raised his bow again. The moonlight caught the tip of the arrow as he drew it back, and frosted the wings of the birds above his head. With his left arm rigid, he held the string at the corner of his lips and waited. And waited. The string hummed suddenly. The arrow flew.

"Got it!" Burge exclaimed, pointing, as Rudi let go a sigh of relief.

A bird plummeted to the street about twenty yards in front of them, where it lay flopping, thrashing with its wings, upon the shaft that impaled its breast. It screamed in a shrill, chirruping voice as it slowly, painfully died. The four watchmen reached it in time to see its final, pitiful twitchings.

When the bird was still, Garett slid from the saddle and went to bend down over it. Then he sprang back, one hand curling around Guardian's hilt.

"What in the hells?" Burge shouted, leaping down and rushing to his captain's side. Rudi snatched another arrow from his quiver. Blossom jumped down and caught the reins of the two loose horses as they began to snort and prance.

"Get back!" Garett ordered, pushing Burge away from the bird as it began to change. He drew Guardian. The blade gave an ominous glow, warning of magic.

The bird underwent a slow metamorphosis. The pinfeathers of its outstretched wings began to lengthen and stiffen and took on the semblance of human fingers. The wings themselves began to melt and reform and grow. The small black body rippled suddenly, like a thick liquid, and the feathers gleamed as wet and smooth as tar before they faded away altogether. The tiny, round, staring eyes, as dark as jet, turned pale in the moonlight as the shape continued to shift and swell.

Garett knew it was over when Guardian lost its glow. He and Burge crept forward again and peered down at the body of a human man. He was fully armed and armored, save for a helm, obviously a soldier, though his garments were all of black and devoid of any rank or insignia that might have revealed his origin.

"Good shot," Blossom muttered over her shoulder to Rudi. "You aim for a black bird and bag us some turkey."

"It's not the sewers!" Garett shouted with sudden understanding. "It's the birds! The damned birds!" He glanced up at the sky. Hundreds of black, moon-frosted shapes winged over the Garden Wall. He could hear them now, hear their high-pitched cries and screeches.

"You were right, Cap'n!" Burge cried, running to his horse and swinging into the saddle. "It's an invasion, all right."

"Congratulations," Blossom added with her usual sarcasm as she handed Garett his reins.

They raced off toward the Garden Gate, but the closer they came to the Processional, the thicker were the crowds that impeded them. "Out of the way!" Garett called uselessly. Few heard or paid any attention. He pushed a man roughly out of the way with his boot. "Move!" he shouted. "Clear the way!"

At the Garden Gate, Garett stopped and shouted to the six watchmen on sentry duty. "Close the gates!" he ordered. No civilians to go through. We're under attack!"

With his comrades close behind, Garett rode under the wall's high arch and paused only long enough to make sure the guards carried out his orders. Even as four of the guards labored to push the heavy doors shut, celebrants protested and tried to force their way into the Garden Quarter. Likewise, some of those already on the north side of the gate looked around in alarm when they saw the great doors closing.

"Get off the streets!" Garett shouted to them.

But Blossom steered her horse to the fore, her blond hair flying in a sudden gust of wind. She brandished her sword. "Or, if you're men enough, take up weapons!" she cried. "The Hierarchs have come to Greyhawk. Show them a fight!"

"Black uniforms!" Burge shouted, raising his own sword. "Know them by black uniforms!"

The music and the dancing went on. Only a few seemed to hear the warning, and they stared back dumbly, as if it were all somehow part of the festivities. Garett wasted no more time. He lashed out with the ends of his reins, cursing loudly, to drive the mob aside. Yelling and screaming curses, Rudi, Blossom, and Burge came after him.

Then a chorus of cries rose over the music, and a surge of human flesh came sweeping south down the Processional. Garett gave out with another curse as he saw the panicked faces that rushed for the closed gate. He grabbed the nearest man by the collar and lifted the frightened fool half off his feet as he bent down from the saddle. "What is it, man! Tell me!" he demanded.

The man's eyes were fear-widened. He stuttered to get

his words out. "Fighting in the High Market!" he managed. "I saw it! Birds! Birds!" He struck at Garett's hand and twisted suddenly, freeing himself, and he disappeared in the crowd.

Now the panic was spreading. The songs and cheers that filled the night turned to screams and shrieking. A wave of men and women crashed against the Garden Gate, crying to be let out as more and more people came running down the Processional and the side streets emptied. It was no use trying to hold them all back, he saw, so he raised an arm and signaled the guards to let them through.

Turning his horse, he rode up the Processional. The clang and clamor of battle soared on the night as a force of black-clad warriors clashed with garrison troops. A dark figure ran into his path suddenly, startling Garett's horse. As the animal reared, the figure raised a sword to strike. In almost the same instant, an arrow sprouted from his chest. The sword tumbled from numbed fingers, and the warrior fell.

"Thanks!" Garett shouted as Rudi nocked another arrow and held it ready on the string.

In the market square, a tent suddenly went up in flames. Revealed in the fire's glow, scores of birds landed and began to transform. Garett cursed and whipped his steed up the Processional and onto High Street. In the shadows of the gardens and groves on either side of the fine road, birds settled to the ground and began to metamorphose.

The fighting had already come to the mayor's house. Garrison troops, stationed there to guard Ellon Thigpen, thanks to Garett's warning, fought furiously against greater numbers. Already the street was slick with blood. Garett drew Guardian from its sheath. It radiated a dull emerald glow that cast an eerie light upon his face. At full speed, he rode his mount into the rear line of black warriors, smashing them aside as he lashed out to the left with his sword. The downward stroke made a green streak through the air as he cut through the nearest foe.

Then Burge was beside him, swinging his own blade. A

warrior rushed up on the half-elf's left side. Burge brought his foot out of the stirrup and crushed the soldier's face with a solid kick.

Blossom and Rudi charged through the line side by side, riding over black-clads, trampling them. A figure flew through the air and swept Blossom from the saddle. With a cry, she went falling. Almost immediately, though, she rose, tall and beautiful and full of rage. She gripped her sword in both hands and swung it right and left as if it were a scythe and the street a field of black wheat.

Rudi wheeled his horse about, knocking a pair of soldiers over with the beast's powerful shoulders. He flung his bow over his back and jumped down, abandoning his mount, then fought his way to Blossom's side. Together, they cut a bloody swath to the marble porch of the mayor's house.

Garett did his best to rally the garrison soldiers. He estimated their number at twenty. Twenty plus the four of them, against unknown scores. From the corner of his eye he saw a black-clad kick a soldier in the stomach and raise his sword for a deathblow as the man sagged. Without thinking, Garett ripped the throwing star from his left arm band and let fly. It caught the black-clad forcefully in the side of the throat, and blood fountained.

"Nice!" said a voice just behind him.

Garett risked a glance over his shoulder. It was another garrison soldier, a sergeant. As he watched, the man blocked an attack with his blade and quickly sidestepped to smash a black warrior's nose with his sword pommel. Instantly, he followed through with a fatal thrust.

"You're not bad, either, Sergeant!" Garett complimented, turning to face his own foe. They traded a swift exchange of strokes. A sudden thrust passed just under Garett's right arm as he leaned away from it. He brought his foot up with all his speed and might into the foe's groin and brought Guardian whistling down. "Look me up if you ever want a job in the watch," he added as the sergeant whirled around and they blocked a pair of blows together.

"You must be Garett Starlen," the soldier said. "I hear you're always trying to recruit from the cream of the garrison. We train 'em, and you take 'em away!" He dropped downward almost to one knee and chopped unexpectedly at his foe's unprotected shin. The black-clad screamed as the blade went to the bone. The sergeant thrust upward, slamming his point under the chin to silence the scream.

"Is the mayor still inside?" Garett demanded when he had breathing space.

"We moved him to the Citadel earlier tonight," the sergeant answered, wiping his forehead with the back of a sleeve. "It's the safest place."

"Not from birds that can fly over any wall or through any window!" Garett shouted back. "Let's not waste lives defending this place then. Run for the Citadel!"

Garett turned and ran along the west side of the estate, calling to Blossom and Rudi as he went past the corner of the porch. Burge and the sergeant were close behind, followed by those few garrison troops who were able to disengage. Through a grove of lemon trees they raced, and over an open lawn. A low ridge rose before them. Scrambling up it, they emerged in another garden and finally into Wizard's Row.

At the end of the road, the broken tower of the wizards' guildhall loomed against the night sky. On either side of it, Kule and Raenei floated, burning and full, pouring silvery light upon the world. Necropolis! Garett thought with a silent curse. Nothing seemed more evil to him than those two full moons and that dark ruin of a tower.

"They're coming up the ridge!" Burge warned, looking back over his shoulder.

Garett could see nothing, but then he didn't have Burge's elven eyesight. He led the way at a run, back toward the Processional. A pair of blue-cloaked night watchmen lay dead in the middle of the street, blood pooling rapidly around them. Garett bent down and snatched up one of their swords, and Burge took the other.

Sounds of combat could still be heard from the High Market. The garrison troops must be holding their own there, Garett reasoned. He turned his party northward and raced for the Citadel. It was the strongest fortress in the city, and the seat of much of Greyhawk's business and government. The city's treasury was also secreted in vaults far below the barracks. It was natural that an enemy would try to take it.

"Didn't think there'd be so many, Cap'n," Burge managed to shout as they ran up the Processional.

Garett hadn't expected it, either. A small force, he'd figured. Enough men to come through the sewers, maybe take a few key points and open the outer gates. He'd alerted gate posts for possible trouble, never guessing the trouble was already inside the city.

Suddenly, the Processional was littered with bodies. Citizens, Garett realized. They were cut and bleeding. Not all were dead yet, and their groans and weeping were pitiful to hear. But Garett could not stop to offer comfort. The sounds of fighting he heard now came from the Grand Citadel, and it was terrible indeed.

He rushed through the massive gates, which were half-closed. Someone had tried to shut them, but too late. Black-clads were everywhere. So were garrison troops and watchmen. A few men fought naked, or in trousers only. Those were day-shifters who had been sleeping in the barracks when the fighting began. A couple of St. Cuthbert followers were also there, swinging their cudgels left and right with consummate fury. They called the name of their deity with every stroke.

A sword came hurtling down out of the shadows at Garett's head. Reflexively, he brought up both his swords in a classic cross-block and caught the descending blade. He kicked out, finding soft flesh, as he drew back with Guardian and thrust. He barely had time to look at the dead man before another warrior was upon him. Garett met the foe and fought intensely with every dirty trick he knew.

A loud crack and the crashing of wooden timbers filled the air, rising even over the noise of the battle. Then another sound, a new tumult of voices, caused Garett to turn and stare toward the Citadel's gate.

Led by watchmen and garrison soldiers, the citizens of Greyhawk surged into the courtyard. They attacked with knives, clubs, rakes, and shovels, with heavy skillets and broom handles. Watchmen fought alongside known thieves, and soldiers beside prostitutes. Yes, even the women fought to defend their city. A huge Rhennee bargeman grabbed a black-clad, lifted him overhead, and flung him with bone-cracking might against the battle wall. An old woman from Old Town flung herself, weaponless, onto the back of another warrior and gouged his eyes as she shrieked with anger.

The tide of battle turned against the black-clad army. The people of Greyhawk forced them to the walls and butchered them mercilessly, and the courtyard ran with blood.

It was then, in their moment of victory, that Garett felt the ground tremble ominously under his feet and Guardian began to shine like a star. His heart thundered with renewed fear. Desperately he turned, raising the enchanted sword high as he sought the source of the powerful magic.

And somehow, through the light of his sword, he saw Kentellen Mar high on the Citadel's roof, his arms outspread as the wind swept through his hair and lashed his robes. A fiery energy surrounded him, an energy that rushed down and stabbed into the heart of the earth itself.

Garett ran to the Citadel's entrance. The doors were sealed. No amount of tugging or pulling would budge them. On impulse, he stood back and struck at them with Guardian. Emerald light flared, and the blade passed through the wood as if it were vapor. When Garett tried the doors again, they opened at his touch.

A mighty wind swirled suddenly around him and swept into the Citadel, extinguishing every torch, every lamp or candle or lantern, leaving darkness in its wake. Utter, frightened darkness. But Garett was not frightened. With Guardian's light to guide him, he went inside to confront Kentellen Mar.

TWENTY-ONE

Garett raced headlong through the corridors of the Citadel. Not a lamp burned anyplace. But for the light of Guardian, he would have been lost and helpless in the absolute dark. Up a flight of stairs he ran, taking them two at a time, and up another flight. Through the stone tiles under his feet he felt the tremors that threatened the city. Tiny streamers of plaster dust cascaded in delicate plumes from the ceiling. He did his best to ignore it all, thinking only of Kentellen Mar.

Higher and higher he went until he came to a wall and a ladder. At the top of the ladder was a trapdoor that opened to the Citadel's roof. He climbed the rungs and set his hand against the door. He hesitated for only a moment, then pushed it open and sprang out.

The two moons, Kule and Raenei, burned spectacularly in the heavens, huge and bloated, more frightening than beautiful as they bled their gleaming light onto the rooftop. They hung poised over the Citadel, like eyes dispassionately watching the battle.

The wizard stood with his back to Garett at the edge of the roof, before a low parapet, his arms high, his hands working mysterious gestures as he wove a cone of energy. The wind blew fiercely at this height. It snatched Garett's cloak and nearly flung him back into the hole from which he'd emerged. He crouched lower against the gusts.

The energy cone rippled suddenly, and coruscating lines of red-orange force lanced groundward. The Citadel gave a violent shudder, and the sound of screaming rose from far below.

Kentellen's wide back presented itself. This was no time to think of honor, Garett told himself, not with a city at stake. He ripped his last throwing star free and hurled it with all his strength. Even as he let fly, a blast of wind caught his arm, and he knew he had missed his mark. The wizard gave a cry of pain and surprise, and lurched forward, clutching at the missile as it sank deep just under his right shoulder blade. With another loud moan, he sagged down onto one knee, and the cone of power dissolved.

Only then did Garett see Ellon Thigpen, bound hand and foot, gagged, bared to the waist. The mayor lay stretched precariously upon the parapet. He dared not even squirm for fear of falling over the side to the earth far below. Wide-eyed, he shot a look of terror at Garett. The wizard clutched at Ellon's arm as he hauled himself to his feet and turned.

"Heirarch!" Garett shouted furiously, moving forward, raising Guardian to strike. It was not Kentellen Mar, he told himself. Kentellen could not have lived so many years among the people of Greyhawk and kept this kind of power hidden. Nor even if he had gone to the Shield Lands could he have learned so much during his time away. Whoever this man was, he had to be one of the great masters of the Horned Society.

The wizard's mouth opened in a snarl. He flung out his hand, and a stream of fire leaped across the roof. Garett hurled himself aside to avoid its searing heat, rolled, and came to his feet again. He gripped Guardian in both hands and ran forward. The wizard's brows knitted together in a hateful glare, and Garett bounced painfully off some invisible wall. The air rushed out of his lungs as he fell backward. Guardian clattered across the rooftop, out of his reach.

Something darted out of the shadows. Cavel! Garett had forgotten the little blond child. The boy snatched up the blade and aimed a blow at Garett head. As he did, he opened his small mouth, and the shrill, high-pitched cry that issued forth was nothing human. The cry was of a savage, angry bird.

Garett rolled aside, dodging the stroke, and scrambled to his feet. As the child delivered a second blow, Garett caught his hands and jerked Guardian from his grasp, reclaiming the sword as his own. In an instant, Cavel was on him, scratching and clawing, screeching that unnatural sound. Somehow, the boy got his legs wrapped around Garett's waist. His young fists thundered and beat at Garett's face.

A red haze of pain flooded Garett's thoughts. Enraged, he flung the boy across the roof and turned again to advance on the wizard.

"Heirarch!" he called again in challenge. Again the invisible wall held him back, but this time Garett raised Guardian above his head and sliced downward through the restraining force. The sword flared, and a greenish rift formed in the air, then faded. The barrier gone, Garett advanced again.

"Stop!" the wizard called, placing a hand on the chest of Ellon Thigpen. "Or this fool goes plummeting over the side!"

The mayor stared in horror at Garett and shook his head frantically. Garett debated within himself, but he stopped, his sword still held at the ready.

The wizard turned only slightly away, grimacing with pain from the throwing star still deep in his shoulder. He mastered himself, though, and drew erect. Keeping one hand on the mayor, he made a gesture with the other and shouted some foreign word into the wind. Just beyond the parapet, the strange cone of energy began to swirl again.

"If I can't rule this city," the wizard snarled at Garett, "then I'll destroy it!"

"You've made a good start already!" Garett cried over the rush of the wind, trying to distract the wizard from his work. "First, it was the seers, because their powers might have detected your coming!"

The man who looked like Kentellen Mar threw back his head and laughed, but the laughter was tinged with pain as he winced suddenly. "Yes, the seers!" he barked. "I was very creative there, striking at them through their own scrying devices!"

The cone rippled like a snake swallowing its dinner. Lines of force shot downward from its heart and struck the earth, and the Citadel quivered and shook.

"Then it was the wizards!" Garett shouted again, stalling as he desperately sought a way to get to his foe without sacrificing Ellon Thigpen's life. "Prestelan Sun nearly beat you. I saw you then, in the form of a giant bird!"

"Hah!" The wizard sneered. "You do not know everything yet, Garett Starlen."

"I know you're a Hierarch of the Horned Society!"

The wizard's eyes narrowed as the cone rippled and the Citadel shook again. Only the hand upon his chest kept Ellon Thigpen from falling off as the parapet shivered under him. "Do you?" the wizard challenged. "Am I?"

"I know you're not Kentellen Mar!" Garett answered, screaming. "You captured or killed him, probably while he was on the border of the Shield Lands."

The wizard's eyes crinkled with horrible mirth. "Yes, that was convenient, though my plan would have worked even without him. Soldiers transformed into birds! A magical work of genius! Who would have expected such a surprise attack?"

Garett advanced a step closer. Before he could do anything, he had to pull Ellon Thigpen from that wall. If he leaped fast enough, he might be able to do it. Then he could deal with his enemy. Time. He had to buy time to get closer.

"But it wasn't a surprise, was it?" Garett taunted, taking another small step while, at the same time, ripping off his chin strap and casting his helmet aside, hoping the wizard would watch the motion of his hands and not his feet. "Some of us were prepared. I guessed enough of your plan to stop you."

The wizard's rage revealed itself in his face. His dark eyes flashed with bits of lightning as the cone of power once more shook the ground. "You've stopped my army!" the wizard shouted. "You haven't stopped me. And you could never have done even that much without outside interference." He pointed an accusing finger. "Who gave you that sword?"

Garett inched another step closer. "I see now," Garett said applaudingly. "If your army had won, you would have ruled Greyhawk. Or, if your army failed but Ellon Thigpen died in the fighting, you, as Kentellen Mar, still stood a high chance of becoming mayor. With your magic, you could have manipulated the election, as long as you had Prestelan Sun out of the way."

The wizard backed up a step. He caught Ellon Thigpen by the hair and twisted his head sharply, eliciting a muffled cry of fear and pain from the mayor. "Come no closer!" the wizard warned. "He is no bird!"

Cursing, Garett backed up a pace. At least no more tremors rocked the Citadel. He had succeeded in some measure at distracting his enemy. "What I still haven't figured," he shouted as the wind roared around him, "is why the murders of the five people in Old Town? What value was their deaths to you?"

The wizard put on a hideous grin. "Ah, but that wasn't me," he answered, attempting a tone of innocence. "I even sent Cavel to investigate."

"Cavel?" Garett glanced quickly around and spotted the blond boy not far away, crouched, ready to spring again, awaiting only a command from his master.

The wizard shook his head and gave a chiding cluck of his tongue. "You should have checked the victims' connections to Sorvesh Kharn, Captain," he sneered. "I believe your master of thieves decided to do a little house cleaning at the guildhall."

"But the altar!" Garett protested. "The sigil painted on the wall!"

Again his foe clucked. "What kind of detective are you, Captain, that you don't realize how many people have access to your reports? And did they not already include information about that old fool, Cat, who managed to escape me, and what you found carved on his wall? Sorvesh Kharn merely took advantage of your suspicions to cover his acts."

It was possible, Garett had to admit. Sorvesh was clever and slippery, and his spies were everywhere. He easily could have gotten those reports. But Garett shook his head. One element didn't fit. "There was a creature down there. It killed two of my men and wounded one."

The wizard pointed, smiling. "Cavel," he answered. "I told you, I sent him to investigate. It was he who altered the symbol, smearing the blood-painted horns into proper wings."

"Then you are a Hierarch!" Garett charged, shaking his fist as he stole forward another pace.

"You sightless fool!" The wizard raised his hands and raked the air with taloned claws. Behind him, the cone of power rippled. The roof under Garett's feet came alive, tilting first one way, then another.

"If you bring this building down, you'll be crushed, too!" Garett shouted, desperately trying to keep his balance.

"Will I?" the wizard answered tauntingly, waving his hands, sending another ripple through the cone.

Ellon Thigpen managed to scream even through the bandage stuffed in his mouth. The parapet cracked and buckled under him, and he pitched over the edge into space. Garett hesitated no more. With an angry shout, he hurled himself at Kentellen Mar's doppelganger. The wizard shrieked and jumped away as Garett swung Guardian. The point drew a bloody streak and, at the same time, flared with emerald fire.

Garett paid no attention. He had forced the wizard back far enough to make a grab for Ellon. He caught the mayor around his legs, dropping Guardian in the process. With all his strength, he held on as Ellon screamed and struggled in terror. His arms were all that saved the man from a swift flight to death.

But another shriek made him turn his head. The wizard touched the bleeding cut on his cheek, but it was not the wound that made him scream. His flesh began to melt and flow, his bones to shift and bend. His frame shrank, becoming smaller. Hair and eyes changed color. So did his skin, turning sallow. Whatever magic had changed him into the image of Kentellen Mar, Guardian's touch had destroyed. It was an older, more frail man who stood there now. He screamed again and clutched once more at the throwing star in his back, unable to reach it.

Again the cone of power faded.

Raging with pain and failure, the wizard cast a baleful glare at Garett, who clung helplessly to Ellon Thigpen. His gaze shifted to Guardian. "I don't know where you got this sword, or what it is," the wizard hissed in an ancient, raspy voice. "But it will end your miserable, meddling life!" He stooped and reached out to claim the enchanted sword.

A dagger clattered against a section of the crumbling parapet. Though it missed, it was enough to make the wizard recoil. Garett strained to see over his shoulder, to see where the dagger had come from.

Blossom pulled herself up from the trapdoor, drawing her sword as she ran across the roof. It was she who had saved him! But Cavel saw her, too. The child flung himself at her, wrapping himself around her legs, sending her sprawling. He was on her then with teeth and nails.

"No!" the wizard wailed. He bent for the sword again. Risking his own precarious balance, Garett kicked out desperately, knocking Guardian out of his reach. "Damn you!" the wizard shrieked. "At least it can't protect you now!" He thrust out his hands over Garett, and a black force radiated from his fingers.

It was Garett's turn to scream as that force touched him. His insides turned to fire, and his brain burned. In horror, he watched his flesh turn black and liquify. A fine sheen of wet feathers appeared on his arms. With all his desperate might, he strained, bones and joints cracking even as they transformed, and he hauled Ellon Thigpen to safety. Garett screamed again, a shriek of purest raw pain as his body changed.

The wizard looked smugly away from Garett. "Get away from her, Cavel!" he ordered, and apparently the boy obeyed. The wizard stretched out his hand and spoke again. "Leeches for you, woman. Lots of leeches!"

Blossom's scream shattered Garett's heart. Resisting the pain of transformation, he rolled and flopped toward Guardian, but when he reached with his left hand to grasp the sword, he had no fingers, only sleek, shining pinfeathers. With a gasp of despair, he twisted over, and his right hand, still human, or near-human, curled around the hilt. He drew the sword to him and hugged the bare blade.

Immediately, the transformation began to reverse. The fire in his body lingered, though, every nerve tingling as if it had been scraped raw. But he had no time to think of himself. Blossom continued to scream as she clawed at the dark slugs that crawled on her flesh and sucked her blood. He struggled up to his hands and knees.

The wizard had no more interest in Garett. "Cavel!" he called, his own voice weak and full of pain. "We've lost! Spread your wings! Carry us away from this cursed city!"

NIGHT WATCH

The blond boy ran to the center of the roof and raised his arms. His transformation was much swifter and far more dramatic than Garett's. An arcane light gleamed in his round eyes. He opened his mouth and screeched a birdlike cry, and his body began to grow and change.

Garett crawled toward Blossom, dragging the sword. His strength returned slowly as the tingling in his body subsided. He rose to his feet. He staggered, walked, and finally ran. Blossom thrashed, driven half mad by the leeches she had learned to hate. Garett didn't hesitate. He struck her on the back with the flat of Guardian, and the sword flared.

Gratefully, she turned around to face him, but the shock had not gone out of her eyes, and she sank into his arms. Garett barely had strength to hold her, so he lowered her gently to the roof.

Cavel's transformation was almost complete. Huge and spectacular, he spread his wings, and their span was greater than the width of the Citadel's roof. His black eyes glittered, and the full moons frosted the crest of his head.

"What is it?" Blossom muttered weakly, lifting her head to stare in fearful wonder.

Garett shook his head as he knelt with his arm around her. "I don't know," he answered simply. "I hate magic."

She forced a weak smile. "I remember." Then she added. "Me, too."

Cavel stretched a wing downward, and the wizard, the Hierarch, climbed carefully upon it and settled himself astride the great bird's neck.

A familiar voice called suddenly from the trapdoor. "Cap'n? Blossom?"

Garett found strength to shout. "Burge! Stay back! Don't come up here!"

But the half-elf poked his head up through the door and gawked in disbelief. The sight was not enough to deter him. As he tried to climb onto the roof, the bird-thing flexed its wings and brushed Burge aside. Then Rudi, too, popped his head up through the door. He, at least, had sense enough to duck as the wondrous beast swept into the sky.

"Captain Starlen?"

Garett twisted around at the sound of Ellon Thigpen's voice. The mayor sat huddled in the shadow of the parapet, hugging his knees.

"If I've been unfair to you in the past," Ellon said weakly, nervously, "I apologize. I'll make up for it. I swear I will."

"You just stay put," Garett warned him. "Don't move from there."

Higher and higher the bird gyred over the Citadel, past the moons and into the night. Then, with a great banking curve, it turned and sailed straight at Garett and his allies. Past the top of the Citadel it flew, and as it skimmed the roof, the wizard leaned out and extended his arm. A blue-white tongue of fire seared away a section of the parapet.

Rudi sprang onto the roof and launched an arrow at the monstrous bird, but if it struck, the shaft had no effect.

Past the moons it swept again, and once more it turned.

"I thought it was the bird alone that fought Prestelan Sun!" Garett exclaimed as Burge and Rudi ran over. "But he rides it! He rides it!"

"Who rides it?" Burge said in bewilderment.

The bird sailed back, moonlight burning on its wings, fire lashing from the wizard's outstretched hand. Rudi dived aside, rolled, and came to his feet with an arrow in his hand. He set it to the string and fired as the bird passed directly overhead. A blazing scorch raced across the roof, straight for the diminutive warrior, and only Burge's quick-thinking tackle knocked Rudi aside in time.

Screeching, the bird turned again, and fire lashed down toward the Citadel. But as it came on this time, Garett remembered Prestelan Sun and his green-glowing shield. He had no shield, but he had Guardian. "Stay down!" he ordered the others. He ran to the edge of the roof. The parapet had been blasted away. Far below, people still stood in the square, too mesmerized by the battle to flee.

Garett searched for the wizard, high on the bird's great neck. For an instant, he fancied their gazes met. The bird screamed, and the wizard yelled as he reached out. A rose of fire blossomed before Garett's eyes. Its heat touched his face.

You might have gotten away, the watch captain thought with a surreal calm as he threw himself aside at the last instant. Now die! A round, blackened circle marked where he had stood a moment before.

He flung Guardian with all his might, and the sword streaked like a shooting star, blazing an emerald light, straight for the heart of the great bird as it passed overhead. Like a bolt it struck, and the thing that was Cavel shrieked a horrible cry as feathers exploded from its chest. Its wings faltered. A crackling green lace-work of energy rippled around the fantastic creature for an instant, then disappeared. Cavel gave another cry. Gigantic wings fluttered uselessly. As it fell, another, far more human cry echoed its own.

EPILOG

Garett sat in Ellon Thigpen's private office in the palace of the lord mayor, his feet propped up on a comfortable stool, a drink of rare wine near his left hand.

"I don't mind telling you," Ellon Thigpen said paternally. He lounged in a plush chair on the other side of the desk, his hands folded over his stomach, his eyes gleaming from the wine. Since his formal investiture in a small, quiet ceremony a few days earlier, Ellon had mellowed considerably. "It was the hells dragging that damned bird's huge carcass out of the river. Cargo shipping was tied up for nearly two days. It crushed part of a major pier when it fell, too, but we finally managed to haul it up onto the west bank, where we burned it. If there'd been some way to roast it properly, we could have fed the Slum Quarter for a year."

Garett knew all that, but he listened patiently. The mayor had grown quite friendly since their adventure on the Citadel's roof. There was no point in mentioning all the complaints from the High Quarter and the Garden

Quarter when the wind carried the smelly smoke over those particular sections of the city. At least they had their streetlights back. Garett had found the twelve missing wizards turned into birds and locked in cages in a basement corner of Kentellen Mar's old house in the Artisan's Quarter. A touch of Guardian's blade was enough to restore them.

"No sign of the imposter's body, I suppose?" Garett asked.

Ellon Thigpen shook his head. He grew quiet for a moment, then looked up pensively. "Have you concluded that other little investigation?" he asked.

Garett nodded as he took a sip from his cup. "All five of the murdered Old Towners were thieves who, despite repeated warnings, had refused to join the guild. That's hearsay, of course, but we interviewed a lot of folks. And of course, there's no concrete proof, and no one will testify. But they all told pretty much the same story."

Ellon shook his head. "Even the little girl?"

Garett nodded again. "Especially the little girl. Turns out that she was quite the pickpocket, single-handedly supporting her mother and a baby sister." Garett shrugged and took another drink of wine. "But you know the guild rules. An independent can work just so long, then it's join or get out of town."

"So Sorvesh had them killed," Ellon Thigpen said wistfully. "Sometimes I hate the way things operate in this town. 'Business as usual' has a very dirty sound to it."

"Well," Garett said, staring into the red liquid in his cup as he swirled it around and around. "No one's in a better position to change things than you."

Ellon got out of his chair and went to his window. The sky beyond was a bright, warm blue. "We'll see," he answered. "We'll just see. Right now, I'm busy trying to choose a new magister. Poor Kentellen Mar. I don't suppose we'll ever know what really happened to him. He was a fine man." Ellon grew quiet again as he looked out the window.

When he turned around again, there was a harder look in

his eye. "I spoke with the ambassadors from Furyondy, Urnst, and Tenh this morning," he said, returning to his chair and his cup of wine. "And I called in a few favors. I'm afraid the Hierarchs in the Shield Lands are going to be encountering some major trade problems in the days to come."

Garett regarded Ellon with new respect. Along with Greyhawk, Furyondy, Urnst, and Tenh pretty much controlled shipping, not only on the Selintan River, but on the great Nyr Dyv as well. If they acted in unison, it was possible to choke off almost all trade into or out of the Shield Lands. Garett doubted, though, that they would go quite that far.

"There is no doubt, then, that he was a Hierarch?"

Ellon put on an ugly sneer. "Not enough to deter me from this course. After the wizards returned to their guildhall, they confirmed the origin of the winged skull sigil as a small but fanatic sect within the Horned Society. They found notes in Prestelan's handwriting in the library with a copy of the sigil. Apparently, he was gone when the wizards were initially attacked and captured. There was further evidence among the cargo of the caravan that brought the wizard to us. Instruments of magic, books of spells written in the society's language, some weapons of Shield Land manufacture." He picked up his cup and took a long drink, then propped his feet up on a corner of his desk as he leaned back. "In any case, we have a number of prisoners from among the invaders. None of them seem to speak a tongue anyone knows, but it's just a matter of time and the proper persuasion before we get some answers from them."

The mayor looked up suddenly and slapped his palm down on the arm of his chair. "So things return to normal. The streets are full of elves and dwarves and orcs again. Even some of the Attloi are drifting back. And thank the gods all this celebration business is over with. I was never very comfortable with a lot of pomp and circumstance." He sipped from his cup again and gave Garett a warm, confident smile. "But enough of all this. You've still got five days of special leave left. What are your plans?"

Garett matched Ellon's smile with a faint one of his own as he rose and went to the window. Looking out, he could just see the tents and booths of High Market Square. "First," he confessed, "I'm going to have dinner and spend the night with a charming, red-haired lady. If she'll have me, that is." Then his hand brushed lightly against Guardian's hilt. He gave a small sigh. "And tomorrow I'm going on a trip."

"A trip!" the mayor exclaimed, brightening. "How nice!"

* * * * *

Garett and Burge sat in their saddles, staring toward the first clumped line of mangaroo trees. The tall grass shifted and stirred as the breeze blew about them, and the water rippled. A light mist hung over everything, a mist that sparkled under the watchful eyes of Kule and Raenei.

"What am I doin' here?" Burge muttered, half to himself. "Blossom had the right idea."

Garett grinned to himself. In response his suggestion that she accompany them on another outing to the Mist Marsh, Blossom made an obscene gesture and announced plans to spend the night at The Tomb, drinking it dry, instead. Not even the gift of earrings made from the two remaining amethyst crystals could change her mind.

"Maybe it's Rudi who has the right idea," Garett ventured.

The half-elf made a face. "Sit home with a wife?" He spat into the mist. "I'm not old enough for that life, and I'm twice his age."

They rode a bit closer to the mangaroo grove, then stopped again. Garett drew Guardian from the sheath. The only glow on the blade was the gleam from the two moons overhead. He turned the weapon over and over, watching the silvery light dance on the edge, watching the flash of the emerald splinters in the eyes of the tiger-shaped tangs. It was a beautiful sword. A wondrous sword.

But it wasn't for him.

Guardian, it was called. One of the Pillars of Heaven, twelve swords that had long ago disappeared from the world. There must have been a reason for that, and Mordenkainen had given dark hints about the abuse of power. Perhaps there was no longer a place in the world for the potent magic Guardian represented. Perhaps times and men had changed too much since the forging of the swords at the beginning of the world.

Garett didn't know if he was right. He only knew that he didn't want to keep Guardian. With an instinct that, itself, bordered on the arcane, he knew the sword didn't belong to him. He had only borrowed it to defend his city.

It was time to give it back.

He rode a few paces ahead of Burge and stared into the dark knot of mangaroos. The leaves rustled, like a raspy song on the breeze, and he remembered how good Rudi's roast goose had smelled on a night not too long ago.

He raised the sword by its hilt, drew back his arm, and threw it. Far out toward the mangaroos it sailed, arcing high, catching the moonlight as it tumbled end over end, and Garett felt his heart soar with the blade. More than ever, he knew that he had done the right thing.

Then an amazing thing happened. Out of the mangaroos, a mighty mouth opened. A great gray worm surged upward out of the mists, through the leafy branches, and caught Guardian. Soundlessly it sank back into the marsh and disappeared.

The water rippled subtly, the grasses waved, and streamers of mist wafted about like timid ghosts. Burge rode up beside Garett. Pale and wide-eyed, he stared toward the trees. "Would it be all right with you if we didn't tell anyone about this?" he asked in a soft whisper.

Garett smiled. He had no doubt that by this time tomorrow Burge would have told the story a dozen times in a dozen different taverns, and with each telling would make it even more fantastic than it truly was.

"Let's go home," was all the watch captain said.

Now you can hear Robin W. Bailey

Robin's first tape of original science fiction and fantasy folk music. Songs on this cassette will take you into deep space and to fantastic worlds of wonder. Without a doubt, Robin's diverse talents are not limited to the written page.

STORYTELLING AT ITS FINEST

To order *Never Too Old To Dream*, or for more information about DAG tapes and products, please write for your complimentary catalog.

DAG Productions
1810 - 14th St. #100
Santa Monica, CA 90404

FORGOTTEN REALMS FANTASY ADVENTURE

EMPIRES TRILOGY

HORSELORDS
David Cook

Between the western Realms and Kara-Tur lies a vast, unexplored domain. The "civilized" people of the Realms have given little notice to these nomadic barbarians. Now, a mighty leader has united these wild horsemen into an army powerful enough to challenge the world. First, they turn to Kara-Tur. Available in May.

DRAGONWALL
Troy Denning

The barbarian horsemen have breached the Dragonwall and now threaten the oriental lands of Kara-Tur. Shou Lung's only hope lies with a general descended from the barbarians, and whose wife must fight the imperial court if her husband is to retain his command. Available in August.

CRUSADE
James Lowder

The barbarian army has turned its sights on the western Realms. Only King Azoun has the strength to forge an army to challenge the horsemen. But Azoun had not reckoned that the price of saving the west might be the life of his beloved daughter. Available in January 1991.

FORGOTTEN REALMS is a trademark owned by TSR, Inc. ©1990 TSR, Inc. All Rights Reserved.

TSR™ BOOKS

Outbanker
Timothy A. Madden

Ian MacKenzie's job as a space policeman is a lonely vigil, until the powerful dreadnaughts of the Corporate Hegemony threaten the home colonies. On sale in August.

The Road West
Gary Wright

Orphaned by the brutal, senseless murder of his parents, Keven rises from the depths of despair to face the menacing danger that threatens Midvale. On sale in October.

The Alien Dark
Diana G. Gallagher

It is one hundred million years in the future. When the ahsin bey, a race of catlike beings, are faced with a slowly dying home planet, they launch six vessels deep into space to search for an uninhibited world suitable for colonization. On sale in December.

TSR is a trademark owned by TSR, Inc. ©1990 TSR, Inc. All Rights Reserved.

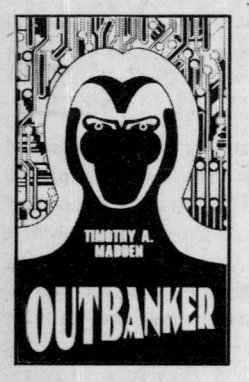